PENGUIN  CLASSICS

THE CONFIDENCE-MAN

Herman Melville was born on 1 August 1819 in New York City, the son of a merchant. Only twelve when his father died bankrupt, young Herman tried work as a bank clerk, as a cabin-boy on a trip to Liverpool, and as an elementary schoolteacher, before shipping in January 1841 on the whaler *Acushnet*, bound for the Pacific. Deserting ship the following year in the Marquesas, he made his way to Tahiti and Honolulu, returning as ordinary seaman on the frigate *United States* to Boston, where he was discharged in October 1844. Books based on these adventures won him immediate success. By 1850 he was married, had acquired a rural estate near Pittsfield, Massachusetts (where he was the impetuous friend and neighbour of Nathaniel Hawthorne), and was hard at work on his masterpiece *Moby-Dick*. But literary success soon faded; his complexity increasingly alienated readers. After a visit to the Holy Land in January 1857, he turned entirely from prose, publishing only poetry in small, privately subsidized editions. In 1863, during the Civil War, he moved back to New York City, where from 1866 to 1885 he was a deputy inspector in the Custom House, and where, on 28 September 1891, he died. A draft of a final prose work, *Billy Budd, Sailor*, was left unfinished and uncollated; packed tidily away by his widow, it was not re-discovered and published until 1924.

Stephen Matterson lectures in American Literature at Trinity College, Dublin. He is the author of *Berryman and Lowell: The Art of Losing*.

HERMAN MELVILLE

THE
CONFIDENCE-
MAN

HIS MASQUERADE

EDITED WITH AN INTRODUCTION
AND NOTES BY
STEPHEN MATTERSON

PENGUIN BOOKS

PENGUIN BOOKS

Published by the Penguin Group
Penguin Books Ltd, 80 Strand, London WC2R 0RL, England
Penguin Putnam Inc., 375 Hudson Street, New York, New York 10014, USA
Penguin Books Australia Ltd, 250 Camberwell Road, Camberwell, Victoria 3124, Australia
Penguin Books Canada Ltd, 10 Alcorn Avenue, Toronto, Ontario, Canada M4V 3B2
Penguin Books India (P) Ltd, 11 Community Centre, Panchsheel Park, New Delhi – 110 017, India
Penguin Books (NZ) Ltd, Cnr Rosedale and Airborne Roads, Albany, Auckland, New Zealand
Penguin Books (South Africa) (Pty) Ltd, 24 Sturdee Avenue, Rosebank 2196, South Africa

Penguin Books Ltd, Registered Offices: 80 Strand, London WC2R 0RL, England

www.penguin.com

First published 1857
Published in Penguin Classics 1990

033

Introduction and Notes copyright © Stephen Matterson, 1990
All rights reserved

The moral right of the editor has been asserted

Printed and bound in Great Britain by Clays Ltd, Elcograf S.p.A.
Filmset in Monotype 10/13 pt Bembo

Except in the United States of America, this book is sold subject
to the condition that it shall not, by way of trade or otherwise, be lent,
re-sold, hired out, or otherwise circulated without the publisher's
prior consent in any form of binding or cover other than that in
which it is published and without a similar condition including this
condition being imposed on the subsequent purchaser

The facsimile of the 1857 title-page on p. 1 is reproduced by permission of the British
Library.

www.greenpenguin.co.uk

MIX
Paper from
responsible sources
FSC
www.fsc.org
FSC® C018179

Penguin Books is committed to a sustainable
future for our business, our readers and our planet.
This book is made from Forest Stewardship
Council™ certified paper.

CONTENTS

———◄●►———

INTRODUCTION

—————

I

The Confidence-Man was the last novel Herman Melville published during his lifetime. As such it completes what had been an extraordinary eleven years; between 1846 and the publication of *The Confidence-Man* in 1857 Melville published nine novels and a collection of short stories. Furthermore, these years had changed Melville. From being a 25-year-old ex-sailor sitting down to write an embellished account of his travels in the South Seas, he had become a sophisticated writer exploring human psychology, motivation, and mythology. 'From my twenty-fifth year I date my life,' he wrote to Nathaniel Hawthorne.[1] However, while it was in this period that he had achieved his breathtaking potential, these years had also seen a steady decline in his literary reputation. The generally established pattern of his literary career had been one of popular acclaim followed by neglect as his works became more ambitious. The 1846 publication of *Typee*, the account of his 'four months' residence' in the Marquesas (in fact, he was only there a little over four weeks), brought him fame, and he was quick to follow its success with *Omoo* (1847). These works satisfied a popular appetite for travel literature; in England they were published by John Murray in the Home and Colonial Library series. This was in spite of Murray's fear that *Typee* and *Omoo* were more fictional than they ought to have been.

1. Letter to Hawthorne, June 1851.

Typee gave Melville a fairly enduring reputation, but it also came to haunt him. It gave him the unwelcome nickname 'Typee' Melville, and he feared he would be known to posterity as 'the man who lived among cannibals'. Each subsequent novel was to be unfavourably compared with *Typee*. Having called *The Confidence-Man* 'indigestible', one reviewer concluded with, 'All we can say, in reply to the brilliant author of *Omoo* and *Typee* is 'the less the merrier'.[2] However, even if *Typee* were a bad book, which it is not, today's readers could be grateful for it. Its success encouraged Melville in the idea that he could live by his pen; were it not for *Typee* there would be no *Moby-Dick*, no *Pierre* and no *The Confidence-Man*. For no matter how badly received the later novels might have been, there were still publishers willing to take a chance on Melville's repeating the popular success of his first novel. In effect, he was able to live on its literary capital for some eleven years, even though the finding of publishers did not grow easier. In December 1846 Melville called on Harper & Brothers in New York to offer them the manuscript of *Omoo*; it was accepted at once, unseen, by Mr Harper, about to start for Europe.[3] It seems that Melville proposed *The Confidence-Man* in 1855 to its eventual American publishers, Dix & Edwards. Their editorial adviser, G. W. Curtis, warned them to 'decline any novel from Melville that is not extremely good'.[4] By 1856 even Melville's family placed little hope in his literary talent. Mrs Melville's step-brother, Lemuel Shaw, Jr, wrote to his brother, 'I believe he is preparing another book for the press . . . I know nothing about it, but I have no great confidence in the success of his productions.'[5] This book was *The Confidence-Man*.

Even Melville's treatment of the novel's manuscript could sug-

2. Unsigned review, *Illustrated Times* (London: 25 April 1857); reprinted in Watson G. Branch (ed.), *Melville: The Critical Heritage* (New York: Methuen, 1985), p. 381.

3. Jay Leyda, *The Melville Log* (New York: Harcourt Brace & Co., 1951), p. 230.

4. ibid., p. 500.

5. ibid., p. 517.

gest that he thought little of the work. With the novel completed in October 1856, he left the USA for Europe and the Holy Land. One copy was left with his family, and when he visited Nathaniel Hawthorne in Liverpool, Melville left the second manuscript with him to arrange the English publication. During this visit he told Hawthorne that he had 'made up his mind to be annihilated'.[6] He saw neither version of *The Confidence-Man* through the press; it was published in New York on 1 April 1857 and in London a few days later. Melville's by now habitual ill-luck intervened. After uncomprehending or hostile reviews, the novel seemed likely to be consigned to oblivion when Dix & Edwards failed in the very month of publication and were dissolved. Melville declined the opportunity to buy the printer's plates, as though agreeing that the novel should be forgotten.

On the surface, Melville's life after *The Confidence-Man* is one of silence and bitterness, culminating in his death in 1891 as a forgotten writer. To support his family he relied no more upon his writing. After a fairly unsuccessful lecture tour and a frustrated attempt to gain a consulship, he eventually took the job of Customs Inspector in the New York Custom House in 1866, working there until his retirement in 1885. As Melville had written almost prophetically of the failed Helmstone in 'The Fiddler', 'to-day he walks Broadway and no man knows him.' He published four books of poetry between 1866 and 1891, three of them privately and two in editions of only twenty-five copies. After his retirement he worked on *Billy Budd*, posthumously published in 1924. The New York paper *The Press* noted his death under the headline 'Death of a Once Popular Author' and pointed out: 'Probably, if the truth were known, even his own generation has long thought him dead, so quiet have been the later years of his life.'[7]

But it is wrong to accept uncritically the pattern of Melville's

6. ibid., p. 529.
7. ibid., p. 836.

decline into misanthropy and bitter silence, as though he were anticipating Mark Twain's later development to works attacking 'the damned human race'. It is also dangerous to do so, because it leads to too much irrelevant emphasis on *The Confidence-Man* as a kind of bitter farewell to prose. Melville's work from 1853 to 1857 can be seen as triumphant in that he was exploring ways of using levels of writing. One level would satisfy an audience, while another would satisfy Melville as expression of his artistic vision, or of the crisis caused by the conflict of vision and audience. Contrary to one of the standard interpretations, Melville's state of mind in 1856, when Hawthorne reported that he was making up his mind 'to be annihilated', probably had little to do with despair over his literary reputation; Melville was talking about the uncertainty of his religious belief. Even the long silence in prose can be misunderstood, since Melville clearly thought highly of his poetry even while acknowledging that there was no likelihood of its selling.

One can see that in his literary career Melville gradually moved away from the kind of work that his established audience wanted. The signals were there in 1848 when he was writing *Mardi* and started to look for a publisher. Melville was certain of the value of his book, and sure that the audience he had found with *Typee* would follow his development into the kind of romance that *Mardi* represented. In its Preface he wrote frankly of *Mardi* as romance with no basis in fact: since his two factual novels had been 'received with incredulity', he had hit upon the idea of writing a work that evaded the issue of factual credibility. *Mardi*, though, was poorly received. Melville returned, almost penitentially, to the factually based narrative in *Redburn* (1849) and in *White-Jacket* (1850). *Redburn*, an intriguing novel which Melville detested, was based upon his first sea voyage, from New York to Liverpool in 1839. For the material in *White-Jacket* he turned to 1843–4 and his time in the US navy. These novels somewhat revived Melville's career, only to encourage him once more to take risks. *Moby-Dick* (1851) was a critical and commercial failure, although it was a blend of what should have appealed to popular taste – a stirring and informative narrative of whaling – and what Melville wrote for his own artistic satisfaction. The novel's dedication to Hawthorne is notable, since it points to the overall significance he had held for Melville since 1850. The admiration is specifically for what Melville saw as Hawthorne's refusal to reduce artistic vision to popular taste: 'He says NO! in thunder; but the Devil himself cannot make him say *yes*.'[8] Melville later applied the lesson to himself: 'What I feel most moved to write, that is banned, – it will not pay. Yet, altogether, write the *other* way I cannot. So the product is a final hash, and all my books are botches.' And again, 'Though I wrote the Gospels in this century, I should die in the gutter.'[9]

However, after the complete failure of the uncompromising *Pierre* (1852), Melville's career was again revived somewhat by the 1856 publication of the six stories and sketches in *The Piazza Tales* (tellingly, *The Confidence-Man*'s 1857 title page refers to Melville as the author of *Piazza Tales*, *Omoo* and *Typee*, omitting any mention of the less successful works). Several of the short stories are successful in somehow being two stories in one. On the surface there is a humorous story or sketch, while underneath there is despair at the situation of the writer. Melville had developed a kind of double, coded writing. His now celebrated 'Bartleby, the Scrivener' won praise from the reviewers, but its textual core is concerned with Melville's alienation from a popular audience, and about the implications of refusing to write in the ways calculated to produce sales.

Bartleby's story is narrated by an easygoing man of the world, a friend of the late John Jacob Astor and a man who thinks 'the easiest way of life is the best'. Bartleby refuses to work, to copy, and eventually refuses to live, starving to death in prison. To the narrator, he is an enigma. To Melville, Bartleby is the

8. Letter to Hawthorne, 16 April 1851.
9. Letter to Hawthorne, June 1851.

uncompromising writer, courageously facing the implications of his refusal. In these terms the narrator too represents a kind of writer, the kind that would take no risks in art, but work to satisfy the demands of the audience. Specifically, he is linked to Washington Irving, one of the most successful authors of the day. Like the narrator, Irving had been a friend of John Jacob Astor; the publication of Irving's *Astoria* in 1836 had stimulated adverse comments on their association. In 1848 Irving had been pallbearer at Astor's funeral and executor of his will. In 1850 Melville had castigated Irving for his 'self acknowledged imitation of a foreign model' and for the 'studied avoidance of all topics but smooth ones'.[10] Irving represents a temptation, that of gaining popular esteem – and wealth – and paying for it with artistic integrity and vision. Ernest Hemingway was to face the same dilemma and to write of it in 'The Snows of Kilimanjaro'; the dying writer's betrayal of talent reflects Hemingway's fear that he will do the same. Melville remained the risk-taker, Bartleby rather than the narrator, the writer for whom 'Failure is the true test of greatness.'[11]

When G. W. Curtis recommended Melville's 'I and My Chimney' for publication in *Putnam's Monthly Magazine*, he wrote that it was 'a capital, genial, humorous sketch.'[12] Indeed, it could still be read as a sort of James Thurber story of struggle between a husband and wife over a chimney. The husband, attached both to his chimney and his pipe, successfully resists his wife's strategies – she is in league also with their daughters – to have the chimney demolished. One tactic involves collusion with a local builder, Hiram Scribe. Scribe inspects the chimney and recommends its demolition, but, the stubborn narrator is able to save the chimney, and to remain by it smoking his pipe.

Beneath the surface comedy, however, the story refers to the concern of Melville's wife and her family over Melville's mental

10. Herman Melville, 'Hawthorne and His Mosses' (1850).
11. ibid.
12. Leyda, *The Melville Log*, p. 507.

and physical state. This worry emerged repeatedly, due mainly to his exhaustion from writing. Their concern grew, so that in June 1855 Dr Oliver Wendell Holmes, a summer neighbour, attended Melville. While the visit was ostensibly due to an attack of sciatica,[13] it seems that Melville's mental state was also under examination. In 'I and My Chimney', written shortly after the visit, Holmes is portrayed as Hiram Scribe. The narrator's sense of triumph at keeping the chimney is tempered, he recognizes, by his resulting alienation. Like Bartleby, he pays a high price for principle:

It is now some seven years since I stirred from home. My city friends all wonder why I don't come to see them, as in former times. They think I am getting sour and unsocial. Some say that I have become a mossy old misanthrope, while all the time the fact is, I am simply standing guard over my mossy old chimney; for it is resolved between me and my chimney, that I and my chimney shall never surrender.

The Confidence-Man too seems to use the kind of double writing Melville had developed in the stories. For instance, in Chapter 40 the story of China Aster's bankruptcy, breakdown and death is very close to the facts of Melville's father's circumstances. Allan Melville was declared bankrupt in 1830, when Herman was eleven, and died in 1832 leaving the family in serious financial difficulties. Yet the interpolated story is told in an almost lighthearted fashion, and Melville actually draws attention in the chapter's title to the disjunction between the style and the substance. The story seems filled with covert personal references[14] to the extent that various possible meanings have been proposed, including the idea that it is about the relationship between Melville and Hawthorne.[15]

13. ibid., p. 502.
14. See Michael Paul Rogin, *Subversive Genealogy: The Politics and Art of Herman Melville* (New York: Alfred A. Knopf, 1983).
15. See Edwin Fussell, *Frontier: American Literature and the American West* (Princeton, N. J: Princeton University Press, 1965).

II

While 'I and My Chimney' ends with a statement of the need to be true to oneself, its narrator is aware of the resulting accusation of misanthropy. And it is as a misanthropical book that *The Confidence-Man* has been generally approached. In writing it, Melville broke out of the restraints imposed by the need to be popular that he had accepted in *Redburn* and *White-Jacket*. In Melville's embittered view the earlier, 'botched' works are now burdens; *Typee* and *Omoo* are referred to as 'Pegee' and 'Hullaballoo'. *The Confidence-Man* is quite different from his other works. It is not set at sea, but on a Mississippi steamer called the *Fidèle*. As in *Pierre* the narrator is not a character in the story; indeed, there is possibly no one central character in *The Confidence-Man*. It is not based on personal experience, as the others tended to be (though Melville had visited the Mississippi in 1840). What little action there is takes place on one day, 1 April.

On the surface *The Confidence-Man* appears to be the bitterest of Melville's novels. In spite of their general bafflement, several 1857 reviewers termed it misanthropical, with the word 'Timonist' recurring in their notices. It was as though Melville had taken over the strategy he had attributed to Shakespeare: 'Through the mouths of the dark characters of Hamlet, Timon, Lear, and Iago, he craftily says, or sometimes insinuates, the things which we feel to be so terrifically true that it were all but madness for any good man . . . to utter.'[16]

The comments of *The Confidence-Man*'s puzzled reviewers seem to have been endorsed by the novel's later critics. During the time of Melville's oblivion it was of course forgotten, along with *Moby-Dick*, but even the Melville revival that started in the 1920s left it neglected or misunderstood. After its first publication in 1857 the novel was not reprinted until 1923, and the first scholarly edition did not appear until 1954. Even Melville's ablest

16. Melville, 'Hawthorne and His Mosses' (1850).

critics tended to dismiss it, or apologize for it; in the 1920s two critics independently termed it 'an abortion'.[17] However, Elizabeth S. Foster's 1954 edition both signalled and stimulated a growing appreciation of the novel. While it is still misunderstood (editions of the *Oxford Guide to American Literature* have consistently called it 'unfinished'), it is no longer possible to dismiss *The Confidence-Man* as an inferior work by an exhausted writer. H. Bruce Franklin's then provocative assessment of the novel in 1963 as 'Melville's most nearly perfect work'[18] has been endorsed by a growing number of critics, and accompanied by a move towards its being more well known. In critical books on Melville the novel now rates more than a chapter of afterthought, and, like *Billy Budd*, it has inspired an opera.[19]

In many respects the increased critical regard for *The Confidence-Man* has derived from two major factors. First, there has been a steadily growing awareness of the importance of masquerade and trickery in American literature, along with a recognition that Melville's novel is central to this tradition. Second, the postmodernist aspects and contemporary relevance of *The Confidence-Man* have started to be emphasized.

When he used the phrase 'confidence man' Melville was certainly up to date; the term itself was coined only in 1849 by the *New York Herald* to cover the activities of one 'William Thompson', a man with a variety of aliases, including that of 'Samuel Willis'. In the following year there had even been a confidence man imitating Melville, rather a 'Curious Fraud', as the *New York Journal* reported in July 1850:

It appears that some individual ambitious of notoriety has become

17. Van Wyck Brooks, 'A Reviewer's Notebook', *The Freeman*, 7 (9 May 1923), pp. 214–15; John Freeman, *Herman Melville* (London: Macmillan, 1926), pp. 62–3, 140–44.

18. H. Bruce Franklin, *The Wake of the Gods* (Stanford, CT: Stanford University Press, 1963), p. 153.

19. Written, by George Rochberg, it was produced by the Santa Fe Opera in 1982. The libretto is published as *The Confidence-Man* (*A Comic Fable*) (Bryn Mawr, PA: Theodore Presser, 1982).

enamoured of the good name and reputation of . . . Herman Melville . . .
and has been so far successful in his attempts to pass himself off for that
gentleman, in remote parts of Georgia and North Carolina, that persons
near the scene of his exploits have been induced to correspond with . . .
Mr Melville's publishers for the purpose of getting reliable information
on the subject of this stranger's claims to the authorship of Mr Melville's
books. It is believed by many that Herman Melville is the assumed name
of the author of *Typee* &c. This is not the fact. Herman Melville is the
real name of the writer of those works.[20]

This incident coincided with an oddly persistent rumour, especially prevalent in Europe, that the very name of Melville was a
hoax. In 1856 the *Dublin University Magazine* referred to Melville
being a 'nom de plume' and linked this 'fact' with 'the mystifi-
cation which this remarkable author dearly loves to indulge in
from the first page to the last of his works'.[21] His imitator may
well have led Melville to the pretence that 'Hawthorne and His
Mosses' was written 'By a Virginian Spending July in Vermont'.

While the figure of the confidence man had already been
present in European life and literature, it was the Americans who,
as it were, gave him, 'a local habitation and a name'. The term 'to
diddle' had already been used; Poe has an essay in which humans
are defined as the 'animal that diddles' (the verb comes from
Jeremy Diddler, a character in an 1803 English farce by James
Kenney). There is actually a peculiarly American delight in confidence tricksters. In part such affection has to do with American
emphasis on and admiration for individual enterprise and ingenuity, which are considered notably 'Yankee' qualities. From
extolling the virtues of enterprise and originality in general, as did
Benjamin Franklin, it is only a short step to appreciating the
enterprise of the confidence man. The American fascination with
confidence games and the confidence man has not lessened over
time, and was one impulse behind the game theories of relation-
ships popularized by Eric Berne. The appeal of the film *The*

20. Leyda, *The Melville Log*, pp. 377–8.
21. ibid., p. 511.

Sting lay partly in the fact that the heroes belonged to the recognizable confidence-man tradition, though, as Gary Lindberg points out in *The Confidence Man in American Literature*, the hoaxers in the film were morally sanitized. They were given noble rather than selfish motives, hence allowing audiences to delight in the confidence trick without feeling any moral discomfort.

At its simplest, *The Confidence-Man* touches a chord in the American character. However much moral condemnation of roguery may exist, the confidence man is actually a figure of covert – and often overt – admiration. After all, as several nineteenth-century commentators pointed out, the confidence trick depended upon the trust of the victim. Therefore, the trickster could exist only in a community where it was natural to trust people. Emerson's rather lofty ideal was that if you trusted someone, then the trust would be repaid. In 'Prudence' (1847) he wrote: 'Trust men, and they will be true to you; treat them greatly, and they will show themselves great, though they make an exception in your favor to all their rules of trade.' (Melville's marginal comment in 1862 was, 'God help the poor fellow who squares his life according to this.')[22] Melville's friend, the editor Evert Duyckinck, wrote in 1849, 'It is not the worst thing that can be said of a country that it gives birth to a confidence man.' Duyckinck went on to approve of a quotation from *The Merchant's Ledger*: 'It is a good thing, and speaks well for human nature, that men *can be swindled*.'[23]

By the strict application of a certain kind of logic it could be shown that the confidence man's existence testified to the general honesty and charity of society. His existence was reassuring in proving that people were not misanthropes; it was those who could not be duped who were the cynics. This idea was expertly put forward by the man who was probably the best-known American of the second half of the nineteenth century:

22. ibid., pp. 648–9.
23. Evert Duyckinck, *The Literary World* (New York: 1849) quoted in Gary Lindberg, *The Confidence Man in American Literature* (New York: Oxford University Press, 1982), p. 6.

The greatest humbug of all is the man who believes — or pretends to believe — that everything and everybody are humbugs. We sometimes meet a person who professes that there is no virtue; that every man has his price, and every woman hers; that any statement from anybody is just as likely to be false as true and that the only way to decide which, is to consider whether truth or a lie was likely to have paid best in that particular case. Religion he thinks one of the smartest dodges extant, a first rate investment, and by all odds the most respectable disguise that a lying or swindling business man can wear. Honor he thinks is a sham. Honesty he considers a plausible word to flourish in the eyes of the greener portion of our race ... Poor fellow! he has exposed his own nakedness. Instead of showing that others are rotten inside, he has proved that he is.[24]

This was Phineas T. Barnum writing in 1865. Melville too had grasped the often perplexing ambiguities that the confidence trick involves, and he uses these in *The Confidence-Man*. Thus Barnum represents an important element of background to the novel. Melville had long been interested in him. For a series of political sketches, 'Authentic Anecdotes of Old Zack', written in 1847, Melville had employed some of the showman's rhetoric and style in his hoax dispatches. In *Mardi* (Chapter 122) the travellers visit an antiquary whose collection clearly parodies the American Museum of Barnum, and in *The Confidence-Man* Melville refers to various Barnum exhibits.

In using Barnum, Melville was seizing on some of the American affection for the hoaxer, which went to the extent of liking to be fooled. In fact, this fondness for being tricked by a clever hoaxer was seen by Baudelaire as a notable American characteristic: '*Ces Américains qui aiment tant à être dupés*,'[25] he wrote; Americans love so much to be fooled. Time and again in *The Life of P. T. Barnum Written by Himself* (1855), the crowds cheer the hoaxer in recognition of his ingenuity. One such incident involved a heavily advertised 'Grand Buffalo Hunt' held in New Jersey.

---

24. P. T. Barnum, *The Humbugs of the World* (New York: 1865), quoted in Irving Wallace, *The Fabulous Showman* (London: Hutchinson, 1960), p. 148.
25. Charles Baudelaire in *Le Pays* (Paris: 20 April 1855).

Everyone was admitted free of charge and crowds flocked across
the river in the ferry boats, expecting a grand spectacle. The catch
was that instead of fully grown buffalo, the crowd saw a few tiny
yearlings being chased around by a dressed-up Indian. However,
the crowd accepted the trick, laughed at themselves and good-
naturedly gave three cheers for whoever had devised it. (Barnum
not only received publicity for his American Museum and kept
up his reputation for ingenuity; he had also chartered the ferry
boats for a day, and made a handsome profit from the 24,000
people who used them.) Oddly, Melville includes 'buffalo hunters'
along with the other hunters on the *Fidèle* (p. 14).

The book in which this and many other stories are told,
Barnum's *Life*, re-titled and updated several times during the
nineteenth century, was to become a phenomenal best seller. It
has been reckoned that, after the Bible, it was the most widely
read book of the second half of the nineteenth century. In this self-
publicity, Barnum presents himself as a rather virtuous man with
respect for the public and a desire to be respected by them. Like
Melville's Confidence Man, he asks for trust and cannot function
without it. 'Without Charity I am nothing,' Barnum said, punning
on his wife's name and the teachings of St Paul, but above all
recognizing the public indulgence upon which his hoaxes relied.
It is unlikely that the cynical remark usually attributed to Barnum,
'There's a sucker born every minute', was actually said by him,
indicating as it does a disrespect for his audience that he never
showed in his writings. Furthermore, as Melville's characters
point out, cynicism is anathema to the hoaxer and to the confidence man. A mysterious stranger appears at the opening of *The
Confidence-Man* and propounds a series of slogans from St Paul
about the need for charity. The stranger could well be an accomplice or an avatar of the Confidence Man, since the act of
reminding the passengers of the need for charity will be played on
later by the other characters.

Nor is money necessarily the hoaxer's objective. Some of
Barnum's exhibits at the Museum cost more than they brought

in, and some of his elaborate hoaxes cost him money with no tangible return at all. Barnum could well claim that even the tricks that lost money brought him publicity and hence more than paid for themselves. But this was by no means always the case. For instance, on 1 April 1851, Barnum, staying in Nashville, sent telegrams to everyone in the hotel; some people were sent on fool's errands, some were given unexpected news. True, the local newspaper picked up on the trick and gave Barnum his usual publicity, but it is clear that the delight of fooling was uppermost in his mind. In *The Confidence-Man* also, the winning of trust, belief and confidence becomes a delight in itself. One reviewer even wondered whether the entire novel was a Barnum-type hoax on the reading public.[26] Surprisingly, Melville's men make very little out of their tricks: the herb-doctor gives away a proportion of the money he has made; the talk of the Cosmopolitan occupies half the novel, yet perhaps he only gulls the barber out of the price of a shave. Another character, a cynical wooden-legged man, points out that deceit and trickery are ends in themselves; there does not need to be any financial reward to delight the deceiver: 'Money, you think, is the sole motive to pains and hazard, deception and deviltry in this world. How much money did the devil make by gulling Eve?' (p. 42).

Barnum eventually became more famous than any of his exhibits, testifying once more to the sense that he was acting out some peculiarly American endeavour (and what better focus for his activities than the 'American Museum'?). People would show up at the Museum simply to convince themselves that Barnum really existed. When the eighteen-year-old Prince of Wales visited in 1860, he was disappointed to find Barnum absent. 'We have missed,' he said, 'the most interesting feature of the establishment.'

While Barnum brought to the fore the relation between confi-

---

26. Unsigned review, *Literary Gazette* (London: 11 April 1857), 348–9, reprinted in Branch, *Melville: The Critical Heritage*, p. 375.

dence and hoax, the American and the trickster, writers before Melville had also considered similar issues. Edgar Allan Poe in particular was interested in the hoax, and in the confidence man. His 1843 essay 'Diddling as One of the Exact Sciences' deals with different types of confidence trick, and it is there that he defines man as 'the animal that diddles'. Some of Poe's tales are themselves hoaxes, or attempts at tricking the reader into belief. 'The Unparalleled Adventure of One Hans Pfaall', 'The Facts in the Case of M. Valdemar', 'Mesmeric Revelation', 'Von Kempelen and His Discovery' and 'The Balloon Hoax' play with the reader's gullibility and rely upon the public's trust in the authority of science. In some other works a fascinated Poe exposes hoaxes; for instance, in 'Maezel's Chess Player' Poe theorized on the principle behind an automaton that could apparently play chess. (Barnum himself had been interested in this automaton when he saw it as a rival attraction; it had been brought to America in 1826. Naturally, it was a hoax; a small man, preferably a competent chess player, was hidden inside it.) Poe was certainly known abroad as a hoaxer; it was while commenting on 'Hans Pfaall' that Baudelaire made his observation about Americans loving so much to be fooled. However, some of Poe's works occupy an unlikely middle ground between respectable scientific inquiry and imaginative rhapsody. *Eureka* (1848) is one of these. Poe claimed to have solved the secret of the universe, yet the style differs little from that used in the hoaxes. He appears in *The Confidence-Man*, hawking a copy of what is probably *Eureka*: '... a haggard, inspired-looking man now approached – a crazy beggar, asking alms under the form of peddling a rhapsodical tract, composed by himself, and setting forth his claims to some rhapsodical apostleship.' The beggar has 'raven curls' over a pale brow, and, as Poe habitually did, he has buttoned his frock coat all the way to the chin.[27]

27. See Harrison Hayford, 'Poe in *The Confidence-Man*', *Nineteenth Century Fiction*, XIV (1959), 207–18.

Poe's appearance in *The Confidence-Man* is rather mysterious; whether or not it was intended as a kind of homage to Poe's influence on Melville, it is certainly uncomplimentary. Poe's use of the hoax as theme is linked closely to the idea that fiction itself is a kind of hoax. A work of fiction is a kind of contract between reader and author. As readers we place our confidence in what the author or narrator tells us. But both Melville and Poe became exploiters of that very confidence. In Poe's story 'The System of Dr Tarr and Prof. Fether' we are duped by a narrator who is himself duped and we are eventually uncertain about who in the story is sane and who mad. In Melville's 'Benito Cereno' (1855) a narrator is similarly deceived by appearances into believing that actually rebellious slaves are acting with deference. In these instances the reader's confidence in the narrator is called into question. In *The Confidence-Man* the narrator, who is supposedly omniscient, at times abdicates his authority. It was unusual for Melville to have such a narrator; typically, his storyteller is a character involved in the action. In this novel we receive no special sense of what characters look like, in spite of the lengthy descriptions given to them. At one point John Ringman, the 'man with the weed', is about to be given some money by a merchant, Roberts. Then, as Ringman continues to elaborate his tale of woe, Roberts changes the banknote, 'for another, possibly of a somewhat larger amount' (p. 29). The narrator does not seem to know how much money Roberts has given. How much confidence, then, can we have in this narrator?

Indeed, once this question of confidence is raised, it can be seen that Melville's playing with the reader has been constant in his work though not quite so extreme as in *The Confidence-Man*. As mentioned above, 'Bartleby' and 'I and my Chimney' employ a kind of double writing. Even Melville's first novel exploited the gullibility of the reader to some degree. In the Introduction to *Typee*, Melville wrote of his hope that the 'desire to speak the unvarnished truth will gain for him the confidence of his readers'. Yet we now know, as was suspected by some at the time, that

Melville had stretched that confidence. Broadly, *Typee* is fiction masquerading as travel literature. *Omoo*, like *Typee*, claims a basis in actuality; the Preface directs us to Melville's 'desire for truth and good' – although he seems to have included a warning to alert readers. In Chapter 2 the description of the boat *Little Jule* (even though based on a real ship called the *Lucy Ann*) makes it into an emblem of the narrative. While seeming fairly safe, she was, after all, 'not to be confided in. Lively enough, and playful she was, but on that very account the more to be distrusted.' By the time of *Mardi* Melville had pretty much dropped any pretence that the narrative could repay the reader's confidence in it as factual. To continue the link between boat and narrative, *The Confidence-Man* advertises itself as a 'daedal boat', and three chapters on the art of fiction are part of its cargo (p. 94). As Pitch puts it, 'In short, the entire ship is a riddle' (p. 145).

Mardi somehow disturbed the necessary confidence between reader and narrator. The works that follow seem to give the readers fair warning. If we are to continue reading, the warning goes, then we must acquiesce in the narrator – give him our confidence – even when we do not rightly know what authority he possesses. If it were a conventional novel, *Moby-Dick* would start with its second sentence: 'Some years ago – never mind how long precisely – having little or no money in my purse, and nothing particular to interest me on shore, I thought I would sail about a little and see the watery part of the world.' But it actually starts, as we know, with 'Call me Ishmael.' In effect, the opening words represent an imperative that as readers we cannot disobey. Once we have acquiesced in this narrator's construction of self, we have made an agreement. In agreeing to call him Ishmael we have accepted his version of events and have agreed to believe him for the rest of the tale. We might see the name he adopts as a strategic evasion, but we cannot challenge it, for we have no grounds for so doing. Thus, by the time we read the 'proper' opening, 'Some years ago . . .' we are already in Ishmael's power – have, in effect, signed a contract to follow him wherever he will take us. Like Wellingborough Redburn signing on with Captain Riga, we are there for the duration. Captain Riga changes character once the ship leaves the harbour; Ishmael too changes (he also disappears), but, like Redburn, we cannot easily renege on a contract, nor can we somehow unread the first three words of *Moby-Dick*.

Ishmael masquerades as Ishmael; the Confidence Man's day on the *Fidèle* is called his masquerade. In effect, it is also Melville's masquerade. Perhaps the very idea for the novel came from a picnic attended by Melville and his family in September 1855. While the others wore fancy costumes, Melville remained aloof, dressed in his usual clothes. As he writes in *The Confidence-Man*, 'Life is a pic-nic *en costume*; one must take a part, assume a character, stand ready in a sensible way to play the fool. To come in plain clothes, with a long face, as a wiseacre, only makes one a discomfort to himself, and a blot upon the scene' (pp. 161).

The masquerade might indeed be an appropriate analogy for American life. The confidence man who becomes a recurring figure in the American novel is related to the masquerader, the role-playing master of disguises. The very process of becoming an American is in part the making of a new self. 'What then is the American, this New Man?' asked De Crèvecoeur in 1782, and writers have often answered with novels of shifting identity. To become American is essentially to divest oneself of a past identity, to make a radical break with the past, and so the construction of identity becomes a significant theme in American writing, present as a recognizable tradition. It is there in the essays of Emerson, and in Hester's rebellion and repentance in Hawthorne's *The Scarlet Letter*. It is there in Thoreau's move to Walden, in *The Adventures of Huckleberry Finn*, in *The Great Gatsby*, in Hemingway's Nick Adams stories, in Jack Kerouac's rides across the continent, in Ralph Ellison's *Invisible Man*, in the figure represented by Ken Kesey's McMurphy. As Harold Beaver has put it, 'America . . . seemed a stage set for masquerade, since Americans by their origins placed a peculiar insistence on rites of transition and

metamorphosis.'[28] Identity is not something given and therefore
fixed; it is something you create from within, something you can
also adapt to fit the circumstances. This is more than being a
confidence man; it is taking the ability to change – to be shifty –
as the capacity to survive. The King and the Duke in *The Adventures of Huckleberry Finn* are entertaining, comic figures. Until the
serious gulling of the Wilks family, when they play cruelly with
the family's grief, they are the standard rogues of the frontier. But
the real confidence man is Huck, whose masquerade of changing
identity ensures his survival. (Even the name on the title page,
'Mark Twain,' is a masquerade adopted by Samuel Clemens.)

If identity is fluid, needs to be changed for purpose of adaptation
and survival, then Melville in *The Confidence-Man* goes further.
Behind the masks we put on, under the fictions of self we create,
there may be nothing; no individual, unique self. Everything is a
masquerade and no one can stand outside. The fluid, shifting
identity of the Confidence Man becomes a strategy of evasion.
The deaf mute's gesture of erasure at the novel's beginning pre-
figures what happens to identity in the novel; character is repeatedly erased and written afresh.

III

While *The Confidence-Man* is already topical in its very use of the
confidence figure, there are themes that make it notably relevant
to the 1850s. In her ambitious and meticulous book *Melville's
Confidence Men and American Politics in the 1850s* Helen Trimpi has
outlined the significance to the novel of the contemporary political
situation. She identifies many of the characters on board the
Fidèle as politicians, and calls the novel a comic political masquerade, or 'pasquinade'. Although, as she admits, many of these
figures were obscure even to Melville's contemporaries, her work

28. Harold Beaver, *The Great American Masquerade* (London: Vision Press,
1985), p. 7.

is important in emphasizing how far *The Confidence-Man* is embedded in current political issues, and in particular that of slavery. The 1854 Kansas–Nebraska Act made slavery the most urgent issue of the time. The Act allowed citizens of newly settled areas to determine whether their territories should become slave states or free states. This made it possible for the Western Territories to become slave states. From the appearance of Black Guinea in Chapter 3, slavery is unavoidable as an issue for the reader of *The Confidence-Man*; Trimpi points out that according to the conventions of contemporary political cartoons the inclusion of a black person indicated a reference to slavery.

However, as usual with Melville, the situation is far from straightforward. In spite of being strongly against slavery, as is evident from *Mardi*, Melville is here satirizing the anti-slavery figures of the newly founded Republican party, the politicians who were prominent before the rise of Lincoln. Trimpi argues that he does so for two reasons. First, the founding of the Republicans effectively made slavery at last a party-political issue. This strategy could result in the break-up of the Union, or lead to a Civil War in which the South might well win and impose slavery nationally. Secondly, the Republicans were confidence men, because

they were founding their appeal upon an inadequate and untrue view of the nature of man and society. In claiming that human nature was good and might be capable of perfection within the nineteenth century they were simply wrong and their motives had to be interpreted as either those of fools (*i.e.* they really believed what they said) or knaves (*i.e.* they said things they did not really believe).[29]

On the face of it, the 1850s were a decade of national confidence, made manifest in levels of investment in Wall Street and confidence in America itself. In the novel, Truman has little trouble in recruiting investors in the 'Black Rapids Coal Company' even

29. Helen P. Trimpi, *Melville's Confidence Men and American Politics in the 1850s* (Hamden, CT: Archon Books, 1987), p. 259.

though the company (if it exists at all) has lately been depressed. The wars to which Melville refers, against the Seminole Indians and against Mexico, were supposedly justified by the idealized concept of the nation's 'manifest destiny': the United States' right to appropriate the American continent. The very situation of *The Confidence-Man* reflects this appropriation, since for the first time Melville is looking to the West, to his continent, rather than voyaging elsewhere. The Mississippi is the artery of trade and commerce, the symbol of manifest destiny, as well as the division between slave states and free. In showing the confidence tricks on board the *Fidèle*, Melville is using the ship to represent the ship of state as well as the ship of fools; as the wooden-legged man puts it, 'you flock of fools, under this captain of fools, in this ship of fools!' (p. 21). Some of the individuals to whom Melville alludes, such as Daniel Boone and Moredock the Indian-hater, are the characteristic figures of frontier life, themselves evidence of the push to take over the continent.

Even the ideas of the transcendentalist philosophy, expressed by Emerson and Thoreau, can be seen as part of a national expression of confidence, an optimism which, however spiritual, is linked to material well-being. When Melville satirizes Emerson and Thoreau in *The Confidence-Man* (they become 'Mark Winsome' and 'Egbert'), he does so on the grounds that their spirituality masks an inherent materialism, and even a lack of charity. Egbert demonstrates that giving a loan to someone is spiritually false and harmful, illustrating this with a short story incorporated into the text, the tale of China Aster, ruined because he took a loan. In the depiction of Emerson and Thoreau, Melville uses their own writings against them; Thoreau's views on friendship in *Walden* and *A Week on the Concord and Merrimack Rivers* and Emerson's 'Essay on Friendship' and 'Compensation' are satirized in *The Confidence-Man*.

In choosing confidence as his theme, Melville is pointing satirically to what lies under the appearance of trust. The 1850s led to serious economic recession, and a republic already deeply divided over slavery was soon to be divided by war. When Melville's 'gentleman with gold sleeve-buttons' comments on 'the happy results' of the confederation of the republic (p. 48), the irony is unmistakable. Further, the American dream itself depends on confidence: confidence in one's own abilities and in American society's openness, its capacity for social mobility. *The Confidence-Man*'s English reviewers were particularly alert to how far Melville was writing on the American situation: 'The money-getting spirit which appears to pervade every class of men in the States ... is vividly portrayed in this satire.'[30]

The confusion between appearance and reality is used carefully by Melville in the novel. Confidence tricksters and hoaxers like Barnum are all very well as admirable figures, but what happens when the disjunction between appearance and reality, exploited by Barnum, extends to religion, politics or economics? The Cosmopolitan may appear to be the devil, but could he not also be a saintly figure? The republic in 1857 may give the appearance of solidity, but what of the division represented by slavery? Throughout the novel Melville insists upon this disjunction between appearance and reality.

IV

Critical disagreements over *The Confidence-Man* have gradually given it the status of perhaps Melville's most puzzling and engaging work. The question, raised in its first reviews, of whether or not it is a novel at all has persisted. One exasperated reviewer wrote: 'A novel it is not, unless a novel means forty-five conversations held on board a steamer, conducted by personages who might pass for the errata of creation, and so far resembling the dialogues of Plato as to be undoubted Greek to ordinary men.'[31]

30. Unsigned review, *Saturday Review* (London: 23 May 1857), 484; reprinted in Branch, *Melville: The Critical Heritage*, p. 383.

31. Unsigned review, *Literary Gazette* (London: 11 April 1857), 348–9; reprinted in Branch, *Melville: The Critical Heritage*, p. 373.

Is it a hoax, a sketch, an allegory, a satire? Melville himself calls it a 'comedy' (p. 87). Even if there were no question of genre, many issues remain to be debated. Are all of the figures who practise as confidence men the same one, undergoing a series of metamorphoses? If so, is the deaf mute of the opening paragraphs one of them? Where are all the people on Black Guinea's list? When he is accused of being an impostor, Black Guinea specifically describes eight figures who will testify to his being genuine. In effect, he is giving us a list of the characters who follow him in the role of Confidence Man, but only six of those on his list can be certainly identified. How do the interpolated stories about the man with the weed, Charlemont, Moredock the Indian-hater and China Aster fit into the novel? What is the function of the chapters on the art of fiction? These are only a few of the issues raised by Melville's text.

As readers we are somehow persuaded that the confidence men are all one figure. They do not appear together; in sequence, the Confidence Man is Black Guinea; the man with the weed, whose name is John Ringman; the man in gray; Mr Truman, who is the agent for the Black Rapids Coal Company; the herb doctor; the Philosophical Intelligence Officer; and, finally, Frank Goodman, the Cosmopolitan. It is uncertain whether the deaf mute at the beginning of the novel should be included in the list. Some actions indicate connections between the characters. For instance, Black Guinea appropriates a card accidentally dropped by the merchant, Mr Roberts. Then the man with the weed introduces himself to Roberts with what is apparently the same card and proceeds to swindle him – a well-publicized confidence trick of pretended acquaintance. Having failed in his attempt to persuade the backwoodsman, Pitch, of the virtue of boys, the Confidence Man reappears as the Philosophical Intelligence Officer and succeeds. However, it is worth pointing out that the confidence men seem not to make very much money. True, Ringman receives an undetermined sum from Roberts, the man in gray is given an unspecified amount by the gentleman with gold sleeve-buttons, and Truman receives money from investors in the Black Rapids Coal Company. But the herb doctor apparently gives away a share of the money he makes on board. The Cosmopolitan apparently swindles the barber only out of the price of a shave. In fact, as a whole, the confidence men seem fairly unconcerned about making money, though, as the cynical wooden-legged man has already warned us, the pleasure of gulling is an end in itself.

The deaf mute brings quotes from I Corinthians about charity; the phrases have their opposite in the barber's sign of 'No Trust'. But the deaf mute well may be an avatar of the Confidence Man, his phrases part of a strategy to soften up the passengers and make them receptive to appeals for charity. In fact, this works; a lady is later seen reading the same text from Corinthians, and when she is appealed to by the man in gray she gives him twenty dollars. However, apart from this possibly revealing action, the deaf mute does nothing to suggest that he is one of the confidence men. Guinea's list presents a further problem in that Melville may have intended further confidence men to appear and then changed his mind. Or perhaps the list itself belongs to the strategy of playing with the reader's confidence. We expect the others to appear and are frustrated when those expectations are thwarted.

Even the features on which critics have agreed contribute to the novel's puzzle. For instance, there is a fairly clear two-part division to the novel. In the first part, Chapters 1 to 23, a number of confidence men appear, six or possibly seven. Thereafter, only one is present: the Cosmopolitan, Frank Goodman. The first half of the book moves along quite quickly, while the pace of the second half is markedly slower. However, the implications of this division are not clear. Is Goodman the 'real' Confidence Man, the force behind the other avatars? Or is he a Confidence Man at all in the sense that the others are? The reader may simply be being duped. In the first half, we are given a series of signals by which we feel we can recognize the Confidence Man. But in the second half of the novel, occupied by the Cosmopolitan, these signals are not so clear, even though the reader accepts that the Cosmopolitan is a Confidence Man. Of the differences between the two halves, Elizabeth S. Foster has argued that the first half concentrates on the dangers of blind trust, the second on the dangers of total distrust.[32]

It was once fairly widely accepted among critics that Goodman and the other confidence men represented the Devil. But this is by no means necessarily the case. Goodman in particular becomes a figure appealing for trust and consideration from others. He is appalled by the coldness of Winsome and Egbert, by the stolid practicality of the barber, William Cream, and is bewildered by readings from scripture that contradict the notion of confidence. Given these attributes and qualities, it is possible that Goodman is actually Christ, come down to test the survival of Christian values in the world, making the novel's theme the gulf between Christian idealism and worldly action. In support of this is the fact that Melville had already explored a similar theme in *Pierre*. In the coach that brings him from Saddle Meadows to the city, Pierre finds a pamphlet of a lecture written by one 'Plotinus Plinlimmon', entitled 'Chronometricals and Horologicals'. The pamphlet's central idea is that Christian ideals are like the ideal of global time set at Greenwich. They can function very well as ideals, but for the practical purposes of life on the planet they do not serve as adequate guides. In several novels Melville satirized figures who achieved worldly material success while paying lip-service to Christian ideals. Plinlimmon is in effect the philosopher of such characters as Falsgrave in *Pierre*, and of Benjamin Franklin as portrayed by Melville in *Israel Potter*. In *The Confidence-Man* Winsome and Egbert represent this philosophy; Winsome, for instance, praises Swedenborg, who had 'one eye on the invisible' and 'the other on the main chance' (p. 235). Like the Cosmopolitan, Pierre finds that worldly success, and even survival,

32. Elizabeth S. Foster (ed.), *The Confidence-Man* (New York: Hendricks House, 1954), p. 300.

are incompatible with Christian charity. As Melville had expressed it in 1851, 'Let any clergyman try to preach the Truth from its very stronghold, the pulpit, and they would ride him out of his church on his own pulpit bannister.'[33]

If the Cosmopolitan is the Devil, *The Confidence-Man* becomes, ironically enough, somewhat less bleak and nihilistic. After all, there are those on the *Fidèle* who resist him. The Devil's very existence is somewhat reassuring, necessarily implying that there could also be redemption and salvation. Eventually, though, the possibilities and alternatives, with their resulting implications for the novel's theme, become almost overwhelming. As John Bryant has forcibly and memorably expressed it, 'Eventually the reader's mind short-circuits.'[34]

However, if the reader sees that there is a choice between the Confidence Man as Devil and as God, something else may be implied: that in possibly being both, he becomes neither. Perhaps the real fear in the novel, the true terror, is not that the Devil walks on earth, or that Christ finds no true believers here below. It is that there is nothing; that there is no order to the universe; that Christianity is a comforting fiction which is, however, little different from an April Fool hoax. The very proximity of the commemoration of Christ's passion, in springtime, to All Fool's Day can provoke some discomforting thoughts for Christians. Indeed, in 1855, the year Melville began the novel, Passion Sunday itself fell on 1 April. This coincidence can readily be used to suggest either that Christians are gullible fools or that Christ himself was on a fool's errand. As readers, we are left wondering if the Confidence Man is God or the Devil. Or perhaps there is no single unifying self under the series of identities; it is this sense of uncertainty in *The Confidence-Man* that has led to its being placed among post-modernist texts with their emphasis on the independent self as illusion.

33. Letter to Hawthorne, June 1851.
34. John Bryant, 'Allegory and Breakdown in *The Confidence-Man*: Melville's Comedy of Doubt', *Philological Quarterly*, LXV (1986), 116.

manifestation of Ringman himself (Truman actually casts cynical doubt on the story's veracity). However, the novel's narrator complicates this situation still further by not giving us the story Roberts tells; the narrator intervenes to tell it in his own words in Chapter 12. A similar strategy of distancing and framing is used with the stories of Indian-hating and of China Aster. The Indian-hating episode is recounted between Chapters 25 and 28 by Charlie Noble, who assumes the character of Judge James Hall. The story of China Aster is told in Chapter 40 by Egbert, but he specifically disclaims the style in which the story is told. (Perhaps this distancing strategy was significant for Melville in that the story of Aster strongly mirrors that of his own father's bankruptcy and death.) Overall, the result of these strategies is to call attention to fiction itself. If we lose belief in God or in any myth assigning meaning and purpose to the universe, then we fall back on fiction to make temporary sense and order, or we make a masquerade of identity. If we do not have myths we at least have fictions.

Critics have often been troubled by the implications the novel has for religion. These are raised particularly in Chapter 34, when the Cosmopolitan tells to Noble the story of Charlemont, the 'gentleman-madman'. Apparently bankrupt, Charlemont disappears from St Louis for some years, then returns and is as before. Questioned by a friend as to his disappearance, Charlemont gives a mysterious and possibly evasive answer, that he has somehow taken a sin to himself and thereby saved another, or even the world. The story makes a variety of pointed references to Christ's sacrifice. Charlemont is aged about thirty when he withdraws from his family. Upon his return he lingers in coffee houses, evoking the New Testament scene in which Christ is recognized in the breaking of bread (Luke 24: 13–35). Melville also alludes particularly to the Last Supper; after a meal, Charlemont's statement is made when the wine glasses are filled and he lifts his. But, given these religious references, it seems that Melville is secularizing and thereby reducing the story of Christ's crucifixion and resurrection. Furthermore, since the Cosmopolitan says that his story, like all stories, is told merely to amuse, Melville is placing the stories of the New Testament on a level with any fiction.

However, this is by no means to solve the problems raised by the Charlemont story. Clearly, the Cosmopolitan has some purpose in telling it, because he uses it to see off Noble, the river-boat operator and inferior confidence man. Noble is distinctly uneasy during the story, and, immediately afterwards, leaves.

Given the uncertainties and complexities of the novel, it is not enough to consider it a satire on optimism and American values. It engages us with its metaphysical and ontological speculations, and yet – ironically if appropriately – denies us confidence in these speculations. We get hold of some slippery part of the novel only to find that our trust is subsequently displaced. This is even indicated in the novel's opening, where the deaf mute writes his mottoes on the slate and then erases each one in order to make room for the next, only the first word, 'Charity', remaining uneffaced. This act can be considered a paradigm of the act of reading *The Confidence-Man*. In fact, while Chapter 1 begins with the silence of the deaf mute, Chapter 2 opens with a babble of unidentified voices seeking to identify him, and the voices displace one another. This technique anticipates the displacing of each Confidence Man by the next, but also establishes something of the reader's uncertainty over voice, character and theme. Even Melville's syntax tends to erase itself; sentences are continually qualified by such words as 'possibly' and 'apparently', and by the use of double and triple negatives, to the extent that the reader is often left with a feeling that in spite of all the words, no concrete information has been provided. For instance, the description of Charlie Noble (pp. 168–9) is almost a minor essay in prevarication, giving the reader virtually no impression of his appearance.

The reviewers who doubted that this was a novel certainly had a point, though Melville had his own antecedents in Burton, Sterne, Swift and Carlyle. Perhaps after the postmodernist novel we can better understand the implications of Melville's shifting perspective and the effacing of the narrative. The playfulness of

Melville's text has even provoked a certain indecorum in others: Hershel Parker's 1971 Norton Critical Edition of the novel includes an article by 'Samuel Willis' on private allusions in Melville. Since Samuel Willis was one of the names used by the original confidence man in 1849, this becomes in effect a private scholarly joke about private writing and scholarship. The same edition includes an apparently non-existent publication in the bibliography compiled by Watson G. Branch. In this spirit it is tempting for even a scrupulous later editor to insert some equivocal piece of information into an edition. For example, one might include a fictive bibliographic item, an unnecessary footnote, or perhaps a cryptic name in the acknowledgements.

Melville's use of uncertainty and doubt impinge on the reader of the novel. As in reading the work of Borges, Nabokov, Barthelme and Pynchon, the reader is often made to assume a position of uncertainty for which there is no apparent solution. Reading *The Confidence-Man* closely is an unusual experience. To be caught in its web of complexity and uncertainty is stimulating and even exhausting. Yet trying to reduce that experience, say, to a paraphrase of the novel, or to fix the work's evanescent meanings is often fruitless. Like the comic characters of *Love's Labour's Lost*, the reader goes to a great feast of language yet somehow comes away only with the scraps.

STEPHEN MATTERSON
Dublin, 1 April 1989

A NOTE ON THE TEXT

The Confidence-Man was first published by Dix, Edwards & Co. in New York on 1 April 1857, and a few days later by Longman, Brown, Green, Longmans & Roberts in London. Melville saw neither edition through the press, since after completion of the novel in 1856 he travelled to Europe and the Holy Land. The English edition was almost certainly set from the proofs of the American edition, since there are corrections to obvious errors in the first printing. In addition to these there are anglicizations, two annotations which explain American terms, and some fresh errors. The novel was not reprinted until 1923, while the first scholarly emended text, edited by Elizabeth S. Foster, appeared in 1954, followed by those of H. Bruce Franklin in 1967 and of Hershel Parker in 1971. The authoritative Northwestern-Newberry Edition was published in 1984 as Volume 10 of *The Writings of Herman Melville*, edited by Harrison Hayford, Hershel Parker and G. Thomas Tanselle. The Northwestern-Newberry editors made 29 word changes and 109 emendations of punctuation from the first American edition, and their extensive editorial apparatus includes details of some of the emendations. Many of these had already been made in the 1857 English edition.

The present text derives from the 1857 English edition. I have emended punctuation where there is an obvious printer's error, and have adopted several of the Northwestern-Newberry readings. In most cases the punctuation changes have been made silently, but all substantive changes have been duly noted.

BIBLIOGRAPHY

The growing reputation of *The Confidence-Man* is reflected in the surge of recent criticism on it. While it was only reprinted once between 1857 and 1954, there are now a variety of editions available. In spite of later critical developments, Elizabeth S. Foster's pioneering 1954 edition maintains its importance for the serious reader, as do the editions by H. Bruce Franklin (1967) and Hershel Parker (1971). The latter usefully includes a selection of critical material. The 1984 Northwestern-Newberry edition, edited by Hayford, Parker and Tanselle, is, in keeping with the standards of the other volumes in the series, meticulous. It includes an Editorial Appendix over 250 pages long. In preparing this edition for Penguin, I am deeply indebted to these previous editors and annotators. The 1989 Oxford edition in the World's Classics series reprints almost without change the 1923 Constable text. It has a good introduction by Tony Tanner.

Several bibliographies for *The Confidence-Man* need to be mentioned. The Norton edition includes an annotated bibliography compiled by Watson G. Branch, though it only includes items up to 1970. The bibliography in the Northwestern-Newberry edition is useful, though the most up to date is that of John Bryant, in his *Companion to Melville Studies*. Bryant also provides an excellent survey of the novel and the criticism it has stimulated. Contemporary reviews of *The Confidence-Man* are available in *Melville: The Critical Heritage*, edited by Watson G. Branch, and a Concordance to the novel has been made by Larry E. Wegener.

The biographies by Newton Arvin and Leon Howard (listed below) have much that is relevant to *The Confidence-Man*, as do the materials collected by Jay Leyda in *The Melville Log*. The novel's context and the notion of 'confidence' are examined in several important recent works; see the books by Wadlington, Kuhlmann, Lindberg, Blair, Lenz, and Beaver, listed below. Helen Trimpi's book identifying the confidence men is important in demonstrating how far the novel's themes are those of the 1850s.

BOOKS

Editions of *The Confidence-Man*

FOSTER, ELIZABETH S. (ed.), *The Confidence-Man* (New York: Hendricks House, 1954).

FRANKLIN, H. BRUCE (ed.), *The Confidence-Man* (Indianapolis: Bobbs-Merrill, 1967).

HAYFORD, HARRISON, HERSHEL PARKER, and G. THOMAS TANSELLE (eds.), *The Confidence-Man* (Vol. 10 of the Northwestern-Newberry Edition of the writings of Herman Melville) (Evanston, IL: Northwestern University Press, 1984).

PARKER, HERSHEL (ed.), *The Confidence-Man* (New York: W. W. Norton, 1971).

Criticism and biography

ALDER, JOYCE SPARER, *War in Melville's Imagination* (New York: New York University Press, 1981).

ARVIN, NEWTON, *Herman Melville* (New York: Sloane Associates, 1950).

BEAVER, HAROLD, *The Great American Masquerade* (London: Vision Press, 1985).

BEPPO, KEIKO (ed.), *Religious and Moral Ambiguity: Essays on Melville's The Confidence-Man* (Kobe, Japan: Kobe College Research Institute, 1985).

BERNSTEIN, JOHN, *Pacifism and Rebellion in the Writings of Herman Melville* (The Hague: Mouton, 1964).

BERTHOFF, WARNER, *The Example of Melville* (Princeton, NJ: Princeton University Press, 1962).

BLAIR, JOHN G., *The Confidence Man in Modern Fiction: A Rogue's Gallery with Six Portraits* (London: Vision Press, 1979).

BOWEN, MERLIN, *The Long Encounter: Self and Experience in the Writings of Herman Melville* (Chicago: University of Chicago Press, 1960).

BRANCH, WATSON G. (ed.), *Melville: The Critical Heritage* (London: Routledge & Kegan Paul, 1974).

BRYANT, JOHN (ed.), *A Companion to Melville Studies* (Westport, CT: Greenwood, 1986).

CHASE, RICHARD, *Herman Melville: A Critical Study* (New York: Macmillan, 1949).

DAVIS, M. R., and W. H. GILMAN (eds.), *The Letters of Herman Melville* (New Haven, CT: Yale University Press, 1960).

DILLINGHAM, WILLIAM, *Melville's Later Novels* (Athens, GA, and London: University of Georgia Press, 1986).

DRINNON, RICHARD, *Facing West: The Metaphysics of Indian-Hating and Empire Building* (Minneapolis: University of Minnesota Press, 1980).

DRYDEN, EDGAR A., *Melville's Thematics of Form: The Great Art of Telling the Truth* (Baltimore, MD: Johns Hopkins University Press, 1968).

DUBAN, JAMES, *Melville's Major Fiction: Politics, Theology and Imagination* (Dekalb: Northern Illinois University Press, 1983).

FIEDELSON, CHARLES, *Symbolism and American Literature* (Chicago: University of Chicago Press, 1953).

FRANKLIN, H. BRUCE, *The Wake of the Gods* (Stanford, CT: Stanford University Press, 1963).

FREEMAN, JOHN, *Herman Melville* (London: Macmillan, 1926).

FUSSELL, EDWIN, *Frontier: American Literature and the American West* (Princeton, NJ: Princeton University Press, 1965).

HAUK, RICHARD BOYD, *A Cheerful Nihilism: Confidence and 'The Absurd' in American Humorous Fiction* (Bloomington: Indiana University Press, 1971).

HOFFMAN, DANIEL G., *Form and Fable in American Fiction* (New York: Oxford University Press, 1961).

HOWARD, LEON, *Herman Melville: A Biography* (Berkeley and Los Angeles: University of California Press, 1951; 2nd edn. 1958).

HUMPHREYS, A. R., *Melville* (Edinburgh: Oliver & Boyd, 1962).

KARCHER, CAROLYN LURY, *Shadow Over the Promised Land: Slavery, Race and Violence in Melville's America* (Baton Rouge: Louisiana University Press, 1980).

KETTERER, DAVID, *New Worlds for Old* (Bloomington and London: Indiana University Press, 1974).

KUHLMANN, SUSAN, *Knave, Fool and Genius; The Confidence Man as He Appears in Nineteenth Century American Fiction* (Chapel Hill: University of North Carolina Press, 1973).

LEBOWITZ, ALAN, *Progress Into Silence: A Study of Melville's Heroes* (Bloomington: Indiana University Press, 1970).

LEE, ROBERT A. (ed.), *Herman Melville: Reassessments* (London: Vision Press, 1984).

LENZ, WILLIAM E., *Fast Talk and Flush Times: The Confidence Man as a Literary Convention* (Columbia, MO: University of Missouri Press, 1985).

LEWIS, R. W. B., *Trials of the Word* (New Haven, CT: Yale University Press, 1965).

LEYDA, JAY, *The Melville Log* (New York: Harcourt Brace & Co., 1951).

LINDBERG, GARY, *The Confidence Man in American Literature* (New York and Oxford: Oxford University Press, 1982).

MASON, RONALD, *The Spirit Above the Dust: A Study of Herman Melville* (London: John Lehmann, 1951).

MATTHIESSON, F. O., *American Renaissance* (Oxford: Oxford University Press, 1941, 1968).

MUSHABAC, JANE, *Melville's Humor: A Critical Study* (Hamden, CT: Archon Books, 1981).

POMMER, HENRY F., *Milton and Melville* (Pittsburgh, PA: University of Pittsburgh Press, 1950).

PORTE, JOEL, *The Romance in America: Studies in Cooper, Poe, Hawthorne, Melville and James* (Middleton, CT: Wesleyan University Press, 1969).

QUIRK, TOM, *Melville's Confidence-Man: From Knave to Knight* (Columbia, MO: University of Missouri Press, 1982).

ROGIN, MICHAEL PAUL, *Subversive Genealogy: The Politics and Art of Herman Melville* (New York: Knopf, 1983).

ROSENBERRY, E. H., *Melville and the Comic Spirit* (Cambridge, MA: Harvard University Press, 1955).

Melville (London: Routledge & Kegan Paul, 1979).

SEDGWICK, WILLIAM, *Herman Melville: The Tragedy of Mind* (Cambridge, MA: Harvard University Press, 1944).

SEELYE, JOHN D., *Melville: The Ironic Diagram* (Evanston, IL: Northwestern University Press, 1970).

THOMPSON, LAWRANCE, *Melville's Quarrel with God* (Princeton, NJ: Princeton University Press, 1952).

TRIMPI, HELEN, *Melville's Confidence Men and American Politics in the 1850s* (Hamden, CT: Archon Books, 1987).

WADLINGTON, WARWICK, *The Confidence Game in American Literature* (Princeton, NJ: Princeton University Press, 1975).

WEGENER, LARRY E. (ed.), *A Concordance to Herman Melville's 'The Confidence-Man'* (New York: Garland, 1987).

WINTERS, YVOR, *In Defense of Reason* (Chicago: Swallow Press, 1937, 1947).

WRIGHT, NATHALIA, *Melville's Use of the Bible* (Durham, NC: Duke University Press, 1949).

ARTICLES

BAYM, NINA, 'Melville's Quarrel with Fiction', *PMLA*, XCIV (1979), 909–23.

BELL, MICHAEL DAVITT, 'Melville and "Romance": Literary Nationalism and Literary Form', *American Transcendental Quarterly*, 24 (1974), 56–62.

BELLIS, PETER, 'Melville's *The Confidence-Man*: An Uncharitable Interpretation', *American Literature*, LIX (1987), 548–69.

BERGMANN, JOHANNES DIETRICH, 'The Original Confidence Man', *American Quarterly*, XXI (1969), 560–77.

BOWEN, MERLIN, 'Tactics of Indirection in Melville's *The Confidence-Man*', *Studies in the Novel*, I (1969), 401–20.

BRANCH, WATSON G., 'The Genesis, Composition and Structure of *The Confidence-Man*', *Nineteenth Century Fiction*, VII (1973), 424–48.

BRODTKORB, PAUL, '*The Confidence-Man*: The Con-Man as Hero', *Studies in the Novel*, I (1969), 421–35.

BROOKS, VAN WYCK, 'A Reviewer's Notebook', *The Freeman*, 7 (9 May 1923), 214–15.

BRYANT, JOHN, 'Allegory and Breakdown in *The Confidence-Man*: Melville's Comedy of Doubt', *Philological Quarterly*, LXV (1986), 113–30.

'Citizens of a World to Come: Melville and the Millennial Cosmopolite', *American Literature*, LIX (1987), 20–36.

'Melville's Comic Debate: Geniality and the Aesthetics of Repose', *American Literature*, LV (1983), 151–70.

'"Nowhere a Stranger": Melville and Cosmopolitanism', *Nineteenth Century Fiction*, XXXIX (1984), 275–91.

CAWELTI, JOHN G., 'Some Notes on the Structure of *The Confidence-Man*', *American Literature*, XXIX (1957), 278–88.

CHABOT, BARRY C., 'Melville's *The Confidence-Man*: A "Poisonous" Reading', *Psychoanalytical Review*, LXIII (1976–7), 571–85.

CHASE, RICHARD, 'Melville's Confidence Man', *Kenyon Review*, XI (1949), 122–40.

DREW, PHILIP, 'Appearance and Reality in Melville's *The Confidence-Man*', *ELH*, XXXI (1964), 418–42.

DUBLER, WALTER, 'Theme and Structure in Melville's *The Confidence-Man*', *American Literature*, XXXIII (1961), 307–19.

DURER, CHRISTOPHER S., 'Melville's *The Confidence-Man* and Jean-Jacques Rousseau', *Comparative Literature Studies*, XXI (1984), 450.

GAUDINO, REBECCA J. KRUGER, 'The Riddle of *The Confidence-Man*', *Journal of Narrative Technique*, XIV (1984), 124–41.

HAYFORD, HARRISON, 'Poe in *The Confidence-Man*', *Nineteenth Century Fiction*, XIV (1959), 207–18.

HOFFMAN, DANIEL, 'Melville's Story of "China Aster"', *American Literature*, XXII (1950), 137–49.

HORSFORD, HOWARD C., 'Evidence for Melville's Plans for a Sequel to *The Confidence-Man*', *American Literature*, XXIV (1952), 85–8.

KARCHER, CAROLYN LURY, 'The Story of Charlemont: A Dramatization of Melville's Concepts of Fiction in *The Confidence-Man*', *Nineteenth Century Fiction*, XXI (1966), 73–84.

KEMPER, STEVEN E., '*The Confidence-Man*: A Knavishly-Packed Deck', *Studies in American Fiction*, VIII (1980), 23–35.

LAMB, ROBERT PAUL, 'The Place of *The Confidence-Man* in Melville's Career', *Southern Review*, XXII (1986), 489–505.

MCHANEY, T. L., '*The Confidence Man* and Satan's Disguises in *Paradise Lost*', *Nineteenth Century Fiction*, XXX (1975), 200–206.

MILLER, JAMES E., JR, '*The Confidence-Man*: His Guises', *PMLA*, LXXIV (1959), 102–11.

NICHOL, JOHN W., 'Melville and the Midwest', *PMLA*, LXVI (1951), 613–25.

NORRIS, WILLIAM, 'Abbott Lawrence in *The Confidence-Man*: American Success or American Failure', *American Studies*, XVII (1976), 25–38.

OLIVER, EGBERT S., 'Melville's Goneril and Fanny Kemble', *New England Quarterly*, XVIII (1945), 489–500.

'Melville's Picture of Emerson and Thoreau in *The Confidence-Man*', *College English*, VIII (1946), 61–72.

PARKER, HERSHEL, 'Melville's Satire of Emerson and Thoreau: An Evaluation of the Evidence', *American Transcendental Quarterly*, 7 (1970), 61–7; ctd in no. 9 (1971), 70.

'The Metaphysics of Indian-hating', *Nineteenth Century Fiction*, XVIII (1963), 165–73.

PEARCE, ROY HARVEY, 'Melville's Indian-Hater: A Note on a Meaning of *The Confidence-Man*', *PMLA*, LXVII (1952), 942–48.

RAMSEY, WILLIAM M., 'Melville's and Barnum's Man with a Weed', *American Literature*, LXI (1979), 101–4.

'The Moot Points of Melville's Indian-Hating', *American Literature*, LII (1980), 224–35.

'Touching Scenes in *The Confidence-Man*', *Emerson Society Quarterly*, 25 (1979), 37–62.

REEVES, PASCHAL, 'The "Deaf Mute" Confidence Man: Melville's Impostor in Action', *Modern Language Notes*, LXXXV (1960), 18–20.

REYNOLDS, MICHAEL S., 'The Prototype for Melville's Confidence-Man', *PMLA*, LXXXVI (1971), 1009–13.

ROSENBERRY, E. H., 'Melville's Ship of Fools', *PMLA*, LXXV (1960), 604–8.

SATTELMEYER, ROBERT, and JAMES BARBOUR, 'A Possible Source and Model for China Aster in Melville's *The Confidence-Man*', *American Literature*, XLVIII (1977), 577–83.

SEELYE, J. D., 'Timothy Flint's "Wicked River" and *The Confidence-Man*', *PMLA*, LXXVIII (1963), 75–9.

'"Ungraspable Phantom": Reflections of Hawthorne in *Pierre* and *The Confidence-Man*', *Studies in the Novel*, I (1969), 436–43.

SELTZER, LEON F., 'Camus's Absurd and the World of Melville's Confidence-Man', *PMLA*, LXXXII (1967), 14–27.

SEWELL, DAVID, 'Mercantile Philosophy and the Dialectics of Confidence: Another Perspective on *The Confidence-Man*', *Emerson Society Quarterly*, 30 (1984), 99–110.

SHROEDER, JOHN W., 'Sources and Symbols for Melville's *The Confidence-Man*', *PMLA*, LXVI (1951), 363–80.

SMITH, PAUL, '*The Confidence-Man* and the Literary World of New York', *Nineteenth Century Fiction*, XVI (1962), 329–37.

STEIN, WILLIAM BYSSHE, 'Melville's *The Confidence-Man*: Quicksands of the Word', *American Transcendental Quarterly*, 24 (1974), 38–50.

STEN, CHRISTOPHER W., 'The Dialogue of Crisis in *The Confidence Man*', *Studies in the Novel*, VI (1974), 165–85.

STRICKLAND, EDWARD, 'The Ruins of Romanticism in *The Confidence Man*', *American Notes and Queries*, XXII (1983), 40–43.

SUSSMAN, HENRY, 'The Deconstructor as Politician: Melville's *The Confidence-Man*', *Glyph*, IV (1978), 32–56.

TICHI, CECELIA, 'Melville's Craft and Theme of Language Debased in *The Confidence-Man*', *ELH*, XXXIX (1972), 639–58.

TRIMPI, HELEN P., 'Harlequin-Confidence-Man: The Satirical Tradition of Commedia Dell'Arte and Pantomime in Melville's *The Confidence-Man*', *Texas Studies in Literature and Language*, XVI (1974), 147–93.

'Three of Melville's Confidence Men', *Texas Studies in Literature and Language*, XXI (1979), 368–95.

TUVESON, ERNEST LEE, 'The Creed of the Confidence-Man', *ELH*, XXXIII (1966), 247–70.

WEISSBUCH, TED N., 'A Note on the Confidence-Man's Counterfeit Detector', *Emerson Society Quarterly*, 19 (1960), 16–18.

WRIGHT, NATHALIA, 'The Confidence Men of Melville and Cooper: An American Indictment', *American Quarterly*, IV (1952), 266–8.

THE

CONFIDENCE - MAN:

HIS MASQUERADE.

BY

HERMAN MELVILLE,

AUTHOR OF "PIAZZA TALES," "OMOO," "TYPEE," ETC. ETC.

Authorised Edition.

LONDON:

LONGMAN, BROWN, GREEN, LONGMANS, & ROBERTS.

1857.

The right of translation is reserved.

Title-page of the first English edition (1857)

CONTENTS

sensible
skeptical
cynical
paranoia

ways to get around this world view!

- charity
- gaslighting
- flattery
- comrades

Speculation → gambling

I

A MUTE GOES ABOARD A BOAT ON THE
MISSISSIPPI

At sunrise on a first of April, there appeared, suddenly as Manco Capac at the lake Titicaca, a man in cream-colours, at the waterside in the city of St Louis.

His cheek was fair, his chin downy, his hair flaxen, his hat a white fur one, with a long fleecy nap. He had neither trunk, valise, carpet-bag, nor parcel. No porter followed him. He was unaccompanied by friends. From the shrugged shoulders, titters, whispers, wonderings of the crowd, it was plain that he was, in the extremest sense of the word, a stranger.

In the same moment with his advent, he stepped aboard the favourite steamer Fidèle, on the point of starting for New Orleans. Stared at, but unsaluted, with the air of one neither courting nor shunning regard, but evenly pursuing the path of duty, lead it through solitudes or cities, he held on his way along the lower deck until he chanced to come to a placard near the captain's office, offering a reward for the capture of a mysterious impostor, supposed to have recently arrived from the East – quite an original genius in his vocation, as would appear, though wherein his originality consisted was not clearly given; but what purported to be a careful description of his person followed.

As if it had been a play-bill, crowds were gathered about the announcement, and among them certain chevaliers, whose eyes, it was plain, were on the capitals, or, at least, earnestly seeking a sight of them from behind intervening coats; but as for their fingers, they were enveloped in some myth; though, during a chance interval, one of these chevaliers somewhat showed his hand in purchasing from another chevalier, ex-officio a peddler of money-belts, one of his popular safe-guards, while another peddler, who was still another versatile chevalier, hawked, in the thick of the throng, the lives of Meason, the bandit of Ohio, Murrel, the pirate of the Mississippi, and the brothers Harpe, the Thugs of the Green River country, in Kentucky — creatures, with others of the sort, one and all exterminated at the time, and for the most part, like the hunted generations of wolves in the same regions, leaving comparatively few successors; which would seem cause for unalloyed gratulation, and is so to all except those who think that in new countries, where the wolves are killed off, the foxes increase.

Pausing at this spot, the stranger so far succeeded in threading his way, as at last to plant himself just beside the placard, when, producing a small slate and tracing some words upon it, he held it up before him on a level with the placard, so that they who read the one might read the other. The words were these:

'Charity thinketh no evil.'

As, in gaining his place, some little perseverance, not to say persistence, of a mildly inoffensive sort, had been unavoidable, it was not with the best relish that the crowd regarded his apparent intrusion; and upon a more attentive survey, perceiving no badge of authority about him, but rather something quite the contrary — he being of an aspect so singularly innocent; an aspect, too, which they took to be somehow inappropriate to the time and place, and inclining to the notion that his writing was of much the same sort: in short, taking him for some strange kind of simpleton, harmless enough, would he keep to himself, but not wholly unobnoxious as an intruder — they made no scruple to jostle him aside; while one, less kind than the rest, or more of a wag, by an unobserved stroke, dexterously flattened down his fleecy hat upon his head. Without readjusting it, the stranger quietly turned, and writing anew upon the slate, again held it up:

'Charity suffereth long, and is kind.'

Ill pleased with his pertinacity, as they thought it, the crowd a second time thrust him aside, and not without epithets and some buffets, all of which were unresented. But, as if at last despairing of so difficult an adventure, wherein one, apparently a non-resistant, sought to impose his presence upon fighting characters, the stranger now moved slowly away, yet not before altering his writing to this:

'Charity endureth all things.'

Shield-like bearing his slate before him, amid stares and jeers he moved slowly up and down, at his turning points again changing his inscription to –

'Charity believeth all things.'

and then –

'Charity never faileth.'

The word charity, as originally traced, remained throughout uneffaced, not unlike the left-hand numeral of a printed date, otherwise left for convenience in blank.

To some observers, the singularity, if not lunacy, of the stranger was heightened by his muteness, and, perhaps also, by the contrast to his proceedings afforded in the actions – quite in the wonted and sensible order of things – of the barber of the boat, whose quarters, under a smoking-saloon, and over against a bar-room, were next door but two to the captain's office. As if the long, wide, covered deck, hereabouts built up on both sides with shop-like windowed spaces, were some Constantinople arcade or bazaar, where more than one trade is plied, this river barber, aproned and slippered, but rather crusty-looking for the moment, it may be from being newly out of bed, was throwing open his premises for the day, and suitably arranging the exterior. With business-like dispatch, having rattled down his shutters, and at a palm-tree angle set out in the iron fixture his little ornamental pole, and this without overmuch tenderness for the elbows and toes of the crowd, he concluded his operations by bidding people stand still more aside, when, jumping on a stool, he hung over his door, on the customary nail, a gaudy sort of illuminated pasteboard sign, skilfully executed by himself, gilt with the likeness of a razor elbowed in readiness to shave, and also, for the public benefit, with two words not unfrequently seen ashore gracing other shops besides barbers':

'NO TRUST' –

an inscription which, though in a sense not less intrusive than the contrasted ones of the stranger, did not, as it seemed, provoke any corresponding derision or surprise, much less indignation; and still less, to all appearances, did it gain for the inscriber the repute of being a simpleton.

Meanwhile, he with the slate continued moving slowly up and down, not without causing some stares to change into jeers, and some jeers into pushes, and some pushes into punches; when suddenly, in one of his turns, he was hailed from behind by two porters carrying a large trunk; but as the summons, though loud, was without effect, they accidentally or otherwise swung their burden against him, nearly overthrowing him; when, by a quick start, a peculiar inarticulate moan, and a pathetic telegraphing of his fingers, he involuntarily betrayed that he was not only dumb but also deaf.

Presently, as if not wholly unaffected by his reception thus far, he went forward, seating himself in a retired spot on the forecastle, near the foot of a ladder there leading to a deck above, up and down which ladder some of the boatmen, in discharge of their duties, were occasionally going.

From his betaking himself to this humble quarter, it was evident that, as a deck-passenger, the stranger, simple though he seemed, was not entirely ignorant of his place, though his taking a deck-passage might have been partly for convenience; as, from his having no luggage, it was probable that his destination was one of the small wayside landings within a few hours' sail. But, though he might not have a long way to go, yet he seemed already to have come from a very long distance.

Though neither soiled nor slovenly, his cream-coloured suit had a tossed look, almost linty, as if, travelling night and day from some far country beyond the prairies, he had long been without the solace of a bed. His aspect was at once gentle and jaded, and, from the moment of seating himself, increasing in tired abstraction and dreaminess. Gradually overtaken by slumber, his flaxen head drooped, his whole lamb-like figure relaxed, and, half reclining against the ladder's foot, lay motionless, as some sugar-snow in March, which, softly stealing down over night, with its white placidity startles the brown farmer peering out from his threshold at daybreak.

2

SHOWING THAT MANY MEN HAVE MANY
MINDS

———◦⊩◦———

'Odd fish!'

'Poor fellow!'

'Who can he be?'

'Casper Hauser.'

'Bless my soul!'

'Uncommon countenance.'

'Green prophet from Utah.'

'Humbug!'

'Singular innocence.'

'Means something.'

'Spirit-rapper.'

'Moon-calf.'

'Piteous.'

'Trying to enlist interest.'

'Beware of him.'

'Fast asleep here, and, doubtless, pick-pockets on board.'

'Kind of daylight Endymion.'

'Escaped convict, worn out with dodging.'

'Jacob dreaming at Luz.'

Such the epitaphic comments, conflictingly spoken or thought, of a miscellaneous company, who, assembled on the overlooking, cross-wise balcony at the forward end of the upper deck hard by, had not witnessed preceding occurrences.

Meantime, like some enchanted man in his grave, happily oblivious of all gossip, whether chiselled or chatted, the deaf and dumb stranger still tranquilly slept, while now the boat started on her voyage.

The great ship-canal of Ving-King-Ching, in the Flowery King-dom, seems the Mississippi in parts, where, amply flowing between low, vine-tangled banks, flat as tow-paths, it bears the huge toppling steamers, bedizened and lacquered within like imperial junks.

Pierced along its great white bulk with two tiers of small embrasure-like windows, well above the water-line, the Fidèle, though, might at distance have been taken by strangers for some whitewashed fort on a floating isle.

Merchants on 'change seem the passengers that buzz on her decks, while, from quarters unseen, comes a murmur as of bees in the comb. Fine promenades, domed saloons, long galleries, sunny balconies, confidential passages, bridal chambers, state-rooms plenty as pigeon-holes, and out-of-the-way retreats like secret drawers in an escritoire, present like facilities for publicity or privacy. Auctioneer or coiner, with equal ease, might somewhere here drive his trade.

Though her voyage of twelve hundred miles extends from apple to orange, from clime to clime, yet, like any small ferry-boat, to right and left, at every landing, the huge Fidèle still receives additional passengers in exchange for those that dis-embark; so that, though always full of strangers, she continually, in some degree, adds to, or replaces them with strangers still more strange; like the Rio Janeiro fountain, fed from the Corcovado mountains, which is ever overflowing with strange waters, but never with the same strange particles in every part.

Though hitherto, as has been seen, the man in cream-colours had by no means passed unobserved, yet by stealing into retire-ment, and there going asleep and continuing so, he seemed to have courted oblivion, a boon not often withheld from so humble an applicant as he. Those staring crowds on the shore were now left far behind, seen dimly clustering like swallows on eaves; while the passengers' attention was soon drawn away to the rapidly shooting high bluffs and shot-towers on the Missouri shore, or the bluff-looking Missourians and towering Kentuckians among the throngs on the decks.

By-and-by – two or three random stoppages having been
made, and the last transient memory of the slumberer vanished,
and he himself, not unlikely, waked up and landed ere now – the
crowd, as is usual, began in all parts to break up from a concourse
into various clusters or squads, which in some cases disintegrated
again into quartettes, trios, and couples, and even solitaires; involuntarily submitting to that natural law which ordains dissolution equally to the mass, as in time to the member.

As among Chaucer's Canterbury pilgrims, or those oriental ones
crossing the Red Sea towards Mecca in the festival month, there
was no lack of variety. Natives of all sorts, and foreigners; men of
business and men of pleasure; parlour men and backwoodsmen;
farm-hunters and fame-hunters; heiress-hunters, gold-hunters,
buffalo-hunters, bee-hunters, happiness-hunters, truth-hunters,
and still keener hunters after all these hunters. Fine ladies in slippers,
and moccasined squaws; Northern speculators and Eastern philosophers; English, Irish, German, Scotch, Danes; Santa Fé traders in
striped blankets, and Broadway bucks in cravats of cloth of gold;
fine-looking Kentucky boatmen, and Japanese-looking Mississippi
cotton-planters; Quakers in full drab, and United States soldiers in
full regimentals; slaves, black, mulatto, quadroon; modish young
Spanish Creoles, and old-fashioned French Jews; Mormons and
Papists; Dives and Lazarus; jesters and mourners, teetotalers and
convivialists, deacons and blacklegs; hard-shell Baptists and clay-
eaters; grinning negroes, and Sioux chiefs solemn as high-priests. In
short, a piebald parliament, an Anacharsis Cloots congress of all
kinds of that multiform pilgrim species, man.

As pine, beech, birch, ash, hackmatack, hemlock, spruce, bass-
wood, maple, interweave their foliage in the natural wood, so
these varieties of mortals blended their varieties of visage and
garb. A Tartar-like picturesqueness; a sort of pagan abandonment
and assurance. Here reigned the dashing and all-fusing spirit of the
West, whose type is the Mississippi itself, which, uniting the
streams of the most distant and opposite zones, pours them along,
helter-skelter, in one cosmopolitan and confident tide.

3

IN WHICH A VARIETY OF CHARACTERS APPEAR

In the forward part of the boat, not the least attractive object, for a time, was a grotesque negro cripple, in tow-cloth attire and an old coal-sifter of a tambourine in his hand, who, owing to something wrong about his legs, was, in effect, cut down to the stature of a Newfoundland dog; his knotted black fleece and good-natured, honest black face rubbing against the upper part of people's thighs as he made shift to shuffle about, making music, such as it was, and raising a smile even from the gravest. It was curious to see him, out of his very deformity, indigence, and houselessness, so cheerily endured, raising mirth in some of that crowd, whose own purses, hearths, hearts, all their possessions, sound limbs included, could not make gay.

'What is your name, old boy?' said a purple-faced drover, putting his large purple hand on the cripple's bushy wool, as if it were the curled forehead of a black steer.

'Der Black Guinea dey calls me, sar.'

'And who is your master, Guinea?'

'Oh sar, I am der dog widout massa.'

'A free dog, eh? Well, on your account, I'm sorry for that, Guinea. Dogs without masters fare hard.'

'So dey do, sar; so dey do. But you see, sar, dese here legs? What ge'mman want to own dese here legs?'

'But where do you live?'

'All 'long shore, sar; dough now I'se going to see brodder at der landing; but chiefly I libs in der city.'

'St Louis, ah? Where do you sleep there of nights?'

'On der floor of der good baker's oven, sar.'

'In an oven? whose, pray? What baker, I should like to know, bakes such black bread in his oven, alongside of his nice white roll, too. Who is that too charitable baker, pray?'

'Dar he be,' with a broad grin, lifting his tambourine high over his head.

'The sun is the baker, eh?'

'Yes sar, in der city dat good baker warms der stones for dis ole darkie when he sleeps out on der pabements o' nights.'

'But that must be in the summer only, old boy. How about winter, when the cold Cossacks come clattering and jingling? How about winter, old boy?'

'Den dis poor old darkie shakes werry bad, I tell you, sar. Oh sar, oh! don't speak ob der winter,' he added, with a reminiscent shiver, shuffling off into the thickest of the crowd, like a half-frozen black sheep nudging itself a cozy berth in the heart of the white flock.

Thus far not very many pennies had been given him, and, used at last to his strange looks, the less polite passengers of those in that part of the boat began to get their fill of him as a curious object; when suddenly the negro more than revived their first interest by an expedient which, whether by chance or design, was a singular temptation at once to *diversion* and charity, though, even more than his crippled limbs, it put him on a canine footing. In short, as in appearance he seemed a dog, so now, in a merry way, like a dog he began to be treated. Still shuffling among the crowd, now and then he would pause, throwing back his head and opening his mouth like an elephant for tossed apples at a menagerie; when, making a space before him, people would have a bout at a strange sort of pitch-penny game, the cripple's mouth being at once target and purse, and he hailing each expertly-caught copper with a cracked bravura from his tambourine. To be the subject of almsgiving is trying, and to feel in duty bound to appear cheerfully grateful under the trial, must be still more so; but whatever his secret emotions, he swallowed them, while still retaining each copper this side the oesophagus. And nearly always he grinned, and only once or twice did he wince, which was when certain coins, tossed by more playful almoners, came inconveniently near his teeth, an accident whose unwelcomeness was not unedged by the circumstance that the pennies thus thrown proved buttons.

While this game of charity was yet at its height, a limping, gimlet-eyed, sour-faced person – it may be some discharged custom-house officer, who, suddenly stripped of convenient means of support, had resolved to be avenged on government and humanity by making himself miserable for life, either by hating or suspecting everything and everybody – this shallow unfortunate, after sundry sorry observations of the negro, began to croak out something about his deformity being a sham, got up for financial purposes, which immediately threw a damp upon the frolic benignities of the pitch-penny players.

But that these suspicions came from one who himself on a wooden leg went halt, this did not appear to strike anybody present. That cripples, above all men, should be companionable, or, at least, refrain from picking a fellow-limper to pieces, in short, should have a little sympathy in common misfortune, seemed not to occur to the company.

Meantime, the negro's countenance, before marked with even more than patient good-nature, drooped into a heavy-hearted expression, full of the most painful distress. So far abased beneath its proper physical level, that Newfoundland-dog face turned in passively hopeless appeal, as if instinct told it that the right or the wrong might not have overmuch to do with whatever wayward mood superior intelligences might yield to.

But instinct, though knowing, is yet a teacher set below reason, which itself says, in the grave words of Lysander in the comedy, after Puck has made a sage of him with his spell:

The will of man is by his reason swayed.

So that, suddenly change as people may, in their dispositions, it is not always waywardness, but improved judgment, which, as in Lysander's case, or the present, operates with them.

Yes, they began to scrutinize the negro curiously enough; when, emboldened by this evidence of the efficacy of his words, the wooden-legged man hobbled up to the negro, and, with the air of a beadle, would, to prove his alleged imposture on the spot, have stripped him and then driven him away, but was prevented by the crowd's clamour, now taking part with the poor fellow, against one who had just before turned nearly all minds the other way. So he with the wooden leg was forced to retire; when the rest, finding themselves left sole judges in the case, could not resist the opportunity of acting the part: not because it is a human weakness to take pleasure in sitting in judgment upon one in a box, as surely this unfortunate negro now was, but that it strangely sharpens human perceptions, when, instead of standing by and having their fellow-feelings touched by the sight of an alleged culprit severely handled by some one justiciary, a crowd suddenly come to be all justiciaries in the same case themselves; as in Arkansas once, a man was found guilty, by law, of murder, but his condemnation being deemed unjust by the people, they rescued him to try him themselves; whereupon, they, as it turned out, found him even guiltier than the court had done, and forthwith proceeded to execution; so that the gallows presented the truly warning spectacle of a man hanged by his friends.

But not to such extremities, or anything like them, did the present crowd come; they, for the time, being content with putting the negro fairly and discreetly to the question; among other things, asking him, had he any documentary proof, any plain paper about him, attesting that his case was not a spurious one.

'No, no, dis poor ole darkie haint none o' dem waloable papers,' he wailed.

'But is there not some one who can speak a good word for you here?' said a person newly arrived from another part of the boat, a young Episcopal clergyman, in a long, straight-bodied black coat; small in stature, but manly; with a clear face and blue eye; innocence, tenderness, and good sense triumvirate in his air.

'Oh yes, oh yes, ge'mmen,' he eagerly answered, as if his memory, before suddenly frozen up by cold charity, as suddenly thawed back into fluidity at the first kindly word. 'Oh yes, oh yes, dar is aboard here a werry nice, good ge'mman wid a weed, and a ge'mman in a gray coat and white tie, what knows all about me; and a ge'mman wid a big book, too; and a yarb-doctor; and a ge'mman in a yaller west; and a ge'mman wid a brass plate; and a ge'mman in a wiolet robe; and a ge'mman as is a sodjer; and ever so many good, kind, honest ge'mmen more aboard what knows me and will speak for me, God bress 'em; yes, and what knows me as well as dis poor ole darkie knows hisself, God bress him! Oh, find 'em, find 'em,' he earnestly added, 'and let 'em come quick, and show you all, ge'mmen, dat dis poor ole darkie is werry well wordy of all you kind ge'mmen's kind confidence.'

'But how are we to find all these people in this great crowd?' was the question of a bystander, umbrella in hand; a middle-aged person, a country merchant apparently, whose natural good-feeling had been made at least cautious by the unnatural ill-feeling of the discharged custom-house officer.

'Where are we to find them?' half-rebukefully echoed the young Episcopal clergyman. 'I will go find one to begin with,' he quickly added, and, with kind haste suiting the action to the word, away he went.

'Wild-goose-chase!' croaked he with the wooden leg, now again drawing near. 'Don't believe there's a soul of them aboard. Did ever beggar have such heaps of fine friends? He can walk fast enough when he tries, a good deal faster than I; but he can lie yet faster. He's some white operator, betwisted and painted up for a decoy. He and his friends are all humbugs.'

'Have you no charity, friend?' here in self-subdued tones, singularly contrasted with his unsubdued person, said a Methodist minister, advancing; a tall, muscular, martial-looking man, a

Tennessean by birth, who in the Mexican war had been volunteer chaplain to a volunteer rifle-regiment.

'Charity is one thing, and truth is another,' rejoined he with the wooden leg: 'he's a rascal, I say.'

'But why not, friend, put as charitable a construction as one can upon the poor fellow?' said the soldier-like Methodist, with increased difficulty maintaining a pacific demeanour towards one whose own asperity seemed so little to entitle him to it: 'he looks honest, don't he?'

'Looks are one thing, and facts are another,' snapped out the other perversely; 'and as to your constructions, what construction can you put upon a rascal, but that a rascal he is?'

'Be not such a Canada thistle,' urged the Methodist, with something less of patience than before. 'Charity, man, charity.'

'To where it belongs with your charity! to heaven with it!' again snapped out the other, diabolically; 'here on earth true charity dotes, and false charity plots. Who betrays a fool with a kiss, the charitable fool has the charity to believe is in love with him, and the charitable knave on the stand gives charitable testimony for his comrade in the box.'

'Surely, friend,' returned the noble Methodist, with much ado restraining his still waxing indignation – 'surely, to say the least, you forget yourself. Apply it home,' he continued, with exterior calmness tremulous with inward emotion. 'Suppose, now, I should exercise no charity in judging your own character by the words which have fallen from you; what sort of vile, pitiless man do you think I would take you for?'

'No doubt' – with a grin – 'some such pitiless man as has lost his piety in much the same way that the jockey loses his honesty.'

'And how is that, friend?' still conscientiously holding back the old Adam in him, as if it were a mastiff he had by the neck.

'Never you mind how it is' – with a sneer; 'but all horses aint virtuous, no more than all men kind; and come close to, and much dealt with, some things are catching. When you find me a virtuous jockey, I will find you a benevolent wise man.'

'Some insinuation there.'

'More fool you that are puzzled by it.'

'Reprobate!' cried the other, his indignation now at last almost boiling over; 'godless reprobate! if charity did not restrain me, I could call you by names you deserve.'

'Could you, indeed?' with an insolent sneer.

'Yea, and teach you charity on the spot,' cried the goaded Methodist, suddenly catching this exasperating opponent by his shabby coat-collar, and shaking him till his timber-toe clattered on the deck like a nine-pin. 'You took me for a non-combatant did you? – thought, seedy coward that you are, that you could abuse a Christian with impunity. You find your mistake' – with another hearty shake.

'Well said and better done, church militant!' cried a voice.

'The white cravat against the world!' cried another.

'Bravo, bravo!' chorused many voices, with like enthusiasm taking sides with the resolute champion.

'You fools!' cried he with the wooden leg, writhing himself loose and inflamedly turning upon the throng; 'you flock of fools, under this captain of fools, in this ship of fools!'

With which exclamations, followed by idle threats against his admonisher, this condign victim to justice hobbled away, as disdaining to hold further argument with such a rabble. But his scorn was more than repaid by the hisses that chased him, in which the brave Methodist, satisfied with the rebuke already administered, was, to omit still better reasons, too magnanimous to join. All he said was, pointing towards the departing recusant, 'There he shambles off on his one lone leg, emblematic of his one-sided view of humanity.'

'But trust your painted decoy,' retorted the other from a distance, pointing back to the black cripple, 'and I have my revenge.'

'But we aint agoing to trust him!' shouted back a voice.

'So much the better,' he jeered back. 'Look you,' he added, coming to a dead halt where he was; 'look you, I have been called a Canada thistle. Very good. And a seedy one: still better. And the seedy Canada thistle has been pretty well shaken among ye; best of all. Dare say some seed has been shaken out; and won't it spring though? And when it does spring, do you cut down the young thistles, and won't they spring the more? It's encouraging and coaxing 'em. Now, when with my thistles your farms shall be well stocked, why then – you may abandon 'em!'

'What does all that mean, now?' asked the country merchant, staring.

'Nothing; the foiled wolf's parting howl,' said the Methodist. 'Spleen, much spleen, which is the rickety child of his evil heart of unbelief: it has made him mad. I suspect him for one naturally reprobate. Oh, friends,' raising his arms as in the pulpit, 'oh beloved, how are we admonished by the melancholy spectacle of this raver. Let us profit by the lesson; and is it not this: that if, next to mistrusting Providence, there be aught that man should pray against, it is against mistrusting his fellow man. I have been in mad-houses full of tragic mopers, and seen there the end of suspicion: the cynic, in the moody madness, muttering in the corner; for years a barren fixture there; head lopped over, gnawing his own lip, vulture of himself; while, by fits and starts, from the corner opposite came the grimace of the idiot at him.'

'What an example,' whispered one.

'Might deter Timon,' was the response.

'Oh, oh, good ge'mmen, have you no confidence in dis poor ole darkie?' now wailed the returning negro, who, during the late scene, had stumped apart in alarm.

'Confidence in you?' echoed he who had whispered, with abruptly changed air turning short round; 'that remains to be seen.'

'I tell you what it is, Ebony,' in similarly changed tones said he who had responded to the whisperer, 'yonder churl,' pointing toward the wooden leg in the distance, 'is, no doubt, a churlish fellow enough, and I would not wish to be like him; but that is no reason why you may not be some sort of black Jeremy Diddler.'

'No confidence in dis poor ole darkie, den?'

'Before giving you our confidence,' said a third, 'we will wait the report of the kind gentleman who went in search of one of your friends who was to speak for you.'

'Very likely, in that case,' said a fourth, 'we shall wait here till Christmas. Shouldn't wonder, did we not see that kind gentleman again. After seeking awhile in vain, he will conclude he has been made a fool of, and so not return to us for pure shame. Fact is, I begin to feel a little qualmish about the darkie myself. Something queer about this darkie, depend upon it.'

Once more the negro wailed, and turning in despair from the last speaker, imploringly caught the Methodist by the skirt of his coat. But a change had come over that before impassioned intercessor. With an irresolute and troubled air, he mutely eyed the suppliant; against whom, somehow, by what seemed instinctive influences, the distrusts first set on foot were now generally reviving, and, if anything, with added severity.

'No confidence in dis poor ole darkie,' yet again wailed the negro, letting go the coat-skirts and turning appealingly all round him.

'Yes, my poor fellow, I have confidence in you,' now exclaimed the country merchant before named, whom the negro's appeal, coming so piteously on the heel of pitilessness, seemed at last humanely to have decided in his favour. 'And here, here is some proof of my trust,' with which, tucking his umbrella under his arm, and diving down his hand into his pocket, he fished forth a purse, and, accidentally, along with it, his business card, which, unobserved, dropped to the deck. 'Here, here, my poor fellow,' he continued, extending a half dollar.

Not more grateful for the coin than the kindness, the cripple's face glowed like a polished copper saucepan, and shuffling a pace nearer, with one upstretched hand he received the alms, while, as unconsciously, his one advanced leather stump covered the card.

Done in despite of the general sentiment, the good deed of the merchant was not, perhaps, without its unwelcome return from the crowd, since that good deed seemed somehow to convey to them a sort of reproach. Still again, and more pertinaciously than ever, the cry arose against the negro, and still again he wailed forth his lament and appeal; among other things, repeating that the friends, of whom already he had partially run off the list, would freely speak for him, would anybody go find them.

'Why don't you go find 'em yourself?' demanded a gruff boatman.

'How can I go find 'em myself? Dis poor ole game-legged darkie's friends must come to him. Oh, whar, whar is dat good friend of dis darkie's, dat good man wid de weed?'

At this point, a steward ringing a bell came along, summoning all persons who had not got their tickets to step to the captain's office; an announcement which speedily thinned the throng about the black cripple, who himself soon forlornly stumped out of sight, probably on much the same errand as the rest.

4

RENEWAL OF OLD ACQUAINTANCE

━━━●∥●━━━

'How do you do, Mr Roberts?'

'Eh?'

'Don't you know me?'

'No, certainly.'

The crowd about the captain's office having in good time melted away, the above encounter took place in one of the side balconies astern, between a man in mourning clean and respectable, but none of the glossiest, a long weed on his hat, and the country-merchant before-mentioned, whom, with the familiarity of an old acquaintance, the former had accosted.

'Is it possible, my dear sir,' resumed he with the weed, 'that you do not recall my countenance? why yours I recall distinctly as if but half an hour, instead of half an age, had passed since I saw you. Don't you recall me, now? Look harder.'

'In my conscience – truly – I protest,' honestly bewildered, 'bless my soul, sir, I don't know you – really, really. But stay, stay,' he hurriedly added, not without gratification, glancing up at the crape on the stranger's hat, 'stay – yes – seems to me, though I have not the pleasure of personally knowing you, yet I am pretty sure I have at least *heard* of you, and recently too, quite recently. A poor negro aboard here referred to you, among others, for a character, I think.'

'Oh, the cripple. Poor fellow, I know him well. They found me. I have said all I could for him. I think I abated their distrust. Would I could have been of more substantial service. And apropos, sir,' he added, 'now that it strikes me, allow me to ask, whether the circumstance of one man, however humble, referring for a character to another man, however afflicted, does not argue more or less of moral worth in the latter?'

The good merchant looked puzzled.

'Still you don't recall my countenance?'

'Still does truth compel me to say that I cannot, despite my best efforts,' was the reluctantly-candid reply.

'Can I be so changed? Look at me. Or is it I who am mistaken? – Are you not, sir, Henry Roberts, forwarding merchant, of Wheeling, Virginia? Pray, now, if you use the advertisement of business cards, and happen to have one with you, just look at it, and see whether you are not the man I take you for.'

'Why,' a bit chafed, perhaps, 'I hope I know myself.'

'And yet self-knowledge is thought by some not so easy. Who knows, my dear sir, but for a time you may have taken yourself for somebody else? Stranger things have happened.'

The good merchant stared.

'To come to particulars, my dear sir, I met you, now some six years back, at Brade Brothers & Co.'s office, I think. I was travelling for a Philadelphia house. The senior Brade introduced us, you remember; some business-chat followed, then you forced me home with you to a family tea, and a family time we had. Have you forgotten about the urn, and what I said about Werther's Charlotte, and the bread and butter, and that capital story you told of the large loaf? A hundred times since, I have laughed over it. At least you must recall my name – Ringman, John Ringman.'

'Large loaf? Invited you to tea? Ringman? Ringman? Ring? Ring?'

'Ah sir,' sadly smiling, 'don't ring the changes that way. I see you have a faithless memory, Mr Roberts. But trust in the faithfulness of mine.'

'Well, to tell the truth, in some things my memory aint of the very best,' was the honest rejoinder. 'But still,' he perplexedly added, 'still I –'

'Oh sir, suffice it that it is as I say. Doubt not that we are all well acquainted.'

'But – but I don't like this going dead against my own memory; I –'

'But didn't you admit, my dear sir, that in some things this memory of yours is a little faithless? Now, those who have faithless memories, should they not have some little confidence in the less faithless memories of others?'

'But, of this friendly chat and tea, I have not the slightest –'

'I see, I see; quite erased from the tablet. Pray, sir,' with a sudden illumination, 'about six years back, did it happen to you to receive any injury on the head? Surprising effects have arisen from such a cause. Not alone unconsciousness as to events for a greater or less time immediately subsequent to the injury, but likewise – strange to add – oblivion, entire and incurable, as to events embracing a longer or shorter period immediately preceding it; that is, when the mind at the time was perfectly sensible of them, and fully competent also to register them in the memory, and did in fact so do; but all in vain, for all was afterwards bruised out by the injury.'

After the first start, the merchant listened with what appeared more than ordinary interest. The other proceeded:

'In my boyhood I was kicked by a horse, and lay insensible for a long time. Upon recovering, what a blank! No faintest trace in regard to how I had come near the horse, or what horse it was, or where it was, or that it was a horse at all that had brought me to that pass. For the knowledge of those particulars I am indebted solely to my friends, in whose statements, I need not say, I place implicit reliance, since particulars of some sort there must have been, and why should they deceive me? You see, sir, the mind is ductile, very much so: but images, ductilely received into it, need a certain time to harden and bake in their impressions, otherwise such a casualty as I speak of will in an instant obliterate them, as though they had never been. We are but clay, sir, potter's clay, as the good book says, clay, feeble, and too-yielding clay. But I will not philosophize. Tell me, was it your misfortune to receive any concussion upon the brain about the period I speak of? If so, I will with pleasure supply the void in your memory by more minutely rehearsing the circumstances of our acquaintance.'

The growing interest betrayed by the merchant had not relaxed as the other proceeded. After some hesitation, indeed, something more than hesitation, he confessed that, though he had never received any injury of the sort named, yet, about the time in question, he had in fact been taken with a brain fever, losing his mind completely for a considerable interval. He was continuing, when the stranger with much animation exclaimed:

'There now, you see, I was not wholly mistaken. That brain fever accounts for it all.'

'Nay; but —'

'Pardon me, Mr Roberts,' respectfully interrupting him, 'but time is short, and I have something private and particular to say to you. Allow me.'

Mr Roberts, good man, could but acquiesce, and the two having silently walked to a less public spot, the manner of the man with the weed suddenly assumed a seriousness almost painful. What might be called a writhing expression stole over him. He seemed struggling with some disastrous necessity inkept. He made one or two attempts to speak, but words seemed to choke him. His companion stood in humane surprise, wondering what was to come. At length, with an effort mastering his feelings, in a tolerably composed tone he spoke:

'If I remember, you are a mason, Mr Roberts?'

'Yes, yes.'

Averting himself a moment, as to recover from a return of agitation, the stranger grasped the other's hand; 'and would you not loan a brother a shilling if he needed it?'

The merchant started, apparently, almost as if to retreat.

'Ah, Mr Roberts, I trust you are not one of those business men, who make a business of never having to do with unfortunates. For God's sake don't leave me. I have something on my heart — on my heart. Under deplorable circumstances thrown among strangers, utter strangers. I want a friend in whom I may confide.

Yours, Mr Roberts, is almost the first known face I've seen for many weeks.'

It was so sudden an outburst; the interview offered such a contrast to the scene around, that the merchant, though not used to be very indiscreet, yet being not entirely inhumane, remained not entirely unmoved.

The other, still tremulous, resumed:

'I need not say, sir, how it cuts me to the soul, to follow up a social salutation with such words as have just been mine. I know that I jeopardize your good opinion. But I can't help it: necessity knows no law, and heeds no risk. Sir, we are masons, one more step aside; I will tell you my story.'

In a low, half-suppressed tone, he began it. Judging from his auditor's expression, it seemed to be a tale of singular interest, involving calamities against which no integrity, no forethought, no energy, no genius, no piety, could guard.

At every disclosure, the hearer's commiseration increased. No sentimental pity. As the story went on, he drew from his wallet a bank note, but after a while, at some still more unhappy revelation, changed it for another, probably of a somewhat larger amount; which, when the story was concluded, with an air studiously disclamatory of alms-giving, he put into the stranger's hands; who, on his side, with an air studiously disclamatory of alms-taking, put it into his pocket.

Assistance being received, the stranger's manner assumed a kind and degree of decorum which, under the circumstances, seemed almost coldness. After some words, not over ardent, and yet not exactly inappropriate, he took leave, making a bow which had one knows not what of a certain chastened independence about it; as if misery, however burdensome, could not break down self-respect, nor gratitude, however deep, humiliate a gentleman.

He was hardly yet out of sight, when he paused as if thinking; then with hastened steps returning to the merchant, 'I am just reminded that the president, who is also transfer-agent, of the Black Rapids Coal Company, happens to be on board here, and, having been subpoenaed as witness in a stock case on the docket in Kentucky, has his transfer-book with him. A month since, in a panic contrived by artful alarmists, some credulous stock-holders sold out; but, to frustrate the aim of the alarmists, the Company, previously advised of their scheme, so managed it as to get into its own hands those sacrificed shares, resolved that, since a spurious panic must be, the panic-makers should be no gainers by it. The Company, I hear, is now ready, but not anxious, to redispose of those shares; and having obtained them at their depressed value, will now sell them at par, though, prior to the panic, they were held at a handsome figure above. That the readiness of the Company to do this is not generally known, is shown by the fact that the stock still stands on the transfer-book in the Company's name offering to one in funds a rare chance for investment. For, the panic subsiding more and more every day, it will daily be seen how it originated; confidence will be more than restored; there will be a reaction; from the stock's descent its rise will be higher than from no fall, the holders trusting themselves to fear no second fate.'

Having listened at first with curiosity, at last with interest, the merchant replied to the effect, that some time since, through friends concerned with it, he had heard of the Company, and heard well of it, but was ignorant that there had latterly been fluctuations. He added that he was no speculator; that hitherto he had avoided having to do with stocks of any sort, but in the present case he really felt something like being tempted. 'Pray,' in conclusion, 'do you think that upon a pinch anything could be transacted on board here with the transfer-agent? Are you acquainted with him?'

'Not personally. I but happened to hear that he was a passenger. For the rest, though it might be somewhat informal, the gentleman might not object to doing a little business on board. Along the Mississippi, you know, business is not so ceremonious as at the East.'

'True,' returned the merchant, and looked down a moment in

thought, then, raising his head quickly, said, in a tone not so benign as his wonted one, 'This would seem a rare chance, indeed; why, upon first hearing it, did you not snatch at it? I mean for yourself!'

'I? – would it had been possible!'

Not without some emotion was this said, and not without some embarrassment was the reply. 'Ah, yes, I had forgotten.'

Upon this, the stranger regarded him with mild gravity, not a little disconcerting; the more so, as there was in it what seemed the aspect not alone of the superior, but, as it were, the rebuker; which sort of bearing, in a beneficiary towards his benefactor, looked strangely enough; none the less, that, somehow, it sat not altogether unbecomingly upon the beneficiary, being free from anything like the appearance of assumption, and mixed with a kind of painful conscientiousness, as though nothing but a proper sense of what he owed to himself swayed him. At length he spoke:

'To reproach a penniless man with remissness in not availing himself of an opportunity for pecuniary investment – but, no, no; it was forgetfulness; and this, charity will impute to some lingering effect of that unfortunate brain-fever, which, as to occurrences dating yet further back, disturbed Mr Roberts's memory still more seriously.'

'As to that,' said the merchant, rallying, 'I am not –'

'Pardon me, but you must admit, that just now, an unpleasant distrust, however vague, was yours. Ah, shallow as it is, yet, how subtle a thing is suspicion, which at times can invade the humanest of hearts and wisest of heads. But, enough. My object, sir, in calling your attention to this stock, is by way of acknowledgment of your goodness. I but seek to be grateful; if my information leads to nothing, you must remember the motive.'

He bowed, and finally retired, leaving Mr Roberts not wholly without self-reproach, for having momentarily indulged injurious thoughts against one who, it was evident, was possessed of a self-respect which forbade his indulging them himself.

5

THE MAN WITH THE WEED MAKES IT AN EVEN QUESTION WHETHER HE BE A GREAT SAGE OR A GREAT SIMPLETON

———◦••◦———

'Well, there is sorrow in the world, but goodness too; and goodness that is not greenness, either, no more than sorrow is. Dear good man. Poor beating heart!'

It was the man with the weed, not very long after quitting the merchant, murmuring to himself with his hand to his side like one with the heart-disease.

Meditation over kindness received seemed to have softened him somewhat, too, it may be, beyond what might, perhaps, have been looked for from one whose unwonted self-respect in the hour of need, and in the act of being aided, might have appeared to some not wholly unlike pride out of place; and pride, in any place, is seldom very feeling. But the truth, perhaps, is, that those who are least touched with that vice, besides being not unsusceptible to goodness, are sometimes the ones whom a ruling sense of propriety makes appear cold, if not thankless, under a favour. For, at such a time, to be full of warm, earnest words, and heart-felt protestations, is to create a scene; and well-bred people dislike few things more than that; which would seem to look as if the world did not relish earnestness; but, not so; because the world, being earnest itself, likes an earnest scene, and an earnest man, very well, but only in their place – the stage. See what sad work they make of it, who, ignorant of this, flame out in Irish enthusiasm and with Irish sincerity, to a benefactor, who, if a man of sense and respectability, as well as kindliness, can but be more or less annoyed by it; and, if of a nervously fastidious nature, as some are, may be led to think almost as much less favourably of the beneficiary paining him by his gratitude, as if he had been guilty of its contrary, instead only of an indiscretion. But, beneficiaries who know better, though they may feel as much, if not more, neither inflict such pain, nor are inclined to run any risk of so doing. And these, being wise, are the majority. By which one sees how inconsiderate those persons are, who, from the absence of its officious manifestations in the world, complain that there is not much gratitude extant; when the truth is, that there is as much of it as there is of modesty; but, both being for the most part votaries of the shade, for the most part keep out of sight.

What started this was, to account, if necessary, for the changed air of the man with the weed, who, throwing off in private the cold garb of decorum and so giving warmly loose to his genuine heart, seemed almost transformed into another being. This subdued air of softness, too, was toned with melancholy, melancholy unreserved; a thing which, however at variance with propriety, still the more attested his earnestness; for one knows not how it is, but it sometimes happens that, where earnestness is, there, also, is melancholy.

At the time, he was leaning over the rail at the boat's side, in his pensiveness, unmindful of another pensive figure near – a young gentleman with a swan-neck, wearing a lady-like open shirt collar thrown back, and tied with a black ribbon. From a square, tableted broach, curiously engraved with Greek characters, he seemed a collegian – not improbably, a sophomore – on his travels; possibly, his first. A small book bound in Roman vellum was in his hand.

Overhearing his murmuring neighbour, the youth regarded him with some surprise, not to say interest. But, singularly for a collegian, being apparently of a retiring nature, he did not speak; when the other still more increased his diffidence by changing from soliloquy to colloquy, in a manner strangely mixed of familiarity and pathos.

'Ah, who is this? You did not hear me, my young friend, did you? Why, you, too, look sad. My melancholy is not catching!'

'Sir, sir,' stammered the other.

'Pray, now,' with a sort of sociable sorrowfulness, slowly sliding along the rail, 'Pray, now, my young friend, what volume have you there? Give me leave,' gently drawing it from him. 'Tacitus!' Then opening it at random, read: 'In general a black and shameful period lies before me.' 'Dear young sir,' touching his arm alarmedly, 'don't read this book. It is poison, moral poison. Even were there truth in Tacitus, such truth would have the operation of falsity, and so still be poison, moral poison. Too well I know this Tacitus. In my college-days he came near souring me into cynicism. Yes, I began to turn down my collar, and go about with a disdainfully joyless expression.'

'Sir, sir, I – I –'

'Trust me. Now, young friend, perhaps you think that Tacitus, like me, is only melancholy; but he's more – he's ugly. A vast difference, young sir, between the melancholy view and the ugly. The one may show the world still beautiful, not so the other. The one may be compatible with benevolence, the other not. The one may deepen insight, the other shallows it. Drop Tacitus. Phrenologically, my young friend, you would seem to have a well-developed head, and large; but cribbed within the ugly view, the Tacitus view, your large brain, like your large ox in the contracted field, will but starve the more. And don't dream, as some of you students may, that, by taking this same ugly view, the deeper meanings of the deeper books will so alone become revealed to you. Drop Tacitus. His subtlety is falsity. To him, in his double-refined anatomy of human nature, is well applied the Scripture saying – "there is a subtle man, and the same is deceived." Drop Tacitus. Come, now, let me throw the book overboard.'

'Sir, I – I –'

'Not a word; I know just what is in your mind, and that is just what I am speaking to. Yes, learn from me that, though the sorrows of the world are great, its wickedness – that is, its ugliness – is small. Much cause to pity man, little to distrust him. I myself have known adversity, and know it still But for that, do I turn cynic? No, no: it is small beer that sours. To my fellow-creatures I owe alleviations. So, whatever I may have undergone, it but deepens my confidence in my kind. Now, then' (winningly), 'this book – will you let me drown it for you?'

'Really, sir – I –'

'I see, I see. But of course you read Tacitus in order to aid you in understanding human nature – as if truth was ever got at by libel. My young friend, if to know human nature is your object, drop Tacitus and go north to the cemeteries of Auburn and Greenwood.'

'Upon my word, I – I –'

'Nay, I foresee all that. But you carry Tacitus, that shallow Tacitus. What do I carry? See' – producing a pocket-volume – 'Akenside – his "Pleasures of Imagination". One of these days you will know it. Whatever our lot, we should read serene and cheery books, fitted to inspire love and trust. But Tacitus! I have long been of opinion that these classics are the bane of colleges; for – not to hint of the immorality of Ovid, Horace, Anacreon, and the rest, and the dangerous theology of Eschylus and others – where will one find views so injurious to human nature as in Thucydides, Juvenal, Lucian, but more particularly Tacitus? When I consider that, ever since the revival of learning, these classics have been the favourites of successive generations of students and studious men, I tremble to think of that mass of unsuspected heresy on every vital topic which for centuries must have simmered unsurmised in the heart of Christendom. But Tacitus – he is the most extraordinary example of a heretic; not one iota of confidence in his kind. What a mockery that such an one should be reputed wise, and Thucydides be esteemed the statesman's manual! But Tacitus – I hate Tacitus; not, though, I trust, with the hate that sins, but a righteous hate. Without confidence himself, Tacitus destroys it in all his readers. Destroys confidence, fraternal confidence, of which God knows that there is in this world none to spare. For, comparatively inexperienced as you are, my dear young friend, did you never observe how little, very little, confidence, there is? I mean between man and man – more particularly between stranger and stranger. In a sad world it is the saddest fact. Confidence! I have sometimes almost thought that confidence is fled; that confidence is the New Astrea – emigrated – vanished – gone.' Then softly sliding nearer, with the softest air, quivering down and looking up, 'could you now, my dear young sir, under such circumstances, by way of experiment, simply have confidence in *me?*'

From the outset, the sophomore, as has been seen, had struggled with an ever-increasing embarrassment, arising, perhaps, from such strange remarks coming from a stranger – such persistent and prolonged remarks, too. In vain had he more than once sought to break the spell by venturing a deprecatory or leave-taking word. In vain. Somehow, the stranger fascinated him. Little wonder, then, that, when the appeal came, he could hardly speak, but, as before intimated, being apparently of a retiring nature, abruptly retired from the spot, leaving the chagrined stranger to wander away in the opposite direction.

AT THE OUTSET OF WHICH CERTAIN
PASSENGERS PROVE DEAF TO THE CALL OF
CHARITY

━━━■━■■━━━

— 'You – pish! Why will the captain suffer these begging fellows on board?'

These pettish words were breathed by a well-to-do gentleman in a ruby-coloured velvet vest, and with a ruby-coloured cheek, a ruby-headed cane in his hand, to a man in a gray coat and white tie, who, shortly after the interview last described, had accosted him for contributions to a Widow and Orphan Asylum recently founded among the Seminoles. Upon a cursory view, this last person might have seemed, like the man with the weed, one of the less unrefined children of misfortune; but, on a closer observation, his countenance revealed little of sorrow, though much of sanctity.

With added words of touchy disgust, the well-to-do gentleman hurried away. But, though repulsed, and rudely, the man in gray did not reproach, for a time patiently remaining in the chilly loneliness to which he had been left, his countenance, however, not without token of latent though chastened reliance.

At length an old gentleman, somewhat bulky, drew near, and from him also a contribution was sought.

'Look, you,' coming to a dead halt, and scowling upon him. 'Look, you,' swelling his bulk out before him like a swaying balloon, 'look, you, you on others' behalf ask for money; you, a fellow with a face as long as my arm. Hark ye, now: there is such a thing as gravity, and in condemned felons it may be genuine; but of long faces there are three sorts; that of grief's drudge, that of the lantern-jawed man, and that of the impostor. You know best which yours is.'

'Heaven give you more charity, sir.'

'And you less hypocrisy, sir.'

With which words, the hard-hearted old gentleman marched off.

While the other still stood forlorn, the young clergyman, before introduced, passing that way, catching a chance sight of him, seemed suddenly struck by some recollection; and, after a moment's pause, hurried up with: 'Your pardon, but shortly since I was all over looking for you.'

'For me?' as marvelling that one of so little account should be sought for.

'Yes, for you; do you know anything about the negro, apparently a cripple, aboard here? Is he, or is he not, what he seems to be?'

'Ah, poor Guinea! have you, too, been distrusted? you, upon whom nature has placarded the evidence of your claims?'

'Then you do really know him, and he is quite worthy? It relieves me to hear it – much relieves me. Come, let us go find him, and see what can be done.'

'Another instance that confidence may come too late. I am sorry to say that at the last landing I myself – just happening to catch sight of him on the gangway-plank – assisted the cripple ashore. No time to talk, only to help. He may not have told you, but he has a brother in that vicinity.'

'Really, I regret his going without my seeing him again; regret it, more, perhaps, than you can readily think. You see, shortly after leaving St Louis, he was on the forecastle, and there, with many others, I saw him, and put trust in him; so much so, that to convince those who did not, I, at his entreaty, went in search of you, you being one of several individuals he mentioned, and whose personal appearance he more or less described, individuals who he said would willingly speak for him. But, after diligent search, not finding you, and catching no glimpse of any of the others he had enumerated, doubts were at last suggested; but doubts indirectly originating, as I can but think, from prior distrust unfeelingly proclaimed by another. Still, certain it is, I began to suspect.'

'Ha, ha, ha!'

A sort of laugh more like a groan than a laugh; and yet, somehow, it seemed intended for a laugh.

Both turned, and the young clergyman started at seeing the wooden-legged man close behind him, morosely grave as a criminal judge with a mustard-plaster on his back. In the present case the mustard-plaster might have been the memory of certain recent biting rebuffs and mortifications.

'Wouldn't think it was I who laughed, would you?'

'But who was it you laughed at? or rather, tried to laugh at?' demanded the young clergyman, flushing, 'me?'

'Neither you nor any one within a thousand miles of you. But perhaps you don't believe it.'

'If he were of a suspicious temper, he might not,' interposed the man in gray calmly, 'it is one of the imbecilities of the suspicious person to fancy that every stranger, however absent-minded, he sees so much as smiling or gesturing to himself in any odd sort of way, is secretly making him his butt. In some moods, the movements of an entire street, as the suspicious man walks down it, will seem an express pantomimic jeer at him. In short, the suspicious man kicks himself with his own foot.'

'Whoever can do that, ten to one he saves other folks' sole-leather,' said the wooden-legged man with a crusty attempt at humour. But with augmented grin and squirm, turning directly upon the young clergyman, 'you still think it was *you* I was laughing at, just now. To prove your mistake, I will tell you what I *was* laughing at; a story I happened to call to mind just then.'

Whereupon, in his porcupine way, and with sarcastic details, unpleasant to repeat, he related a story, which might, perhaps, in a good-natured version, be rendered as follows:

A certain Frenchman of New Orleans, an old man, less slender in purse than limb, happening to attend the theatre one evening, was so charmed with the character of a faithful wife, as there represented to the life, that nothing would do but he must marry upon it. So marry he did, a beautiful girl from Tennessee, who had first attracted his attention by her liberal mould, and was subsequently recommended to him through her kin, for her equally liberal education and disposition. Though large, the praise proved not too much. For, ere long, rumour more than corroborated it, by whispering that the lady was liberal to a fault. But though various circumstances, which by most Benedicts would have been deemed all but conclusive, were duly recited to the old Frenchman by his friends, yet such was his confidence that not a syllable would he credit, till, chancing one night to return unexpectedly from a journey, upon entering his apartment, a stranger burst from the alcove: 'Begar!' cried he, 'now I *begin* to suspec.'

His story told, the wooden-legged man threw back his head, and gave vent to a long, gasping, rasping sort of taunting cry, intolerable as that of a high-pressure engine jeering off steam; and that done, with apparent satisfaction hobbled away.

'Who is that scoffer?' said the man in gray, not without warmth. 'Who is he, who even were truth on his tongue, his way of speaking it would make truth almost as offensive as falsehood? Who is he?'

'He whom I mentioned to you as having boasted his suspicion of the negro,' replied the young clergyman, recovering from disturbance, 'in short, the person to whom I ascribe the origin of my own distrust; he maintained that Guinea was some white scoundrel, betwisted and painted up for a decoy. Yes, these were his very words, I think.'

'Impossible! he could not be so wrong-headed. Pray, will you call him back, and let me ask him if he were really in earnest?'

The other complied; and, at length, after no few surly objections, prevailed upon the one-legged individual to return for a moment. Upon which, the man in gray thus addressed him: 'This reverend gentleman tells me, sir, that a certain cripple, a poor negro, is by you considered an ingenious impostor. Now, I am not unaware that there are some persons in this world, who, unable to give better proof of being wise, take a strange delight in showing what they think they have sagaciously read in mankind by uncharitable suspicions of them. I hope you are not one of these. In short, would you tell me now, whether you were not merely joking in the notion you threw out about the negro? Would you be so kind?'

'No, I won't be so kind, I'll be so cruel.'

'As you please about that.'

'Well, he's just what I said he was.'

'A white masquerading as a black?'

'Exactly.'

The man in gray glanced at the young clergyman a moment, then quietly whispered to him, 'I thought you represented your friend here as a very distrustful sort of person, but he appears endued with a singular credulity. – Tell me, sir, do you really think that a white could look the negro so? For one, I should call it pretty good acting.'

'Not much better than any other man acts.'

'How? Does all the world act? Am *I*, for instance, an actor? Is my reverend friend here, too, a performer?'

'Yes, don't you both perform acts? To do is to act; so all doers are actors.'

'You trifle. – I ask again, if a white, how could he look the negro so?'

'Never saw the negro-minstrels, I suppose?'

'Yes, but they are apt to overdo the ebony; exemplifying the old saying, not more just than charitable, that "the devil is never so black as he is painted". But his limbs, if not a cripple, how could he twist his limbs so?'

'How do other hypocritical beggars twist theirs? Easy enough to see how they are hoisted up.'

'The sham is evident, then?'

'To the discerning eye,' with a horrible screw of his gimlet one.

'Well, where is Guinea?' said the man in gray; 'where is he? Let us at once find him, and refute beyond cavil this injurious hypothesis.'

'Do so,' cried the one-legged man, 'I'm just in the humour now for having him found, and leaving the streaks of these fingers on his paint, as the lion leaves the streaks of his nails on a Caffre. They wouldn't let me touch him before. Yes, find him, I'll make wool fly, and him after.'

'You forget,' here said the young clergyman to the man in gray, 'that yourself helped poor Guinea ashore.'

'So I did, so I did; how unfortunate. But look now,' to the other, 'I think that without personal proof I can convince you of your mistake. For I put it to you, is it reasonable to suppose that a man with brains, sufficient to act such a part as you say, would take all that trouble, and run all that hazard, for the mere sake of those few paltry coppers, which, I hear, was all that he got for his pains, if pains they were?'

'That puts the case irrefutably,' said the young clergyman, with a challenging glance towards the one-legged man.

'You two green-horns! Money, you think, is the sole motive to pains and hazard, deception and devilry, in this world. How much money did the devil make by gulling Eve?'

Whereupon he hobbled off again with a repetition of his intolerable jeer.

The man in gray stood silently eyeing his retreat a while, and then, turning to his companion, said: 'A bad man, a dangerous man; a man to be put down in any Christian community. – And this was he who was the means of begetting your distrust? Ah, we should shut our ears to distrust, and keep them open only for its opposite.'

'You advance a principle, which, if I had acted upon it this morning, I should have spared myself what I now feel. – That but one man, and he with one leg, should have such ill power given him; his one sour word leavening into congenial sourness (as, to my knowledge, it did) the dispositions, before sweet enough, of a numerous company. But, as I hinted, with me at the time his ill words went for nothing; the same as now; only afterwards they had effect; and I confess, this puzzles me.'

'It should not. With humane minds, the spirit of distrust works something as certain potions do; it is a spirit which may enter such minds, and yet, for a time, longer or shorter, lie in them quiescent; but only the more deplorable its ultimate activity.'

'An uncomfortable solution; for, since that baneful man did but just now anew drop on me his bane, how shall I be sure that my present exemption from its effects will be lasting?'

'You cannot be sure, but you can strive against it.'

'How?'

'By strangling the least symptom of distrust, of any sort, which hereafter, upon whatever provocation, may arise in you.'

'I will do so.' Then added as in soliloquy, 'Indeed, indeed, I was to blame in standing passive under such influences as that one-legged man's. My conscience upbraids me. – The poor negro: you see him occasionally, perhaps?'

'No, not often; though in a few days, as it happens, my engagements will call me to the neighbourhood of his present retreat; and, no doubt, honest Guinea, who is a grateful soul, will come to see me there.'

'Then you have been his benefactor?'

'His benefactor? I did not say that. I have known him.'

'Take this mite. Hand it to Guinea when you see him; say it comes from one who has full belief in his honesty, and is sincerely sorry for having indulged, however transiently, in a contrary thought.'

'I accept the trust. And, by-the-way, since you are of this truly charitable nature, you will not turn away an appeal in behalf of the Seminole Widow and Orphan Asylum?'

'I have not heard of that charity.'

'But recently founded.'

After a pause, the clergyman was irresolutely putting his hand in his pocket, when, caught by something in his companion's expression, he eyed him inquisitively, almost uneasily.

'Ah, well,' smiled the other wanly, 'if that subtle bane, we were speaking of but just now, is so soon beginning to work, in vain my appeal to you. Good-bye.'

'Nay,' not untouched, 'you do me injustice; instead of indulging present suspicions, I had rather make amends for previous ones. Here is something for your asylum. Not much; but every drop helps. Of course you have papers?'

'Of course,' producing a memorandum book and pencil. 'Let me take down name and amount. We publish these names. And now let me give you a little history of our asylum, and the providential way in which it was started.'

CON:
ask for small favor
(like Ben Franklin
lending a book)
and them ask for
bigger favor

charity as a selfish act
b charitable act is like
a con because it
decieves one's true
motives

A GENTLEMAN WITH GOLD SLEEVE-BUTTONS

At an interesting point of the narration, and at the moment when, with much curiosity, indeed, urgency, the narrator was being particularly questioned upon that point, he was, as it happened, altogether diverted both from it and his story, by just then catching sight of a gentleman who had been standing in sight from the beginning, but, until now, as it seemed, without being observed by him.

'Pardon me,' said he, rising, 'but yonder is one who I know will contribute, and largely. Don't take it amiss if I quit you.'

'Go: duty before all things,' was the conscientious reply.

The stranger was a man of more than winning aspect. There he stood apart and in repose, and yet, by his mere look, lured the man in gray from his story, much as by its graciousness of bearing, some full-leaved elm, alone in a meadow, lures the noon sickleman to throw down his sheaves, and come and apply for the alms of its shade.

But, considering that goodness is no such rare thing among men – the world familiarly know the noun; a common one in every language – it was curious that what so signalized the stranger, and made him look like a kind of foreigner, among the crowd (as to some it may make him appear more or less unreal in this portraiture), was but the expression of so prevalent a quality. Such goodness seemed his, allied with such fortune, that, so far as his own personal experience could have gone, scarcely could he have known ill, physical or moral; and as for knowing or suspecting the latter in any serious degree (supposing such degree of it to be), by observation or philosophy; for that, probably, his nature, by its opposition, imperfectly qualified, or from it wholly exempted him. For the rest, he might have been five and fifty, perhaps sixty, but tall, rosy, between plump and portly, with a primy, palmy air, and for the time and place, not to hint of his years, dressed with a strangely festive finish and elegance. The inner side of his coat skirts was of white satin, which might have looked especially inappropriate, had it not seemed less a bit of mere tailoring than something of an emblem, as it were; an involuntary emblem, let us say, that what seemed so good about him was not all outside; no, the fine covering had a still finer lining. Upon one hand he wore a white kid glove, but the other hand, which was ungloved, looked hardly less white. Now, as the Fidèle, like most steamboats, was upon deck a little soot-streaked here and there, especially about the railings, it was a marvel how, under such circumstances, these hands retained their spotlessness. But, if you watched them a while, you noticed that they avoided touching anything; you noticed, in short, that a certain negro body-servant, whose hands nature had dyed black, perhaps with the same purpose that millers wear white, this negro servant's hands did most of his master's handling for him; having to do with dirt on his account, but not to his prejudices. But if, with the same undefiledness of consequences to himself, a gentleman could also sin by deputy, how shocking would that be! But it is not permitted to be; and even if it were, no judicious moralist would make proclamation of it.

This gentleman, therefore, there is reason to affirm, was one who, like the Hebrew governor, knew how to keep his hands clean, and who never in his life happened to be run suddenly against by hurrying house-painter, or sweep; in a word, one whose very good luck it was to be a very good man.

Not that he looked as if he were a kind of Wilberforce at all, that superior merit, probably, was not his; nothing in his manner bespoke him righteous, but only good; and though to be good is much below being righteous, and though there is a difference between the two, yet not, it is to be hoped, so incompatible as that a righteous man cannot be a good man; though, conversely, in the pulpit it has been with much cogency urged, that a merely good man, that is, one good merely by his nature, is so far from thereby being righteous, that nothing short of a total change and conversion can make him so; which is something which no honest mind, well read in the history of righteousness, will care to deny; nevertheless, since St Paul himself, agreeing in a sense with the pulpit distinction, though not altogether in the pulpit deduction, and also pretty plainly intimating which of the two qualities in question enjoys his apostolic preference; I say, since St Paul has so meaningly said, that, 'scarcely for a righteous man will one die, yet peradventure for a good man some would even dare to die'; therefore, when we repeat of this gentleman, that he was only a good man, whatever else by severe censors may be objected to him, it is still to be hoped that his goodness will not at least be considered criminal in him. At all events, no man, not even a righteous man, would think it quite right to commit this gentleman to prison for the crime, extraordinary as he might deem it; more especially, as, until everything could be known, there would be some chance that the gentleman might after all be quite as innocent of it as he himself.

It was pleasant to mark the good man's reception of the salute of the righteous man, that is, the man in gray; his inferior, apparently, not more in the social scale than in stature. Like the benign elm again, the good man seemed to wave the canopy of his goodness over that suitor, not in conceited condescension, but with that even amenity of true majesty, which can be kind to any one without stooping to it.

To the plea in behalf of the Seminole widows and orphans, the gentleman, after a question or two duly answered, responded by producing an ample pocket-book in the good old capacious style, of fine green French morocco and workmanship, bound with silk of the same colour, not to omit bills crisp with newness, fresh from the bank, no muckworms' grime upon them. Lucre those bills might be, but as yet having been kept unspotted from the world, not of the filthy sort. Placing now three of those virgin bills in the applicant's hands, he hoped that the smallness of the contribution would be pardoned; to tell the truth, and this at last accounted for his toilet, he was bound but a short run down the river, to attend, in a festive grove, the afternoon wedding of his niece; so did not carry much money with him.

The other was about expressing his thanks when the gentleman in his pleasant way checked him: the gratitude was on the other side. To him, he said, charity was in one sense not an effort, but a luxury; against too great indulgence in which his steward, a humourist, had sometimes admonished him.

In some general talk which followed, relative to organized modes of doing good, the gentleman expressed his regrets that so many benevolent societies as there were, here and there isolated in the land, should not act in concert by coming together, in the way that already in each society the individuals composing it had done, which would result, he thought, in like advantages upon a larger scale. Indeed, such a confederation might, perhaps, be attended with as happy results as politically attended that of the states.

Upon his hitherto moderate enough companion, this suggestion had an effect illustrative in a sort of that notion of Socrates, that the soul is a harmony; for as the sound of a flute, in any particular key, will, it is said, audibly affect the corresponding chord of any harp in good tune within hearing, just so now did some string in him respond, and with animation.

Which animation, by the way, might seem more or less out of character in the man in gray, considering his unsprightly manner when first introduced, had he not already, in certain after colloquies, given proof, in some degree, of the fact that, with certain natures, a soberly continent air at times, so far from arguing emptiness of stuff, is good proof it is there, and plenty of it, because unwasted, and may be used the more effectively, too, when opportunity offers. What now follows on the part of the man in gray will still further exemplify, perhaps somewhat strikingly, the truth, or what appears to be such, of this remark.

'Sir,' said he eagerly, 'I am before you. A project, not dissimilar to yours, was by me thrown out at the World's Fair in London.'

'World's Fair? You there? Pray how was that?'

'First, let me —'

'Nay, but first tell me what took you to the Fair?'

'I went to exhibit an invalid's easy-chair I had invented.'

'Then you have not always been in the charity business?'

'Is it not charity to ease human suffering? I am, and always have been, as I always will be, I trust, in the charity business, as you call it; but charity is not like a pin, one to make the head, and the other the point; charity is a work to which a good workman may be competent in all its branches. I invented my Protean easy-chair in odd intervals stolen from meals and sleep.'

'You call it the Protean easy-chair; pray describe it.'

'My Protean easy-chair is a chair so all over bejointed, behinged, and bepadded, everyway so elastic, springy, and docile to the airiest touch, that in some one of its endlessly-changeable accommodations of back, seat, footboard, and arms, the most restless body, the body most racked, nay, I had almost added the most tormented conscience must, somehow and somewhere, find rest. Believing that I owed it to suffering humanity to make known such a chair to the utmost, I scraped together my little means and off to the World's Fair with it.'

'You did right. But your scheme; how did you come to hit upon that?'

'I was going to tell you. After seeing my invention duly catalogued and placed, I gave myself up to pondering the scene about me. As I dwelt upon that shining pageant of arts, and moving concourse of nations, and reflected that here was the pride of the world glorying in a glass house, a sense of the fragility of worldly grandeur profoundly impressed me. And I said to myself, I will see if this occasion of vanity cannot supply a hint toward a better profit than was designed. Let some world-wide

good to the world-wide cause be now done. In short, inspired by
the scene, on the fourth day I issued at the World's Fair my
prospectus of the World's Charity.'

'Quite a thought. But, pray explain it.'

'The World's Charity is to be a society whose members shall
comprise deputies from every charity and mission extant; the one
object of the society to be the methodization of the world's
benevolence; to which end, the present system of voluntary and
promiscuous contribution to be done away, and the Society to be
empowered by the various governments to levy, annually, one
grand benevolence tax upon all mankind; as in Augustus Caesar's
time, the whole world to come up to be taxed; a tax which, for
the scheme of it, should be something like the income-tax in
England, a tax, also, as before hinted, to be a consolidation-tax of
all possible benevolence taxes; as in America here, the state-tax,
and the county-tax, and the town-tax, and the poll-tax, are by the
assessors rolled into one. This tax, according to my tables, calculated with care, would result in the yearly raising of a fund little
short of eight hundred millions; this fund to be annually applied
to such objects, and in such modes, as the various charities and
missions, in general congress represented, might decree; whereby,
in fourteen years, as I estimate, there would have been devoted to
good works the sum of eleven thousand two hundred millions;
which would warrant the dissolution of the society, as that fund
judiciously expended, not a pauper or heathen could remain the
round world over.'

'Eleven thousand two hundred millions! And all by passing
round a *hat*, as it were.'

'Yes, I am no Fourier, the projector of an impossible scheme,
but a philanthropist and a financier, setting forth a philanthropy
and a finance which are practicable.'

'Practicable?'

'Yes. Eleven thousand two hundred millions; it will frighten
none but a retail philanthropist. What is it but eight hundred
millions for each of fourteen years? Now eight hundred millions –

what is that, to average it, but one little dollar a head for the population of the planet? And who will refuse, what Turk or Dyak even, his own little dollar for sweet charity's sake? Eight hundred millions! More than that sum is yearly expended by mankind, not only in vanities, but miseries. Consider that bloody spendthrift, War. And are mankind so stupid, so wicked, that, upon the demonstration of these things they will not, amending their ways, devote their superfluities to blessing the world instead of cursing it? Eight hundred millions! They have not to make it, it is theirs already; they have but to direct it from ill to good. And to this, scarce a self-denial is demanded. Actually, they would not in the mass be one farthing the poorer for it; as certainly would they be all the better and happier. Don't you see? But admit, as you must, that mankind is not mad, and my project is practicable. For what creature, but a madman, would not rather do good than ill, when it is plain that, good or ill, it must return upon himself?'

'Your sort of reasoning,' said the good gentleman, adjusting his gold sleeve-buttons, 'seems all reasonable enough, but with mankind it won't do.'

'Then mankind are not reasoning beings, if reason won't do with them.'

'That is not to the purpose. By the way, from the manner in which you alluded to the world's census, it would appear that, according to your world-wide scheme, the pauper not less than the nabob is to contribute to the relief of pauperism, and the heathen not less than the Christian to the conversion of heathenism. How is that?'

'Why, that – pardon me – is quibbling. Now, no philanthropist likes to be opposed with quibbling.'

'Well, I won't quibble any more. But, after all, if I understand your project, there is little specially new in it, further than the magnifying of means now in operation.'

'Magnifying and energizing. For one thing, missions I would thoroughly reform. Missions I would quicken with the Wall street spirit.'

'The Wall street spirit?'

'Yes; for if, confessedly, certain spiritual ends are to be gained but through the auxiliary agency of worldly means, then, to the surer gaining of such spiritual ends, the example of worldly policy in worldly projects should not by spiritual projectors be slighted. In brief, the conversion of the heathen, so far, at least, as depending on human effort, would, by the World's Charity, be let out on contract. So much by bid for converting India, so much for Borneo, so much for Africa. Competition allowed, stimulus would be given. There would be no lethargy of monopoly. We should have no mission-house or tract-house of which slanderers could, with any plausibility, say that it had degenerated in its clerkships into a sort of custom-house. But the main point is the Archimedean money-power that would be brought to bear.'

'You mean the eight hundred million power?'

'Yes. You see, this doing good to the world by driblets amounts to just nothing. I am for doing good to the world with a will. I am for doing good to the world once for all and having done with it. Do but think, my dear sir, of the eddies and maëlstroms of pagans in China. People here have no conception of it. Of a frosty morning in Hong Kong, pauper pagans are found dead in the streets like so many nipped peas in a bin of peas. To be an immortal being in China is no more distinction than to be a snow-flake in a snow-squall. What are a score or two of missionaries to such a people? A pinch of snuff to the kraken. I am for sending ten thousand missionaries in a body and converting the Chinese *en masse* within six months of the debarkation. The thing is then done, and turn to something else.'

'I fear you are too enthusiastic.'

'A philanthropist is necessarily an enthusiast; for without enthusiasm what was ever achieved but commonplace? But again: consider the poor in London. To that mob of misery, what is a joint here and a loaf there? I am for voting to them twenty thousand bullocks and one hundred thousand barrels of flour to begin with. They are then comforted, and no more hunger for one while among the poor of London. And so all round.'

'Sharing the character of your general project, these things, I take it, are rather examples of wonders that were to be wished, than wonders that will happen.'

'And is the age of wonders past? Is the world too old? Is it barren? Think of Sarah.'

'Then I am Abraham reviling the angel (with a smile). But still, as to your design at large, there seems a certain audacity.'

'But if to the audacity of the design there be brought a commensurate circumspectness of execution, how then?'

'Why, do you really believe that your World's Charity will ever go into operation?'

'I have confidence that it will.'

'But may you not be over-confident?'

'For a Christian to talk so!'

'But think of the obstacles!'

'Obstacles? I have confidence to remove obstacles, though mountains. Yes, confidence in the World's Charity to that degree, that, as no better person offers to supply the place, I have nominated myself provisional treasurer, and will be happy to receive subscriptions, for the present to be devoted to striking off a million more of my prospectuses.'

The talk went on; the man in gray revealed a spirit of benevolence which, mindful of the millennial promise, had gone abroad over all the countries of the globe, much as the diligent spirit of the husbandman, stirred by forethought of the coming seed-time, leads him, in March reveries at his fire-side, over every field of his farm. The master chord of the man in gray had been touched, and it seemed as if it would never cease vibrating. A not unsilvery tongue, too, was his, with gestures that were a Pentecost of added ones, and persuasiveness before which granite hearts might crumble into gravel.

Strange, therefore, how his auditor, so singularly good-hearted as he seemed, remained proof to such eloquence; though not, as it turned out, to such pleadings. For, after listening a little longer with pleasant incredulity, presently, as the boat touched his place of destination, the gentleman, with a look of half humour, half pity, put another bank-note into his hands; charitable to the last, if only to the dreams of enthusiasm.

8

A CHARITABLE LADY

If a drunkard in a sober fit is the dullest of mortals, an enthusiast in a reason-fit is not the most lively. And this, without prejudice to his greatly improved understanding: for, if his elation was the height of his madness, his despondency is but the extreme of his sanity. Something thus now, to all appearance, with the man in gray. Society his stimulus, loneliness was his lethargy. Loneliness, like the sea-breeze, blowing off from a thousand leagues of blankness, he did not find, as veteran solitaires do, if anything, too bracing. In short, left to himself, with none to charm forth his latent lymphatic, he insensibly resumes his original air, a quiescent one blended of sad humility and demureness.

Ere long he goes laggingly into the ladies' saloon, as in spiritless quest of somebody; but, after some disappointed glances about him, seats himself upon a sofa with an air of melancholy exhaustion and depression.

At the sofa's further end sits a plump and pleasant person, whose aspect seems to hint that, if she have any weak point, it must be anything rather than her excellent heart. From her twilight dress, neither dawn nor dark, apparently she is a widow just breaking the chrysalis of her mourning. A small gilt testament is in her hand, which she has just been reading. Half-relinquished, she holds the book in reverie, her finger inserted at the thirteenth of 1st Corinthians, to which chapter possibly her attention might have recently been turned, by witnessing the scene of the monitory mute and his slate.

The sacred page no longer meets her eye; but, as at evening, when for a time the western hills shine on though the sun be set, her thoughtful face retains its tenderness though the teacher is forgotten.

Meantime, the expression of the stranger is such as ere long to attract her glance. But no responsive one. Presently, in her somewhat inquisitive survey, her volume drops. It is restored. No encroaching politeness in the act, but kindness, unadorned. The eyes of the lady sparkle. Evidently, she is not now unprepossessed. Soon, bending over, in a low, sad tone, full of deference, the stranger breathes, 'Madam, pardon my freedom, but there is something in that face which strangely draws me. May I ask, are you a sister of the Church?'

'Why – really – you –'

In concern for her embarrassment, he hastens to relieve it, but without seeming so to do. 'It is very solitary for a brother here,' eyeing the showy ladies brocaded in the background. 'I find none to mingle souls with. It may be wrong – I *know* it is – but I cannot force myself to be easy with the people of the world. I prefer the company, however silent, of a brother or sister in good standing. By the way, madam, may I ask if you have confidence?'

'Really, sir – why, sir – really – I –'

'Could you put confidence in *me*, for instance?'

'Really, sir – as much – I mean, as one may wisely put in a – a – stranger – an entire stranger, I had almost said,' rejoined the lady, hardly yet at ease in her affability, drawing aside a little in body, while at the same time her heart might have been drawn as far the other way. A natural struggle between charity and prudence.

'Entire stranger!' with a sigh. 'Ah, who would be a stranger? In vain, I wander; no one will have confidence in me.'

'You interest me,' said the good lady, in mild surprise. 'Can I any way befriend you?'

'No one can befriend me who has not confidence.'

'But I – I have – at least to that degree – I mean that –'

'Nay, nay, you have none – none at all. Pardon, I see it. No confidence. Fool, fond fool that I am to seek it!'

'You are unjust, sir,' rejoins the good lady with heightened interest; 'but it may be that something untoward in your experiences has unduly biassed you. Not that I would cast reflections. Believe me, I – yes, yes – I may say that – that –'

'That you have confidence? Prove it. Let me have twenty dollars.'

'Twenty dollars!'

'There, I told you, madam, you had no confidence.'

The lady was, in an extraordinary way, touched. She sat in a sort of restless torment, knowing not which way to turn. She began twenty different sentences, and left off at the first syllable of each. At last, in desperation, she hurried out, 'Tell me, sir, for what you want the twenty dollars?'

'And did I not?' – then glancing at her half-mourning, – 'for the widow and the fatherless. I am travelling agent of the Widow and Orphan Asylum, recently founded among the Seminoles.'

'And why did you not tell me your object before?' as not a little relieved. 'Poor souls – Indians, too – those cruelly-used Indians. Here, here; how could I hesitate? I am so sorry it is no more.'

'Grieve not for that, madam,' rising and folding up the banknotes. 'This is an inconsiderable sum, I admit, but,' taking out his pencil and book, 'though I here but register the amount, there is another register, where is set down the motive. Good-bye; you have confidence. Yea, you can say to me as the apostle said to the Corinthians, "I rejoice that I have confidence in you in all things."'

9

TWO BUSINESS MEN TRANSACT A LITTLE
BUSINESS

———— •••• ————

— 'Pray, sir, have you seen a gentleman with a weed hereabouts, rather a saddish gentleman? Strange where he can have gone to. I was talking with him not twenty minutes since.'

By a brisk, ruddy-cheeked man in a tasseled travelling-cap, carrying under his arm a ledger-like volume, the above words were addressed to the collegian before introduced, suddenly accosted by the rail to which, not long after his retreat, as in a previous chapter recounted, he had returned, and there remained.

'Have you seen him, sir?'

Rallied from his apparent diffidence by the genial jauntiness of the stranger, the youth answered with unwonted promptitude: 'Yes, a person with a weed was here not very long ago.'

'Saddish?'

'Yes, and a little cracked, too, I should say.'

'It was he. Misfortune, I fear, has disturbed his brain. Now quick, which way did he go?'

'Why just in the direction from which you came, the gangway yonder.'

'Did he? Then the man in the gray coat, whom I just met, said right: he must have gone ashore. How unlucky!'

He stood vexedly twitching at his cap-tassel, which fell over by his whisker, and continued: 'Well, I am very sorry. In fact, I had something for him here.' —Then drawing nearer, 'You see, he applied to me for relief — no, I do him injustice, not that, but he began to intimate, you understand. Well, being very busy just then, I declined; quite rudely, too, in a cold, morose, unfeeling way, I fear. At all events, not three minutes afterwards I felt self-reproach, with a kind of prompting, very peremptory, to deliver over into that unfortunate man's hands a ten dollar bill. You smile. Yes, it may be superstition, but I can't help it; I have my weak side, thank God. Then again,' he rapidly went on, 'we have been so very prosperous lately in our affairs – by we, I mean the Black Rapids Coal Company – that, really, out of my abundance, associative and individual, it is but fair that a charitable investment or two should be made, don't you think so?'

'Sir,' said the collegian without the least embarrassment, 'do I understand that you are officially connected with the Black Rapids Coal Company?'

'Yes, I happen to be president and transfer-agent.'

'You are?'

'Yes, but what is it to you? You don't want to invest?'

'Why, do you sell the stock?'

'Some might be bought, perhaps; but why do you ask? you don't want to invest?'

'But supposing I did,' with cool self-collectedness, 'could you do up the thing for me, and here?'

'Bless my soul,' gazing at him in amaze, 'really, you are quite a businessman. Positively, I feel afraid of you.'

'Oh, no need of that. – You could sell me some of that stock, then?'

'I don't know, I don't know. To be sure, there are a few shares under peculiar circumstances bought in by the Company; but it would hardly be the thing to convert this boat into the Company's office. I think you had better defer investing. So,' with an indifferent air, 'you have seen the unfortunate man I spoke of?'

'Let the unfortunate man go his ways. – What is that large book you have with you?'

'My transfer-book. I am subpoenaed with it to court.'

'Black Rapids Coal Company,' obliquely reading the gilt inscription on the back; 'I have heard much of it. Pray do you happen to have with you any statement of the condition of your company?'

'A statement has lately been printed.'

'Pardon me, but I am naturally inquisitive. Have you a copy with you?'

'I tell you again, I do not think that it would be suitable to convert this boat into the Company's office. – That unfortunate man, did you relieve him at all?'

'Let the unfortunate man relieve himself. – Hand me the statement.'

'Well, you are such a business-man, I can hardly deny you. Here,' handing a small printed pamphlet.

The youth turned it over sagely.

'I hate a suspicious man,' said the other, observing him; 'but I must say I like to see a cautious one.'

'I can gratify you there,' languidly returning the pamphlet; 'for, as I said before, I am naturally inquisitive; I am also circumspect. No appearances can deceive me. Your statement,' he added, 'tells a very fine story; but pray, was not your stock a little heavy a while ago? downward tendency? Sort of low spirits among holders on the subject of that stock?'

'Yes, there was a depression. But how came it? who devised it? The "bears", sir. The depression of our stock was solely owing to the growling, the hypocritical growling, of the bears.'

'How hypocritical?'

'Why, the most monstrous of all hypocrites are these bears: hypocrites by inversion; hypocrites in the simulation of things dark instead of bright; souls that thrive, less upon depression, than the fiction of depression; professors of the wicked art of manufacturing depressions; spurious Jeremiahs; sham Heraclituses, who, the lugubrious day done, return, like sham Lazaruses among the beggars, to make merry over the gains got by their pretended sore heads – scoundrelly bears!'

'You are warm against these bears?'

'If I am, it is less from the remembrance of their stratagems as to our stock, than from the persuasion that these same destroyers of confidence, and gloomy philosophers of the stock-market, though false in themselves, are yet true types of most destroyers of confidence and gloomy philosophers, the world over. Fellows who, whether in stocks, politics, bread-stuffs, morals, metaphysics, religion – be it what it may – trump up their black panics in the naturally quiet brightness, solely with a view to some sort of covert advantage. That corpse of calamity which the gloomy philosopher parades, is but his Good-Enough-Morgan.'

'I rather like that,' knowingly drawled the youth. 'I fancy these gloomy souls as little as the next one. Sitting on my sofa after a champagne dinner, smoking my plantation cigar, if a gloomy fellow come to me – what a bore!'

'You tell him it's all stuff, don't you?'

'I tell him it ain't natural. I say to him, you are happy enough, and you know it; and everybody else is as happy as you, and you know that, too; and we shall all be happy after we are no more, and you know that, too; but no, still you must have your sulk.'

'And do you know whence this sort of fellow gets his sulk? not from life; for he's often too much of a recluse, or else too young to have seen anything of it. No, he gets it from some of those old plays he sees on the stage, or some of those old books he finds up in garrets. Ten to one, he has lugged home from auction a musty old Seneca, and sets about stuffing himself with that stale old hay; and, thereupon, thinks it looks wise and antique to be a croaker, thinks it's taking a stand 'way above his kind.'

'Just so,' assented the youth, 'I've lived some, and seen a good many such ravens at second hand. By the way, strange how that man with the weed, you were inquiring for, seemed to take me for some soft sentimentalist, only because I kept quiet, and thought, because I had a copy of Tacitus with me, that I was reading him for his gloom, instead of his gossip. But I let him talk. And, indeed, by my manner humoured him.'

'You shouldn't have done that, now. Unfortunate man, you must have made quite a fool of him.'

'His own fault if I did. But I like prosperous fellows, comfortable fellows; fellows that talk comfortably and prosperously, like you. Such fellows are generally honest. And, I say now, I happen to have a superfluity in my pocket, and I'll just –'

'– Act the part of a brother to that unfortunate man?'

'Let the unfortunate man be his own brother. What are you dragging him in for all the time? One would think you didn't care to register any transfers, or dispose of any stock – mind running on something else. I say I will invest.'

'Stay, stay, here come some uproarious fellows – this way, this way.'

And with off-handed politeness, the man with the book escorted his companion into a private little haven removed from the brawling swells without.

Business transacted, the two came forth, and walked the deck.

'Now tell me, sir,' said he with the book, 'how comes it that a young gentleman like you, a sedate student at the first appearance, should dabble in stocks and that sort of thing?'

'There are certain sophomorean errors in the world,' drawled the sophomore, deliberately adjusting his shirt-collar, 'not the least of which is the popular notion touching the nature of the modern scholar, and the nature of the modern scholastic sedateness.'

'So it seems, so it seems. Really, this is quite a new leaf in my experience.'

'Experience, sir,' originally observed the sophomore, 'is the only teacher.'

'Hence am I your pupil; for it's only when experience speaks, that I can endure to listen to speculation.'

'My speculations, sir,' dryly drawing himself up, 'have been chiefly governed by the maxim of Lord Bacon; I speculate in those philosophies which come home to my business and bosom – pray, do you know of any other good stocks?'

'You wouldn't like to be concerned in the New Jerusalem, would you?'

'New Jerusalem?'

'Yes, the new and thriving city, so called in northern Minnesota. It was originally founded by certain fugitive Mormons. Hence the name. It stands on the Mississippi. Here, here is the map,' producing a roll. 'There – there, you see are the public buildings – here the landing – there the park – yonder the botanic gardens – and this, this little dot here, is a perpetual fountain, you understand. You observe there are twenty asterisks. Those are for the lyceums. They have lignum-vitae rostrums.'

'And are all these buildings now standing?'

'All standing – *bona fide.*'

'These marginal squares here, are they the water-lots?'

'Water-lots in the city of New Jerusalem? All terra firma – you don't seem to care about investing, though?'

'Hardly think I should read my title clear, as the law students say,' yawned the collegian.

'Prudent – you are prudent. Don't know that you are wholly out, either. At any rate, I would rather have one of your shares of coal stock than two of this other. Still, considering that the first settlement was by two fugitives, who had swum over naked from the opposite shore – it's a surprising place. It is *bona fide.* – But dear me, I must go. Oh, if by possibility you should come across that unfortunate man –'

'– In that case,' with drawling impatience, 'I will send for the steward, and have him and his misfortunes consigned overboard.'

'Ha, ha! – Now were some gloomy philosopher here, some theological bear, for ever taking occasion to growl down the stock of human nature (with ulterior views, d'ye see, to a fat benefice in the gift of the worshippers of Arimanius), he would pronounce that the sign of a hardening heart and a softening brain. Yes, that would be his sinister construction. But it's nothing more than the oddity of a genial humour – genial but dry. Confess it. Good-bye.'

Stools, settees, sofas, divans, ottomans; occupying them are clusters of men, old and young, wise and simple; in their hands are cards spotted with diamonds, spades, clubs, hearts; the favourite games are whist, cribbage, and brag. Lounging in arm-chairs or sauntering among the marble-topped tables, amused with the scene, are the comparatively few, who, instead of having hands in the games, for the most part keep their hands in their pockets. These may be the *philosophes*. But here and there, with a curious expression, one is reading a small sort of handbill of anonymous poetry, rather wordily entitled:

ODE

ON THE INTIMATIONS

OF

DISTRUST IN MAN,

UNWILLINGLY INFERRED FROM REPEATED REPULSES,

IN DISINTERESTED ENDEAVOURS

TO PROCURE HIS

CONFIDENCE.

On the floor are many copies, looking as if fluttered down from a balloon. The way they came there was this: A somewhat elderly person, in the quaker dress, had quietly passed through the cabin, and, much in the manner of those railway book-peddlers who precede their proffers of sale by a distribution of puffs, direct or indirect, of the volumes to follow, had, without speaking, handed about the odes, which, for the most part, after a cursory glance, had been disrespectfully tossed aside, as no doubt the moon-struck production of some wandering rhapsodist.

In due time, book under arm, in trips the ruddy man with the travelling-cap, who, lightly moving to and fro, looks animatedly about him, with a yearning sort of gratulatory affinity and longing, expressive of the very soul of sociality; as much as to say, 'Oh, boys, would that I were personally acquainted with each mother's son of you, since what a sweet world, to make sweet acquaintance in, is ours, my brothers; yea, and what dear, happy dogs are we all!'

And just as if he had really warbled it forth, he makes fraternally up to one lounging stranger or another, exchanging with him some pleasant remark.

'Pray, what have you there?' he asked of one newly accosted, a little, dried-up man, who looked as if he never dined.

'A little ode, – rather queer, too,' was the reply, 'of the same sort you see strewn on the floor here.'

'I did not observe them. Let me see;' picking one up and looking it over. 'Well now, this is pretty; plaintive, especially the opening –

> Alas for man, he hath small sense
> Of genial trust and confidence.

– If it be so, alas for him, indeed. Runs off very smoothly, sir. Beautiful pathos. But do you think the sentiment just?'

'As to that,' said the little dried-up man, 'I think it a kind of queer thing altogether, and yet I am almost ashamed to add, it really has set me to thinking; yes and to feeling. Just now, somehow, I feel as it were trustful and genial. I don't know that ever I felt so much so before. I am naturally numb in my sensibilities; but this ode, in its way, works on my numbness not unlike a sermon, which, by lamenting over my lying dead in trespasses and sins, thereby stirs me up to be all alive in well-doing.'

'Glad to hear it, and hope you will do well, as the doctors say. But who snowed the odes about here?'

'I cannot say; I have not been here long.'

'Wasn't an angel, was it? Come, you say you feel genial, let us do as the rest, and have cards.'

'Thank you, I never play cards.'

'A bottle of wine?'

'Thank you, I never drink wine.'

'Cigars?'

'Thank you, I never smoke cigars.'

'Tell stories?'

'To speak truly, I hardly think I know one worth telling.'

'Seems to me, then, this geniality you say you feel waked in you is as water-power in a land without mills. Come, you had better take a genial hand at the cards. To begin, we will play for as small a sum as you please; just enough to make it interesting.'

'Indeed, you must excuse me. Somehow I distrust cards.'

'What, distrust cards? Genial cards? Then for once I join with our sad Philomel here:

> Alas for man, he hath small sense
> Of genial trust and confidence.

Good-bye!'

Sauntering and chatting here and there, again, he with the book at length seems fatigued, looks round for a seat, and spying a partly-vacant settee drawn up against the side, drops down there; soon, like his chance neighbour, who happens to be the good merchant, becoming not a little interested in the scene more immediately before him; a party at whist; two cream-faced, giddy, unpolished youths, the one in a red cravat, the other in a green, opposed to two bland, grave, handsome, self-possessed men of middle age, decorously dressed in a sort of professional black, and apparently doctors of some eminence in the civil law.

By-and-by, after a preliminary scanning of the new-comer next him, the good merchant, sideways leaning over, whispers behind a crumpled copy of the Ode which he holds: 'Sir, I don't like the looks of those two, do you?'

'Hardly,' was the whispered reply; 'those coloured cravats are not in the best taste, at least not to mine; but my taste is no rule for all.'

'You mistake; I mean the other two, and I don't refer to dress, but countenance. I confess I am not familiar with such gentry any further than reading about them in the papers – but those two are – are sharpers, ain't they?'

'Far be from us the captious and fault-finding spirit, my dear sir.'

'Indeed, sir, I would not find fault; I am little given that way; but certainly, to say the least, these two youths can hardly be adepts, while the opposed couple may be even more.'

'You would not hint that the coloured cravats would be so bungling as to lose, and the dark cravats so dextrous as to cheat? – Sour imaginations, my dear sir. Dismiss them. To little purpose have you read the Ode you have there. Years and experience, I trust, have not sophisticated you. A fresh and liberal construction would teach us to regard those four players – indeed, this whole cabin-full of players – as playing at games in which every player plays fair, and not a player but shall win.'

'Now, you hardly mean that; because games in which all may win, such games remain as yet in this world uninvented, I think.'

'Come, come,' luxuriously laying himself back, and casting a free glance upon the players, 'fares all paid; digestion sound; care, toil, penury, grief, unknown; lounging on this sofa, with waistband relaxed, why not be cheerfully resigned to one's fate, nor peevishly pick holes in the blessed fate of the world?'

Upon this, the good merchant, after staring long and hard, and then rubbing his forehead, fell into meditation, at first uneasy, but at last composed, and in the end, once more addressed his companion: 'Well, I see it's good to out with one's private thoughts now and then. Somehow, I don't know why, a certain misty suspiciousness seems inseparable from most of one's private notions about some men and some things; but once out with these misty notions, and their mere contact with other men's soon dissipates, or, at least, modifies them.'

'You think I have done you good, then? may be, I have. But don't thank me, don't thank me. If by words, casually delivered in the social hour, I do any good to right or left, it is but involuntary influence – locust-tree sweetening the herbage under it; no merit at all; mere wholesome accident, of a wholesome nature. – Don't you see?'

Another stare from the good merchant, and both were silent again.

Finding his book, hitherto resting on his lap, rather irksome there, the owner now places it edgewise on the settee, between himself and neighbour; in so doing, chancing to expose the lettering on the back – *Black Rapids Coal Company* – which the good merchant, scrupulously honourable, had much ado to avoid reading, so directly would it have fallen under his eye, had he not conscientiously averted it. On a sudden, as if just reminded of something, the stranger starts up, and moves away, in his haste leaving his book; which the merchant observing, without delay takes it up, and, hurrying after, civilly returns it; in which act he could not avoid catching sight by an involuntary glance of part of the lettering.

'Thank you, thank you, my good sir,' said the other, receiving the volume, and was resuming his retreat, when the merchant spoke: 'Excuse me, but are you not in some way connected with the – the Coal Company I have heard of?'

'There is more than one Coal Company that may be heard of, my good sir,' smiled the other, pausing with an expression of painful impatience, disinterestedly mastered.

'But you are connected with one in particular. – The "Black Rapids", are you not?'

'How did you find that out?'

'Well, sir, I have heard rather tempting information of your Company.'

'Who is your informant, pray?' somewhat coldly.

'A – a person by the name of Ringman.'

'Don't know him. But, doubtless, there are plenty who know

our Company, whom our Company does not know; in the same way that one may know an individual, yet be unknown to him. – Known this Ringman long? Old friend, I suppose. – But pardon, I must leave you.'

'Stay, sir, that – that stock.'

'Stock?'

'Yes, it's a little irregular, perhaps, but –'

'Dear me, you don't think of doing any business with me, do you? In my official capacity I have not been authenticated to you. This transfer-book, now,' holding it up so as to bring the lettering in sight, 'how do you know that it may not be a bogus one? And I, being personally a stranger to you, how can you have confidence in me?'

'Because,' knowingly smiled the good merchant, 'if you were other than I have confidence that you are, hardly would you challenge distrust that way.'

'But you have not examined my book.'

'What need to, if already I believe that it is what it is lettered to be?'

'But you had better. It might suggest doubts.'

'Doubts, may be, it might suggest, but not knowledge; for how, by examining the book, should I think I knew any more than I now think I do; since, if it be the true book, I think it so already; and since if it be otherwise, then I have never seen the true one, and don't know what that ought to look like.'

'Your logic I will not criticize, but your confidence I admire, and earnestly, too, jocose as was the method I took to draw it out. Enough, we will go to yonder table, and if there be any business which, either in my private or official capacity, I can help you do, pray command me.'

The transaction concluded, the two still remained seated, falling into familiar conversation, by degrees verging into that confidental sort of sympathetic silence, the last refinement and luxury of unaffected good feeling. It is a kind of social superstition to suppose that to be truly friendly one must be saying friendly words all the time, any more than be doing friendly deeds continually; – true friendliness, like true religion, being in a sort independent of works.

At length, the good merchant, whose eyes were pensively resting upon the gay tables in the distance, broke the spell by saying that, from the spectacle before them, one would little divine what other quarters of the boat might reveal. He cited the case, accidentally encountered but an hour or two previous, of a shrunken old miser, clad in shrunken old moleskin, stretched out, an invalid, on a bare plank in the emigrants' quarters, eagerly clinging to life and lucre, though the one was gasping for outlet, and about the other he was in torment lest death, or some other unprincipled cut-purse, should be the means of his losing it; by like feeble tenure holding lungs and pouch, and yet knowing and desiring nothing beyond them; for his mind, never raised above mould, was now all but mouldered away; – to such a degree, indeed, that he had no trust in anything, not even in his parchment bonds, which, the better to preserve from the tooth of time, he had packed down and sealed up, like brandy peaches, in a tin case of spirits.

The worthy man proceeded at some length with these dispiriting particulars. Nor would his cheery companion wholly deny that there might be a point of view from which such a case of extreme want of confidence might, to the humane mind, present features not altogether welcome as wine and olives after dinner. Still, he was not without compensatory considerations, and, upon the whole, took his companion to task for evincing what, in a good-natured, round-about way, he hinted to be a somewhat jaundiced sentimentality. Nature, he added, in Shakespeare's words, had meal and bran; and, rightly regarded, the bran in its way was not to be condemned.

The other was not disposed to question the justice of Shakespeare's thought, but would hardly admit the propriety of the application in this instance, much less of the comment. So, after some further temperate discussion of the pitiable miser, finding that they could not entirely harmonize, the merchant cited another case, that of the negro cripple. But his companion suggested whether the alleged hardships of that alleged unfortunate might not exist more in the pity of the observer than the experience of the observed. He knew nothing about the cripple, nor had seen him, but ventured to surmise that, could one but get at the real state of his heart, he would be found about as happy as most men, if not, in fact, full as happy as the speaker himself. He added that negroes were by nature a singularly cheerful race; no one ever heard of a native-born African Zimmermann or Torquemada; that even from religion they dismissed all gloom; in their hilarious rituals they danced, so to speak, and, as it were, cut pigeon-wings. It was improbable, therefore, that a negro, however reduced to his stumps by fortune, could be ever thrown off the legs of a laughing philosophy.

Foiled again, the good merchant would not desist, but ventured still a third case, that of the man with the weed, whose story, as narrated by himself, and confirmed and filled out by the testimony of a certain man in a gray coat, whom the merchant had afterwards met, he now proceeded to give; and that without holding back those particulars disclosed by the second informant, but which delicacy had prevented the unfortunate man himself from touching upon.

But as the good merchant could, perhaps, do better justice to the man than the story, we shall venture to tell it in other words than his, though not to any other effect.

crackers and brawn of ham. She liked lemons, and the only kind
of candy she loved were little dried sticks of blue clay, secretly
carried in her pocket. Withal she had hard, steady health like a
squaw's, with as firm a spirit and resolution. Some other points
about her were likewise such as pertain to the women of savage
life. Lithe though she was, she loved supineness, but upon occasion
could endure like a stoic. She was taciturn, too. From early
morning till about three o'clock in the afternoon she would
seldom speak – it taking that time to thaw her, by all accounts,
into but talking terms with humanity. During the interval she did
little but look, and keep looking out of her large metallic eyes,
which her enemies called cold as a cuttle-fish's, but which by her
were esteemed gazelle-like; for Goneril was not without vanity.
Those who thought they best knew her, often wondered what
happiness such a being could take in life, considering the happiness
which is to be had by some natures in the very easy way of simply
causing pain to those around them. Those who suffered from
Goneril's strange nature might, with one of those hyperboles to
which the resentful incline, have pronounced her some kind of
toad; but her worst slanderers could never, with any show of
justice, have accused her of being a toady. In a large sense she
possessed the virtue of independence of mind. Goneril held it
flattery to hint praise even of the absent, and even if merited; but
honesty, to fling people's imputed faults into their faces. This was
thought malice, but it certainly was not passion. Passion is human.
Like an icicle-dagger, Goneril at once stabbed and froze; so at least
they said; and when she saw frankness and innocence tyrannized
into sad nervousness under her spell, according to the same authority, inly she chewed her blue clay, and you could mark that she
chuckled. These peculiarities were strange and unpleasing; but
another was alleged, one really incomprehensible. In company she
had a strange way of touching, as by accident, the hand or arm of
comely young men, and seemed to reap a secret delight from it,
but whether from the humane satisfaction of having given the
evil-touch, as it is called, or whether it was something else in her,

not equally wonderful, but quite as deplorable, remained an enigma.

Needless to say what distress was the unfortunate man's, when, engaged in conversation with company, he would suddenly perceive his Goneril bestowing her mysterious touches, especially in such cases where the strangeness of the thing seemed to strike upon the touched person, notwithstanding good-breeding forbade his proposing the mystery, on the spot, as a subject of discussion for the company. In these cases, too, the unfortunate man could never endure so much as to look upon the touched young gentleman afterwards, fearful of the mortification of meeting in his countenance some kind of more or less quizzingly-knowing expression. He would shudderingly shun the young gentleman. So that here, to the husband, Goneril's touch had the dread operation of the heathen taboo. Now Goneril brooked no chiding. So, at favourable times, he, in a wary manner, and not indelicately, would venture in private interviews gently to make distant allusions to this questionable propensity. She divined him. But, in her cold loveless way, said it was witless to be telling one's dreams, especially foolish ones; but if the unfortunate man liked connubially to rejoice his soul with such chimeras, much connubial joy might they give him. All this was sad – a touching case – but all might, perhaps, have been borne by the unfortunate man – conscientiously mindful of his vow – for better or for worse – to love and cherish his dear Goneril so long as kind heaven might spare her to him – but when, after all that had happened, the devil of jealousy entered her, a calm, clayey, cakey devil, for none other could possess her, and the object of that deranged jealousy, her own child, a little girl of seven, her father's consolation and pet; when he saw Goneril artfully torment the little innocent, and then play the maternal hypocrite with it, the unfortunate man's patient long-suffering gave way. Knowing that she would neither confess nor amend, and might, possibly, become even worse than she was, he thought it but duty, as a father, to withdraw the child from her; but, loving it as he did, he could not do so without accompanying it into domestic exile himself. Which, hard though it was, he did. Whereupon the whole female neighbourhood, who till now had little enough admired dame Goneril, broke out in indignation against a husband who, without assigning a cause, could deliberately abandon the wife of his bosom, and sharpen the sting to her, too, by depriving her of the solace of retaining her offspring. To all this, self-respect, with Christian charity towards Goneril, long kept the unfortunate man dumb. And well had it been had he continued so; for when, driven to desperation, he hinted something of the truth of the case, not a soul would credit it; while for Goneril, she pronounced all he said to be a malicious invention.

Ere long, at the suggestion of some woman's-rights women, the injured wife began a suit, and, thanks to able counsel and accommodating testimony, succeeded in such a way, as not only to recover custody of the child, but to get such a settlement awarded upon a separation, as to make penniless the unfortunate man (so he averred), besides, through the legal sympathy she enlisted, effecting a judicial blasting of his private reputation. What made it yet more lamentable was, that the unfortunate man, thinking that, before the court, his wisest plan, as well as the most Christian besides, being, as he deemed, not at variance with the truth of the matter, would be to put forth the plea of the mental derangement of Goneril, which done, he could, with less of mortification to himself, and odium to her, reveal in self-defence those eccentricities which had led to his retirement from the joys of wedlock, had much ado in the end to prevent this charge of derangement from fatally recoiling upon himself —. especially, when, among other things, he alleged her mysterious touchings. In vain did his counsel, striving to make out the derangement to be where, in fact, if anywhere, it was, urge that, to hold otherwise, to hold that such a being as Goneril was sane, this was constructively a libel upon womankind. Libel be it. And all ended by the unfortunate man's subsequently getting wind of Goneril's intention to procure him to be permanently committed for a lunatic. Upon which he fled, and was now an innocent outcast, wandering forlorn in the great valley of the Mississippi, with a weed on his hat for the loss of his Goneril; for he had lately seen by the papers that she was dead, and thought it but proper to comply with the prescribed form of mourning in such cases. For some days past he had been trying to get money enough to return to his child, and was but now started with inadequate funds.

Now all of this, from the beginning, the good merchant could not but consider rather hard for the unfortunate man.

13

THE MAN WITH THE TRAVELLING-CAP
EVINCES MUCH HUMANITY, AND IN A WAY
WHICH WOULD SEEM TO SHOW HIM TO BE
ONE OF THE MOST LOGICAL OF OPTIMISTS

◆━━━◆━■━◆━━━◆

Years ago, a grave American *savan*, being in London, observed at an evening party there, a certain coxcombical fellow, as he thought, an absurd ribbon in his lapel, and full of smart persiflage, whisking about to the admiration of as many as were disposed to admire. Great was the *savan*'s disdain; but, chancing ere long to find himself in a corner with the jackanapes, got into conversation with him, when he was somewhat ill-prepared for the good sense of the jackanapes, but was altogether thrown aback, upon subsequently being whispered by a friend, that the jackanapes was almost as great a *savan* as himself, being no less a personage than Sir Humphry Davy.

The above anecdote is given just here by way of an anticipative reminder to such readers as, from the kind of jaunty levity, or what may have passed for such, hitherto for the most part appearing in the man with the travelling-cap, may have been tempted into a more or less hasty estimate of him; that such readers, when they find the same person, as they presently will, capable of philosophic and humanitarian discourse – no mere casual sentence or two as heretofore at times, but solidly sustained throughout an almost entire sitting; that they may not, like the American *savan*, be thereupon betrayed into any surprise incompatible with their own good opinion of their previous penetration.

The merchant's narration being ended, the other would not deny but that it did in some degree affect him. He hoped he was not without proper feeling for the unfortunate man. But he begged to know in what spirit he bore his alleged calamities. Did he despond or have confidence?

The merchant did not, perhaps, take the exact import of the last member of the question; but answered, that, if whether the unfortunate man was becomingly resigned under his affliction or no, was the point, he could say for him that resigned he was, and to an exemplary degree: for not only, so far as known, did he refrain from any one-sided reflections upon human goodness and human justice, but there was observable in him an air of chastened reliance, and at times tempered cheerfulness.

Upon which the other observed, that since the unfortunate man's alleged experience could not be deemed very conciliatory towards a view of human nature better than human nature was, it largely redounded to his fair-mindedness, as well as piety, that under the alleged dissuasives, apparently so, from philanthropy, he had not, in a moment of excitement, been warped over to the ranks of the misanthropes. He doubted not, also, that with such a man his experience would, in the end, act by a complete and beneficent inversion, and so far from shaking his confidence in his kind, confirm it, and rivet it. Which would the more surely be the case, did he (the unfortunate man) at last become satisfied (as sooner or later he probably would be) that in the distraction of his mind his Goneril had not in all respects had fair play. At all events, the description of the lady, charity could not but regard as more or less exaggerated, and so far unjust. The truth probably was that she was a wife with some blemishes mixed with some beauties. But when the blemishes were displayed, her husband, no adept in the female nature, had tried to use reason with her, instead of something more persuasive. Hence his failure to convince and convert. The act of withdrawing from her seemed, under the circumstances, abrupt. In brief, there were probably small faults on both sides, more than balanced by large virtues; and one should not be hasty in judging.

When the merchant, strange to say, opposed views so calm and impartial, and again, with some warmth, deplored the case of the unfortunate man, his companion, not without seriousness, checked him, saying, that this would never do; that though but in the most exceptional case, to admit the existence of unmerited misery, more particularly if alleged to have been brought about by unhindered arts of the wicked, such an admission was, to say the least, not prudent; since, with some, it might unfavourably bias their most important persuasions. Not that those persuasions were legitimately servile to such influences. Because, since the common occurrences of life could never, in the nature of things, steadily look one way and tell one story, as flags in the trade-wind; hence, if the conviction of a Providence, for instance, were in any way made dependent upon such variabilities as everyday events, the degree of that conviction would, in thinking minds, be subject to fluctuations akin to those of the stock-exchange during a long and uncertain war. Here he glanced aside at his transfer-book, and after a moment's pause continued. It was of the essence of a right conviction of the divine nature, as with a right conviction of the human, that, based less on experience than intuition, it rose above the zones of weather.

When now the merchant, with all his heart, coincided with this (as being a sensible, as well as religious person, he could not but do), his companion expressed satisfaction, that, in an age of some distrust on such subjects, he could yet meet with one who shared with him, almost to the full, so sound and sublime a confidence.

Still, he was far from the illiberality of denying that philosophy duly bounded was not permissible. Only he deemed it at least desirable that when such a case as that alleged of the unfortunate man was made the subject of philosophic discussion, it should be so philosophized upon, as not to afford handles to those unblessed with the true light. For, but to grant that there was so much as a mystery about such a case, might by those persons be held for a tacit surrender of the question. And as for the apparent licence temporarily permitted sometimes, to the bad over the good (as was by implication alleged with regard to Goneril and the unfortunate man), it might be injudicious there to lay too much polemic stress upon the doctrine of future retribution as the vindication of present impunity. For though, indeed, to the right-minded that doctrine was true, and of sufficient solace, yet with the perverse the polemic mention of it might but provoke the shallow, though mischievous conceit, that such a doctrine was but tantamount to the one which should affirm that Providence was not now, but was going to be. In short, will all sorts of cavillers, it was best, both for them and everybody, that whoever had the true light should stick behind the secure Malakoff of confidence, nor be tempted forth to hazardous skirmishes on the open ground of reason. Therefore, he deemed it unadvisable in the good man, even in the privacy of his own mind, or in communion with a congenial one, to indulge in too much latitude of philosophizing, or, indeed, of compassionating, since this might beget an indiscreet habit of thinking and feeling which might unexpectedly betray him upon unsuitable occasions. Indeed, whether in private or public, there was nothing which a good man was more bound to guard himself against than, on some topics, the emotional un-reserve of his natural heart; for, that the natural heart in certain points was not what it might be, men had been authoritatively ad-monished.

But he thought he might be getting dry.

The merchant, in his good-nature, thought otherwise, and said that he would be glad to refresh himself with such fruit all day. It was sitting under a ripe pulpit, and better such a seat than under a ripe peach-tree.

The other was pleased to find that he had not, as he feared, been prosing; but would rather not be considered in the formal light of a preacher; he preferred being still received in that of the equal and genial companion. To which end, throwing still more of sociability into his manner, he again reverted to the unfortunate man. Take the very worst view of that case: admit that his Goneril was, indeed, a Goneril; how fortunate to be at last rid of this Goneril, both by nature and by law! If he were acquainted with the unfortunate man, instead of condoling with him, he would congratulate him. Great good fortune had this unfortunate man. Lucky dog, he dared say, after all.

To which the merchant replied, that he earnestly hoped it might be so, and at any rate he tried his best to comfort himself with the persuasion that if the unfortunate man was not happy in this world, he would, at least, be so in another.

His companion made no question of the unfortunate man's happiness in both worlds; and presently calling for some champagne, invited the merchant to partake, upon the playful plea that, whatever notions other than felicitous ones he might associate with the unfortunate man, a little champagne would readily bubble away.

At intervals they slowly quaffed several glasses in silence and thoughtfulness. At last the merchant's expressive face flushed, his eye moistly beamed, his lips trembled with an imaginative and feminine sensibility. Without sending a single fume to his head, the wine seemed to shoot to his heart, and begin soothsaying there. 'Ah,' he cried, pushing his glass from him, 'ah, wine is good, and confidence is good; but can wine or confidence percolate down through all the stony strata of hard considerations, and drop warmly and ruddily into the cold cave of truth? Truth will *not* be comforted. Led by dear charity, lured by sweet hope, fond fancy essays this feat; but in vain; mere dreams and ideals, they explode in your hand, leaving nought but the scorching behind!'

'Why, why, why!' in amaze, at the burst; 'bless me, if *In vino veritas* be a true saying, then, for all the fine confidence you professed with me, just now, distrust, deep distrust, underlies it; and ten thousand strong, like the Irish Rebellion, breaks out in you now. That wine, good wine, should do it! Upon my soul,' half seriously, half humorously, securing the bottle, 'you shall drink no more of it. Wine was meant to gladden the heart, not grieve it; to heighten confidence, not depress it.'

Sobered, shamed, all but confounded, by this raillery, the most telling rebuke under such circumstances, the merchant stared about him, and then, with altered mien, stammeringly confessed, that he was almost as much surprised as his companion, at what had escaped him. He did not understand it; was quite at a loss to account for such a rhapsody popping out of him unbidden. It could hardly be the champagne; he felt his brain unaffected; in fact, if anything, the wine had acted upon it something like white of egg in coffee, clarifying and brightening.

'Brightening? brightening it may be, but less like the white of egg in coffee, than like stove-lustre on a stove – black, brightening. Seriously, I repent calling for the champagne. To a temperament like yours, champagne is not to be recommended. Pray, my dear sir, do you feel quite yourself again? Confidence restored?'

'I hope so; I think I may say it is so. But we have had a long talk, and I think I must retire now.'

So saying, the merchant rose, and making his adieus, left the table with the air of one, mortified at having been tempted by his own honest goodness, accidentally stimulated into making mad disclosures – to himself as to another – of the queer, unaccountable caprices of his natural heart.

14

WORTH THE CONSIDERATION OF THOSE TO
WHOM IT MAY PROVE WORTH CONSIDERING

As the last chapter was begun with a reminder looking forwards, so the present must consist of one glancing backwards.

To some, it may raise a degree of surprise that one so full of confidence, as the merchant has throughout shown himself, up to the moment of his late sudden impulsiveness, should, in that instance, have betrayed such a depth of discontent. He may be thought inconsistent, and even so he is. But for this is the author to be blamed? True, it may be urged that there is nothing a writer of fiction should more carefully see to, as there is nothing a sensible reader will more carefully look for, than that, in the depicting of any character, its consistency should be preserved. But this, though at first blush, seeming reasonable enough, may, upon a closer view, prove not so much so. For how does it couple with another requirement – equally insisted upon, perhaps – that, while to all fiction is allowed some play of invention, yet, fiction based on fact should never be contradictory to it; and is it not a fact, that, in real life, a consistent character is a *rara avis*? Which being so, the distaste of readers to the contrary sort in books can hardly arise from any sense of their untrueness. It may rather be from perplexity as to understanding them. But if the acutest sage be often at his wits' ends to understand living character, shall those who are not sages expect to run and read character in those mere phantoms which flit along a page like shadows along a wall? That fiction, where every character can, by reason of its consistency, be comprehended at a glance, either exhibits but sections of character, making them appear for wholes, or else is very untrue to reality;

while, on the other hand, that author who draws a character, even though to common view incongruous in its parts, as the flying-squirrel, and, at different periods, as much at variance with itself as the caterpillar is with the butterfly into which it changes, may yet, in so doing, be not false but faithful to facts.

If reason be judge, no writer has produced such inconsistent characters as nature herself has. It must call for no small sagacity in a reader unerringly to discriminate in a novel between the inconsistencies of conception and those of life. As elsewhere, experience is the only guide here; but as no one man's experience can be coextensive with *what is*, it may be unwise in every case to rest upon it. When the duck-billed beaver of Australia was first brought stuffed to England, the naturalists, appealing to their classifications, maintained that there was, in reality, no such creature; the bill in the specimen must needs be, in some way, artificially stuck on.

But let nature, to the perplexity of the naturalists, produce her duck-billed beavers as she may, lesser authors, some may hold, have no business to be perplexing readers with duck-billed characters. Always, they should represent human nature not in obscurity, but transparency, which, indeed, is the practice with most novelists, and is, perhaps, in certain cases, someway felt to be a kind of honour rendered by them to their kind. But whether it involve honour or otherwise might be mooted, considering that, if these waters of human nature can be so readily seen through, it may be either that they are very pure or very shallow. Upon the whole, it might rather be thought, that he, who, in view of its inconsistencies, says of human nature the same that, in view of its contrasts, is said of the divine nature, that it is past finding out, thereby evinces a better appreciation of it than he who, by always representing it in a clear light, leaves it to be inferred that he clearly knows all about it.

But though there is a prejudice against inconsistent characters in books, yet the prejudice bears the other way, when what seemed at first their inconsistency, afterwards, by the skill of the writer, turns out to be their good keeping. The great masters excel in nothing so much as in this very particular. They challenge astonishment at the tangled web of some character, and then raise admiration still greater at their satisfactory unravelling of it; in this way throwing open, sometimes to the understanding even of school misses, the last complications of that spirit which is affirmed by its Creator to be fearfully and wonderfully made.

At least something like this is claimed for certain psychological novelists; nor will the claim be here disputed. Yet, as touching this point, it may prove suggestive, that all those sallies of ingenuity, having for their end the revelation of human nature on fixed principles, have, by the best judges, been excluded with contempt from the ranks of the sciences — palmistry, physiognomy, phrenology, psychology. Likewise, the fact, that in all ages such conflicting views have, by the most eminent minds, been taken of mankind, would, as with other topics, seem some presumption of a pretty general and pretty thorough ignorance of it, — which may appear the less improbable if it be considered that, after poring over the best novels professing to portray human nature, the studious youth will still run risk of being too often at fault upon actually entering the world; whereas, had he been furnished with a true delineation, it ought to fare with him somewhat as with a stranger entering, map in hand, Boston town; the streets may be very crooked, he may often pause; but, thanks to his true map, he does not hopelessly lose his way. Nor, to this comparison, can it be an adequate objection, that the twistings of the town are always the same, and those of human nature subject to variation. The grand points of human nature are the same to-day they were a thousand years ago. The only variability in them is in expression, not in feature.

But as, in spite of seeming discouragement, some mathematicians are yet in hopes of hitting upon an exact method of determining the longitude, the more earnest psychologists may, in the face of previous failures, still cherish expectations with regard to some mode of infallibly discovering the heart of man.

But enough has been said by way of apology for whatever may have seemed amiss or obscure in the character of the merchant; so nothing remains but to turn to our comedy, or, rather, to pass from the comedy of thought to that of action.

15

AN OLD MISER, UPON SUITABLE REPRESENTATIONS, IS PREVAILED UPON TO VENTURE AN INVESTMENT

The merchant having withdrawn, the other remained seated alone for a time, with the air of one who, after having conversed with some excellent man, carefully ponders what fell from him, however intellectually inferior it may be, that none of the profit may be lost; happy if from any honest word he has heard he can derive some hint, which, besides confirming him in the theory of virtue, may, likewise, serve for a finger-post to virtuous action.

Ere long his eye brightened, as if some such hint was now caught. He rises, book in hand, quits the cabin, and enters upon a sort of corridor, narrow and dim, a by-way to a retreat less ornate and cheery than the former; in short, the emigrants' quarters; but which, owing to the present trip being a down-river one, will doubtless be found comparatively tenantless. Owing to obstructions against the side windows, the whole place is dim and dusky; very much so, for the most part; yet, by starts, haggardly lit here and there by narrow, capricious skylights in the cornices. But there would seem no special need for light, the place being designed more to pass the night in, than the day; in brief, a pine barrens dormitory, of knotty pine bunks, without bedding. As with the nests in the geometrical towns of the associate penguin and pelican, these bunks were disposed with Philadelphian regularity, but, like the cradle of the oriole, they were pendulous, and moreover, were, so to speak, three-story cradles; the description of one of which will suffice for all.

Four ropes, secured to the ceiling, passed downwards through

auger-holes bored in the corners of three rough planks, which at
equal distances rested on knots vertically tied in the ropes, the
lowermost plank but an inch or two from the floor, the whole
affair resembling, on a large scale, rope book-shelves; only, instead
of hanging firmly against a wall, they swayed to and fro at the
least suggestion of motion, but were more especially lively upon
the provocation of a green emigrant sprawling into one, and trying
to lay himself out there, when the cradling would be such as
almost to toss him back whence he came. In consequence, one less
inexperienced, essaying repose on the uppermost shelf, was liable
to serious disturbance, should a raw beginner select a shelf beneath.
Sometimes a throng of poor emigrants, coming at night in a
sudden rain to occupy these oriole nests, would – through ignorance of their peculiarity – bring about such a rocking uproar of
carpentry, joining to it such an uproar of exclamations, that it
seemed as if some luckless ship, with all its crew, was being dashed
to pieces among the rocks. They were beds devised by some
sardonic foe of poor travellers, to deprive them of that tranquillity
which should precede, as well as accompany, slumber. Procrustean
beds, on whose hard grain humble worth and honesty writhed,
still invoking repose, while but torment responded. Ah, did any
one make such a bunk for himself, instead of having it made
for him, it might be just, but how cruel, to say, You must lie
on it!

But, purgatory as the place would appear, the stranger advances
into it; and, like Orpheus in his gay descent to Tartarus, lightly
hums to himself an opera snatch.

Suddenly there is a rustling, then a creaking, one of the cradles
swings out from a murky nook, a sort of wasted penguin-flipper
is supplicatingly put forth, while a wail like that of Dives is heard:
'Water, water!'

It was the miser of whom the merchant had spoken.

Swift as a sister-of-charity, the stranger hovers over him:

'My poor, poor sir, what can I do for you?'

'Ugh, ugh – water!'

Darting out, he procures a glass, returns, and, holding it to the sufferer's lips, supports his head while he drinks: 'And did they let you lie here, my poor sir, racked with this parching thirst?'

The miser, a lean old man, whose flesh seemed salted cod-fish, dry as combustibles; head, like one whittled by an idiot out of a knot; flat, bony mouth, nipped between buzzard nose and chin; expression, flitting between hunks and imbecile – now one, now the other – he made no response. His eyes were closed, his cheek lay upon an old white moleskin coat, rolled under his head like a wizened apple upon a grimy snow-bank.

Revived at last, he inclined towards his ministrant, and, in a voice disastrous with a cough, said: 'I am old and miserable, a poor beggar, not worth a shoe-string – how can I repay you?'

'By giving me your confidence.'

'Confidence!' he squeaked, with changed manner, while the pallet swung, 'little left at my age, but take the stale remains, and welcome.'

'Such as it is, though, you give it. Very good. Now give me a hundred dollars.'

Upon this the miser was all panic. His hands groped towards his waist, then suddenly flew upward beneath his moleskin pillow, and there lay clutching something out of sight. Meantime, to himself he incoherently mumbled: 'Confidence? Cant, gammon! Confidence? hum, bubble! – Confidence? fetch, gouge! – Hundred dollars? – hundred devils!'

Half spent, he lay mute awhile, then feebly raising himself, in a voice for the moment made strong by the sarcasm, said, 'A hundred dollars? rather high price to put upon confidence. But don't you see I am a poor, old rat here, dying in the wainscot? You have served me; but, wretch that I am, I can but cough you my thanks, – ugh, ugh, ugh!'

This time his cough was so violent that its convulsions were imparted to the plank, which swung him about like a stone in a sling preparatory to its being hurled.

'Ugh, ugh, ugh!'

'What a shocking cough. I wish, my friend, the herb–doctor was here now; a box of his Omni-Balsamic Reinvigorator would do you good.'

'Ugh, ugh, ugh!'

'I've a good mind to go find him. He's aboard somewhere. I saw his long, snuff-coloured surtout. Trust me, his medicines are the best in the world.'

'Ugh, ugh, ugh!'

'Oh, how sorry I am.'

'No doubt of it,' squeaked the other again, 'but go, get your charity out on deck. There parade the pursy peacocks; they don't cough down here in desertion and darkness, like poor old me. Look how scaly a pauper I am, clove with this churchyard cough. Ugh, ugh, ugh!'

'Again, how sorry I feel, not only for your cough, but your poverty. Such a rare chance made unavailable. Did you have but the sum named, how I could invest it for you. Treble profits. But confidence – I fear that, even had you the precious cash, you would not have the more precious confidence I speak of.'

'Ugh, ugh, ugh!' flightingly raising himself. 'What's that? How, how? Then you don't want the money for yourself?'

'My dear, *dear* sir, how could you impute to me such preposterous self-seeking? To solicit out of hand, for my private behoof, a hundred dollars from a perfect stranger? I am not mad, my dear sir.'

'How, how?' still more bewildered, 'do you, then, go about the world, gratis, seeking to invest people's money for them?'

'My humble profession, sir. I live not for myself; but the world will not have confidence in me, and yet confidence in me were great gain.'

'But, but,' in a kind of vertigo, 'what do – do you do – do with people's money? Ugh, ugh! How is the gain made?'

'To tell that would ruin me. That known, every one would be going into the business, and it would be overdone. A secret, a mystery – all I have to do with you is to receive your confidence, and all you have to do with me is, in due time, to receive it back, thrice paid in trebling profits.'

'What, what?' imbecility in the ascendant once more; 'but the vouchers, the vouchers,' suddenly hunkish again.

'Honesty's best voucher is honesty's face.'

'Can't see yours, though,' peering through the obscurity.

From this last alternating flicker of rationality, the miser fell back, sputtering, into his previous gibberish, but it took now an arithmetical turn. Eyes closed, he lay muttering to himself –

'One hundred, one hundred – two hundred, two hundred – three hundred, three hundred.'

He opened his eyes, feebly stared, and still more feebly said –

'It's a little dim here, ain't it? Ugh, ugh! But, as well as my poor old eyes can see, you look honest.'

'I am glad to hear that.'

'If – if, now, I should put' – trying to raise himself, but vainly, excitement having all but exhausted him – 'if, if now, I should put, put –'

'No ifs. Downright confidence, or none. So help me heaven, I will have no half-confidences.'

He said it with an indifferent and superior air, and seemed moving to go.

'Don't, don't leave me, friend; bear with me; age can't help some distrust; it can't friend, it can't. Ugh, ugh, ugh! Oh, I am so old and miserable. I ought to have a guardeean. Tell me , if –'

'If? No more!'

'Stay! how soon – ugh, ugh! – would my money be trebled? How soon, friend?'

'You won't confide. Good-bye!'

'Stay, stay,' falling back now like an infant, 'I confide, I confide; help, friend, my distrust!'

From an old buckskin pouch, tremulously dragged forth, ten hoarded eagles, tarnished into the appearance of ten old horn-buttons, were taken, and half-eagerly, half-reluctantly, offered.

'I know not whether I should accept this slack confidence,' said the other coldly, receiving the gold, 'but an eleventh-hour confidence, a sick-bed confidence, a distempered, death-bed confidence, after all. Give me the healthy confidence of healthy men, with their healthy wits about them. But let that pass. All right. Goodbye!'

'Nay, back, back – receipt, my receipt! Ugh, ugh, ugh! Who are you? What have I done? Where go you? My gold, my gold! Ugh, ugh, ugh!'

But, unluckily for this final flicker of reason, the stranger was now beyond ear-shot, nor was any one else within hearing of so feeble a call.

16

A SICK MAN, AFTER SOME IMPATIENCE, IS
INDUCED TO BECOME A PATIENT

The sky slides into blue, the bluffs into bloom, the rapid Mississippi expands; runs sparkling and gurgling all over in eddies; one magnified wake of a seventy-four. The sun comes out, a golden hussar, from his tent, flashing his helm on the world. All things, warmed in the landscape, leap. Speeds the daedal boat as a dream.

But, withdrawn in a corner, wrapped about in a shawl, sits an unparticipating man, visited, but not warmed, by the sun – a plant whose hour seems over while buds are blowing and seeds are astir. On a stool at his left sits a stranger in a snuff-coloured surtout, the collar thrown back, his hand waving in persuasive gesture, his eye beaming with hope. But not easily may hope be awakened in one long tranced into hopelessness by a chronic complaint.

To some remark the sick man, by word or look, seemed to have just made an impatiently querulous answer, when, with a deprecatory air, the other resumed:

'Nay, think not I seek to cry up my treatment by crying down that of others. And yet, when one is confident he has truth on his side, and that it is not on the other, it is no very easy thing to be charitable; not that temper is the bar, but conscience; for charity would beget toleration, you know, which is a kind of implied permitting, and in effect a kind of countenancing; and that which is countenanced is so far furthered. But should untruth be furthered? Still, while for the world's good I refuse to further the cause of these mineral doctors, I would fain regard them, not as wilful wrong-doers, but good Samaritans erring. And is this – I

put it to you, sir – is this the view of an arrogant rival and pre-
tender?'

His physical power all dribbled and gone, the sick man replied
not by voice or by gesture; but, with feeble dumb-show of his
face, seemed to be saying, 'Pray leave me; who was ever cured by
talk?'

But the other, as if not unused to make allowances for such
despondency, proceeded; and kindly, yet firmly:

'You tell me, that by advice of an eminent physiologist in
Louisville, you took tincture of iron. For what? To restore your
lost energy. And how? Why, in healthy subjects iron is naturally
found in the blood, and iron in the bar is strong; ergo, iron is the
source of animal invigoration. But you being deficient in vigour,
it follows that the cause is deficiency of iron. Iron, then, must be
put into you; and so your tincture. Now as to the theory here, I
am mute. But in modesty assuming its truth, and then, as a plain
man viewing that theory in practice, I would respectfully question
your eminent physiologist: "Sir," I would say, "though by natural
processes, lifeless natures taken as nutriment become vitalized, yet
is a lifeless nature, under any circumstances, capable of a living
transmission, with all its qualities as a lifeless nature unchanged? If,
sir, nothing can be incorporated with the living body but by
assimilation, and if that implies the conversion of one thing to a
different thing (as, in a lamp, oil is assimilated into flame), is it, in
this view, likely, that by banquetting on fat, Calvin Edson will
fatten? That is, will what is fat on the board prove fat on the
bones? If it will, then, sir, what is iron in the vial will prove iron
in the vein." Seems that conclusion too confident?'

But the sick man again turned his dumb-show look, as much as
to say, 'Pray leave me. Why, with painful words, hint the vanity
of that which the pains of this body have too painfully proved?'

But the other, as if unobservant of that querulous look, went
on:

'But this notion, that science can play farmer to the flesh,
making there what living soil it pleases, seems not so strange as

that other conceit – that science is now-a-days so expert, that in consumptive cases, as yours, it can, by prescription of the inhalation of certain vapours, achieve the sublimest act of omnipotence, breathing into all but lifeless dust the breath of life. For did you not tell me, my poor sir, that by order of the great chemist in Baltimore, for three weeks you were never driven out without a respirator, and for a given time of every day sat bolstered up in a sort of gasometer, inspiring vapours generated by the burning of drugs? as if this concocted atmosphere of man were an antidote to the poison of God's natural air. Oh, who can wonder at that old reproach against science, that it is atheistical? And here is my prime reason for opposing these chemical practitioners, who have sought out so many inventions. For what do their inventions indicate, unless it be that kind and degree of pride in human skill, which seems scarce compatible with reverential dependence upon the power above? Try to rid my mind of it as I may, yet still these chemical practitioners with their tinctures, and fumes, and braziers, and occult incantations, seem to me like Pharaoh's vain sorcerers, trying to beat down the will of heaven. Day and night, in all charity, I intercede for them, that heaven may not, in its own language, be provoked to anger with their inventions; may not take vengeance of their inventions. A thousand pities that you should ever have been in the hands of these Egyptians.'

But again came nothing but the dumb-show look, as much as to say, 'Pray leave me; quacks, and indignation against quacks, both are vain.'

But, once more, the other went on: 'How different we herb-doctors! who claim nothing, invent nothing; but staff in hand, in glades, and upon hillsides, go about in nature, humbly seeking her cures. True Indian doctors, though not learned in names we are not unfamiliar with essences – successors of Solomon the Wise, who knew all vegetables, from the cedar of Lebanon, to the hyssop on the wall. Yes, Solomon was the first of herb-doctors. Nor were the virtues of herbs unhonoured by yet older ages. Is it not writ, that on a moonlight night,

"Medea gathered the enchanted herbs
That did renew old Aeson"?

Ah, would you but have confidence, you should be the new
Aeson, and I your Medea. A few vials of my Omni-Balsamic
Reinvigorator would, I am certain, give you some strength.'

Upon this, indignation and abhorrence seemed to work by
their excess the effect promised of the balsam. Roused from
that long apathy of impotence, the cadaverous man started, and,
in a voice that was as the sound of obstructed air gurgling
through a maze of broken honey-combs, cried: 'Begone! You
are all alike. The name of doctor, the dream of helper, con-
demns you. For years I have been but a gallipot for your experi-
mentizers to rinse your experiments into, and now, in this livid
skin, partake of the nature of my contents. Begone! I hate
ye.'

'I were inhuman, could I take affront at a want of confidence,
born of too bitter an experience of betrayers. Yet, permit one
who is not without feeling –'

'Begone! Just in that voice talked to me, not six months ago,
the German doctor at the water cure, from which I now return,
six months and sixty pangs nigher my grave.'

'The water-cure? Oh, fatal delusion of the well-meaning Priessnitz! – Sir, trust me –'

'Begone!'

'Nay, an invalid should not always have his own way. Ah, sir,
reflect how untimely this distrust in one like you. How weak you
are; and weakness, is it not the time for confidence? Yes, when
through weakness everything bids despair, then is the time to get
strength by confidence.'

Relenting in his air, the sick man cast upon him a long glance
of beseeching, as if saying, 'With confidence must come hope;
and how can hope be?'

The herb-doctor took a sealed paper box from his surtout
pocket, and holding it towards him, said solemnly, 'Turn not

away. This may be the last time of health's asking. Work upon yourself; invoke confidence, though from ashes; rouse it; for your life, rouse it, and invoke it, I say.'

The other trembled, was silent; and then, a little commanding himself, asked the ingredients of the medicine.

'Herbs.'

'What herbs? And the nature of them? And the reason for giving them?'

'It cannot be made known.'

'Then I will none of you.'

Sedately observant of the juiceless, joyless form before him, the herb-doctor was mute a moment, then said: 'I give up.'

'How?'

'You are sick, and a philosopher.'

'No, no – not the last.'

'But, to demand the ingredient, with the reason for giving, is the mark of a philosopher; just as the consequence is the penalty of a fool. A sick philosopher is incurable.'

'Why?'

'Because he has no confidence.'

'How does that make him incurable?'

'Because either he spurns his powder, or, if he take it, it proves a blank cartridge, though the same given to a rustic in like extremity, would act like a charm. I am no materialist; but the mind so acts upon the body, that if the one have no confidence, neither has the other.'

Again, the sick man appeared not unmoved. He seemed to be thinking what in candid truth could be said to all this. At length, 'You talk of confidence. How comes it that when brought low himself, the herb-doctor, who was most confident to prescribe in other cases, proves least confident to prescribe in his own; having small confidence in himself for himself?'

'But he has confidence in the brother he calls in. And that he does so, is no reproach to him, since he knows that when the body is prostrated, the mind is not erect. Yes, in this hour the herb-doctor does distrust himself, but not his art.'

The sick man's knowledge did not warrant him to gainsay this. But he seemed not grieved at it; glad to be confuted in a way tending towards his wish.

'Then you give me hope?' his sunken eye turned up.

'Hope is proportioned to confidence. How much confidence you give me, so much hope do I give you. For this,' lifting the box, 'if all depended upon this, I should rest. It is nature's own.'

'Nature!'

'Why do you start?'

'I know not,' with a sort of shudder, 'but I have heard of a book entitled "Nature in Disease."'

'A title I cannot approve; it is suspiciously scientific. "Nature in Disease"? As if nature, divine nature, were aught but health; as if through nature disease is decreed! But did I not before hint of the tendency of science, that forbidden tree? Sir, if despondency is yours from recalling that title, dismiss it. Trust me, nature is health; for health is good, and nature cannot work ill. As little can she work error. Get nature, and you get well. Now, I repeat, this medicine is nature's own.'

Again the sick man could not, according to his light, conscientiously disprove what was said. Neither, as before, did he seem over-anxious to do so; the less, as in his sensitiveness it seemed to him, that hardly could he offer so to do without something like the appearance of a kind of implied irreligion; nor in his heart was he ungrateful, that since a spirit opposite to that pervaded all the herb-doctor's hopeful words, therefore, for hopefulness, he (the sick man) had not alone medical warrant, but also doctrinal.

'Then you do really think,' hectically, 'that if I take this medicine,' mechanically reaching out for it, 'I shall regain my health?'

'I will not encourage false hopes,' relinquishing to him the box, 'I will be frank with you. Though frankness is not always the weakness of the mineral practitioner, yet the herb-doctor must be frank, or nothing. Now then, sir, in your case, a radical cure – such a cure, understand, as should make you robust – such a cure, sir, I do not and cannot promise.'

'Oh, you need not! only restore me the power of being something else to others than a burdensome care, and to myself a droning grief. Only cure me of this misery of weakness; only make me so that I can walk about in the sun and not draw the flies to me, as lured by the coming of decay. Only do that – but that.'

'You ask not much; you are wise; not in vain have you suffered. That little you ask, I think, can be granted. But remember, not in a day, nor a week, nor perhaps a month, but sooner or later; I say not exactly when, for I am neither prophet nor charlatan. Still, if, according to the directions in your box there, you take my medicine steadily, without assigning an especial day, near or remote, to discontinue it, then may you calmly look for some eventual result of good. But again I say, you must have confidence.'

Feverishly he replied that he now trusted he had, and hourly should pray for its increase. When suddenly relapsing into one of those strange caprices peculiar to some invalids, he added: 'But to one like me, it is so hard, so hard. The most confident hopes so often have failed me, and as often have I vowed never, no, never, to trust them again. Oh,' feebly wringing his hands, 'you do not know, you do not know.'

'I know this, that never did a right confidence come to nought. But time is short; you hold your cure, to retain or reject?'

'I retain,' with a clinch, 'and now how much?'

'As much as you can evoke from your heart and heaven.'

'How? – the price of this medicine?'

'I thought it was confidence you meant; how much confidence you should have. The medicine, – that is half a dollar a vial. Your box holds six.'

The money was paid.

'Now, sir,' said the herb-doctor, 'my business calls me away, and it may so be that I shall never see you again; if then –'

He paused, for the sick man's countenance fell blank.

'Forgive me,' cried the other, 'forgive that imprudent phrase "never see you again". Though I solely intended it with reference to myself, yet I had forgotten what your sensitiveness might be. I repeat, then, that it may be that we shall not soon have a second interview, so that hereafter, should another of my boxes be needed, you may not be able to replace it except by purchase at the shops; and in so doing, you may run more or less risk of taking some not salutary mixture. For such is the popularity of the Omni-Balsamic Reinvigorator – thriving not by the credulity of the simple, but the trust of the wise – that certain contrivers have not been idle, though I would not, indeed, hastily affirm of them that they are aware of the sad consequences to the public. Homicides and murderers, some call those contrivers; but I do not; for murder (if such a crime be possible) comes from the heart, and these men's motives come from the purse. Were they not in poverty, I think they would hardly do what they do. Still, the public interests forbid that I should let their needy device for a living succeed. In short, I have adopted precautions. Take the wrapper from any of my vials and hold it to the light, you will see water-marked in capitals the word *confidence*, which is the countersign of the medicine, as I wish it was of the world. The wrapper bears that mark or else the medicine is counterfeit. But if still any lurking doubt should remain, pray enclose the wrapper to this address,' handing a card, 'and by return mail I will answer.'

At first the sick man listened, with the air of vivid interest, but gradually, while the other was still talking, another strange caprice came over him, and he presented the aspect of the most calamitous dejection.

'How now?' said the herb-doctor.

'You told me to have confidence, said that confidence was indispensable, and here you preach to me distrust. Ah, truth will out!'

'I told you, you must have confidence, unquestioning confidence; I meant confidence in the genuine medicine, and the genuine *me*.'

'But in your absence, buying vials purporting to be yours, it seems I cannot have unquestioning confidence.'

'Prove all the vials; trust those which are true.'

'But to doubt, to suspect, to prove – to have all this wearing work to be doing continually – how opposed to confidence. It is evil!'

'From evil comes good. Distrust is a stage to confidence. How has it proved in our interview? But your voice is husky; I have let you talk too much. You hold your cure; I leave you. But stay – when I hear that health is yours, I will not, like some I know, vainly make boasts; but, giving glory where all glory is due, say, with the devout herb-doctor, Iapis in Virgil, when, in the unseen but efficacious presence of Venus, he with simples healed the wound of Aeneas:

"This is no mortal work, no cure of mine,
  Nor art's effect, but done by power divine."'

17

TOWARDS THE END OF WHICH THE HERB-DOCTOR PROVES HIMSELF A FORGIVER OF INJURIES

In a kind of ante-cabin, a number of respectable looking people, male and female, way-passengers, recently come on board, are listlessly sitting in a mutually shy sort of silence.

Holding up a small, square bottle, ovally labelled with the engraving of a countenance full of soft pity as that of the Romish-painted Madonna, the herb-doctor passes slowly among them, benignly urbane, turning this way and that, saying:

'Ladies and gentlemen, I hold in my hand here the Samaritan Pain Dissuader, thrice-blessed discovery of that disinterested friend of humanity whose portrait you see. Pure vegetable extract. Warranted to remove the acutest pain within less than ten minutes. Five hundred dollars to be forfeited on failure. Especially efficacious in heart disease and tic-douloureux. Observe the expression of this pledged friend of humanity. – Price only fifty cents.'

In vain. After the first idle stare, his auditors, – in pretty good health, it seemed – instead of encouraging his politeness, appeared, if anything, impatient of it; and, perhaps, only diffidence, or some small regard for his feelings, prevented them from telling him so. But, insensible to their coldness, or charitably overlooking it, he more wooingly than ever resumed: 'May I venture upon a small supposition? Have I your kind leave, ladies and gentlemen?'

To which modest appeal, no one had the kindness to answer a syllable.

'Well,' said he, resignedly, 'silence is at least not denial, and may be consent. My supposition is this: Possibly some lady, here present, has a dear friend at home, a bed-ridden sufferer from spinal complaint. If so, what gift more appropriate to that sufferer than this tasteful little bottle of Pain Dissuader?'

Again he glanced about him, but met much the same reception as before. Those faces, alien alike to sympathy or surprise, seemed patiently to say, 'We are travellers; and, as such, must expect to meet, and quietly put up with, many antic fools, and more antic quacks.'

'Ladies and gentlemen,' (deferentially fixing his eyes upon their now self-complacent faces) 'ladies and gentlemen, might I, by your kind leave, venture upon one other small supposition? It is this: that there is scarce a sufferer, this noonday, writhing on his bed, but in his hour he sat satisfactorily healthy and happy; that the Samaritan Pain Dissuader is the one only balm for that to which each living creature – who knows? – may be a draughted victim, present or prospective. In short: – Oh, Happiness on my right hand, and oh, Security on my left, can ye wisely adore a Providence, and not think it wisdom to provide? – Provide!' (Uplifting the bottle.)

What immediate effect, if any, this appeal might have had, is uncertain. For just then the boat touched at a houseless landing, scooped, as by a land-slide, out of sombre forests; back through which led a road, the sole one, which, from its narrowness, and its being walled up with story on story of dusk, matted foliage, presented the vista of some cavernous old gorge in a city, like haunted Cock Lane in London. Issuing from that road, and crossing that landing, there stooped his shaggy form in the doorway, and entered the ante-cabin, with a step so burdensome that shot seemed in his pockets, a kind of invalid Titan in homespun; his beard blackly pendant, like the Carolina-moss, and dank with cypress dew; his countenance tawny and shadowy as an iron-ore country in a clouded day. In one hand he carried a heavy walking-stick of swamp-oak; with the other, led a puny girl, walking in moccasins, not improbably his child, but evidently of alien maternity, perhaps Creole, or even

Camanche. Her eye would have been large for a woman, and was inky as the pools of falls among mountain-pines. An Indian blanket, orange-hued, and fringed with bead tassel-work, appeared that morning to have shielded the child from heavy showers. Her limbs were tremulous; she seemed a little Cassandra, in nervousness.

No sooner was the pair spied by the herb-doctor, than, with a cheerful air, both arms extended like a host's, he advanced, and taking the child's reluctant hand, said, trippingly: 'On your travels, ah, my little May Queen? Glad to see you. What pretty moccasins. Nice to dance in.' Then with a half caper sang –

> 'Hey diddle, diddle, the cat and the fiddle;
> The cow jumped over the moon.

Come, chirrup, chirrup, my little robin!'

Which playful welcome drew no responsive playfulness from the child, nor appeared to gladden or conciliate the father; but rather, if anything, to dash the dead weight of his heavy-hearted expression with a smile hypochondriacally scornful.

Sobering down now, the herb-doctor addressed the stranger in a manly, business-like way – a transition which, though it might seem a little abrupt, did not appear constrained, and, indeed, served to show that his recent levity was less the habit of a frivolous nature, than the frolic condescension of a kindly heart.

'Excuse me,' said he, 'but, if I err not, I was speaking to you the other day; – on a Kentucky boat wasn't it?'

'Never to me,' was the reply; the voice deep and lonesome enough to have come from the bottom of an abandoned coal-shaft.

'Ah! – But am I again mistaken (his eye falling on the swamp-oak stick), or don't you go a little lame, sir?'

'Never was lame in my life.'

'Indeed? I fancied I had perceived not a limp, but a hitch, a slight hitch; – some experience in these things – divined some hidden cause of the hitch – buried bullet, may be – some dragoons in the Mexican war, discharged with such, you know. – Hard fate!' he sighed; 'little pity for it, for who sees it? – have you dropped anything?'

Why, there is no telling, but the stranger was bowed over, and might have seemed bowing for the purpose of picking up something, were it not that, as arrested in the imperfect posture, he for the moment so remained; slanting his tall stature like a mainmast yielding to the gale, or Adam to the thunder.

The little child pulled him. With a kind of a surge he righted himself; for an instant looked toward the herb-doctor; but, either from emotion or aversion, or both together, withdrew his eyes, saying nothing. Presently, still stooping, he seated himself, drawing his child between his knees, his massy hands tremulous, and still averting his face, while up into the compassionate one of the herb-doctor the child turned a fixed, melancholy glance of repugnance.

The herb-doctor stood observant a moment, then said:

'Surely you have pain, strong pain, somewhere; in strong frames pain is strongest. Try, now, my specific' (holding it up). 'Do but look at the expression of this friend of humanity. Trust me, certain cure for any pain in the world. Won't you look?'

'No,' choked the other.

'Very good. Merry time to you, little May Queen.'

And so, as if he would intrude his cure upon no one, moved pleasantly off, again crying his wares, nor now at last without result. A new-comer, not from the shore, but another part of the boat, a sickly young man, after some questions, purchased a bottle. Upon this, others of the company began a little to wake up as it were; the scales of indifference or prejudice fell from their eyes; now, at last, they seemed to have an inkling that here was something not undesirable which might be had for the buying.

But while, ten times more briskly bland than ever, the herb-doctor was driving his benevolent trade, accompanying each sale with added praises of the thing graded, all at once the dusk giant, seated at some distance, unexpectedly raised his voice with –

'What was that you last said?'

The question was put distinctly, yet resonantly, as when a great clock-bell – stunning admonisher – strikes one; and the stroke, though single, comes bedded in the belfry clamor.

All proceedings were suspended. Hands held forth for the specific were withdrawn, while every eye turned towards the direction whence the question came. But, no way abashed, the herb-doctor, elevating his voice with even more than wonted self-possession, replied –

'I was saying what, since you wish it, I cheerfully repeat, that the Samaritan Pain Dissuader, which I here hold in my hand, will either cure or ease any pain you please, within ten minutes after its application.'

'Does it produce insensibility?'

'By no means. Not the least of its merits is, that it is not an opiate. It kills pain without killing feeling.'

'You lie! Some pains cannot be eased but by producing insensibility, and cannot be cured but by producing death.'

Beyond this the dusk giant said nothing; neither, for impairing the other's market, did there appear much need to. After eyeing the rude speaker a moment with an expression of mingled admiration and consternation, the company silently exchanged glances of mutual sympathy under unwelcome conviction. Those who had purchased looked sheepish or ashamed; and a cynical-looking little man, with a thin flaggy beard, and a countenance ever wearing the rudiments of a grin, seated alone in a corner commanding a good view of the scene, held a rusty hat before his face.

But, again, the herb-doctor, without noticing the retort, overbearing though it was, began his panegyrics anew, and in a tone more assured than before, going so far now as to say that his specific was sometimes almost as effective in cases of mental suffering as in cases of physical; or rather, to be more precise, in cases when, through sympathy, the two sorts of pain cooperated into a climax of both – in such cases, he said, the specific had done very well. He cited an example: Only three bottles, faithfully taken, cured a Louisiana widow (for three weeks sleepless in a darkened chamber) of neuralgic sorrow for the loss of husband and child, swept off in one night by the last epidemic. For the truth of this, a printed voucher was produced, duly signed.

While he was reading it aloud, a sudden side-blow all but felled him.

It was the giant, who, with a countenance lividly epileptic with hypochondriac mania, exclaimed —

'Profane fiddler on heart-strings! Snake!'

More he would have added, but, convulsed, could not; so, without another word, taking up the child, who had followed him, went with a rocking pace out of the cabin.

'Regardless of decency, and lost to humanity!' exclaimed the herb-doctor, with much ado recovering himself. Then, after a pause, during which he examined his bruise, not omitting to apply externally a little of his specific, and with some success, as it would seem, complained to himself:

'No, no, I won't seek redress; innocence is my redress. But,' turning upon them all, 'if that man's wrathful blow provokes me to no wrath, should his evil distrust arouse you to distrust? I do devoutly hope,' proudly raising voice and arm, 'for the honour of humanity — hope that, despite this coward assault, the Samaritan Pain Dissuader stands unshaken in the confidence of all who hear me!'

But, injured as he was, and patient under it, too, somehow his case excited as little compassion as his oratory now did enthusiasm. Still, pathetic to the last, he continued his appeals, notwithstanding the frigid regard of the company, till, suddenly interrupting himself, as if in reply to a quick summons from without, he said hurriedly, 'I come, I come,' and so, with every token of precipitate dispatch, out of the cabin the herb-doctor went.

18

INQUEST INTO THE TRUE CHARACTER OF THE
HERB-DOCTOR

'Shan't see that fellow again in a hurry,' remarked an auburn-haired gentleman, to his neighbour with a hook-nose. 'Never knew an operator so completely unmasked.'

'But do you think it the fair thing to unmask an operator that way?'

'Fair? It is right.'

'Supposing that at high 'change on the Paris Bourse, Asmodeus should lounge in, distributing hand-bills, revealing the true thoughts and designs of all the operators present – would that be the fair thing in Asmodeus? Or, as Hamlet says, were it "to consider the thing too curiously"?'

'We won't go into that. But since you admit the fellow to be a knave –'

'I don't admit it. Or, if I did, I take it back. Shouldn't wonder if, after all, he is no knave at all, or, but little of one. What can you prove against him?'

'I can prove that he makes dupes.'

'Many held in honour do the same; and many, not wholly knaves, do it too.'

'How about that last?'

'He is not wholly at heart a knave, I fancy, among whose dupes is himself. Did you not see our quack friend apply to himself his own quackery? A fanatic quack; essentially a fool, though effectively a knave.'

Bending over, and looking down between his knees on the floor, the auburn-haired gentleman meditatively scribbled there awhile with his cane, then, glancing up, said:

'I can't conceive how you, in any way, can hold him a fool. How he talked – so glib, so pat, so well.'

'A smart fool always talks well: takes a smart fool to be tonguey.'

In much the same strain the discussion continued – the hook-nosed gentleman talking at large and excellently, with a view of demonstrating that a smart fool always talks just so. Ere long he talked to such purpose as almost to convince.

Presently, back came the person of whom the auburn-haired gentleman had predicted that he would not return. Conspicuous in the door-way he stood saying, in a clear voice, 'Is the agent of the Seminole Widow and Orphan Asylum within here?'

No one replied.

'Is there within here any agent or any member of any charitable institution whatever?'

No one seemed competent to answer, or, no one thought it worth while to.

'If there be within here any such person, I have in my hand two dollars for him.'

Some interest was manifested.

'I was called away so hurriedly, I forgot this part of my duty. With the proprietor of the Samaritan Pain Dissuader it is a rule, to devote, on the spot, to some benevolent purpose, the half of the proceeds of sales. Eight bottles were disposed of among this company. Hence, four half-dollars remain to charity. Who, as steward, takes the money?'

One or two pair of feet moved upon the floor, as with a sort of itching; but nobody rose.

'Does diffidence prevail over duty? If, I say, there be any gentleman, or any lady either, here present, who is in any connection with any charitable institution whatever, let him or her come forward. He or she happening to have at hand no certificate of such connection, makes no difference. Not of a suspicious temper, thank God, I shall have confidence in whoever offers to take the money.'

A demure-looking woman, in a dress rather tawdry and rumpled, here drew her veil well down and rose; but, marking every eye upon her, thought it advisable, upon the whole, to sit down again.

'Is it to be believed that, in this Christian company, there is no one charitable person? I mean, no one connected with any charity? Well then, is there no object of charity here?'

Upon this, an unhappy-looking woman, in a sort of mourning, neat, but sadly worn, hid her face behind a meagre bundle, and was heard to sob. Meantime, as not seeing or hearing her, the herb-doctor again spoke, and this time not unpathetically:

'Are there none here who feel in need of help, and who, in accepting such help, would feel that they, in their time, have given or done more than may ever be given or done to them? Man or woman, is there none such here?'

The sobs of the woman were more audible, though she strove to repress them. While nearly every one's attention was bent upon her, a man of the appearance of a day-labourer, with a white bandage across his face, concealing the side of the nose, and who, for coolness' sake, had been sitting in his red-flannel shirt-sleeves, his coat thrown across one shoulder, the darned cuffs drooping behind – this man shufflingly rose, and, with a pace that seemed the lingering memento of the lock-step of convicts, went up for a duly-qualified claimant.

'Poor wounded hussar!' sighed the herb-doctor, and dropping the money into the man's clam-shell of a hand turned and departed.

The recipient of the alms was about moving after, when the auburn-haired gentleman staid him: 'Don't be frightened, you; but I want to see those coins. Yes, yes; good silver, good silver. There, take them again, and while you are about it, go bandage the rest of yourself behind something. D'ye hear? Consider yourself, wholly, the scar of a nose, and be off with yourself.'

Being of a forgiving nature, or else from emotion not daring to trust his voice, the man silently, but not without some precipitancy, withdrew.

'Strange,' said the auburn-haired gentleman, returning to his friend, 'the money was good money.'

'Aye, and where your fine knavery now? Knavery to devote the half of one's receipts to charity? He's a fool I say again.'

'Others might call him an original genius.'

'Yes, being original in his folly. Genius? His genius is a cracked pate, and, as this age goes, not much originality about that.'

'May he not be knave, fool, and genius all together?'

'I beg pardon,' here said a third person with a gossiping expression who had been listening, 'but you are somewhat puzzled by this man, and well you may be.'

'Do you know anything about him?' asked the hook-nosed gentleman.

'No, but I suspect him for something.'

'Suspicion. We want knowledge.'

'Well, suspect first, and know next. True knowledge comes but by suspicion or revelation. That's my maxim.'

'And yet,' said the auburn-haired gentleman, 'since a wise man will keep even some certainties to himself, much more some suspicions, at least he will at all events so do till they ripen into knowledge.'

'Do you hear that about the wise man?' said the hook-nosed gentleman, turning upon the new comer. 'Now what is it you suspect of this fellow?'

'I shrewdly suspect him,' was the eager response, 'for one of those Jesuit emissaries prowling all over our country. The better to accomplish their secret designs, they assume, at times, I am told, the most singular masques; sometimes, in appearance, the absurdest.'

This, though indeed for some reason causing a droll smile upon the face of the hook-nosed gentleman, added a third angle to the discussion, which now became a sort of triangular duel, and ended, at last, with but a triangular result.

19

A SOLDIER OF FORTUNE

—————•‖•—————

'Mexico? Molino del Rey? Resaca de la Palma?'

'Resaca de la *Tombs!*'

Leaving his reputation to take care of itself, since, as is not seldom the case, he knew nothing of its being in debate, the herb-doctor, wandering towards the forward part of the boat, had there espied a singular character in a grimy old regimental coat, a countenance at once grim and wizened, interwoven paralysed legs, stiff as icicles, suspended between rude crutches, while the whole rigid body, like a ship's long barometer on gimbals, swung to and fro, mechanically faithful to the motion of the boat. Looking downward while he swung, the cripple seemed in a brown study.

As moved by the sight, and conjecturing that here was some battered hero from the Mexican battle-fields, the herb-doctor had sympathetically accosted him as above, and received the above rather dubious reply. As, with a half moody, half surly sort of air that reply was given, the cripple, by a voluntary jerk, nervously increased his swing (his custom when seized by emotion), so that one would have thought some squall had suddenly rolled the boat and with it the barometer.

'Tombs? my friend,' exclaimed the herb-doctor in mild surprise. 'You have not descended to the dead, have you? I had imagined you a scarred campaigner, one of the noble children of war, for your dear country a glorious sufferer. But you are Lazarus, it seems.'

'Yes, he who had sores.'

'Ah, the *other* Lazarus. But I never knew that either of them was in the army,' glancing at the dilapidated regimentals.

'That will do now. Jokes enough.'

'Friend,' said the other reproachfully, 'you think amiss. On principle, I greet unfortunates with some pleasant remark, the better to call off their thoughts from their troubles. The physician who is at once wise and humane seldom unreservedly sympathizes with his patient. But come, I am a herb-doctor, and also a natural bone-setter. I may be sanguine, but I think I can do something for you. You look up now. Give me your story. Ere I undertake a cure, I require a full account of the case.'

'You can't help me,' returned the cripple gruffly. 'Go away.'

'You seem sadly destitute of –'

'No I ain't destitute; to-day, at least, I can pay my way.'

'The Natural Bone-setter is happy, indeed, to hear that. But you were premature. I was deploring your destitution, not of cash, but of confidence. You think the Natural Bone-setter can't help you. Well, suppose he can't, have you any objection to telling him your story? You, my friend, have, in a signal way, experienced adversity. Tell me, then, for my private good, how, without aid from the noble cripple, Epictetus, you have arrived at his heroic sang-froid in misfortune.'

At these words the cripple fixed upon the speaker the hard ironic eye of one toughened and defiant in misery, and, in the end, grinned upon him with his unshaven face like an ogre.

'Come, come, be sociable – be human, my friend. Don't make that face; it distresses me.'

'I suppose,' with a sneer, 'you are the man I've long heard of – The Happy Man.'

'Happy? my friend. Yes, at least I ought to be. My conscience is peaceful. I have confidence in everybody. I have confidence that, in my humble profession, I do some little good to the world. Yes, I think that, without presumption, I may venture to assent to the proposition that I am the Happy Man – the Happy Bone-setter.'

'Then you shall hear my story. Many a month I have longed to get hold of the Happy Man, drill him, drop the powder, and leave him to explode at his leisure.'

'What a demoniac unfortunate!' exclaimed the herb-doctor, retreating. 'Regular infernal machine!'

'Look ye,' cried the other, stumping after him, and with his horny hand catching him by a horn button, 'my name is Thomas Fry. Until my –'

– 'Any relation of Mrs Fry?' interrupted the other. 'I still correspond with that excellent lady on the subject of prisons. Tell me, are you any way connected with *my* Mrs Fry?'

'Blister Mrs Fry! What do them sentimental souls know of prisons or any other black fact? I'll tell ye a story of prisons. Ha, ha!'

The herb-doctor shrank, and with reason, the laugh being strangely startling.

'Positively, my friend,' said he, 'you must stop that; I can't stand that; no more of that. I hope I have the milk of kindness, but your thunder will soon turn it.'

'Hold, I haven't come to the milk-turning part yet. My name is Thomas Fry. Until my twenty-third year I went by the nickname of Happy Tom – happy – ha, ha! They called me Happy Tom, d'ye see? because I was so good-natured and laughing all the time, just as I am now – ha, ha!'

Upon this the herb-doctor would, perhaps, have run, but once more the hyaena clawed him. Presently, sobering down, he continued:

'Well, I was born in New York, and there I lived a steady, hard-working man, a cooper by trade. One evening I went to a political meeting in the Park – for you must know, I was in those days a great patriot. As bad luck would have it, there was trouble near, between a gentleman who had been drinking wine, and a pavior who was sober. The pavior chewed tobacco, and the gentleman said it was beastly in him, and pushed him, wanting to have his place. The pavior chewed on and pushed back. Well, the gentleman carried a sword-cane, and presently the pavior was down – skewered.'

'How was that?'

'Why you see the pavior undertook something above his strength.'

'The other must have been a Samson then. "Strong as a pavior", is a proverb.'

'So it is, and the gentleman was in body a rather weakly man, but for all that, I say again, the pavior undertook something above his strength.'

'What are you talking about? He tried to maintain his rights, didn't he?'

'Yes; but for all that, I say again, he undertook something above his strength.'

'I don't understand you. But go on.'

'Along with the gentleman, I, with other witnesses, was taken to the Tombs. There was an examination, and, to appear at the trial, the gentleman and witnesses all gave bail – I mean all but me.'

'And why didn't you?'

'Couldn't get it.'

'Steady, hard-working cooper like you; what was the reason you couldn't get bail?'

'Steady, hard-working cooper hadn't no friends. Well, souse I went into a wet cell, like a canal-boat splashing into the lock; locked up in pickle, d'ye see? against the time of the trial.'

'But what had you done?'

'Why, I hadn't got any friends, I tell ye. A worse crime than murder, as ye'll see afore long.'

'Murder? Did the wounded man die?'

'Died the third night.'

'Then the gentleman's bail didn't help him. Imprisoned now, wasn't he?'

'Had too many friends. No, it was *I* that was imprisoned. – But I was going on: They let me walk about the corridor by day; but at night I must into lock. There the wet and the damp struck into my bones. They doctored me, but no use. When the trial came, I was boosted up and said my say.'

'And what was that?'

'My say was that I saw the steel go in, and saw it sticking in.'

'And that hung the gentleman.'

'Hung him with a gold chain! His friends called a meeting in the Park, and presented him with a gold watch and chain upon his acquittal.'

'Acquittal?'

'Didn't I say he had friends?'

There was a pause, broken at last by the herb-doctor's saying: 'Well, there is a bright side to everything. If this speak prosaically for justice, it speaks romantically for friendship! But go on, my fine fellow.'

'My say being said, they told me I might go. I said I could not without help. So the constables helped me, asking *where* would I go? I told them back to the Tombs. I knew no other place. "But where are your friends?" said they. "I have none." So they put me into a hand-barrow with an awning to it, and wheeled me down to the dock and on board a boat, and away to Blackwell's Island to the Corporation Hospital. There I got worse – got pretty much as you see me now. Couldn't cure me. After three years, I grew sick of lying in a grated iron bed alongside of groaning thieves and mouldering burglars. They gave me five silver dollars, and these crutches, and I hobbled off. I had an only brother who went to Indiana, years ago. I begged about, to make up a sum to go to him; got to Indiana at last, and they directed me to his grave. It was on a great plain, in a log-church yard with a stump fence, the old gray roots sticking all ways like moose-antlers. The bier, set over the grave, it being the last dug, was of green hickory; bark on, and green twigs sprouting from it. Some one had planted a bunch of violets on the mound, but it was a poor soil (always choose the poorest soils for grave-yards), and they were all dried to tinder. I was going to sit and rest myself on the bier and think about my brother in heaven, but the bier broke down, the legs being only tacked. So, after driving some hogs out of the yard that were rooting there, I came away, and, not to make too long a story of it, here I am, drifting down stream like any other bit of wreck.'

The herb-doctor was silent for a time, buried in thought. At last, raising his head, he said: 'I have considered your whole story, my friend, and strove to consider it in the light of a commentary on what I believe to be the system of things; but it so jars with all, is so incompatible with all, that you must pardon me, if I honestly tell you, I cannot believe it.'

'That don't surprise me.'

'How?'

'Hardly anybody believes my story, and so to most I tell a different one.'

'How, again?'

'Wait here a bit and I'll show ye.'

With that, taking off his rag of a cap, and arranging his tattered regimentals the best he could, off he went stumping among the passengers in an adjoining part of the deck, saying with a jovial kind of air: 'Sir, a shilling for Happy Tom, who fought at Buena Vista. Lady, something for General Scott's soldier, crippled in both pins at glorious Contreras.'

Now, it so chanced that, unbeknown to the cripple, a prim-looking stranger had overheard part of his story. Beholding him, then, on his present begging adventure, this person, turning to the herb-doctor, indignantly said: 'Is it not too bad, sir, that yonder rascal should lie so?'

'Charity never faileth, my good sir,' was the reply. 'The vice of this unfortunate is pardonable. Consider, he lies not out of wanton-ness.'

'Not out of wantonness. I never heard more wanton lies. In one breath to tell you what would appear to be his true story, and, in the next, away and falsify it.'

'For all that, I repeat, he lies not out of wantonness. A ripe philosopher, turned out of the great Sorbonne of hard times, he thinks that woes, when told to strangers for money, are best sugared. Though the inglorious lock-jaw of his knee-pans in a wet dungeon is a far more pitiable ill than to have been crippled at glorious Contreras, yet he is of opinion that this lighter and false ill shall attract, while the heavier and real one might repel.'

'Nonsense; he belongs to the Devil's regiment; and I have a great mind to expose him.'

'Shame upon you. Dare to expose that poor unfortunate, and by heaven – don't you do it, sir.'

Noting something in his manner, the other thought it more prudent to retire than retort. By-and-by, the cripple came back, and with glee, having reaped a pretty good harvest.

'There,' he laughed, 'you know now what sort of soldier I am.'

'Aye, one that fights not the stupid Mexican, but a foe worthy your tactics – Fortune!'

'Hi, hi!' clamoured the cripple, like a fellow in the pit of a sixpenny theatre, then said, 'don't know much what you meant, but it went off well.'

This over, his countenance capriciously put on a morose ogre-ness. To kindly questions he gave no kindly answers. Unhandsome notions were thrown out about 'free Ameriky', as he sarcastically called his country. These seemed to disturb and pain the herb-doctor, who, after an interval of thoughtfulness, gravely addressed him in these words:

'You, my worthy friend, to my concern, have reflected upon the government under which you live and suffer. Where is your patriotism? Where your gratitude? True, the charitable may find something in your case, as you put it, partly to account for such reflections as coming from you. Still, be the facts how they may, your reflections are none the less unwarrantable. Grant, for the moment, that your experiences are as you give them; in which case I would admit that government might be thought to have more or less to do with what seems undesirable in them. But it is never to be forgotten that human government, being subordinate to the divine, must needs, therefore, in its degree, partake of the characteristics of the divine. That is, while in general efficacious to happiness, the world's law may yet, in some cases, have, to the eye of reason, an unequal operation, just as, in the same imperfect view, some inequalities may appear in the operations of heaven's law; nevertheless, to one who has a right confidence, final benignity is, in every instance, as sure with the one law as the other. I expound the point at some length, because these are the considerations, my poor fellow, which, weighed as they merit, will enable you to sustain with unimpaired trust the apparent calamities which are yours.'

'What do you talk your hog-latin to me for?' cried the cripple, who, throughout the address, betrayed the most illiterate obduracy; and, with an incensed look, anew he swung himself.

Glancing another way till the spasm passed, the other continued:

'Charity marvels not that you should be somewhat hard of conviction, my friend, since you, doubtless, believe yourself hardly dealt by; but forget not that those who are loved are chastened.'

'Mustn't chasten them too much, though, and too long, because their skin and heart get hard, and feel neither pain nor tickle.'

'To mere reason, your case looks something piteous, I grant. But never despond; many things – the choicest – yet remain. You breathe this bounteous air, are warmed by this gracious sun, and, though poor and friendless, indeed, nor so agile as in your youth, yet, how sweet to roam, day by day, through the groves, plucking the bright mosses and flowers, till forlornness itself becomes a hilarity, and, in your innocent independence, you skip for joy.'

'Fine skipping with these 'ere horse-posts – ha, ha!'

'Pardon; I forgot the crutches. My mind, figuring you after receiving the benefit of my art, overlooked you as you stand before me.'

'Your art? You call yourself a bone-setter – a natural bone-setter, do ye? Go, bone-set the crooked world, and then come bone-set crooked me.'

'Truly, my honest friend, I thank you for again recalling me to my original object. Let me examine you,' bending down; 'ah, I see, I see; much such a case as the negro's. Did you see him? Oh no, you came aboard since. Well, his case was a little something like yours. I prescribed for him, and I shouldn't wonder at all if, in a very short time, he were able to walk almost as well as myself. Now, have you no confidence in my art?'

'Ha, ha!'

The herb–doctor averted himself; but, the wild laugh dying away, resumed:

'I will not force confidence on you. Still, I would fain do the friendly thing by you. Here, take this box; just rub that liniment on the joints night and morning. Take it. Nothing to pay. God bless you. Good–bye.'

'Stay,' pausing in his swing, not untouched by so unexpected an act; 'stay – thank'ee – but will this really do me good? Honour bright, now; will it? Don't deceive a poor fellow,' with changed mien and glistening eye.

'Try it. Good–bye.'

'Stay, stay! *Sure* it will do me good?'

'Possibly, possibly; no harm in trying. Good–bye.'

'Stay, stay; give me three more boxes, and here's the money.'

'My friend,' returning towards him with a sadly pleased sort of air, 'I rejoice in the birth of your confidence and hopefulness. Believe me that, like your crutches, confidence and hopefulness will long support a man when his own legs will not. Stick to confidence and hopefulness, then, since how mad for the cripple to throw his crutches away. You ask for three more boxes of my liniment. Luckily, I have just that number remaining. Here they are. I sell them at half–a–dollar apiece. But I shall take nothing from you. There; God bless you again; good–bye.'

'Stay,' in a convulsed voice, and rocking himself, 'stay, stay! You have made a better man of me. You have borne with me like a good Christian, and talked to me like one, and all that is enough without making me a present of these boxes. Here is the money. I won't take nay. There, there; and may Almighty goodness go with you.'

20

REAPPEARANCE OF ONE WHO MAY BE REMEMBERED

The herb-doctor had not moved far away, when, in advance of him, this spectacle met his eye. A dried-up old man, with the stature of a boy of twelve, was tottering about like one out of his mind, in rumpled clothes of old moleskin, showing recent contact with bedding, his ferret eyes, blinking in the sunlight of the snowy boat, as imbecilely eager, and, at intervals, coughing, he peered hither and thither as if in alarmed search for his nurse. He presented the aspect of one who, bed-rid, has, through over-ruling excitement, like that of a fire, been stimulated to his feet.

'You seek some one,' said the herb-doctor, accosting him. 'Can I assist you?'

'Do, do; I am so old and miserable,' coughed the old man. 'Where is he? This long time I've been trying to get up and find him. But I haven't any friends, and couldn't get up till now. Where is he?'

'Who do you mean?' drawing closer, to stay the further wanderings of one so weakly.

'Why, why, why,' now marking the other's dress, 'why you, yes you – you, you – ugh, ugh, ugh!'

'I?'

'Ugh, ugh, ugh! – you are the man he spoke of. Who is he?'

'Faith, that is just what I want to know.'

'Mercy, mercy!' coughed the old man, bewildered, 'ever since seeing him, my head spins round so. I ought to have a guardeean.

Is this a snuff-coloured surtout of yours, or ain't it? Somehow, can't trust my senses any more, since trusting him – ugh, ugh, ugh!'

'Oh, you have trusted somebody? Glad to hear it. Glad to hear of any instance of that sort. Reflects well upon all men. But you inquire whether this is a snuff-coloured surtout. I answer it is; and will add that a herb-doctor wears it.'

Upon this the old man, in his broken way, replied that then he (the herb-doctor) was the person he sought – the person spoken of by the other person as yet unknown. He then, with flighty eagerness, wanted to know who this last person was, and where he was, and whether he could be trusted with money to treble it.

'Aye, now, I begin to understand; ten to one you mean my worthy friend, who, in pure goodness of heart, makes people's fortunes for them – their everlasting fortunes, as the phrase goes – only charging his one small commission of confidence. Aye, aye; before intrusting funds with my friend, you want to know about him. Very proper – and, I am glad to assure you, you need have no hesitation; none, none, just none in the world; *bona fide*, none. Turned me in a trice a hundred dollars the other day into as many eagles.'

'Did he? did he? But where is he? Take me to him.'

'Pray, take my arm! The boat is large! We may have something of a hunt! Come on! Ah, is that he?'

'Where? where?'

'O, no; I took yonder coat-skirts for his. But no, my honest friend would never turn tail that way. Ah! –'

'Where? where?'

'Another mistake. Surprising resemblance. I took yonder clergyman for him. Come on!'

Having searched that part of the boat without success, they went to another part, and, while exploring that, the boat sided up to a landing, when, as the two were passing by the open guard, the herb-doctor suddenly rushed towards the disembarking throng, crying out: 'Mr Truman, Mr Truman! There he goes –

that's he. Mr Truman, Mr Truman! – Confound that steam-pipe. Mr Truman! for God's sake, Mr Truman! – No, no. – There, the plank's in – too late – we're off.'

With that, the huge boat, with a mighty walrus wallow, rolled away from the shore, resuming her course.

'How vexatious!' exclaimed the herb-doctor, returning. 'Had we been but one single moment sooner. There he goes, now, towards yon hotel, his portmanteau following. You see him, don't you?'

'Where? where?'

'Can't see him any more. Wheel-house shot between. I am very sorry. I should have so liked you to have let him have a hundred or so of your money. You would have been pleased with the investment, believe me.'

'Oh, I *have* let him have some of my money,' groaned the old man.

'You have? My dear sir,' seizing both the miser's hands in both his own and heartily shaking them. 'My dear sir, how I congratulate you. You don't know.'

'Ugh, ugh! I fear I don't,' with another groan. 'His name is Truman, is it?'

'John Truman.'

'Where does he live?'

'In St Louis.'

'Where's his office?'

'Let me see. Jones Street, number one hundred and – no, no – anyway, it's somewhere or other upstairs in Jones Street.'

'Can't you remember the number? Try, now.'

'One hundred – two hundred – three hundred –'

'Oh, my hundred dollars! I wonder whether it will be one hundred, two hundred, three hundred, with them! Ugh, ugh! Can't remember the number?'

'Positively, though I once knew, I have forgotten, quite forgotten it. Strange. But never mind. You will easily learn in St Louis. He is well known there.'

'But I have no receipt – ugh, ugh! Nothing to show – don't know where I stand – ought to have a guardeean – ugh, ugh! Don't know anything. Ugh, ugh!'

'Why, you know that you gave him your confidence, don't you?'

'Oh, yes.'

'Well, then?'

'But what, what – how, how – ugh, ugh!'

'Why, didn't he tell you?'

'No.'

'What! Didn't he tell you that it was a secret, a mystery?'

'Oh – yes.'

'Well, then?'

'But I have no bond.'

'Don't need any with Mr Truman. Mr Truman's word is his bond.'

'But how am I to get my profits – ugh, ugh! – and my money back? Don't know anything. Ugh, ugh!'

'Oh, you must have confidence.'

'Don't say that word again. Makes my head spin so. Oh, I'm so old and miserable, nobody caring for me, everybody fleecing me, and my head spins so – ugh, ugh! – and this cough racks me so. I say again, I ought to have a guardeean.'

'So you ought; and Mr Truman is your guardian to the extent you invested with him. Sorry we missed him just now. But you'll hear from him, all right. It's imprudent, though, to expose yourself this way. Let me take you to your berth.'

Forlornly enough the old miser moved slowly away with him. But, while descending a stairway, he was seized with such coughing that he was fain to pause.

'That is a very bad cough.'

'Church-yard – ugh, ugh! – church-yard cough. – Ugh!'

'Have you tried anything for it?'

'Tired of trying. Nothing does me any good – ugh! ugh! Not even the Mammoth Cave. Ugh! ugh! Denned there six months, but coughed so bad the rest of the coughers – ugh! ugh! – black-balled me out. Ugh, ugh! Nothing does me good.'

'But have you tried the Omni-Balsamic Reinvigorator, sir?'

'That's what that Truman – ugh, ugh! – said I ought to take. Yarb-medicine; you are that yarb-doctor, too?'

'The same. Suppose you try one of my boxes now. Trust me, from what I know of Mr Truman, he is not the gentleman to recommend, even in behalf of a friend, anything of whose excellence he is not conscientiously satisfied.'

'Ugh! – how much?'

'Only two dollars a box.'

'Two dollars? Why don't you say two millions? ugh, ugh! Two dollars, that's two hundred cents; that's eight hundred farthings; that's two thousand mills; and all for one little box of yarb-medicine. My head, my head! – oh, I ought to have a guardeean for my head. Ugh, ugh, ugh, ugh!'

'Well, if two dollars a box seems too much, take a dozen boxes at twenty dollars; and that will be getting four boxes for nothing, and you need use none but those four, the rest you can retail out at a premium, and so cure your cough, and make money by it. Come, you had better do it. Cash down. Can fill an order in a day or two. Here now,' producing a box; 'pure herbs.'

At that moment, seized with another spasm, the miser snatched each interval to fix his half-distrustful, half-hopeful eye upon the medicine, held alluringly up. 'Sure – ugh! Sure it's all nat'ral? Nothing but yarbs? If I only thought it was a purely nat'ral medicine now – all yarbs – ugh, ugh! – oh this cough, this cough – ugh, ugh! – shatters my whole body. Ugh, ugh, ugh!'

'For heaven's sake try my medicine, if but a single box. That it is pure nature you may be confident. Refer you to Mr Truman.'

'Don't know his number – ugh, ugh, ugh, ugh! – Oh this cough. He did speak well of this medicine though; said solemnly it would cure me – ugh, ugh, ugh, ugh! – take off a dollar and I'll have a box.'

'Can't sir, can't.'

'Say a dollar-and-half. Ugh!'

'Can't. Am pledged to the one-price system, only honourable one.'

'Take off a shilling – ugh, ugh!'

'Can't.'

'Ugh, ugh, ugh – I'll take it. – There.'

Grudgingly he handed eight silver coins, but while still in his hand, his cough took him, and they were shaken upon the deck.

One by one, the herb-doctor picked them up, and, examining them, said: 'These are not quarters, these are pistareens; and clipped, and sweated, at that.'

'Oh don't be so miserly – ugh, ugh! – better a beast than a miser – ugh, ugh!'

'Well, let it go. Anything rather than the idea of your not being cured of such a cough. And I hope, for the credit of humanity, you have not made it appear worse than it is, merely with a view to working upon the weak point of my pity, and so getting my medicine the cheaper. Now, mind, don't take it till night. Just before retiring is the time. There, you can get along now, can't you? I would attend you further, but I land presently, and must go hunt up my luggage.'

'Yarbs, yarbs; natur, natur; you foolish old file you! He diddled you with that hocus-pocus, did he? Yarbs and natur will cure your incurable cough, you think?'

It was a rather eccentric-looking person who spoke, somewhat ursine in aspect; sporting a shaggy spencer of the cloth called bear's-skin; a high-peaked cap of racoon-skin, the long bushy tail switching over behind; raw-hide leggings; grim stubble chin; and, to end, a double-barrelled gun in hand – a Missouri bachelor, a Hoosier gentleman, of Spartan leisure and fortune, and equally Spartan manners and sentiments; and, as the sequel may show, not less acquainted, in a Spartan way of his own, with philosophy and books, than with woodcraft and rifles.

He must have overheard some of the talk between the miser and the herb-doctor; for, just after the withdrawal of the one, he made up to the other – now at the foot of the stairs leaning against the baluster there – with the 'greeting' above.

'Think it will cure me?' coughed the miser in echo; 'why shouldn't it? The medicine is nat'ral yarbs, pure yarbs; yarbs must cure me.'

'Because a thing is nat'ral, as you call it, you think it must be good. But who gave you that cough? Was it, or was it not, nature?'

'Sure, you don't think that natur, Dame Natur, will hurt a body, do you?'

'Natur is good Queen Bess; but who's responsible for the cholera?'

'But yarbs, yarbs; yarbs are good?'

'What's deadly-nightshade? Yarb, ain't it?'

'Oh, that a Christian man should speak agin natur and yarbs – ugh, ugh, ugh! – ain't sick men sent out into the country; sent out to natur and grass?'

'Aye, and poets send out the sick spirit to green pastures, like lame horses turned out unshod to the turf to renew their hoofs. A sort of yarb-doctors in their way, poets have it that for sore hearts, as for sore lungs, nature is the grand cure. But who froze to death my teamster on the prairie? And who made an idiot of Peter the Wild Boy?'

'Then you don't believe in these 'ere yarb-doctors?'

'Yarb-doctors? I remember the lank yarb-doctor I saw once on a hospital-cot in Mobile. One of the faculty passing round and seeing who lay there, said with professional triumph, "Ah, Dr Green, your yarbs don't help ye now, Dr Green. Have to come to us and the mercury now, Dr Green." – Natur! Y-a-r-b-s!'

'Did I hear something about herbs and herb-doctors?' here said a flute-like voice, advancing.

It was the herb-doctor in person. Carpet-bag in hand, he happened to be strolling back that way.

'Pardon me,' addressing the Missourian, 'but if I caught your words aright, you would seem to have little confidence in nature; which, really, in my way of thinking, looks like carrying the spirit of distrust pretty far.'

'And who of my sublime species may you be?' turning short round upon him, clicking his rifle-lock, with an air which would have seemed half cynic, half wild-cat, were it not for the grotesque excess of the expression, which made its sincerity appear more or less dubious.

'One who has confidence in nature, and confidence in man, with some little modest confidence in himself.'

'That's your Confession of Faith, is it? Confidence in man, eh? Pray, which do you think are most, knaves or fools?'

'Having met with few or none of either, I hardly think I am competent to answer.'

'I will answer for you. Fools are most.'

'Why do you think so?'

'For the same reason that I think oats are numerically more than horses. Don't knaves munch up fools just as horses do oats?'

'A droll, sir; you are a droll. I can appreciate drollery – ha, ha, ha!'

'But I'm in earnest.'

'That's the drollery, to deliver droll extravagance with an earnest air – knaves munching up fools as horses oats. – Faith, very droll, indeed, ha, ha, ha! Yes, I think I understand you now, sir. How silly I was to have taken you seriously, in your droll conceits, too, about having no confidence in nature. In reality you have just as much as I have.'

'*I* have confidence in nature? *I?* I say again, there is nothing I am more suspicious of. I once lost ten thousand dollars by nature. Nature embezzled that amount from me; absconded with ten thousand dollars' worth of my property; a plantation on this stream, swept clean away by one of those sudden shiftings of the banks in a freshet; ten thousand dollars' worth of alluvion thrown broad off upon the waters.'

'But have you no confidence that by a reverse shifting that soil will come back after many days? – ah, here is my venerable friend,' observing the old miser, – 'not in your berth yet? Pray, if you *will* keep afoot, don't lean against that baluster; take my arm.'

It was taken; and the two stood together; the old miser leaning against the herb-doctor with something of that air of trustful fraternity with which, when standing, the less strong of the Siamese twins habitually leans against the other.

The Missourian eyed them in silence, which was broken by the herb-doctor.

'You look surprised, sir. Is it because I publicly take under my protection a figure like this? But I am never ashamed of honesty, whatever his coat.'

'Look you,' said the Missourian, after a scrutinizing pause, 'you are a queer sort of chap. Don't know exactly what to make of you. Upon the whole though, you somewhat remind me of the last boy I had on my place.'

'Good, trustworthy boy, I hope?'

'Oh, very! I am now started to get me made some kind of machine to do the sort of work which boys are supposed to be fitted for.'

'Then you have passed a veto upon boys?'

'And men, too.'

'But, my dear sir, does not that again imply more or less lack of confidence? – (Stand up a little, just a very little, my venerable friend; you lean rather hard.) – No confidence in boys, no confidence in men, no confidence in nature. Pray, sir, who or what may you have confidence in?'

'I have confidence in distrust; more particularly as applied to you and your herbs.'

'Well,' with a forbearing smile, 'that is frank. But pray, don't forget that when you suspect my herbs you suspect nature.'

'Didn't I say that before?'

'Very good. For the argument's sake I will suppose you are in earnest. Now, can you, who suspect nature, deny that this same nature, not only kindly brought you into being, but has faithfully nursed you to your present vigorous and independent condition? Is it not to nature that you are indebted for that robustness of mind which you so unhandsomely use to her scandal? Pray, is it not to nature that you owe the very eyes by which you criticize her?'

'No! for the privilege of vision I am indebted to an oculist, who in my tenth year operated upon me in Philadelphia. Nature made me blind, and would have kept me so. My oculist counterplotted her.'

'And yet, sir, by your complexion, I judge you live an out-of-door life; without knowing it, you are partial to nature; you fly to nature, the universal mother.'

'Very motherly! Sir, in the passion-fits of nature, I've known birds fly from nature to me, rough as I look; yes, sir, in a tempest, refuge here,' smiting the folds of his bearskin. 'Fact, sir, fact. Come, come, Mr Palaverer, for all your palavering, did you yourself never shut out nature of a cold, wet night? Bar her out? Bolt her out? Lint her out?'

'As to that,' said the herb-doctor calmly, 'much may be said.'

'Say it, then,' ruffling all his hairs. 'You can't, sir, can't.' Then, as in apostrophe: 'Look you, nature! I don't deny but your clover is sweet, and your dandelions don't roar; but whose hailstones smashed my windows?'

'Sir,' with unimpaired affability, producing one of his boxes, 'I am pained to meet with one who holds nature a dangerous character. Though your manner is refined, your voice is rough; in short, you seem to have a sore throat. In the calumniated name of nature, I present you with this box; my venerable friend here has a similar one; but to you, a free gift, sir. Through her regularly-authorized agents, of whom I happen to be one, nature delights in benefiting those who most abuse her. Pray, take it.'

'Away with it! Don't hold it so near. Ten to one there is a torpedo in it. Such things have been. Editors been killed that way. Take it further off, I say.'

'Good heavens! my dear sir –'

'I tell you I want none of your boxes,' snapping his rifle.

'Oh, take it – ugh, ugh! do take it,' chimed in the old miser; 'I wish he would give me one for nothing.'

'You find it lonely, eh,' turning short round; 'gulled yourself, you would have a companion.'

'How can he find it lonely,' returned the herb-doctor, 'or how desire a companion, when here I stand by him; I, even I, in whom he has trust? For the gulling, tell me, is it humane to talk so to this poor old man? Granting that his dependence on my medicine is vain, is it kind to deprive him of what, in mere imagination, if nothing more, may help eke out, with hope, his disease? For you, if you have no confidence, and, thanks to your native health, can get along without it, so far, at least, as trusting in my medicine goes; yet, how cruel an argument to use, with this afflicted one here. Is it not for all the world as if some brawny pugilist, aglow in December, should rush in and put out a hospital-fire, because, forsooth, he feeling no need of artificial heat, the shivering patients shall have none? Put it to your conscience, sir, and you will admit, that whatever be the nature of this afflicted one's trust, you, in opposing it, evince either an erring head or a heart amiss. Come, own, are you not pitiless?'

'Yes, poor soul,' said the Missourian, gravely eyeing the old man — 'yes, it *is* pitiless in one like me to speak too honestly to one like you. You are a late sitter-up in this life; past man's usual bed-time; and truth, though with some it makes a wholesome breakfast, proves to all a supper too hearty. Hearty food, taken late, gives bad dreams.'

'What, in wonder's name — ugh, ugh! — is he talking about?' asked the old miser, looking up to the herb-doctor.

'Heaven be praised for that!' cried the Missourian.

'Out of his mind, ain't he?' again appealed the old miser.

'Pray, sir,' said the herb-doctor to the Missourian, 'for what were you giving thanks just now?'

'For this: that, with some minds, truth is, in effect, not so cruel a thing after all, seeing that, like a loaded pistol found by poor devils of savages, it raises more wonder than terror — its peculiar virtue being unguessed, unless, indeed, by indiscreet handling, it should happen to go off of itself.'

'I pretend not to divine your meaning there,' said the herb-doctor, after a pause, during which he eyed the Missourian with a kind of pinched expression, mixed of pain and curiosity, as if he grieved at his state of mind, and, at the same time, wondered what had brought him to it, — 'but this much I know,' he added, 'that the general cast of your thoughts is, to say the least, unfortunate. There is strength in them, but a strength, whose source, being physical, must wither. You will yet recant.'

'Recant?'

'Yes, when, as with this old man, your evil days of decay come on, when a hoary captive in your chamber, then will you, something like the dungeoned Italian we read of, gladly seek the breast of that confidence begot in the tender time of your youth, blessed beyond telling if it return to you in age.'

'Go back to nurse again, eh? Second childhood, indeed. You are soft.'

'Mercy, mercy!' cried the old miser, 'what is all this? – ugh, ugh! Do talk sense, my good friends. Ain't you,' to the Missourian, 'going to buy some of that medicine?'

'Pray, my venerable friend,' said the herb-doctor, now trying to straighten himself, 'don't lean *quite* so hard, my arm grows numb; abate a little, just a very little.'

'Go,' said the Missourian, 'go lay down in your grave, old man, if you can't stand of yourself. It's a hard world for a leaner.'

'As to his grave,' said the herb-doctor, 'that is far enough off, so he but faithfully take my medicine.'

'Ugh, ugh, ugh! – He says true. No, I ain't – ugh! a going to die yet – ugh, ugh, ugh! Many years to live yet, ugh, ugh, ugh!'

'I approve your confidence,' said the herb-doctor; 'but your coughing distresses me, besides being injurious to you. Pray, let me conduct you to your berth. You are best there. Our friend here will wait till my return, I know.'

With which he led the old miser away, and then, coming back, the talk with the Missourian was resumed.

'Sir,' said the herb-doctor, with some dignity and more feeling, 'now that our infirm friend is withdrawn, allow me, to the full, to express my concern at the words you allowed to escape you in his hearing. Some of those words, if I err not, besides being calculated to beget deplorable distrust in the patient, seemed fitted to convey unpleasant imputations against me, his physician.'

'Suppose they did?' with a menacing air.

'Why, then – then, indeed,' respectfully retreating, 'I fall back upon my previous theory of your general facetiousness. I have the fortune to be in company with a humorist – a wag.'

'Fall back you had better, and wag it is,' cried the Missourian, following him up, and wagging his racoon tail almost into the herb-doctor's face, 'look you!'

'At what?'

'At this coon. Can you, the fox, catch him?'

'If you mean,' returned the other, not unselfpossessed, 'whether I flatter myself that I can in any way dupe you, or impose upon you, or pass myself off upon you for what I am not, I, as an honest man, answer that I have neither the inclination nor the power to do aught of the kind.'

'Honest man? Seems to me you talk more like a craven.'

'You in vain seek to pick a quarrel with me, or put any affront upon me. The innocence in me heals me.'

'A healing like your own nostrums. But you are a queer man — a very queer and dubious man; upon the whole, about the most so I ever met.'

The scrutiny accompanying this seemed unwelcome to the diffidence of the herb-doctor. As if at once to attest the absence of resentment, as well as to change the subject, he threw a kind of familiar cordiality into his air, and said: 'So you are going to get some machine made to do your work? Philanthropic scruples, doubtless, forbid your going as far as New Orleans for slaves?'

'Slaves?' morose again in a twinkling, 'won't have 'em! Bad enough to see whites ducking and grinning round for a favour, without having those poor devils of niggers congeeing round for their corn. Though, to me, the niggers are the freer of the two. You are an abolitionist, ain't you?' he added, squaring himself with both hands on his rifle, used for a staff, and gazing in the herb-doctor's face with no more reverence than if it were a target. 'You are an abolitionist, ain't you?'

'As to that, I cannot so readily answer. If by abolitionist you mean a zealot, I am none; but if you mean a man, who, being a man, feels for all men, slaves included, and by any lawful act, opposed to nobody's interest, and therefore rousing nobody's enmity, would willingly abolish suffering (supposing it, in its degree, to exist) from among mankind, irrespective of colour, then am I what you say.'

'Picked and prudent sentiments. You are the moderate man,

the invaluable understrapper of the wicked man. You, the moderate man, may be used for wrong, but are useless for right.'

'From all this,' said the herb-doctor, still forgivingly, 'I infer, that you, a Missourian, though living in a slave-state, are without slave sentiments.'

'Aye, but are you? Is not that air of yours, so spiritlessly enduring and yielding, the very air of a slave? Who is your master, pray; or are you owned by a company?'

'*My* master?'

'Aye, for come from Maine or Georgia, you come from a slave-state, and a slave-pen, where the best breeds are to be bought up at any price from a livelihood to the Presidency. Abolitionism, ye gods, but expresses the fellow-feeling of slave for slave.'

'The back-woods would seem to have given you rather eccentric notions,' now with polite superiority smiled the herb-doctor, still with manly intrepidity forbearing each unmanly thrust. 'But to return: since, for your purpose, you will have neither man nor boy, bond nor free, truly, then some sort of machine for you is all there is left. My desires for your success attend you, sir. – Ah!' glancing shoreward, 'here is Cape Girardeau; I must leave you.'

IN THE POLITE SPIRIT OF THE TUSCULAN
DISPUTATIONS

━━━━◆◆◆━━━━

– '"Philosophical Intelligence Office" – novel idea! But how did you come to dream that I wanted anything in your absurd line, eh?'

About twenty minutes after leaving Cape Girardeau, the above was growled out over his shoulder by the Missourian to a chance stranger who had just accosted him; a round-backed, baker-kneed man, in a mean five-dollar suit, wearing, collar-wise by a chain, a small brass plate, inscribed P.I.O., and who, with a sort of canine deprecation, slunk obliquely behind.

'How did you come to dream that I wanted anything in your line, eh?'

'Oh, respected sir,' whined the other, crouching a pace nearer, and, in his obsequiousness, seeming to wag his very coat-tails behind him, shabby though they were, 'oh, sir, from long experience, one glance tells me the gentleman who is in need of our humble services.'

'But suppose I did want a boy – what they jocosely call a good boy – how could your absurd office help me? – Philosophical Intelligence Office?'

'Yes, respected sir, an office founded on strictly philosophical and physio–'

'Look you – come up here – how, by philosophy or physiology either, make good boys to order? Come up here. Don't give me a crick in the neck. Come up here, come, sir, come,' calling as if to his pointer. 'Tell me, how put the requisite assortment of good qualities into a boy, as the assorted mince into the pie?'

'Respected sir, our office –'

'You talk much of that office. Where is it? On board this boat?'

'Oh no, sir, I just came aboard. Our office –'

'Came aboard at that last landing, eh? Pray, do you know a herb-doctor there? Smooth scamp in a snuff-coloured surtout?'

'Oh, sir, I was but a sojourner at Cape Girardeau. Though, now that you mention a snuff-coloured surtout, I think I met such a man as you speak of stepping ashore as I stepped aboard, and 'pears to me I have seen him somewhere before. Looks like a very mild Christian sort of person, I should say. Do you know him, respected sir?'

'Not much, but better than you seem to. Proceed with your business.'

With a low, shabby bow, as grateful for the permission, the other began: 'Our office –'

'Look you,' broke in the bachelor with ire, 'have you the spinal complaint? What are you ducking and grovelling about? Keep still. Where's your office?'

'The branch one which I represent is at Alton, sir, in the free state we now pass' (pointing somewhat proudly ashore).

'Free, eh? You a freeman, you flatter yourself? With those coat-tails and that spinal complaint of servility? Free? Just cast up in your private mind who is your master, will you?'

'Oh, oh, oh! I don't understand – indeed – indeed. But, re-spected sir, as before said, our office, founded on principles wholly new –'

'To the devil with your principles! Bad sign when a man begins to talk of his principles. Hold, come back, sir; back here, back, sir, back! I tell you no more boys for me. Nay, I'm a Mede and Persian. In my old home in the woods I'm pestered enough with squirrels, weasels, chipmunks, skunks. I want no more wild vermin to spoil my temper and waste my substance. Don't talk of boys; enough of your boys; a plague of your boys; chilblains on your boys! As for Intelligence Offices, I've lived in the East, and know 'em. Swindling concerns kept by low-born cynics, under a fawning exterior wreaking their cynic malice upon mankind. You are a fair specimen of 'em.'

'Oh dear, dear, dear!'

'Dear? Yes, a thrice dear purchase one of your boys would be to me. A rot on your boys!'

'But, respected sir, if you will not have boys, might we not, in our small way, accommodate you with a man?'

'Accommodate? Pray, no doubt you could accommodate me with a bosom-friend too, couldn't you? Accommodate! Obliging word accommodate: there's accommodation notes now, where one accommodates another with a loan, and if he don't pay it pretty quickly, accommodates him with a chain to his foot. Accommodate! God forbid that I should ever be accommodated. No, no. Look you, as I told that cousin-german of yours, the herb-doctor, I'm now on the road to get me made some sort of machine to do my work. Machines for me. My cider-mill – does that ever steal my cider? My mowing-machine – does that ever lay a-bed mornings? My corn-husker – does that ever give me insolence? No: cider-mill, mowing-machine, corn-husker – all faithfully attend to their business. Disinterested, too; no board, no wages; yet doing good all their lives long; shining examples that virtue is its own reward – the only practical Christians I know.'

'Oh dear, dear, dear, dear!'

'Yes, sir: – boys? Start my soul-bolts, what a difference, in a moral point of view, between a corn-husker and a boy! Sir, a corn-husker, for its patient continuance in well-doing, might not unfitly go to heaven. Do you suppose a boy will?'

'A corn-husker in heaven! (turning up the whites of his eyes). Respected sir, this way of talking as if heaven were a kind of Washington patent office museum – oh, oh, oh! – as if mere machine-work and puppet-work went to heaven – oh, oh, oh! Things incapable of free agency, to receive the eternal reward of well-doing – oh, oh, oh.'

'You Praise-God-Barebones you, what are you groaning about? Did I say anything of that sort? Seems to me, though you talk so good, you are mighty quick at a hint the other way, or else you want to pick a polemic quarrel with me.'

'It may be so or not, respected sir,' was now the demure reply; 'but if it be, it is only because as a soldier out of honour is quick in taking affront, so a Christian out of religion is quick, sometimes perhaps a little too much so, in spying heresy.'

'Well,' after an astonished pause, 'for an unaccountable pair, you and the herb-doctor ought to yoke together.'

So saying, the bachelor was eyeing him rather sharply, when he with the brass plate recalled him to the discussion by a hint, not unflattering, that he (the man with the brass plate) was all anxiety to hear him further on the subject of servants.

'About that matter,' exclaimed the impulsive bachelor, going off at the hint like a rocket, 'all thinking minds are, now-a-days, coming to the conclusion – one derived from an immense hereditary experience – see what Horace and others of the ancients say of servants – coming to the conclusion, I say, that boy or man, the human animal is, for most work-purposes, a losing animal. Can't be trusted; less trustworthy than oxen; for conscientiousness a turn-spit dog excels him. Hence these thousand new inventions – carding machines, horse-shoe machines, tunnel-boring machines, reaping machines, apple-paring machines, boot-blacking machines, sewing machines, shaving machines, run-of-errand machines, dumb-waiter machines, and the Lord-only-knows-what-machines; all of which announce the era when that refractory animal, the working or serving man, shall be a buried by-gone, a superseded fossil. Shortly prior to which glorious time, I doubt not that a price will be put upon their peltries as upon the knavish 'possums, especially the boys. Yes, sir (ringing his rifle down on the deck), I rejoice to think that the day is at hand, when, prompted to it by law, I shall shoulder this gun and go out a boy-shooting.'

'Oh, now! Lord, Lord, Lord! – But *our* office, respected sir, conducted as I ventured to observe –'

'No, sir,' bristlingly settling his stubble chin in his coon-skins.

'Don't try to oil me; the herb-doctor tried that. My experience, carried now through a course – worse than salivation – a course of five and thirty boys, proves to me that boyhood is a natural state of rascality.'

'Save us, save us!'

'Yes, sir, yes. My name is Pitch; I stick to what I say. I speak from fifteen years' experience; five and thirty boys; American, Irish, English, German, African, Mulatto; not to speak of that China boy sent me by one who well knew my perplexities, from California; and that Lascar boy from Bombay. Thug! I found him sucking the embryo life from my spring eggs. All rascals, sir, every soul of them; Caucasian or Mongol. Amazing the endless variety of rascality in human nature of the juvenile sort. I remember that, having discharged, one after another, twenty-nine boys – each, too, for some wholly unforeseen species of viciousness peculiar to that one peculiar boy – I remember saying to myself: Now, then, surely, I have got to the end of the list, wholly exhausted it; I have only now to get me a boy, any boy different from those twenty-nine preceding boys, and he infallibly shall be that virtuous boy I have so long been seeking. But, bless me! this thirtieth boy – by the way, having at the time long forsworn your intelligence offices, I had him sent to me from the Commissioners of Emigration, all the way from New York, culled out carefully, in fine, at my particular request, from a standing army of eight hundred boys, the flowers of all nations, so they wrote me, temporarily in barracks on an East River island – I say, this thirtieth boy was in person not ungraceful; his deceased mother a lady's maid, or something of that sort; and in manner, why, in a plebeian way, a perfect Chesterfield; very intelligent, too – quick as a flash. But, such suavity! "Please sir! please sir!" always bowing and saying, "Please sir." In the strangest way, too, combining a filial affection with a menial respect. Took such warm, singular interest in my affairs. Wanted to be considered one of the family – sort of adopted son of mine, I suppose. Of a morning, when I

would go out to my stable, with what childlike good nature he
would trot out my nag, "Please sir, I think he's getting fatter and
fatter." "But, he don't look very clean, does he?" unwilling to be
downright harsh with so affectionate a lad; "and he seems a little
hollow inside the haunch there, don't he? or no, perhaps I don't
see plain this morning." "Oh, please sir, it's just there I think he's
gaining so, please." Polite scamp! I soon found he never gave that
wretched nag his oats of nights; didn't bed him either. Was
above that sort of chambermaid work. No end to his wilful
neglects. But the more he abused my service, the more polite
he grew.'

'Oh, sir, some way you mistook him.'

'Not a bit of it. Besides, sir, he was a boy who under a
Chesterfieldian exterior hid strong destructive propensities. He
cut up my horse-blanket for the bits of leather, for hinges to his
chest. Denied it point-blank. After he was gone, found the shreds
under his mattress. Would slyly break his hoe-handle, too, on
purpose to get rid of hoeing. Then be so gracefully penitent for
his fatal excess of industrious strength. Offer to mend all by
taking a nice stroll to the nighest settlement – cherry-trees in full
bearing all the way – to get the broken thing cobbled. Very
politely stole my pears, odd pennies, shillings, dollars, and nuts;
regular squirrel at it. But I could prove nothing. Expressed to him
my suspicions. Said I, moderately enough, "A little less politeness,
and a little more honesty would suit me better." He fired up;
threatened to sue for libel. I won't say anything about his afterwards, in Ohio, being found in the act of gracefully putting a bar
across a railroad track, for the reason that a stoker called him the
rogue that he was. But enough: polite boys or saucy boys, white
boys or black boys, smart boys or lazy boys, Caucasian boys or
Mongol boys – all are rascals.'

'Shocking, shocking!' nervously tucking his frayed cravat-end
out of sight. 'Surely, respected sir, you labour under a deplorable
hallucination. Why, pardon again, you seem to have not the
slightest confidence in boys. I admit, indeed, that boys, some of

them at least, are but too prone to one little foolish foible or other. But, what then, respected sir, when, by natural laws, they finally outgrow such things, and wholly?'

Having until now vented himself mostly in plaintive dissent of canine whines and groans, the man with the brass-plate seemed beginning to summon courage to a less timid encounter. But, upon his maiden essay, was not very encouragingly handled, since the dialogue immediately continued as follows:

'Boys outgrow what is amiss in them? From bad boys spring good men? Sir, "the child is father of the man"; hence, as all boys are rascals, so are all men. But, God bless me, you must know these things better than I; keeping an intelligence office as you do; a business which must furnish peculiar facilities for studying mankind. Come, come up here, sir; confess you know these things pretty well, after all. Do you not know that all men are rascals, and all boys, too?'

'Sir,' replied the other, spite of his shocked feelings seeming to pluck up some spirit, but not to an indiscreet degree, 'Sir, heaven be praised, I am far, very far from knowing what you say. True,' he thoughtfully continued, 'with my associates, I keep an intelligence office, and for ten years, come October, have, one way or other, been concerned in that line; for no small period in the great city of Cincinnati, too; and though, as you hint, within that long interval, I must have had more or less favourable opportunity for studying mankind – in a business way, scanning not only the faces, but ransacking the lives of several thousands of human beings, male and female, of various nations, both employers and employed, genteel and ungenteel, educated and uneducated; yet – of course, I candidly admit, with some random exceptions, I have, so far as my small observation goes, found that mankind thus domestically viewed, confidentially viewed, I may say; they, upon the whole – making some reasonable allowances for human imperfection – present as pure a moral spectacle as the purest angel could wish. I say it, respected sir, with confidence.'

'Gammon! You don't mean what you say. Else you are like a

landsman at sea: don't know the ropes, the very things everlast-ingly pulled before your eyes. Serpent-like, they glide about, travelling blocks too subtle for you. In short, the entire ship is a riddle. Why, you green ones wouldn't know if she were un-seaworthy; but still, with thumbs stuck back into your arm-holes, pace the rotten planks, singing, like a fool, words put into your green mouth by the cunning owner, the man who, heavily insuring it, sends his ship to be wrecked –

> A wet sheet and a flowing sea!

– and, sir, now that it occurs to me, your talk, the whole of it, is but a wet sheet and a flowing sea, and an idle wind that follows fast, offering a striking contrast to my own discourse.'

'Sir,' exclaimed the man with the brass-plate, his patience now more or less tasked, 'permit me with deference to hint that some of your remarks are injudiciously worded. And thus we say to our patrons, when they enter our office full of abuse of us because of some worthy boy we may have sent them – some boy wholly misjudged for the time. Yes, sir, permit me to remark that you do not sufficiently consider, that, though a small man, I may have my small share of feelings.'

'Well, well, I didn't mean to wound your feelings at all. And that they are small, very small, I take your word for it. Sorry, sorry. But truth is like a thrashing-machine; tender sensibilities must keep out of the way. Hope you understand me. Don't want to hurt you. All I say is, what I said in the first place, only now I swear it, that all boys are rascals.'

'Sir,' lowly replied the other, still forbearing like an old lawyer badgered in court, or else like a good-hearted simpleton, the butt of mischievous wags, 'Sir, since you come back to the point, will you allow me, in my small, quiet way, to submit to you certain small, quiet views of the subject in hand?'

'Oh, yes!' with insulting indifference, rubbing his chin and looking the other way. 'Oh, yes; go on.'

'Well, then, respected sir,' continued the other, now assuming as genteel an attitude as the irritating set of his pinched five-dollar suit would permit; 'well, then, sir, the peculiar principles, the strictly philosophical principles, I may say,' guardedly rising in dignity, as he guardedly rose on his toes, 'upon which our office is founded, have led me and my associates, in our small, quiet way, to a careful analytical study of man, conducted, too, on a quiet theory, and with an unobtrusive aim wholly our own. That theory I will not now at large set forth. But some of the discoveries resulting from it, I will, by your permission, very briefly mention; such of them, I mean, as refer to the state of boyhood scientifically viewed.'

'Then you have studied the thing? expressly studied boys, eh? Why didn't you out with that before?'

'Sir, in my small business way, I have not conversed with so many masters, gentlemen masters, for nothing. I have been taught that in this world there is a precedence of opinions as well as of persons. You have kindly given me your views, I am now, with modesty, about to give you mine.'

'Stop flunkying – go on.'

'In the first place, sir, our theory teaches us to proceed by analogy from the physical to the moral. Are we right there, sir? Now, sir, take a young boy, a young male infant rather, a man-child in short – what sir, I respectfully ask, do you in the first place remark?'

'A rascal, sir! present and prospective, a rascal!'

'Sir, if passion is to invade, surely science must evacuate. May I proceed? Well, then, what, in the first place, in a general view, do you remark, respected sir, in that male baby or man-child?'

The bachelor privily growled, but this time, upon the whole, better governed himself than before, though not, indeed, to the degree of thinking it prudent to risk an articulate response.

'What do you remark? I respectfully repeat.' But, as no answer came, only the low, half-suppressed growl, as of Bruin in a hollow trunk, the questioner continued: 'Well, sir, if you will permit me, in my small way, to speak for you, you remark, respected sir, an incipient creation; loose sort of sketchy thing; a little preliminary rag-paper study, or careless cartoon, so to speak, of a man. The idea, you see, respected sir, is there; but, as yet, wants filling out. In a word, respected sir, the man-child is at present but little, every way; I don't pretend to deny it; but, then, he *promises* well, does he not? Yes, promises very well indeed, I may say. (So, too, we say to our patrons in reference to some noble little youngster objected to for being a *dwarf*.) But, to advance one step further,' extending his thread-bare leg, as he drew a pace nearer, 'we must now drop the figure of the rag-paper cartoon, and borrow one – to use presently, when wanted – from the horticultural kingdom. Some bud, lily-bud, if you please. Now, such points as the new-born man-child has – as yet not all that could be desired, I am free to confess – still, such as they are, there they are, and palpable as those of an adult. But we stop not here,' taking another step. 'The man-child not only possesses these present points, small though they are, but, likewise – now our horticultural image comes into play – like the bud of the lily, he contains concealed rudiments of others; that is, points at present invisible, with beauties at present dormant.'

'Come, come, this talk is getting too horticultural and beautiful altogether. Cut it short, cut it short!'

'Respected sir,' with a rustily martial sort of gesture, like a decayed corporal's, 'when deploying into the field of discourse the vanguard of an important argument, much more in evolving the grand central forces of a new philosophy of boys, as I may say, surely you will kindly allow scope adequate to the movement in hand, small and humble in its way as that movement may be. Is it worth my while to go on, respected sir?'

'Yes, stop flunkying and go on.'

Thus encouraged, again the philosopher with the brass-plate proceeded:

'Supposing, sir, that worthy gentleman (in such terms, to an applicant for service, we allude to some patron we chance to have in our eye), supposing, respected sir, that worthy gentleman,

Adam, to have been dropped overnight in Eden, as a calf in the pasture; supposing that, sir – then how could even the learned serpent himself have foreknown that such a downy-chinned little innocent would eventually rival the goat in a beard? Sir, wise as the serpent was, that eventuality would have been entirely hidden from his wisdom.'

'I don't know about that. The devil is very sagacious. To judge by the event, he appears to have understood man better even than the Being who made him.'

'For God's sake, don't say that, sir! To the point. Can it now with fairness be denied that, in his beard, the man-child prospectively possesses an appendix, not less imposing than patriarchal; and for this goodly beard, should we not by generous anticipation give the man-child, even in his cradle, credit? Should we not now, sir? respectfully I put it.'

'Yes, if like pig-weed he mows it down soon as it shoots,' porcinely rubbing his stubble-chin against his coon-skins.

'I have hinted at the analogy,' continued the other, calmly disregardful of the digression; 'now to apply it. Suppose a boy evince no noble quality. Then generously give him credit for his prospective one. Don't you see? So we say to our patrons when they would fain return a boy upon as unworthy: "Madam, or sir (as the case may be), has this boy a beard?" "No." "Has he, we respectfully ask, as yet, evinced any noble quality?" "No, indeed." "Then, madam, or sir, take him back, we humbly beseech; and keep him till that same noble quality sprouts; for, have confidence, it, like the beard, is in him."'

'Very fine theory,' scornfully exclaimed the bachelor, yet in secret, perhaps, not entirely undisturbed by these strange new views of the matter; 'but what trust is to be placed in it?'

'The trust of perfect confidence, sir. To proceed. Once more, if you please, regard the man-child.'

'Hold!' paw-like thrusting out his bear-skin arm, 'don't intrude that man-child upon me too often. He who loves not bread dotes not on dough. As little of your man-child as your logical arrangements will admit.'

'Anew regard the man-child,' with inspired intrepidity repeated he with the brass-plate, 'in the perspective of his developments, I mean. At first the man-child has no teeth, but about the sixth month – am I right, sir?'

'Don't know anything about it.'

'To proceed then: though at first deficient in teeth, about the sixth month the man-child begins to put forth in that particular. And sweet those tender little puttings-forth are.'

'Very, but blown out of his mouth directly, worthless enough.'

'Admitted. And, therefore, we say to our patrons returning with a boy alleged not only to be deficient in goodness, but redundant in ill: "The lad, madam or sir, evinces very corrupt qualities, does he?" "No end to them." "But, have confidence, there will be; for pray, madam, in this lad's early childhood, were not those frail first teeth, then his, followed by his present sound, even, beautiful and permanent set? And the more objectionable those first teeth became, was not that, madam, we respectfully submit, so much the more reason to look for their speedy substitution by the present sound, even, beautiful and permanent ones?" "True, true, can't deny that." "Then, madam, take him back, we respectfully beg, and wait till, in the now swift course of nature, dropping those transient moral blemishes you complain of, he replacingly buds forth in the sound, even, beautiful and permanent virtues."'

'Very philosophical again,' was the contemptuous reply – the outward contempt, perhaps, proportioned to the inward misgiving. 'Vastly philosophical, indeed, but tell me – to continue your analogy – since the second teeth followed – in fact, came from – the first, is there no chance the blemish may be transmitted?'

'Not at all.' Abating in humility as he gained in the argument. 'The second teeth follow, but do not come from, the first; successors, not sons. The first teeth are not like the germ blossom of the apple, at once the father of, and incorporated into, the growth it foreruns; but they are thrust from their place by the independent undergrowth of the succeeding set – an illustration, by the way, which shows more for me than I meant, though not more than I wish.'

'What does it show?' Surly-looking as a thunder-cloud with the inkept unrest of unacknowledged conviction.

'It shows this, respected sir, that in the case of any boy, especially an ill one, to apply unconditionally the saying, that the "child is father of the man," is, besides implying an uncharitable aspersion of the race, affirming a thing very wide of –'

'– Your analogy,' like a snapping turtle.

'Yes, respected sir.'

'But is analogy argument? You are a punster.'

'Punster, respected sir?' with a look of being aggrieved.

'Yes, you pun with ideas as another man may with words.'

'Oh well, sir, whoever talks in that strain, whoever has no confidence in human reason, whoever despises human reason, in vain to reason with him. Still, respected sir,' altering his air, 'permit me to hint that, had not the force of analogy moved you somewhat, you would hardly have offered to contemn it.'

'Talk away,' disdainfully; 'but pray tell me what has that last analogy of yours to do with your intelligence office business?'

'Everything to do with it, respected sir. From that analogy we derive the reply made to such a patron as, shortly after being supplied by us with an adult servant, proposes to return him upon our hands; not that, while with the patron, said adult has given any cause of dissatisfaction, but the patron has just chanced to hear something unfavourable concerning him from some gentleman who employed said adult long before, while a boy. To which too fastidious patron, we, taking said adult by the hand, and graciously reintroducing him to the patron, say: "Far be it from you, madam, or sir, to proceed in your censure against this adult, in anything of the spirit of an ex-post-facto law. Madam, or sir, would you visit upon the butterfly the sins of the caterpillar? In the natural advance of all creatures, do they not bury themselves over and over again in the endless resurrection of better and better? Madam, or sir, take back this adult; he may have been a caterpillar, but is now a butterfly."'

'Pun away; but even accepting your analogical pun, what does it amount to? Was the caterpillar one creature, and is the butterfly another? The butterfly is the caterpillar in a gaudy cloak; stripped of which, there lies the impostor's long spindle of a body, pretty much worm-shaped as before.'

'You reject the analogy. To the facts then. You deny that a youth of one character can be transformed into a man of an opposite character. Now then — yes, I have it. There's the founder of La Trappe, and Ignatius Loyola; in boyhood, and someway into manhood, both devil-may-care bloods, and yet, in the end, the wonders of the world for anchoritish self-command. These two examples, by-the-way, we cite to such patrons as would hastily return rakish young waiters upon us. "Madam, or sir — patience; patience," we say; "good madam, or sir, would you discharge forth your cask of good wine, because, while working, it riles more or less? Then discharge not forth this young waiter; the good in him is working." "But he is a sad rake." "Therein is his promise; the rake being crude material for the saint."'

'Ah, you are a talking man — what I call a wordy man. You talk, talk.'

'And with submission, sir, what is the greatest judge, bishop or prophet, but a talking man? He talks, talks. It is the peculiar vocation of a teacher to talk. What's wisdom itself but table-talk? The best wisdom in this world, and the last spoken by its teacher, did it not literally and truly come in the form of table-talk?'

'You, you, you!' rattling down his rifle.

'To shift the subject, since we cannot agree. Pray, what is your opinion, respected sir, of St Augustine?'

'St Augustine? What should I, or you either, know of him? Seems to me, for one in such a business, to say nothing of such a coat, that though you don't know a great deal, indeed, yet you know a good deal more than you ought to know, or than you have a right to know, or than it is safe or expedient for you to know, or than, in the fair course of life, you could have honestly come to know. I am of opinion you should be served like a Jew in the middle ages with his gold; this knowledge of yours, which you haven't enough knowledge to know how to make a right use of, it should be taken from you. And so I have been thinking all along.'

'You are merry, sir. But you have a little looked into St Augustine I suppose.'

'St Augustine on Original Sin is my text book. But you, I ask again, where do you find time or inclination for these out-of-the-way speculations? In fact, your whole talk, the more I think of it, is altogether unexampled and extraordinary.'

'Respected sir, have I not already informed you that the quite new method, the strictly philosophical one, on which our office is founded, has led me and my associates to an enlarged study of mankind. It was my fault, if I did not, likewise, hint, that these studies directed always to the scientific procuring of good servants of all sorts, boys included, for the kind gentlemen, our patrons – that these studies, I say, have been conducted equally among all books of all libraries, as among all men of all nations. Then, you rather like St Augustine, sir?'

'Excellent genius!'

'In some points he was; yet, how comes it that under his own hand, St Augustine confesses that, until his thirtieth year, he was a very sad dog?'

'A saint a sad dog?'

'Not the saint, but the saint's irresponsible little forerunner – the boy.'

'All boys are rascals, and so are all men,' again flying off at his tangent; 'my name is Pitch; I stick to what I say.'

'Ah, sir, permit me – when I behold you on this mild summer's eve, thus eccentrically clothed in the skins of wild beasts, I cannot but conclude that the equally grim and unsuitable habit of your mind is likewise but an eccentric assumption, having no basis in your genuine soul, no more than in nature herself.'

'Well, really, now – really,' fidgeted the bachelor, not unaffected in his conscience by these benign personalities, 'really,

really, now, I don't know but that I may have been a little bit too hard upon those five and thirty boys of mine.'

'Glad to find you a little softening, sir. Who knows now, but that flexile gracefulness, however questionable at the time of that thirtieth boy of yours, might have been the silky husk of the most solid qualities of maturity. It might have been with him as with the ear of the Indian corn.'

'Yes, yes, yes,' excitedly cried the bachelor, as the light of this new illustration broke in, 'yes, yes; and now that I think of it, how often I've sadly watched my Indian corn in May, wondering whether such sickly, half-eaten sprouts, could ever thrive up into the stiff, stately spear of August.'

'A most admirable reflection, sir, and you have only, according to the analogical theory first started by our office, to apply it to that thirtieth boy in question, and see the result. Had you but kept that thirtieth boy – been patient with his sickly virtues, cultivated them, hoed round them, why what a glorious guerdon would have been yours, when at last you should have had a St Augustine for an ostler.'

'Really, really – well, I am glad I didn't send him to jail, as at first I intended.'

'Oh that would have been too bad. Grant he was vicious. The petty vices of boys are like the innocent kicks of colts, as yet imperfectly broken. Some boys know not virtue only for the same reason they know not French; it was never taught them. Established upon the basis of parental charity, juvenile asylums exist by law for the benefit of lads convicted of acts which, in adults, would have received other requital. Why? Because, do what they will, society, like our office, at bottom has a Christian confidence in boys. And all this we say to our patrons.'

'Your patrons, sir, seem your marines, to whom you may say anything,' said the other, relapsing. 'Why do knowing employers shun youths from asylums, though offered them at the smallest wages? I'll none of your reformado boys.'

'Such a boy, respected sir, I would not get for you, but a boy that never needed reform. Do not smile, for as whooping-cough and measles are juvenile diseases, and yet some juveniles never have them, so are there boys equally free from juvenile vices. True, for the best of boys, measles may be contagious, and evil communications corrupt good manners; but a boy with a sound mind in a sound body – such is the boy I would get you. If hitherto, sir, you have struck upon a peculiarly bad vein of boys, so much the more hope now of your hitting a good one.'

'That sounds a kind of reasonable, as it were – a little so, really. In fact, though you have said a great many foolish things, very foolish and absurd things, yet, upon the whole, your conversation has been such as might almost lead one less distrustful than I to repose a certain conditional confidence in you, I had almost added in your office, also. Now, for the humour of it, supposing that even I, I myself, really had this sort of conditional confidence, though but a grain, what sort of a boy, in sober fact, could you send me? And what would be your fee?'

'Conducted,' replied the other somewhat loftily, rising now in eloquence as his proselyte, for all his pretences, sunk in conviction, 'conducted upon principles involving care, learning, and labour, exceeding what is usual in kindred institutions, the Philosophical Intelligence Office is forced to charges somewhat higher than customary. Briefly, our fee is three dollars in advance. As for the boy, by a lucky chance, I have a very promising little fellow now in my eye – a very likely little fellow, indeed.'

'Honest?'

'As the day is long. Might trust him with untold millions. Such, at least, were the marginal observations on the phrenological chart of his head, submitted to me by the mother.'

'How old?'

'Just fifteen.'

'Tall? Stout?'

'Uncommonly so, for his age, his mother remarked.'

'Industrious?'

'The busy bee.'

The bachelor fell into a troubled reverie. At last, with much hesitancy, he spoke:

'Do you think now, candidly, that – I say candidly – candidly – could I have some small, limited – some faint, conditional degree of confidence in that boy? Candidly, now?'

'Candidly, you could.'

'A sound boy? A good boy?'

'Never knew one more so.'

The bachelor fell into another irresolute reverie; then said: 'Well, now, you have suggested some rather new views of boys, and men, too. Upon those views in the concrete I at present decline to determine. Nevertheless, for the sake purely of a scientific experiment, I will try that boy. I don't think him an angel, mind. No, no. But I'll try him. There are my three dollars, and here is my address. Send him along this day two weeks. Hold, you will be wanting the money for his passage. There,' handing it somewhat reluctantly.

'Ah, thank you. I had forgotten his passage'; then, altering in manner, and gravely holding the bills, continued: 'Respected sir, never willingly do I handle money not with perfect willingness, nay, with a certain alacrity paid. Either tell me that you have a perfect and unquestioning confidence in me (never mind the boy now) or permit me respectfully to return these bills.'

'Put 'em up, put 'em up!'

'Thank you. Confidence is the indispensable basis of all sorts of business transactions. Without it, commerce between man and man, as between country and country, would, like a watch, run down and stop. And now, supposing that against present expectation the lad should, after all, evince some little undesirable trait, do not, respected sir, rashly dismiss him. Have but patience, have but confidence. Those transient vices will, ere long, fall out, and be replaced by the sound, firm, even and permanent virtues. Ah,' glancing shoreward, towards a grotesquely-shaped bluff, 'there's the Devil's Joke, as they call it; the bell for landing will shortly ring. I must go look up the cook I brought for the innkeeper at Cairo.'

23

IN WHICH THE POWERFUL EFFECT OF NATURAL SCENERY IS EVINCED IN THE CASE OF THE MISSOURIAN, WHO, IN VIEW OF THE REGION ROUND ABOUT CAIRO, HAS A RETURN OF HIS CHILLY FIT

At Cairo, the old established firm of Fever & Ague is still settling up its unfinished business; that Creole grave-digger, Yellow Jack – his hand at the mattock and spade has not lost its cunning; while Don Saturninus Typhus, taking his constitutional with Death, Calvin Edson and three undertakers, in the morass, snuffs up the mephitic breeze with zest.

In the dank twilight, fanned with mosquitoes, and sparkling with fire-flies, the boat now lies before Cairo. She has landed certain passengers, and tarries for the coming of expected ones. Leaning over the rail on the inshore side, the Missourian eyes through the dubious medium that swampy and squalid domain; and over it audibly mumbles his cynical mind to himself, as Apemantus' dog may have mumbled his bone. He bethinks him that the man with the brass-plate was to land on this villainous bank, and for that cause, if no other, begins to suspect him. Like one beginning to rouse himself from a dose of chloroform treacherously given, he half divines, too, that he, the philosopher, had unwittingly been betrayed into being an unphilosophical dupe. To what vicissitudes of light and shade is man subject! He ponders the mystery of human subjectivity in general. He thinks he perceives with Crossbones, his favourite author, that, as one may wake up well in the morning, very well, indeed, and brisk as a buck, I thank you, but ere bedtime get under the weather, there is no telling how – so one may wake up wise, and slow of assent, very wise and very slow, I assure you, and for all that, before night, by like trick in the atmosphere, be left in the lurch a ninny. Health and wisdom equally precious, and equally little as un-fluctuating possessions to be relied on.

But where was slipped in the entering wedge? Philosophy, knowledge, experience – were those trusty knights of the castle recreant? No, but unknown to them, the enemy stole on the castle's south side, its genial one, where Suspicion, the warder, parleyed. In fine, his too indulgent, too artless and companionable nature betrayed him. Admonished by which, he thinks he must be a little splenetic in his intercourse henceforth.

He revolves the crafty process of sociable chat, by which, as he fancies, the man with the brass-plate wormed into him, and made such a fool of him as insensibly to persuade him to waive, in his exceptional case, that general law of distrust systematically applied to the race. He revolves, but cannot comprehend, the operation, still less the operator. Was the man a trickster, it must be more for the love than the lucre. Two or three dirty dollars the motive to so many nice wiles? And yet how full of mean needs his seeming. Before his mental vision the person of that threadbare Talleyrand, that impoverished Machiavelli, that seedy Rosicrucian – for some-thing of all these he vaguely deems him – passes now in puzzled review. Fain, in his disfavour, would he make out a logical case. The doctrine of analogies recurs. Fallacious enough doctrine when wielded against one's prejudices, but in corroboration of cherished suspicions not without likelihood. Analogically, he couples the slanting cut of the equivocator's coat-tails with the sinister cast in his eye; he weighs slyboot's sleek speech in the light imparted by the oblique import of the smooth slope of his worn boot-heels; the insinuator's undulating flunkyisms dovetail into those of the flunky beast that windeth his way on his belly.

From these uncordial reveries he is roused by a cordial slap on the shoulder, accompanied by a spicy volume of tobacco smoke, out of which came a voice, sweet as a seraph's:

'A penny for your thoughts, my fine fellow.'

24

A PHILANTHROPIST UNDERTAKES TO
CONVERT A MISANTHROPE, BUT DOES NOT
GET BEYOND CONFUTING HIM

'Hands off!' cried the bachelor, involuntarily covering dejection with moroseness.

'Hands off? that sort of label won't do in our Fair. Whoever in our Fair has fine feelings loves to feel the nap of fine cloth, especially when a fine fellow wears it.'

'And who of my fine-fellow species may you be? From the Brazils, ain't you? Toucan fowl. Fine feathers on foul meat.'

This ungentle mention of the toucan was not improbably suggested by the parti-hued, and rather plumagy aspect of the stranger, no bigot it would seem, but a liberalist, in dress, and whose wardrobe, almost anywhere but on the liberal Mississippi, used to all sorts of fantastic informalities, might, even to observers less critical than the bachelor, have looked, if anything, a little out of the common; but not more so perhaps, than, considering the bear and raccoon costume, the bachelor's own appearance. In short, the stranger sported a vesture barred with various hues, that of the cochineal predominating, in style participating of a Highland plaid, Emir's robe, and French blouse; from its plaited sort of front peeped glimpses of a flowered regatta-shirt, while, for the rest, white trowsers of ample duck flowed over maroon-coloured slippers, and a jaunty smoking-cap of regal purple crowned him off at top; king of travelled good-fellows, evidently. Grotesque as all was, nothing looked stiff or unused; all showed signs of easy service, the least wonted thing setting like a wonted glove. That genial hand, which had just been laid on the ungenial shoulder, was now carelessly thrust down before him, sailor-fashion, into a sort of Indian belt, confining the redundant vesture; the other held, by its long bright cherry-stem, a Nuremberg pipe in blast, its great porcelain bowl painted in miniature with linked crests and arms of interlinked nations – a florid show. As by subtle saturations of its mellowing essence the tobacco had ripened the bowl, so it looked as if something similar of the interior spirit came rosily out on the cheek. But rosy pipe-bowl, or rosy countenance, all was lost on that unrosy man, the bachelor, who, waiting a moment till the commotion, caused by the boat's renewed progress, had a little abated, thus continued:

'Hark ye,' jeeringly eyeing the cap and belt, 'did you ever see Signor Marzetti in the African pantomime?'

'No; – good performer?'

'Excellent; plays the intelligent ape till he seems it. With such naturalness can a being endowed with an immortal spirit enter into that of a monkey. But where's your tail? In the pantomime, Marzetti, no hypocrite in his monkery, prides himself on that.'

The stranger, now at rest, sideways and genially, on one hip, his right leg cavalierly crossed before the other, the toe of his vertical slipper pointed easily down on the deck, whiffed out a long, leisurely sort of indifferent and charitable puff, betokening him more or less of the mature man of the world, a character which, like its opposite, the sincere Christian's, is not always swift to take offence; and then, drawing near, still smoking, again laid his hand, this time with mild impressiveness, on the ursine shoulder, and not unamiably said: 'That in your address there is a sufficiency of the *fortiter in re* few unbiassed observers will question; but that this is duly attempered with the *suaviter in modo* may admit, I think, of an honest doubt. My dear fellow,' beaming his eyes full upon him, 'what injury have I done you, that you should receive my greeting with a curtailed civility?'

'Off hands'; once more shaking the friendly member from him. 'Who in the name of the great chimpanzee, in whose likeness, you, Marzetti, and the other chatterers are made, who in thunder are you?'

'A cosmopolitan, a catholic man; who, being such, ties himself to no narrow tailor or teacher, but federates, in heart as in costume, something of the various gallantries of men under various suns. Oh, one roams not over the gallant globe in vain. Bred by it, is a fraternal and fusing feeling. No man is a stranger. You accost anybody. Warm and confiding, you wait not for measured advances. And though, indeed, mine, in this instance, have met with no very hilarious encouragement, yet the principle of a true citizen of the world is still to return good for ill. – My dear fellow, tell me how I can serve you.'

'By dispatching yourself, Mr Popinjay-of-the-world, into the heart of the Lunar Mountains. You are another of them. Out of my sight!'

'Is the sight of humanity so very disagreeable to you then? Ah, I may be foolish, but for my part, in all its aspects, I love it. Served up à la Pole, or à la Moor, à la Ladrone, or à la Yankee, that good dish, man, still delights me; or rather is man a wine I never weary of comparing and sipping; wherefore am I a pledged cosmopolitan, a sort of London-Dock-Vault connoisseur, going about from Teheran to Natchitoches, a taster of races; in all his vintages, smacking my lips over this racy creature, man, continually. But as there are teetotal palates which have a distaste even for Amontillado, so I suppose there may be teetotal souls which relish not even the very best brands of humanity. Excuse me, but it just occurs to me that you, my dear fellow, possibly lead a solitary life.'

'Solitary?' starting as at a touch of divination.

'Yes: in a solitary life one insensibly contracts oddities, – talking to one's self now.'

'Been eaves-dropping, eh?'

'Why, a soliloquist in a crowd can hardly but be overheard, and without much reproach to the hearer.'

'You are an eaves-dropper.'

'Well. Be it so.'

'Confess yourself an eaves-dropper.'

'I confess that when you were muttering here I, passing by, caught a word or two, and, by like chance, something previous of your chat with the intelligence-office man; – a rather sensible fellow, by the way; much of my style of thinking; would, for his own sake, he were of my style of dress. Grief to good minds, to see a man of superior sense forced to hide his light under the bushel of an inferior coat. – Well, from what little I heard, I said to myself, Here now is one with the unprofitable philosophy of disesteem for man. Which disease, in the main, I have observed – excuse me – to spring from a certain lowness, if not sourness, of spirits inseparable from sequestration. Trust me, one had better mix in, and do like others. Sad business, this holding out against having a good time. Life is a pic-nic *en costume*; one must take a part, assume a character, stand ready in a sensible way to play the fool. To come in plain clothes, with a long face, as a wiseacre, only makes one a discomfort to himself, and a blot upon the scene. Like your jug of cold water among the wine-flasks, it leaves you unelated among the elated ones. No, no. This austerity won't do. Let me tell you too – *en confiance* – that while revelry may not always merge into ebriety, soberness, in too deep potations, may become a sort of sottishness. Which sober sottishness, in my way of thinking, is only to be cured by beginning at the other end of the horn, to tipple a little.'

'Pray, what society of vintners and old topers are you hired to lecture for?'

'I fear I did not give my meaning clearly. A little story may help. The story of the worthy old woman of Goshen, a very moral old woman, who wouldn't let her shoats eat fattening apples in fall, for fear the fruit might ferment upon their brains, and so make them swinish. Now, during a green Christmas, inauspicious to the old, this worthy old woman fell into a moping decline, took to her bed, no appetite, and refused to see her best friends. In much concern her good man sent for the doctor, who, after seeing the patient and putting a question or two, beckoned the husband out, and said: "Deacon, do you want her cured?"

"Indeed I do." "Go directly, then, and buy a jug of Santa Cruz." "Santa Cruz? my wife drink Santa Cruz?" "Either that or die." "But how much?" "As much as she can get down." "But she'll get drunk!" "That's the cure." Wise men, like doctors, must be obeyed. Much against the grain, the sober deacon got the unsober medicine, and, equally against her conscience, the poor old woman took it; but, by so doing, ere long recovered health and spirits, famous appetite, and glad again to see her friends; and having by this experience broken the ice of arid abstinence, never afterwards kept herself a cup too low.'

This story had the effect of surprising the bachelor into interest, though hardly into approval.

'If I take your parable right,' said he, sinking no little of his former churlishness, 'the meaning is, that one cannot enjoy life with gusto unless he renounce the too-sober view of life. But since the too-sober view is, doubtless, nearer true than the too-drunken; I, who rate truth, though cold water, above untruth, though Tokay, will stick to my earthen jug.'

'I see,' slowly spirting upward a spiral staircase of lazy smoke, 'I see; you go in for the lofty.'

'How?'

'Oh, nothing! but if I wasn't afraid of prosing, I might tell another story about an old boot in a pieman's loft, contracting there between sun and oven an unseemly, dry-seasoned curl and warp. You've seen such leathery old garretteers, haven't you? Very high, sober, solitary, philosophic, grand, old boots, indeed; but I, for my part, would rather be the pieman's trodden slipper on the ground. Talking of piemen, humble-pie before proud-cake for me. This notion of being lone and lofty is a sad mistake. Men I hold in this respect to be like roosters; the one that betakes himself to a lone and lofty perch is the hen-pecked one, or the one that has the pip.'

'You are abusive!' cried the bachelor, evidently touched.

'Who is abused? You, or the race? You won't stand by and see the human race abused? Oh then, you have some respect for the human race.'

'I have some respect for *myself*,' with a lip not so firm as before.

'And what race may *you* belong to? now don't you see, my dear fellow, in what inconsistencies one involves himself by affecting disesteem for men? To a charm, my little stratagem succeeded. Come, come, think better of it, and, as a first step to a new mind, give up solitude. I fear, by the way, you have at some time been reading Zimmermann, that old Mr Megrims of a Zimmermann, whose book on Solitude is as vain as Hume's on Suicide, as Bacon's on Knowledge; and, like these, will betray him who seeks to steer soul and body by it, like a false religion. All they, be they what boasted ones you please, who, to the yearning of our kind after a founded rule of content, offer aught not in the spirit of fellowly gladness based on due confidence in what is above, away with them for poor dupes, or still poorer impostors.'

His manner here was so earnest that scarcely any auditor, perhaps, but would have been more or less impressed by it, while, possibly, nervous opponents might have a little quailed under it. Thinking within himself a moment, the bachelor replied: 'Had you experience, you would know that your tippling theory, take it in what sense you will, is poor as any other. And Rabelais's pro-wine Koran no more trustworthy than Mahomet's anti-wine one.'

'Enough,' for a finality knocking the ashes from his pipe, 'we talk and keep talking, and still stand where we did. What do you say for a walk? My arm, and let's a turn. They are to have dancing on the hurricane-deck to-night. I shall fling them off a Scotch jig, while, to save the pieces, you hold my loose change; and following that, I propose that you, my dear fellow, stack your gun, and throw your bearskins in a sailor's hornpipe – I holding your watch. What do you say?'

At this proposition the other was himself again, all racoon.

'Look you,' thumping down his rifle, 'are you Jeremy Diddler No. 3?'

'Jeremy Diddler? I have heard of Jeremy the prophet, and Jeremy Taylor the divine, but your other Jeremy is a gentleman I am unacquainted with.'

'You are his confidential clerk, ain't you?'

'*Whose*, pray? Not that I think myself unworthy of being confided in, but I don't understand.'

'You are another of them. Somehow I meet with the most extraordinary metaphysical scamps to-day. Sort of visitation of them. And yet that herb-doctor Diddler somehow takes off the raw edge of the Diddlers that come after him.'

'Herb-doctor? who is he?'

'Like you – another of them.'

'*Who*?' Then drawing near, as if for a good long explanatory chat, his left hand spread, and his pipe-stem coming crosswise down upon it like a ferule, 'You think amiss of me. Now to undeceive you, I will just enter into a little argument and –'

'No you don't. No more little arguments for me. Had too many little arguments to-day.'

'But put a case. Can you deny – I dare you to deny – that the man leading a solitary life is peculiarly exposed to the sorriest misconceptions touching strangers?'

'Yes, I *do* deny it,' again, in his impulsiveness, snapping at the controversial bait, 'and I will confute you there in a trice. Look, you –'

'Now, now, now, my dear fellow,' thrusting out both vertical palms for double shields, 'you crowd me too hard. You don't give one a chance. Say what you will, to shun a social proposition like mine, to shun society in any way, evinces a churlish nature – cold, loveless; as, to embrace it, shows one warm and friendly, in fact, sunshiny.'

Here the other, all agog again, in his perverse way, launched forth into the unkindest references to deaf old worldlings keeping in the deafening world; and gouty gluttons limping to their gouty gourmandizings; and corsetted coquettes clasping their corsetted cavaliers in the waltz, all for disinterested society's sake; and thousands, bankrupt through lavishness, ruining themselves out of pure love of the sweet company of man – no envies, rivalries, or other unhandsome motive to it.

'Ah, now,' deprecating with his pipe, 'irony is so unjust; never could abide irony; something Satanic about irony. God defend me from Irony, and Satire his bosom friend.'

'A right knave's prayer, and a right fool's, too,' snapping his rifle-lock.

'Now be frank. Own that was a little gratuitous. But, no, no, you didn't mean it; any way, I can make allowances. Ah, did you but know it, how much pleasanter to puff at this philanthropic pipe, than still to keep fumbling at that misanthropic rifle. As for your worldling, glutton, and coquette, though, doubtless, being such, they may have their little foibles — as who has not? — yet not one of the three can be reproached with that awful sin of shunning society; awful I call it, for not seldom it presupposes a still darker thing than itself — remorse.'

'Remorse drives man away from man? How came your fellow-creature, Cain, after the first murder, to go and build the first city? And why is it that the modern Cain dreads nothing so much as solitary confinement?'

'My dear fellow, you get excited. Say what you will, I for one must have my fellow-creatures round me. Thick, too — I must have them thick.'

'The pick-pocket, too, loves to have his fellow-creatures round him. Tut, man! no one goes into the crowd but for his end; and the end of too many is the same as the pick-pocket's — a purse.'

'Now, my dear fellow, how can you have the conscience to say that, when it is as much according to natural law that men are social as sheep gregarious. But grant that, in being social, each man has his end, do you, upon the strength of that, do you yourself, I say, mix with man, now, immediately, and be your end a more genial philosophy. Come, let's take a turn.'

Again he offered his fraternal arm; but the bachelor once more flung it off, and, raising his rifle in energetic invocation, cried: 'Now the high-constable catch and confound all knaves in towns and rats in grain-bins, and if in this boat, which is a human grain-bin for the time, any sly, smooth, philandering rat be dodging now, pin him, thou high rat-catcher, against this rail.'

'A noble burst! shows you at heart a trump. And when a card's that, little matters it whether it be spade or diamond. You are good wine that, to be still better, only needs a shaking up. Come, let's agree that we'll to New Orleans, and there embark for London – I staying with my friends nigh Primrose Hill, and you putting up at the Piazza, Covent Garden – Piazza, Covent Garden; for tell me – since you will not be a disciple to the full – tell me, was not that humour of Diogenes, which led him to live, a merry-andrew, in the flower-market, better than that of the less wise Athenian, which made him a skulking scare-crow in pine-barrens? An injudicious gentleman, Lord Timon.'

'Your hand!' seizing it.

'Bless me, how cordial a squeeze. It is agreed we shall be brothers, then?'

'As much so as a brace of misanthropes can be,' with another and terrific squeeze. 'I had thought that the moderns had degener-ated beneath the capacity of misanthropy. Rejoiced, though but in one instance, and that disguised, to be undeceived.'

The other stared in blank amaze.

'Won't do. You are Diogenes, Diogenes in disguise. I say Diogenes masquerading as a cosmopolitan.' With ruefully altered mien, the stranger still stood mute awhile. At length, in a pained tone spoke: 'How hard the lot of that pleader who, in his zeal conceding too much, is taken to belong to a side which he but labours, however ineffectually, to convert!' Then, with another change of air: 'To you, an Ishmael, disguising in sportiveness my intent, I came ambassador from the human race, charged with the assurance that for your mislike they bore no answering grudge, but sought to conciliate accord between you and them. Yet you take me not for the honest envoy, but I know not what sort of unheard-of spy. Sir,' he less lowly added, 'this mistaking of your man should teach you how you may mistake all men. For God's sake,' laying both hands upon him, 'get you confidence. See how distrust has duped you. I, Diogenes? I, he who, going a step beyond misanthropy, was less a man-hater than a man-hooter? Better were I stark and stiff!'

With which the philanthropist moved away less lightsome than he had come, leaving the discomfited misanthrope to the solitude he held so sapient.

25

THE COSMOPOLITAN MAKES AN
ACQUAINTANCE

In the act of retiring, the cosmopolitan was met by a passenger, who, with the bluff *abord* of the West, thus addressed him, though a stranger.

'Queer 'coon, your friend. Had a little skrimmage with him myself. Rather entertaining old 'coon, if he wasn't so deuced analytical. Reminded me somehow of what I've heard about Colonel John Moredock of Illinois, only your friend ain't quite so good a fellow at bottom, I should think.'

It was in the semicircular porch of a cabin, opening a recess from the deck, lit by a zoned lamp swung overhead, and sending its light vertically down, like the sun at noon. Beneath the lamp stood the speaker, affording to any one disposed to it no unfavourable chance for scrutiny; but the glance now resting on him betrayed no such rudeness.

A man neither tall nor stout, neither short nor gaunt; but with a body fitted, as by measure, to the service of his mind. For the rest, one less favoured perhaps in his features than his clothes; and of these the beauty may have been less in the fit than the cut; to say nothing of the fineness of the nap, seeming out of keeping with something the reverse of fine in the skin; and the unsuitableness of a violet vest, sending up sunset hues to a countenance betokening a kind of bilious habit.

But, upon the whole, it could not be fairly said that his appearance was unprepossessing; indeed, to the congenial, it would have been doubtless not uncongenial; while to others, it could not fail to be at least curiously interesting, from the warm air of florid cordiality, contrasting itself with one knows not what kind of aguish sallowness of saving discretion lurking behind it. Ungracious critics might have thought that the manner flushed the man, something in the same fictitious way that the vest flushed the cheek. And though his teeth were singularly good, those same ungracious ones might have hinted that they were too good to be true; or rather, were not so good as they might be; since the best false teeth are those made with at least two or three blemishes, the more to look like life. But fortunately for better constructions, no such critics had the stranger now in eye; only the cosmopolitan, who, after, in the first place, acknowledging his advances with a mute salute – in which acknowledgment, if there seemed less of spirit than in his way of accosting the Missourian, it was probably because of the saddening sequel of that late interview – thus now replied: 'Colonel John Moredock,' repeating the words abstractedly; 'that surname recalls reminiscences. Pray,' with enlivened air, 'was he any way connected with the Moredocks of Moredock Hall, Northamptonshire, England?'

'I know no more of the Moredocks of Moredock Hall than of the Burdocks of Burdock Hut,' returned the other, with the air somehow of one whose fortunes had been of his own making; 'all I know is, that the late Colonel John Moredock was a famous one in his time; eye like Lochiel's; finger like a trigger; nerve like a catamount's; and with but two little oddities – seldom stirred without his rifle, and hated Indians like snakes.'

'Your Moredock, then, would seem a Moredock of Misanthrope Hall – the Woods. No very sleek creature, the colonel, I fancy.'

'Sleek or not, he was no uncombed one, but silky bearded and curly headed, and to all but Indians juicy as a peach. But Indians – how the late Colonel John Moredock, Indian-hater of Illinois, did hate Indians, to be sure!'

'Never heard of such a thing. Hate Indians? Why should he or anybody else hate Indians? *I* admire Indians. Indians I have always heard to be one of the finest of the primitive races, possessed of many heroic virtues. Some noble women, too. When I think of Pocahontas, I am ready to love Indians. Then there's Massasoit, and Philip of Mount Hope, and Tecumseh, and Red-Jacket, and Logan – all heroes; and there's the Five Nations, and Araucanians – federations and communities of heroes. God bless me; hate Indians? Surely the late Colonel John Moredock must have wandered in his mind.'

'Wandered in the woods considerably, but never wandered elsewhere, that I ever heard.'

'Are you in earnest? Was there ever one who so made it his particular mission to hate Indians that, to designate him, a special word has been coined – Indian-hater?'

'Even so.'

'Dear me, you take it very calmly. – But really, I would like to know something about this Indian-hating. I can hardly believe such a thing to be. Could you favour me with a little history of the extraordinary man you mentioned?'

'With all my heart,' and immediately stepping from the porch, gestured the cosmopolitan to a settee near by, on deck. 'There, sir, sit you there, and I will sit here beside you – you desire to hear of Colonel John Moredock. Well, a day in my boyhood is marked with a white stone – the day I saw the colonel's rifle, powder-horn attached, hanging in a cabin on the West bank of the Wabash river. I was going westward a long journey through the wilderness with my father. It was high noon, and we had stopped at the cabin to unsaddle and bait. The man at the cabin pointed out the rifle, and told whose it was, adding that the colonel was that moment sleeping on wolf-skins in the corn-loft above, so we must not talk very loud, for the colonel had been out all night hunting (Indians, mind), and it would be cruel to disturb his sleep. Curious to see one so famous, we waited two hours over, in hopes he would come forth; but he did not. So, it being necessary to get to the next cabin before nightfall, we had at last to ride off without the wished-for satisfaction. Though, to tell the truth, I for one, did not go away entirely ungratified, for, while my father was watering the horses, I slipped back into the cabin, and stepping a round or two up the ladder, pushed my head through the trap, and peered about. Not much light in the loft; but off in the further corner, I saw what I took to be the wolf-skins, and on them a bundle of something, like a drift of leaves; and at one end, what seemed a moss-ball; and over it, deer-antlers branched; and close by, a small squirrel sprang out from a maple-bowl of nuts, brushed the moss-ball with his tail, through a hole, and vanished squeaking. That bit of woodland scene was all I saw. No Colonel Moredock there, unless that moss-ball was his curly head, seen in the back view. I would have gone clear up, but the man below had warned me, that though, from his camping habits, the colonel could sleep through thunder, he was for the same cause amazing quick to waken at the sound of footsteps, however soft, and especially if human.'

'Excuse me,' said the other, softly laying his hand on the narrator's wrist, but I fear the colonel was of a distrustful nature – little or no confidence. He *was* a little suspicious-minded, wasn't he?'

'Not a bit. Knew too much. Suspected nobody, but was not ignorant of Indians. Well: though, as you may gather, I never fully saw the man, yet, have I, one way and another, heard about as much of him as any other; in particular, have I heard his history again and again from my father's friend, James Hall, the judge, you know. In every company being called upon to give this history, which none could better do, the judge at last fell into a style so methodic, you would have thought he spoke less to mere auditors than to an invisible amanuensis; seemed talking for the press; very impressive way with him indeed. And I, having an equally impressible memory, think that, upon a pinch, I can render you the judge upon the colonel almost word for word.'

'Do so, by all means,' said the cosmopolitan, well pleased.

'Shall I give you the judge's philosophy, and all?'

'As to that,' rejoined the other gravely, pausing over the pipe-bowl he was filling, 'the desirableness, to a man of a certain mind, of having another man's philosophy given, depends considerably upon what school of philosophy that other man belongs to. Of what school or system was the judge, pray?'

'Why, though he knew how to read and write, the judge never had much schooling. But I should say he belonged, if anything, to the free-school system. Yes, a true patriot, the judge went in strong for free-schools.'

'In philosophy? The man of a certain mind, then, while respecting the judge's patriotism, and not blind to the judge's capacity for narrative, such as he may prove to have, might, perhaps with prudence, waive an opinion of the judge's probable philosophy. But I am no rigorist; proceed, I beg; his philosophy or not, as you please.'

'Well, I would mostly skip that part, only, to begin, some reconnoitring of the ground in a philosophical way the judge always deemed indispensable with strangers. For you must know that Indian-hating was no monopoly of Colonel Moredock's; but a passion, in one form or other, and to a degree, greater or less, largely shared among the class to which he belonged. And Indian-hating still exists; and, no doubt, will continue to exist, so long as Indians do. Indian-hating, then, shall be my first theme, and Colonel Moredock, the Indian-hater, my next and last.'

With which the stranger, settling himself in his seat, commenced – the hearer paying marked regard, slowly smoking, his glance, meanwhile, steadfastly abstracted towards the deck, but his right ear so disposed towards the speaker that each word came through as little atmospheric intervention as possible. To intensify the sense of hearing, he seemed to sink the sense of sight. No complaisance of mere speech could have been so flattering, or expressed such striking politeness as this mute eloquence of thoroughly digesting attention.

26

CONTAINING THE METAPHYSICS OF INDIAN-HATING, ACCORDING TO THE VIEWS OF ONE EVIDENTLY NOT SO PREPOSSESSED AS ROUSSEAU IN FAVOUR OF SAVAGES

'The judge always began in these words: "The backwoodsman's hatred of the Indian has been a topic for some remark. In the earlier times of the frontier the passion was thought to be readily accounted for. But Indian rapine having mostly ceased through regions where it once prevailed, the philanthropist is surprised that Indian-hating has not in like degree ceased with it. He wonders why the backwoodsman still regards the red man in much the same spirit that a jury does a murderer, or a trapper a wild cat – a creature, in whose behalf mercy were not wisdom; truce is vain; he must be executed.

'"A curious point," the judge would continue, "which perhaps not everybody, even upon explanation, may fully understand; while, in order for any one to approach to an understanding, it is necessary for him to learn, or if he already know, to bear in mind, what manner of man the backwoodsman is; as for what manner of man the Indian is, many know, either from history or experience.

'"The backwoodsman is a lonely man. He is a thoughtful man. He is a man strong and unsophisticated. Impulsive, he is what some might call unprincipled. At any rate, he is self-willed; being one who less hearkens to what others may say about things, than looks for himself, to see what are things themselves. If in straits, there are few to help; he must depend upon himself; he must continually look to himself. Hence self-reliance, to the degree of standing by his own judgment, though it stand alone. Not that he deems himself infallible; too many mistakes in following trails prove the contrary; but he thinks that nature destines such sagacity as she has given him, as she destines it to the 'possum. To these fellow-beings of the wilds their untutored sagacity is their best dependence. If with either it prove faulty, if the 'possum's betray it to the trap, or the backwoodsman's mislead him into ambuscade, there are consequences to be undergone, but no self-blame. As with the 'possum, instincts prevail with the backwoodsman over precepts. Like the 'possum the backwoodsman presents the spectacle of a creature dwelling exclusively among the works of God, yet these, truth must confess, breed little in him of a godly mind. Small bowing and scraping is his, further than when with bent knee he points his rifle, or picks its flint. With few companions, solitude by necessity his lengthened lot, he stands the trial – no slight one, since, next to dying, solitude, rightly borne, is perhaps of fortitude the most rigorous test. But not merely is the backwoodsman content to be alone, but in no few cases is anxious to be so. The sight of smoke ten miles off is provocation to one more remove from man, one step deeper into nature. Is it that he feels that whatever man may be, man is not the universe? that glory, beauty, kindness, are not all engrossed by him? that as the presence of man frights birds away, so, many bird-like thoughts? Be that how it will, the backwoodsman is not without some fineness to his nature. Hairy Orson as he looks, it may be with him as with the Shetland seal – beneath the bristles lurks the fur.

'"Though held in a sort a barbarian, the backwoodsman would seem to America what Alexander was to Asia – captain in the vanguard of conquering civilization. Whatever the nation's growing opulence or power, does it not lackey his heels? Pathfinder, provider of security to those who come after him, for himself he asks nothing but hardship. Worthy to be compared with Moses in the Exodus, or the Emperor Julian in Gaul, who on foot, and bare-browed, at the head of covered or mounted legions, marched so through the elements, day after day. The tide of emigration, let it roll as it will, never overwhelms the backwoodsman into itself; he rides upon advance, as the Polynesian upon the comb of the surf.

'"Thus, though he keep moving on through life, he maintains with respect to nature much the same unaltered relation throughout; with her creatures, too, including panthers and Indians. Hence, it is not unlikely that, accurate as the theory of the Peace Congress may be with respect to those two varieties of beings, among others, yet the backwoodsman might be qualified to throw out some practical suggestions.

'"As the child born to a backwoodsman must in turn lead his father's life – a life which, as related to humanity, is related mainly to Indians – it is thought best not to mince matters, out of delicacy; but to tell the boy pretty plainly what an Indian is, and what he must expect from him. For however charitable it may be to view Indians as members of the Society of Friends, yet to affirm them such to one ignorant of Indians, whose lonely path lies a long way through their lands, this, in the event, might prove not only injudicious but cruel. At least something of this kind would seem the maxim upon which backwoods education is based. Accordingly, if in youth the backwoodsman incline to knowledge, as is generally the case, he hears little from his schoolmasters, the old chroniclers of the forest, but histories of Indian lying, Indian theft, Indian double-dealing, Indian fraud and perfidy, Indian want of conscience, Indian blood-thirstiness, Indian diabolism – histories which, though of wild woods, are almost as full of things unangelic as the Newgate Calendar or the Annals of Europe. In these Indian narratives and traditions the lad is thoroughly grounded. 'As the twig is bent the tree's inclined.' The instinct of antipathy against an Indian grows in the backwoodsman with the sense of good and bad, right and wrong. In one breath he learns that a brother is to be loved, and an Indian to be hated.

'"Such are the facts," the judge would say, "upon which, if one seek to moralize, he must do so with an eye to them. It is terrible that one creature should so regard another, should make it conscience to abhor an entire race. It is terrible; but is it surprising? Surprising, that one should hate a race which he believes to be red from a cause akin to that which makes some tribes of garden insects green? A race whose name is upon the frontier a *memento mori*; painted to him in every evil light; now a horse-thief like those in Moyamensing; now an assassin like a New York rowdy; now a treaty-breaker like an Austrian; now a Palmer with poisoned arrows; now a judicial murderer and Jeffries, after a fierce farce of trial condemning his victim to bloody death; or a Jew with hospitable speeches cozening some fainting stranger into ambuscade, there to burke him, and account it a deed grateful to Manitou, his god.

'"Still, all this is less advanced as truths of the Indians than as examples of the backwoodsman's impression of them – in which the charitable may think he does them some injustice. Certain it is, the Indians themselves think so; quite unanimously, too. The Indians, indeed, protest against the backwoodsman's view of them; and some think that one cause of their returning his antipathy so sincerely as they do, is their moral indignation at being so libelled by him, as they really believe and say. But whether, on this or any point, the Indians should be permitted to testify for themselves, to the exclusion of other testimony, is a question that may be left to the Supreme Court. At any rate, it has been observed that when an Indian becomes a genuine proselyte to Christianity (such cases, however, not being very many; though, indeed, entire tribes are sometimes nominally brought to the true light), he will not in that case conceal his enlightened conviction, that his race's portion by nature is total depravity; and, in that way, as much as admits that the backwoodsman's worst idea of it is not very far from true; while, on the other hand, those red men who are the greatest sticklers for the theory of Indian virtue, and Indian loving-kindness, are sometimes the arrantest horse-thieves and tomahawkers among them. So, at least, avers the backwoodsman. And though, knowing the Indian nature, as he thinks he does, he fancies he is not ignorant that an Indian may in some points deceive himself almost as effectually as in bush-tactics he can another, yet his theory and his practice as above contrasted seem to involve an inconsistency so extreme, that the backwoodsman only accounts for it on the supposition that when a tomahawking red man advances the notion of the benignity of the red race, it is but part and parcel of that subtle strategy which he finds so useful in war, in hunting, and the general conduct of life."

'In further explanation of that deep abhorrence with which the backwoodsman regards the savage, the judge used to think it might perhaps a little help, to consider what kind of stimulus to it is furnished in those forest histories and traditions before spoken of. In which behalf, he would tell the story of the little colony of Wrights and Weavers, originally seven cousins from Virginia, who, after successive removals with their families, at last established themselves near the southern frontier of the Bloody Ground, Kentucky: "They were strong, brave men; but, unlike many of the pioneers in those days, theirs was no love of conflict for conflict's sake. Step by step they had been lured to their lonely resting-place by the ever-beckoning seductions of a fertile and virgin land, with a singular exemption, during the march, from Indian molestation. But clearings made and houses built, the bright shield was soon to turn its other side. After repeated persecutions and eventual hostilities, forced on them by a dwindled tribe in their neighbourhood – persecutions resulting in loss of crops and cattle; hostilities in which they lost two of their number, ill to be spared, besides others getting painful wounds – the five remaining cousins made, with some serious concessions, a kind of treaty with Mocmohoc, the chief – being to this induced by the harryings of the enemy, leaving them no peace. But they were further prompted, indeed, first incited, by the suddenly changed ways of Mocmohoc, who, though hitherto deemed a savage almost perfidious as Caesar Borgia, yet now put on a seeming the reverse of this, engaging to bury the hatchet, smoke the pipe, and be friends for ever; not friends in the mere sense of renouncing enmity, but in the sense of kindliness, active and familiar.

'"But what the chief now seemed, did not wholly blind them to what the chief had been; so that, though in no small degree influenced by his change of bearing, they still distrusted him enough to covenant with him, among other articles on their side, that though friendly visits should be exchanged between the wigwams and the cabins, yet the five cousins should never, on any account, be expected to enter the chief's lodge together. The intention was, though they reserved it, that if ever, under the guise of amity, the chief should mean them mischief, and effect it, it should be but partially; so that some of the five might survive, not only for their families' sake, but also for retribution's. Nevertheless, Mocmohoc did, upon a time, with such fine art and pleasing carriage win their confidence, that he brought them all together to a feast of bear's meat, and there, by stratagem, ended them. Years after, over their calcined bones and those of all their families, the chief, reproached for his treachery by a proud hunter whom he had made captive, jeered out, 'Treachery? pale face! 'Twas they who broke their covenant first, in coming all together; they that broke it first, in trusting Mocmohoc.'"

'At this point the judge would pause, and lifting his hand, and rolling his eyes, exclaim in a solemn enough voice, "Circling wiles and bloody lusts. The acuteness and genius of the chief but make him the more atrocious."

'After another pause, he would begin an imaginary kind of dialogue between a backwoodsman and a questioner:

'"But are all Indians like Mocmohoc? – Not all have proved such; but in the least harmful may lie his germ. There is an Indian nature. 'Indian blood is in me,' is the half-breed's threat. – But are not some Indians kind? – Yes, but kind Indians are mostly lazy, and reputed simple – at all events, are seldom chiefs; chiefs among the red men being taken from the active, and those accounted wise. Hence, with small promotion, kind Indians have but proportionate influence. And kind Indians may be forced to do unkind biddings. So 'beware the Indian, kind or unkind,' said Daniel Boone, who lost his sons by them. – But, have all you backwoodsmen been some way victimized by Indians? – No. – Well, and in certain cases may not at least some few of you be favoured by them? – Yes, but scarce one among us so self-important, or so selfish-minded, as to hold his personal exemption from Indian outrage such a set-off against the contrary experience of so many others, as that he must needs, in a general way, think well of Indians; or, if he do, an arrow in his flank might suggest a pertinent doubt.

' "In short," according to the judge, "if we at all credit the backwoodsman, his feeling against Indians, to be taken aright, must be considered as being not so much on his own account as on others', or jointly on both accounts. True it is, scarce a family he knows but some member of it, or connection, has been by Indians maimed or scalped. What avails, then, that some one Indian, or some two or three, treat a backwoodsman friendly-like? He fears me, he thinks. Take my rifle from me, give him motive, and what will come? Or if not so, how know I what involuntary preparations may be going on in him for things as unbeknown in present time to him as me – a sort of chemical preparation in the soul for malice, as chemical preparation in the body for malady."

'Not that the backwoodsman ever used those words, you see, but the judge found him expression for his meaning. And this point he would conclude with saying, that, "What is called a 'friendly Indian' is a very rare sort of creature; and well it was so, for no ruthlessness exceeds that of a 'friendly Indian' turned enemy. A coward friend, he makes a valiant foe.

' "But, thus far the passion in question has been viewed in a general way as that of a community. When to his due share of this the backwoodsman adds his private passion, we have then the stock out of which is formed, if formed at all, the Indian-hater *par excellence*."

'The Indian-hater *par excellence* the judge defined to be one "who, having with his mother's milk drank in small love for red men, in youth or early manhood, ere the sensibilities become osseous, receives at their hand some signal outrage, or, which in effect is much the same, some of his kin have, or some friend. Now, nature all around him by her solitudes wooing or bidding

him muse upon this matter, he accordingly does so, till the
thought develops such attraction, that much as straggling vapours
troop from all sides to a storm-cloud, so straggling thoughts of
other outrages troop to the nucleus thought, assimilate with it,
and swell it. At last, taking counsel with the elements, he comes to
his resolution. An intenser Hannibal, he makes a vow, the hate of
which is a vortex from whose suction scarce the remotest chip of
the guilty race may reasonably feel secure. Next, he declares
himself and settles his temporal affairs. With the solemnity of a
Spaniard turned monk, he takes leave of his kin; or rather, these
leave-takings have something of the still more impressive finality
of death-bed adieus. Last, he commits himself to the forest pri-
meval; there, so long as life shall be his, to act upon a calm,
cloistered scheme of strategical, implacable, and lonesome vengeance. Ever on the noiseless trail; cool, collected, patient; less seen
than felt; snuffing, smelling – a Leather-stocking Nemesis. In the
settlements he will not be seen again; in eyes of old companions
tears may start at some chance thing that speaks of him; but they
never look for him, nor call; they know he will not come. Suns
and seasons fleet; the tiger-lily blows and falls; babes are born and
leap in their mothers' arms; but, the Indian-hater is good as gone
to his long home, and 'Terror' is his epitaph."

'Here the judge, not unaffected, would pause again, but
presently resume: "How evident that in strict speech there can be
no biography of an Indian-hater *par excellence*, any more than one
of a sword-fish, or other deep sea denizen; or, which is still less
imaginable, one of a dead man. The career of the Indian-hater *par
excellence* has the impenetrability of the fate of a lost steamer.
Doubtless, events, terrible ones, have happened, must have
happened; but the powers that be in nature have taken order that
they shall never become news.

'"But, luckily for the curious, there is a species of diluted
Indian-hater, one whose heart proves not so steely as his brain. Soft
enticements of domestic life too often draw him from the ascetic
trail; a monk who apostatizes to the world at times. Like a

mariner, too, though much abroad, he may have a wife and family in some green harbour which he does not forget. It is with him as with the Papist converts in Senegal; fasting and mortification prove hard to bear."

'The judge, with his usual judgment, always thought that the intense solitude to which the Indian-hater consigns himself, has, by its overawing influence, no little to do with relaxing his vow. He would relate instances where, after some months' lonely scoutings, the Indian-hater is suddenly seized with a sort of calenture; hurries openly towards the first smoke, though he knows it is an Indian's, announces himself as a lost hunter, gives the savage his rifle, throws himself upon his charity, embraces him with much affection, imploring the privilege of living a while in his sweet companionship. What is too often the sequel of so distempered a procedure may be best known by those who best know the Indian. Upon the whole, the judge, by two and thirty good and sufficient reasons, would maintain that there was no known vocation whose consistent following calls for such self-containings as that of the Indian-hater *par excellence*. In the highest view, he considered such a soul one peeping out but once an age.

'For the diluted Indian-hater, although the vacations he permits himself impair the keeping of the character, yet, it should not be overlooked that this is the man who, by his very infirmity, enables us to form surmises, however inadequate, of what Indian-hating in its perfection is.'

'One moment,' gently interrupted the cosmopolitan here, 'and let me refill my calumet.'

Which being done, the other proceeded:—

27

SOME ACCOUNT OF A MAN OF QUESTIONABLE MORALITY, BUT WHO, NEVERTHELESS, WOULD SEEM ENTITLED TO THE ESTEEM OF THAT EMINENT ENGLISH MORALIST WHO SAID HE LIKED A GOOD HATER

'Coming to mention the man to whose story all thus far said was but the introduction, the judge, who, like you, was a great smoker, would insist upon all the company taking cigars, and then lighting a fresh one himself, rise in his place, and, with the solemnest voice, say – "Gentlemen, let us smoke to the memory of Colonel John Moredock"; when, after several whiffs taken standing in deep silence and deeper reverie, he would resume his seat and his discourse, something in these words:

'"Though Colonel John Moredock was not an Indian-hater *par excellence*, he yet cherished a kind of sentiment towards the red man, and in that degree, and so acted out his sentiment as sufficiently to merit the tribute just rendered to his memory.

'"John Moredock was the son of a woman married thrice, and thrice widowed by a tomahawk. The three successive husbands of this woman had been pioneers, and with them she had wandered from wilderness to wilderness, always on the frontier. With nine children, she at last found herself at a little clearing, afterwards Vincennes. There she joined a company about to remove to the new country of Illinois. On the eastern side of Illinois there were then no settlements; but on the west side, the shore of the Mississippi, there were, near the mouth of the Kaskaskia, some old hamlets of French. To the vicinity of those hamlets, very innocent and pleasant places, a new Arcadia, Mrs Moredock's party was

destined; for thereabouts, among the vines, they meant to settle.
They embarked upon the Wabash in boats, proposing to descend
that stream into the Ohio, and the Ohio into the Mississippi, and
so, northwards, towards the point to be reached. All went well till
they made the rock of the Grand Tower on the Mississippi, where
they had to land and drag their boats round a point swept by a
strong current. Here a party of Indians, lying in wait, rushed out
and murdered nearly all of them. The widow was among the
victims with her children, John excepted, who, some fifty miles
distant, was following with a second party.

'"He was just entering upon manhood, when thus left in nature
sole survivor of his race. Other youngsters might have turned
mourners; he turned avenger. His nerves were electric wires –
sensitive, but steel. He was one who, from self-possession, could
be made neither to flush nor pale. It is said that when the tidings
were brought him, he was ashore sitting beneath a hemlock
eating his dinner of venison – and as the tidings were told him,
after the first start he kept on eating, but slowly and deliberately,
chewing the wild news with the wild meat, as if both together,
turned to chyle, together should sinew him to his intent. From
that meal he rose an Indian-hater. He rose; got his arms, prevailed
upon some comrades to join him, and without delay started to
discover who were the actual transgressors. They proved to belong
to a band of twenty renegades from various tribes, outlaws even
among Indians, and who had formed themselves into a marauding
crew. No opportunity for action being at the time presented, he
dismissed his friends; told them to go on, thanking them, and
saying he would ask their aid at some future day. For upwards of
a year, alone in the wilds, he watched the crew. Once, what he
thought a favourable chance having occurred – it being mid-
winter, and the savages encamped, apparently to remain so – he
anew mustered his friends, and marched against them; but, getting
wind of his coming, the enemy fled, and in such panic that
everything was left behind but their weapons. During the winter,
much the same thing happened upon two subsequent occasions.
The next year he sought them at the head of a party pledged to

serve him for forty days. At last the hour came. It was on the shore of the Mississippi. From their covert, Moredock and his men dimly descried the gang of Cains in the red dusk of evening, paddling over to a jungled island in mid-stream, there the more securely to lodge; for Moredock's retributive spirit in the wilderness spoke ever to their trepidations now, like the voice calling through the garden. Waiting until dead of night, the whites swam the river, towing after them a raft laden with their arms. On landing, Moredock cut the fastenings of the enemy's canoes, and turned them, with his own raft, adrift; resolved that there should be neither escape for the Indians, nor safety, except in victory, for the whites. Victorious the whites were; but three of the Indians saved themselves by taking to the stream. Moredock's band lost not a man.

'"Three of the murderers survived. He knew their names and persons. In the course of three years each successively fell by his own hand. All were now dead. But this did not suffice. He made no avowal, but to kill Indians had become his passion. As an athlete, he had few equals; as a shot, none; in single combat, not to be beaten. Master of that woodland-cunning enabling the adept to subsist where the tyro would perish, and expert in all those arts by which an enemy is pursued for weeks, perhaps months, without once suspecting it, he kept to the forest. The solitary Indian that met him, died. When a number was descried, he would either secretly pursue their track for some chance to strike at least one blow; or if, while thus engaged, he himself was discovered, he would elude them by superior skill.

'"Many years he spent thus; and though after a time he was, in a degree, restored to the ordinary life of the region and period, yet it is believed that John Moredock never let pass an opportunity of quenching an Indian. Sins of commission in that kind may have been his, but none of omission.

'"It were to err to suppose," the judge would say, "that this gentleman was naturally ferocious, or peculiarly possessed of those qualities which, unhelped by provocation of events, tend to

withdraw man from social life. On the contrary, Moredock was
an example of something apparently self-contradicting, certainly
curious, but, at the same time, undeniable: namely, that nearly all
Indian-haters have at bottom loving hearts; at any rate, hearts, if
anything, more generous than the average. Certain it is that, to
the degree in which he mingled in the life of the settlements,
Moredock showed himself not without humane feelings. No cold
husband or colder father, he; and, though often and long away
from his household, bore its needs in mind, and provided for
them. He could be very convivial; told a good story (though
never of his more private exploits), and sung a capital song.
Hospitable, not backward to help a neighbour; by report, benevolent, as retributive in secret; while, in a general manner, though
sometimes grave – as is not unusual with men of his complexion,
a sultry and tragical brown – yet with nobody, Indians excepted,
otherwise than courteous in a manly fashion; a moccasined gentleman, admired and loved. In fact, no one more popular, as an
incident to follow may prove.

'"His bravery, whether in Indian fight or any other, was
unquestionable. An officer in the ranging service during the war
of 1812, he acquitted himself with more than credit. Of his
soldierly character, this anecdote is told: Not long after Hull's
dubious surrender at Detroit, Moredock with some of his rangers
rode up at night to a log-house, there to rest till morning. The
horses being attended to, supper over, and sleeping-places assigned
the troop, the host showed the colonel his best bed, not on the
ground like the rest, but a bed that stood on legs. But out of
delicacy, the guest declined to monopolize it, or, indeed, to
occupy it at all; when, to increase the inducement, as the host
thought, he was told that a general officer had once slept in that
bed. 'Who, pray?' asked the colonel. 'General Hull.' 'Then you
must not take offence,' said the colonel, buttoning up his coat,
'but, really, no coward's bed for me, however comfortable.'
Accordingly he took up with valour's bed – a cold one on the
ground.

'"At one time the colonel was a member of the territorial council of Illinois, and at the formation of the state government, was pressed to become candidate for governor, but begged to be excused. And, though he declined to give his reasons for declining, yet by those who best knew him the cause was not wholly unsurmised. In his official capacity he might be called upon to enter into friendly treaties with Indian tribes, a thing not to be thought of. And even did no such contingency arise, yet he felt there would be an impropriety in the Governor of Illinois stealing out now and then, during a recess of the legislative bodies, for a few days' shooting at human beings, within the limits of his paternal chief-magistracy. If the governorship offered large honours, from Moredock it demanded larger sacrifices. These were incompatibles. In short, he was not unaware that to be a consistent Indian-hater involves the renunciation of ambition, with its objects – the pomps and glories of the world; and since religion, pronouncing such things vanities, accounts it merit to renounce them, therefore, so far as this goes, Indian-hating, whatever may be thought of it in other respects, may be regarded as not wholly without the efficacy of a devout sentiment."'

Here the narrator paused. Then, after his long and irksome sitting, started to his feet, and regulating his disordered shirt-frill, and at the same time adjustingly shaking his legs down in his rumpled pantaloons, concluded: 'There, I have done; having given you, not my story, mind, or my thoughts, but another's. And now, for your friend Coonskins, I doubt not, that, if the judge were here, he would pronounce him a sort of comprehensive Colonel Moredock, who, too much spreading his passion, shallows it.'

28

MOOT POINTS TOUCHING THE LATE COLONEL
JOHN MOREDOCK

'Charity, charity!' exclaimed the cosmopolitan, 'never a sound judgment without charity. When man judges man, charity is less a bounty from our mercy than just allowance for the insensible lee-way of human fallibility. God forbid that my eccentric friend should be what you hint. You do not know him, or but imperfectly. His outside deceived you; at first it came near deceiving even me. But I seized a chance, when, owing to indignation against some wrong, he laid himself a little open; I seized that lucky chance, I say, to inspect his heart, and found it an inviting oyster in a forbidding shell. His outside is but put on. Ashamed of his own goodness, he treats mankind as those strange old uncles in romances do their nephews – snapping at them all the time and yet loving them as the apple of their eye.'

'Well, my words with him were few. Perhaps he is not what I took him for. Yes, for aught I know, you may be right.'

'Glad to hear it. Charity, like poetry, should be cultivated, if only for its being graceful. And now, since you have renounced your notion, I should be happy would you, so to speak, renounce your story, too. That story strikes me with even more incredulity than wonder. To me some parts don't hang together. If the man of hate, how could John Moredock be also the man of love? Either his lone campaigns are fabulous as Hercules'; or else, those being true, what was thrown in about his geniality is but garnish. In short, if ever there was such a man as Moredock, he, in my way of thinking, was either misanthrope or nothing; and his misanthropy the more intense from being focused on one race of men. Though, like suicide, man-hatred would seem peculiarly a Roman and a Grecian passion – that is, Pagan; yet, the annals of neither Rome nor Greece can produce the equal in man-hatred of Colonel Moredock, as the judge and you have painted him. As for this Indian-hating in general, I can only say of it what Dr Johnson said of the alleged Lisbon earthquake: "Sir, I don't believe it." '

'Didn't believe it? Why not? Clashed with any little prejudice of his?'

'Dr Johnson had no prejudice; but, like a certain other person,' with an ingenuous smile, 'he had sensibilities, and those were pained.'

'Dr Johnson was a good Christian, wasn't he?'

'He was.'

'Suppose he had been something else?'

'Then small incredulity as to the alleged earthquake.'

'Suppose he had been also a misanthrope?'

'Then small incredulity as to the robberies and murders alleged to have been perpetrated under the pall of smoke and ashes. The infidels of the time were quick to credit those reports and worse. So true it is that, while religion, contrary to the common notion, implies, in certain cases, a spirit of slow reserve as to assent, infidelity, which claims to despise credulity, is sometimes swift to it.'

'You rather jumble together misanthropy and infidelity.'

'I do not jumble them; they are coordinates. For misanthropy, springing from the same root with disbelief of religion, is twin with that. It springs from the same root, I say; for, set aside materialism, and what is an atheist, but one who does not, or will not, see in the universe a ruling principle of love; and what a misanthrope, but one who does not, or will not, see in man a ruling principle of kindness? Don't you see? In either case the vice consists in a want of confidence.'

'What sort of a sensation is misanthropy?'

'Might as well ask me what sort of sensation is hydrophobia.

Don't know; never had it. But I have often wondered what it can be like. Can a misanthrope feel warm, I ask myself; take ease? be companionable with himself? Can a misanthrope smoke a cigar and muse? How fares he in solitude? Has the misanthrope such a thing as an appetite? Shall a peach refresh him? The effervescence of champagne, with what eye does he behold it? Is summer good to him? Of long winters how much can he sleep? What are his dreams? How feels he, and what does he, when suddenly awakened, alone, at dead of night, by fusilades of thunder?'

'Like you,' said the stranger, 'I can't understand the misanthrope. So far as my experience goes, either mankind is worthy one's best love, or else I have been lucky. Never has it been my lot to have been wronged, though but in the smallest degree. Cheating, back-biting, superciliousness, disdain, hard-heartedness, and all that brood, I know but by report. Cold regards tossed over the sinister shoulder of a former friend, ingratitude in a beneficiary, treachery in a confidant − such things may be; but I must take somebody's word for it. Now the bridge that has carried me so well over, shall I not praise it?'

'Ingratitude to the worthy bridge not to do so. Man is a noble fellow, and in an age of satirists, I am not displeased to find one who has confidence in him, and bravely stands up for him.'

'Yes, I always speak a good word for man; and what is more, am always ready to do a good deed for him.'

'You are a man after my own heart,' responded the cosmopolitan, with a candour which lost nothing by its calmness. 'Indeed,' he added, 'our sentiments agree so, that were they written in a book, whose was whose, few but the nicest critics might determine.'

'Since we are thus joined in mind,' said the stranger, 'why not be joined in hand?'

'My hand is always at the service of virtue,' frankly extending it to him as to virtue personified.

'And now,' said the stranger, cordially retaining his hand, 'you know our fashion here at the West. It may be a little low, but it is kind. Briefly, we being newly-made friends must drink together. What say you?'

'Thank you; but indeed, you must excuse me.'

'Why?'

'Because, to tell the truth, I have to-day met so many old friends, all free-hearted, convivial gentlemen, that really, really, though for the present I succeed in mastering it, I am at bottom almost in the condition of a sailor who, stepping ashore after a long voyage, ere night reels with loving welcomes, his head of less capacity than his heart.'

At the allusion to old friends, the stranger's countenance a little fell, as a jealous lover's might at hearing from his sweetheart of former ones. But rallying, he said: 'No doubt they treated you to something strong; but wine – surely, that gentle creature, wine; come, let us have a little gentle wine at one of these little tables here. Come, come.' Then essaying to roll about like a full pipe in the sea, sang in a voice which had had more of good-fellowship, had there been less of a latent squeak to it:

> 'Let us drink of the wine of the vine benign,
> That sparkles warm in Sansovine.'

The cosmopolitan, with longing eye upon him, stood as sorely tempted and wavering a moment; then, abruptly stepping towards him, with a look of dissolved surrender, said: 'When mermaid songs move figure-heads, then may glory, gold, and women try their blandishments on me. But a good fellow, singing a good song, he woos forth my every spike, so that my whole hull, like a ship's, sailing by a magnetic rock, caves in with acquiescence. Enough: when one has a heart of a certain sort, it is in vain trying to be resolute.'

29

THE BOON COMPANIONS

━━◆━◆━◆━━

The wine, port, being called for, and the two seated at the little table, a natural pause of convivial expectancy ensued; the stranger's eye turned towards the bar near by, watching the red-cheeked, white-aproned man there, blithely dusting the bottle, and invitingly arranging the salver and glasses; when, with a sudden impulse turning round his head towards his companion, he said, 'Ours is friendship at first sight, ain't it?'

'It is,' was the placidly pleased reply: 'and the same may be said of friendship at first sight as of love at first sight: it is the only true one, the only noble one. It bespeaks confidence. Who would go sounding his way into love or friendship, like a strange ship by night, into an enemy's harbour?'

'Right. Boldly in before the wind. Agreeable, how we always agree. By-the-way, though but a formality, friends should know each other's names. What is yours, pray?'

'Francis Goodman. But those who love me call me Frank. And yours?'

'Charles Arnold Noble. But do you call me Charlie.'

'I will, Charlie; nothing like preserving in manhood the fraternal familiarities of youth. It proves the heart a rosy boy to the last.'

'My sentiments again. Ah!'

It was a smiling waiter, with the smiling bottle, the cork drawn; a common quart bottle, but for the occasion fitted at bottom into a little bark basket, braided with porcupine quills, gaily tinted in the Indian fashion. This being set before the entertainer, he regarded it with affectionate interest, but seemed not to understand, or else to pretend not to, a handsome red label pasted on the bottle, bearing the capital letters, P.W.

'P.W.,' said he at last, perplexedly eyeing the pleasing poser, 'now what does P.W. mean?'

'Shouldn't wonder,' said the cosmopolitan gravely, 'if it stood for port wine. You called for port wine, didn't you?'

'Why so it is, so it is!'

'I find some little mysteries not very hard to clear up,' said the other, quietly crossing his legs.

This commonplace seemed to escape the stranger's hearing, for, full of his bottle, he now rubbed his somewhat sallow hands over it, and with a strange kind of cackle, meant to be a chirrup, cried: 'Good wine, good wine; is it not the peculiar bond of good feeling?' Then brimming both glasses, pushed one over, saying, with what seemed intended for an air of fine disdain: 'Ill betide those gloomy sceptics who maintain that now-a-days pure wine is unpurchasable; that almost every variety on sale is less the vintage of vineyards than laboratories; that most bar-keepers are but a set of male Brinvillierses, with complaisant arts practising against the lives of their best friends, their customers.'

A shade passed over the cosmopolitan. After a few minutes' down-cast musing, he lifted his eyes and said: 'I have long thought, my dear Charlie, that the spirit in which wine is regarded by too many in these days is one of the most painful examples of want of confidence. Look at these glasses. He who could mistrust poison in this wine would mistrust consumption in Hebe's cheek. While, as for suspicions against the dealers in wine and sellers of it, those who cherish such suspicions can have but limited trust in the human heart. Each human heart they must think to be much like each bottle of port, not such port as this, but such port as they hold to. Strange traducers, who see good faith in nothing, however sacred. Not medicines, not the wine in sacraments, has escaped them. The doctor with his phial, and the priest with his chalice, they deem equally the unconscious dispensers of bogus cordials to the dying.'

'Dreadful!'

'Dreadful indeed,' said the cosmopolitan solemnly. 'These distrusters stab at the very soul of confidence. If this wine,' impressively holding up his full glass, 'if this wine with its bright promise be not true, how shall man be, whose promise can be no brighter? But if wine be false, while men are true, whither shall fly convivial geniality? To think of sincerely-genial souls drinking each other's health at unawares in perfidious and murderous drugs!'

'Horrible!'

'Much too much so to be true, Charlie. Let us forget it. Come, you are my entertainer on this occasion, and yet you don't pledge me. I have been waiting for it.'

'Pardon, pardon,' half confusedly and half ostentatiously lifting his glass. 'I pledge you, Frank, with my whole heart, believe me,' taking a draught too decorous to be large, but which, small though it was, was followed by a slight involuntary wryness to the mouth.

'And I return you the pledge, Charlie, heart-warm as it came to me, and honest as this wine I drink it in,' reciprocated the cosmopolitan with princely kindliness in his gesture, taking a generous swallow, concluding in a smack, which, though audible, was not so much so as to be unpleasing.

'Talking of alleged spuriousness of wines,' said he, tranquilly setting down his glass, and then sloping back his head and with friendly fixedness eyeing the wine, 'perhaps the strangest part of those allegings is, that there is, as claimed, a kind of man who, while convinced that on this continent most wines are shams, yet still drinks away at them; accounting wine so fine a thing, that even the sham article is better than none at all. And if the temperance people urge that, by this course, he will sooner or later be undermined in health, he answers, "And do you think I don't know that? But health without cheer I hold a bore; and cheer, even of the spurious sort, has its price, which I am willing to pay."'

'Such a man, Frank, must have a disposition ungovernably bac-chanalian.'

'Yes, if such a man there be, which I don't credit. It is a fable, but a fable from which I once heard a person of less genius than grotesqueness draw a moral even more extravagant than the fable itself. He said that it illustrated, as in a parable, how that a man of a disposition ungovernably good-natured might still familiarly associate with men, though, at the same time, he believed the greater part of men false-hearted – accounting society so sweet a thing that even the spurious sort was better than none at all. And if the Rochefoucaultites urge that, by this course, he will sooner or later be undermined in security, he answers, "And do you think I don't know that? But security without society I hold a bore; and society, even of the spurious sort, has its price, which I am willing to pay."'

'A most singular theory,' said the stranger with a slight fidget, eyeing his companion with some inquisitiveness, 'indeed, Frank, a most slanderous thought,' he exclaimed in sudden heat and with an involuntary look almost of being personally aggrieved.

'In one sense it merits all you say, and more,' rejoined the other with wonted mildness, 'but, for a kind of drollery in it, charity might, perhaps, overlook something of the wickedness. Humour is, in fact, so blessed a thing, that even in the least virtuous product of the human mind, if there can be found but nine good jokes, some philosophers are clement enough to affirm that those nine good jokes should redeem all the wicked thoughts, though plenty as the populace of Sodom. At any rate, this same humour has something, there is no telling what, of beneficence in it, it is such a catholicon and charm – nearly all men agreeing in relishing it, though they may agree in little else – and in its way it undeniably does such a deal of familiar good in the world, that no wonder it is almost a proverb, that a man of humour, a man capable of a good loud laugh – seem how he may in other things – can hardly be a heartless scamp.'

'Ha, ha, ha!' laughed the other, pointing to the figure of a pale

pauper-boy on the deck below, whose pitiableness was touched, as
it were, with ludicrousness by a pair of monstrous boots, apparently some mason's discarded ones, cracked with drouth, half
eaten by lime, and curled up about the toe like a bassoon. 'Look –
ha, ha, ha!'

'I see,' said the other, with what seemed quiet appreciation, but
of a kind expressing an eye to the grotesque, without blindness to
what in this case accompanied it, 'I see; and the way in which it
moves you, Charlie, comes in very apropos to point the proverb I
was speaking of. Indeed, had you intended this effect, it could not
have been more so. For who that heard that laugh, but would as
naturally argue from it a sound heart as sound lungs? True, it is
said that a man may smile, and smile, and smile, and be a villain;
but it is not said that a man may laugh, and laugh, and laugh, and
be one, is it, Charlie?'

'Ha, ha, ha! – no no, no no.'

'Why Charlie, your explosions illustrate my remarks almost as
aptly as the chemist's imitation volcano did his lectures. But even
if experience did not sanction the proverb, that a good laugher
cannot be a bad man, I should yet feel bound in confidence to
believe it, since it is a saying current among the people, and I
doubt not originated among them, and hence *must* be true; for the
voice of the people is the voice of truth. Don't you think so?'

'Of course I do. If Truth don't speak through the people, it
never speaks at all; so I heard one say.'

'A true saying. But we stray. The popular notion of humour,
considered as index to the heart, would seem curiously confirmed
by Aristotle – I think, in his "Politics" (a work, by-the-by, which,
however it may be viewed upon the whole, yet, from the tenor of
certain sections, should not, without precaution, be placed in the
hands of youth) – who remarks that the least lovable men in
history seem to have had for humour not only a disrelish, but a
hatred; and this, in some cases, along with an extraordinary dry
taste for practical punning. I remember it is related of Phalaris, the
capricious tyrant of Sicily, that he once caused a poor fellow to be

beheaded on a horse-block, for no other cause than having a
horse-laugh.'

'Funny Phalaris!'

'Cruel Phalaris!'

As after fire-crackers, there was a pause, both looking downward on the table as if mutually struck by the contrast of exclamations, and pondering upon its significance, if any. So, at least, it
seemed; but on one side it might have been otherwise; for presently
glancing up, the cosmopolitan said: 'In the instance of the moral,
drolly cynic, drawn from the queer bacchanalian fellow we were
speaking of, who had his reasons for still drinking spurious wine,
though knowing it to be such – there, I say, we have an example
of what is certainly a wicked thought, but conceived in humour. I
will now give you one of a wicked thought conceived in wickedness. You shall compare the two, and answer, whether in the
one case the sting is not neutralized by the humour, and whether
in the other the absence of humour does not leave the sting free
play. I once heard a wit, a mere wit, mind, an irreligious Parisian
wit, say, with regard to the temperance movement, that none, to
their personal benefit, joined it sooner than niggards and knaves;
because, as he affirmed, the one by it saved money and the other
made money, as in ship-owners cutting off the spirit ration
without giving its equivalent, and gamblers and all sorts of subtle
tricksters sticking to cold water, the better to keep a cool head for
business.'

'A wicked thought, indeed!' cried the stranger, feelingly.

'Yes,' leaning over the table on his elbow and genially gesturing
at him with his forefinger: 'yes, and, as I said, you don't remark
the sting of it?'

'I do, indeed. Most calumnious thought, Frank!'

'No humour in it?'

'Not a bit!'

'Well now, Charlie,' eyeing him with moist regard, 'let us
drink. It appears to me you don't drink freely.'

'Oh, oh – indeed, indeed – I am not backward there. I protest, a freer drinker than friend Charlie you will find nowhere,' with feverish zeal snatching his glass, but only in the sequel to dally with it. 'By-the-way, Frank,' said he, perhaps, or perhaps not, to draw attention from himself, 'by-the-way, I saw a good thing the other day; capital thing; a panegyric on the press. It pleased me so, I got it by heart at two readings. It is a kind of poetry, but in a form which stands in something the same relation to blank verse which that does to rhyme. A sort of free-and-easy chant with refrains to it. Shall I recite it?'

'Anything in praise of the press I shall be happy to hear,' rejoined the cosmopolitan, 'the more so,' he gravely proceeded, 'as of late I have observed in some quarters a disposition to disparage the press.'

'Disparage the press?'

'Even so; some gloomy souls affirming that it is proving with that great invention as with brandy or eau-de-vie, which, upon its first discovery, was believed by the doctors to be, as its French name implies, a panacea – a notion which experience, it may be thought, has not fully verified.'

'You surprise me, Frank. Are there really those who so decry the press? Tell me more. Their reasons.'

'Reasons they have none, but affirmations they have many; among other things affirming that, while under dynastic despotisms, the press is to the people little but an improvisatore, under popular ones it is too apt to be their Jack Cade. In fine, these sour sages regard the press in the light of a Colt's revolver, pledged to no cause but his in whose chance hands it may be; deeming the one invention an improvement upon the pen, much akin to what the other is upon the pistol; involving along with the multiplication of the barrel, no consecration of the aim. The term "freedom of the press" they consider on a par with *freedom of Colt's revolver*. Hence, for truth and the right, they hold, to indulge hopes from the one is little more sensible than for Kossuth and Mazzini to indulge hopes from the other. Heart-breaking views enough, you think; but their refutation is in every true reformer's contempt. Is it not so?'

'Without doubt. But go on, go on. I like to hear you,' flatteringly brimming up his glass for him.

'For one,' continued the cosmopolitan, grandly swelling his chest, 'I hold the press to be neither the people's improvisatore, nor Jack Cade; neither their paid fool, nor conceited drudge. I think interest never prevails with it over duty. The press still speaks for truth though impaled, in the teeth of lies though intrenched. Disdaining for it the poor name of cheap diffuser of news, I claim for it the independent apostleship of Advancer of Knowledge – the iron Paul! Paul, I say; for not only does the press advance knowledge, but righteousness. In the press, as in the sun, resides, my dear Charlie, a dedicated principle of beneficent force and light. For the Satanic press, by its coappearance with the apostolic, it is no more an aspersion to that, than to the true sun is the coappearance of the mock one. For all the baleful-looking parhelion, god Apollo dispenses the day. In a word, Charlie, what the sovereign of England is titularly, I hold the press to be actually – Defender of the Faith! – defender of the faith in the final triumph of truth over error, metaphysics over superstition, theory over falsehood, machinery over nature, and the good man over the bad. Such are my views, which, if stated at some length, you, Charlie, must pardon, for it is a theme upon which I cannot speak with cold brevity. And now I am impatient for your panegyric, which, I doubt not, will put mine to the blush.'

'It is rather in the blush-giving vein,' smiled the other; 'but such as it is, Frank, you shall have it.'

'Tell me when you are about to begin,' said the cosmopolitan, 'for, when at public dinners the press is toasted, I always drink the toast standing, and shall stand while you pronounce the panegyric.'

'Very good, Frank; you may stand up now.'

He accordingly did so, when the stranger likewise rose, and uplifting the ruby wine-flask began.

30

OPENING WITH A POETICAL EULOGY OF THE PRESS, AND CONTINUING WITH TALK INSPIRED BY THE SAME

━━━━◼◼━━━━

'"Praise be unto the press, not Faust's, but Noah's; let us extol and magnify the press, the true press of Noah, from which breaketh the true morning. Praise be unto the press, not the black press but the red; let us extol and magnify the press, the red press of Noah, from which cometh inspiration. Ye pressmen of the Rhineland and the Rhine, join in with all ye who tread out the glad tidings on isle Madeira or Mitylene. – Who giveth redness of eyes by making men long to tarry at the fine print? – Praise be unto the press, the rosy press of Noah, which giveth rosiness of hearts, by making men long to tarry at the rosy wine. – Who hath babblings and contentions? Who, without cause, inflicteth wounds? Praise be unto the press, the kindly press of Noah, which knitteth friends, which fuseth foes. – Who may be bribed? – Who may be bound? – Praise be unto the press, the free press of Noah, which will not lie for tyrants, but make tyrants speak the truth. – Then praise be unto the press, the frank old press of Noah; then let us extol and magnify the press, the brave old press of Noah; then let us with roses garland and enwreath the press, the grand old press of Noah, from which flow streams of knowledge which give man a bliss no more unreal than his pain."'

'You deceived me,' smiled the cosmopolitan, as both now resumed their seats; 'you roguishly took advantage of my simplicity; you archly played upon my enthusiasm. But never mind; the offence, if any, was so charming, I almost wish you would offend again. As for certain poetic left-handers in your panegyric, those I cheerfully concede to the indefinite privileges of the poet.

Upon the whole, it was quite in the lyric style – a style I always admire on account of that spirit of Sibyllic confidence and assurance which is, perhaps, its prime ingredient. But come,' glancing at his companion's glass, 'for a lyrist, you let the bottle stay with you too long.'

'The lyre and the vine for ever!' cried the other in his rapture, or what seemed such, heedless of the hint, 'the vine, the vine! is it not the most graceful and bounteous of all growths? And, by its being such, is not something meant – divinely meant? As I live, a vine, a Catawba vine, shall be planted on my grave!'

'A genial thought; but your glass there.'

'Oh, oh,' taking a moderate sip, 'but you, why don't you drink?'

'You have forgotten, my dear Charlie, what I told you of my previous convivialities to-day.'

'Oh,' cried the other, now in manner quite abandoned to the lyric mood, not without contrast to the easy sociability of his companion. 'Oh, one can't drink too much of good old wine – the genuine, mellow old port. Pooh, pooh! drink away.'

'Then keep me company.'

'Of course,' with a flourish, taking another sip – 'suppose we have cigars. Never mind your pipe there; a pipe is best when alone. I say, waiter, bring some cigars – your best.'

They were brought in a pretty little bit of western pottery, representing some kind of Indian utensil, mummy-coloured, set down in a mass of tobacco leaves, whose long, green fans, fancifully grouped, formed with peeps of red the sides of the receptacle.

Accompanying it were two accessories, also bits of pottery, but smaller, both globes; one in guise of an apple flushed with red and gold to the life, and, through a cleft at top, you saw it was hollow. This was for the ashes. The other, gray, with wrinkled surface. in the likeness of a wasp's nest, was the match-box.

'There,' said the stranger, pushing over the cigar-stand, 'help yourself, and I will touch you off,' taking a match. 'Nothing like tobacco,' he added, when the fumes of the cigar began to wreathe, glancing from the smoker to the pottery, 'I will have a Virginia tobacco-plant set over my grave beside the Catawba vine.'

'Improvement upon your first idea, which by itself was good – but you don't smoke.'

'Presently, presently – let me fill your glass again. You don't drink.'

'Thank you; but no more just now. Fill *your* glass.'

'Presently, presently; do you drink on. Never mind me. Now that it strikes me, let me say, that he who, out of superfine gentility or fanatic morality, denies himself tobacco, suffers a more serious abatement in the cheap pleasures of life than the dandy in his iron boot, or the celibate on his iron cot. While for him who would fain revel in tobacco, but cannot, it is a thing at which philanthropists must weep, to see such an one, again and again, madly returning to the cigar, which, for his incompetent stomach, he cannot enjoy, while still, after each shameful repulse, the sweet dream of the impossible good goads him on to his fierce misery once more – poor eunuch!'

'I agree with you,' said the cosmopolitan, still gravely social, 'but you don't smoke.'

'Presently, presently, do you smoke on. As I was saying about –'

'But *why* don't you smoke – come. You don't think that tobacco, when in league with wine, too much enhances the latter's vinous quality – in short, with certain constitutions tends to impair self-possession, do you?'

'To think that, were treason to good fellowship,' was the warm disclaimer. 'No, no. But the fact is, there is an unpropitious flavour in my mouth just now. Ate of a diabolical ragout at dinner, so I shan't smoke till I have washed away the lingering memento of it with wine. But smoke away, you, and pray, don't forget to drink. By-the-way, while we sit here so companionably, giving loose to any companionable nothing, your uncompanion-able friend, Coonskins, is, by pure contrast, brought to recollection. If he were but here now, he would see how much of real heart-joy he denies himself by not hob-a-nobbing with his kind.'

'Why,' with loitering emphasis, slowly withdrawing his cigar, 'I thought I had undeceived you there. I thought you had come to a better understanding of my eccentric friend.'

'Well, I thought so, too; but first impressions will return, you know. In truth, now that I think of it, I am led to conjecture from chance things, which dropped from Coonskins, during the little interview I had with him, that he is not a Missourian by birth, but years ago came West here, a young misanthrope from the other side of the Alleghenies, less to make his fortune, than to flee man. Now, since they say trifles sometimes effect great results, I shouldn't wonder, if his history were probed, it would be found that what first indirectly gave his sad bias to Coonskins was his disgust at reading in boyhood the advice of Polonius to Laertes – advice which, in the selfishness it inculcates, is almost on a par with a sort of ballad upon the economies of money-making, to be occasionally seen pasted against the desk of small retail traders in New England.'

'I do hope now, my dear fellow,' said the cosmopolitan with an air of bland protest, 'that, in my presence at least, you will throw out nothing to the prejudice of the sons of the Puritans.'

'Hey-day and high times indeed,' exclaimed the other, nettled, 'sons of the Puritans forsooth! And who be Puritans, that I, an Alabamaian, must do them reverence? A set of sourly conceited old Malvolios, whom Shakespeare laughs his fill at in his comedies.'

'Pray, what were you about to suggest with regard to Polonius,' observed the cosmopolitan with quiet forbearance, expressive of the patience of a superior mind at the petulance of an inferior one; 'how do you characterize his advice to Laertes?'

'As false, fatal, and calumnious,' exclaimed the other, with a degree of ardour befitting one resenting a stigma upon the family escutcheon, 'and for a father to give his son – monstrous. The case you see is this: The son is going abroad, and for the first time.

What does the father? Invoke God's blessing upon him? Put the blessed Bible in his trunk? No. Crams him with maxims smacking of my lord Chesterfield, with maxims of France, with maxims of Italy.'

'No, no, be charitable, not that. Why, does he not among other things say:

> "The friends thou hast, and their adoption tried,
> Grapple them to thy soul with hooks of steel"?

Is that compatible with maxims of Italy?'

'Yes it is, Frank. Don't you see? Laertes is to take the best of care of his friends – his proved friends, on the same principle that a wine-corker takes the best of care of his proved bottles. When a bottle gets a sharp knock and don't break, he says, "Ah, I'll keep that bottle." Why? Because he loves it? No, he has particular use for it.'

'Dear, dear!' appealingly turning in distress, 'that – that kind of criticism is – is – in fact – it won't do.'

'Won't truth do, Frank? You are so charitable with everybody, do but consider the tone of the speech. Now I put it to you, Frank; is there anything in it hortatory to high, heroic, dis-interested effort? Anything like "sell all thou hast and give to the poor"? And, in other points, what desire seems most in the father's mind, that his son should cherish nobleness for himself, or be on his guard against the contrary thing in others? An irreligious warner, Frank – no devout counsellor, is Polonius. I hate him. Nor can I bear to hear your veterans of the world affirm, that he who steers through life by the advice of old Polonius will not steer among the breakers.'

'No, no – I hope nobody affirms that,' rejoined the cos-mopolitan, with tranquil abandonment; sideways reposing his arm at full length upon the table. 'I hope nobody affirms that; because, if Polonius' advice be taken in your sense, then the recommendation of it by men of experience would appear to involve more or less of an unhandsome sort of reflection upon human nature. And yet,' with a perplexed air, 'your suggestions have put things in such a strange light to me as in fact a little to disturb my previous notions of Polonius and what he says. To be frank by your ingenuity you have unsettled me there, to that degree that were it not for our coincidence of opinion in general, I should almost think I was now at length beginning to feel the ill effect of an immature mind, too much consorting with a mature one, except on the ground of first principles in common.'

'Really and truly,' cried the other with a kind of tickled modesty and pleased concern, 'mine is an understanding too weak to throw out grapnels and hug another to it. I have indeed heard of some great scholars in these days, whose boast is less that they have made disciples than victims. But for me, had I the power to do such things, I have not the heart to desire.'

'I believe you, my dear Charlie. And yet, I repeat, by your commentaries on Polonius you have, I know not how, unsettled me; so that now I don't exactly see how Shakespeare meant the words he put in Polonius' mouth.'

'Some say that he meant them to open people's eyes; but I don't think so.'

'Open their eyes?' echoed the cosmopolitan, slowly expanding his; 'what is there in this world for one to open his eyes to? I mean in the sort of invidious sense you cite?'

'Well, others say he meant to corrupt people's morals; and still others, that he had no express intention at all, but in effect opens their eyes and corrupts their morals in one operation. All of which I reject.'

'Of course you reject so crude an hypothesis; and yet, to confess, in reading Shakespeare in my closet, struck by some passage, I have laid down the volume, and said: "This Shakespeare is a queer man." At times seeming irresponsible, he does not always seem reliable. There appears to be a certain – what shall I call it? – hidden sun, say, about him, at once enlightening and mystifying. Now, I should be afraid to say what I have sometimes thought that hidden sun might be.'

'Do you think it was the true light?' with clandestine geniality again filling the other's glass.

'I would prefer to decline answering a categorical question there. Shakespeare has got to be a kind of deity. Prudent minds, having certain latent thoughts concerning him, will reserve them in a condition of lasting probation. Still, as touching avowable speculations, we are permitted a tether. Shakespeare himself is to be adored, not arraigned; but, so we do it with humility, we may a little canvass his characters. There's his Autolycus now, a fellow that always puzzled me. How is one to take Autolycus? A rogue so happy, so lucky, so triumphant, of so almost captivatingly vicious a career that a virtuous man reduced to the poor-house (were such a contingency conceivable), might almost long to change sides with him. And yet, see the words put into his mouth: "Oh," cries Autolycus, as he comes galloping, gay as a buck, upon the stage, "oh," he laughs, "oh, what a fool is Honesty, and Trust, his sworn brother, a very simple gentleman". Think of that. Trust, that is, confidence – that is, the thing in this universe the sacredest – is rattlingly pronounced just the simplest. And the scenes in which the rogue figures seem purposely devised for verification of his principles. Mind, Charlie, I do not say it *is* so, far from it; but I *do* say it seems so. Yes, Autolycus would seem a needy varlet acting upon the persuasion that less is to be got by invoking pockets than picking them, more to be made by an expert knave than a bungling beggar; and for this reason, as he thinks, that the soft heads outnumber the soft hearts. The devil's drilled recruit, Autolycus is joyous as if he wore the livery of heaven. When disturbed by the character and career of one thus wicked and thus happy, my sole consolation is in the fact that no such creature ever existed, except in the powerful imagination which evoked him. And yet, a creature, a living creature, he is, though only a poet was his maker. It may be, that in that paper-and-ink investiture of his, Autolycus acts more effectively upon mankind than he would in a flesh-and-blood one. Can his influence be salutary? True, in Autolycus there is humour; but though, according to my principle, humour is in general to be held a saving quality, yet the case of Autolycus is an exception; because it is his humour which, so to speak, oils his mischievousness. The bravadoing mischievousness of Autolycus is slid into the world on humour, as a pirate schooner, with colours flying, is launched into the sea on greased ways.'

'I approve of Autolycus as little as you,' said the stranger, who, during his companion's commonplaces, had seemed less attentive to them than to maturing within his own mind the original conceptions destined to eclipse them. 'But I cannot believe that Autolycus, mischievous as he must prove upon the stage, can be near so much so as such a character as Polonius.'

'I don't know about that,' bluntly, and yet not impolitely, returned the cosmopolitan; 'to be sure, accepting your view of the old courtier, then if between him and Autolycus you raise the question of unprepossessingness, I grant you the latter comes off best. For a moist rogue may tickle the midriff, while a dry worldling may but wrinkle the spleen.'

'But Polonius is not dry,' said the other excitedly; 'he drules. One sees the fly-blown old fop drule and look wise. His vile wisdom is made the viler by his vile rheuminess. The bowing and cringing, time-serving old sinner – is such an one to give manly precepts to youth? The discreet, decorous, old dotard-of-state; senile prudence; fatuous soullessness! The ribanded old dog is paralytic all down one side, and that the side of nobleness. His soul is gone out. Only nature's automatonism keeps him on his legs. As with some old trees, the bark survives the pith, and will still stand stiffly up, though but to rim round punk, so the body of old Polonius has outlived his soul.'

'Come, come,' said the cosmopolitan with serious air, almost displeased; 'though I yield to none in admiration of earnestness, yet, I think, even earnestness may have limits. To humane minds, strong language is always more or less distressing. Besides, Polonius is an old man – as I remember him upon the stage – with snowy locks. Now charity requires that such a figure – think of it how you will – should at least be treated with civility. Moreover old age is ripeness, and I once heard say, "Better ripe than raw."'

'But not better rotten than raw!' bringing down his hand with energy on the table.

'Why, bless me,' in mild surprise contemplating his heated comrade, 'how you fly out against this unfortunate Polonius – a being that never was, nor will be. And yet, viewed in a Christian light,' he added pensively, 'I don't know that anger against this man of straw is a whit less wise than anger against a man of flesh. Madness, to be mad with anything.'

'That may be, or may not be,' returned the other, a little testily perhaps; 'but I stick to what I said, that it is better to be raw than rotten. And what is to be feared on that head, may be known from this: that it is with the best of hearts as with the best of pears – a dangerous experiment to linger too long upon the scene. This did Polonius. Thank fortune, Frank, I am young, every tooth sound in my head, and if good wine can keep me where I am, long shall I remain so.'

'True,' with a smile. 'But wine, to do good, must be drunk. You have talked much and well, Charlie; but drunk little and indifferently – fill up.'

'Presently, presently,' with a hasty and preoccupied air. 'If I remember right, Polonius hints as much as that one should, under no circumstances, commit the indiscretion of aiding in a pecuniary way an unfortunate friend. He drules out some stale stuff about "loan losing both itself and friend", don't he? But our bottle; is it glued fast? Keep it moving, my dear Frank. Good wine, and upon my soul I begin to feel it, and through me old Polonius – yes, this wine, I fear, is what excites me so against that detestable old dog without a tooth.'

Upon this, the cosmopolitan, cigar in mouth, slowly raised the bottle, and brought it slowly to the light, looking at it steadfastly, as one might at a thermometer in August, to see not how low it was, but how high. Then whiffing out a puff, set it down, and said: 'Well, Charlie, if what wine you have drunk came out of this bottle, in that case I should say that if – supposing a case – that if one fellow had an object in getting another fellow fuddled, and this fellow to be fuddled was of your capacity, the operation would be comparatively inexpensive. What do you think, Charlie?'

'Why, I think I don't much admire the supposition,' said Charlie, with a look of resentment; 'it ain't safe, depend upon it, Frank, to venture upon too jocose suppositions with one's friends.'

'Why, bless you, Charlie, my supposition wasn't personal, but general. You mustn't be so touchy.'

'If I am touchy it is the wine. Sometimes, when I freely drink it, it has a touchy effect on me, I have observed.'

'Freely drink? you haven't drunk the perfect measure of one glass yet. While for me, this must be my fourth or fifth, thanks to your importunity; not to speak of all I drank this morning, for old acquaintance sake. Drink, drink; you must drink.'

'Oh, I drink while you are talking,' laughed the other; 'you have not noticed it, but I have drunk my share. Have a queer way I learned from a sedate old uncle, who used to tip off his glass unperceived. Do you fill up, and my glass too. There! Now away with that stump, and have a new cigar. Good fellowship for ever!' again in the lyric mood. 'Say, Frank, are we not men? I say are we not human? Tell me, were they not human who engendered us, as before heaven I believe they shall be whom we shall engender? Fill up, up, up, my friend. Let the ruby tide aspire, and all ruby aspirations with it! Up, fill up! Be we convivial. And conviviality, what is it? The word, I mean; what expresses it? A living together. But bats live together, and did you ever hear of convivial bats?'

'If I ever did,' observed the cosmopolitan, 'it has quite slipped my recollection.'

'But *why* did you never hear of convivial bats, nor anybody else? Because bats, though they live together, live not together genially. Bats are not genial souls. But men are; and how delightful to think that the word which among men signifies the highest pitch of geniality, implies, as indispensable auxiliary, the cheery benediction of the bottle. Yes, Frank, to live together in the finest sense, we must drink together. And so, what wonder that he who loves not wine, that sober wretch, has a lean heart – a heart like a wrung-out old bluing-bag, and loves not his kind? Out upon him, to the rag-house with him, hang him – the ungenial soul!'

'Oh, now, now, can't you be convivial without being censorious? I like easy, unexcited conviviality. For the sober man, really, though for my part I naturally love a cheerful glass, I will not prescribe my nature as the law to other natures. So don't abuse the sober man. Conviviality is one good thing, and sobriety is another good thing. So don't be one-sided.'

'Well, if I am one-sided, it is the wine. Indeed, indeed, I have indulged too genially. My excitement upon slight provocation shows it. But yours is a stronger head; drink you. By the way, talking of geniality, it is much on the increase in these days, ain't it?'

'It is, and I hail the fact. Nothing better attests the advance of the humanitarian spirit. In former and less humanitarian ages – the ages of amphitheatres and gladiators – geniality was mostly confined to the fireside and table. But in our age – the age of joint-stock companies and free-and-easies – it is with this precious quality as with precious gold in old Peru, which Pizarro found making up the scullion's sauce-pot as the Inca's crown. Yes, we golden boys, the moderns, have geniality everywhere – a bounty broadcast like moonlight.'

'True, true; my sentiments again. Geniality has invaded each department and profession. We have genial senators, genial authors, genial lecturers, genial doctors, genial clergymen, genial surgeons, and the next thing we shall have genial hangmen.'

'As to the last-named sort of person,' said the cosmopolitan, 'I trust that the advancing spirit of geniality will at last enable us to dispense with him. No murderers – no hangmen. And surely, when the whole world shall have been genialized, it will be as out of place to talk of murderers, as in a Christianized world to talk of sinners.'

'To pursue the thought,' said the other, 'every blessing is attended with some evil, and –'

'Stay,' said the cosmopolitan, 'that may be better let pass for a loose saying, than for hopeful doctrine.'

'Well, assuming that saying's truth, it would apply to the future supremacy of the genial spirit, since then it will fare with the hangman as it did with the weaver when the spinning-jenny whizzed into the ascendant. Thrown out of employment, what could Jack Ketch turn his hand to? Butchering?'

'That he could turn his hand to it seems probable; but that, under the circumstances, it would be appropriate, might in some minds admit of a question. For one, I am inclined to think – and I trust it will not be held fastidiousness – that it would hardly be suitable to the dignity of our nature, that an individual, once employed in attending the last hours of human unfortunates, should, that office being extinct, transfer himself to the business of attending the last hours of unfortunate cattle. I would suggest that the individual turn valet – a vocation to which he would, perhaps, appear not wholly inadapted by his familiar dexterity about the person. In particular, for giving a finishing tie to a gentleman's cravat, I know few who would, in all likelihood, be, from previous occupation, better fitted than the professional person in question.'

'Are you in earnest?' regarding the serene speaker with unaffected curiosity; 'are you really in earnest?'

'I trust I am never otherwise,' was the mildly earnest reply; 'but talking of the advance of geniality, I am not without hopes that it will eventually exert its influence even upon so difficult a subject as the misanthrope.'

'A genial misanthrope! I thought I had stretched the rope pretty hard in talking of genial hangmen. A genial misanthrope is no more conceivable than a surly philanthropist.'

'True,' lightly depositing in an unbroken little cylinder the ashes of his cigar, 'true, the two you name are well opposed.'

'Why, you talk as if there *was* such a being as a surly philanthropist.'

'I do. My eccentric friend, whom you call Coonskins, is an example. Does he not, as I explained to you, hide under a surly air a philanthropic heart? Now, the genial misanthrope, when in the process of eras, he shall turn up, will be the converse of this; under an affable air, he will hide a misanthropical heart. In short, the genial misanthrope will be a new kind of monster, but still no small improvement upon the original one, since, instead of making faces and throwing stones at people, like that poor old crazy man, Timon, he will take steps, fiddle in hand, and set the tickled world a'dancing. In a word, as the progress of Christianization mellows those in manner whom it cannot mend in mind, much the same will it prove with the progress of genialization. And so, thanks to geniality, the misanthrope, reclaimed from his boorish address, will take on refinement and softness – to so genial a degree, indeed, that it may possibly fall out that the misanthrope of the coming century will be almost as popular as, I am sincerely sorry to say, some philanthropists of the present time would seem not to be, as witness my eccentric friend named before.'

'Well,' cried the other, a little weary, perhaps, of a speculation so abstract, 'well, however it may be with the century to come, certainly in the century which is, whatever else one may be, he must be genial or he is nothing. So fill up, fill up, and be genial!'

'I am trying my best,' said the cosmopolitan, still calmly companionable. 'A moment since, we talked of Pizarro, gold, and Peru; no doubt, now, you remember that when the Spaniard first entered Atahalpa's treasure-chamber, and saw such profusion of plate stacked up, right and left, with the wantonness of old barrels in a brewer's yard, the needy fellow felt a twinge of misgiving, of want of confidence, as to the genuineness of an opulence so profuse. He went about rapping the shining vases with his knuckles. But it was all gold, pure gold, good gold, sterling gold, which how cheerfully would have been stamped such at Goldsmiths' Hall. And just so those needy minds, which, through their own insincerity, having no confidence in mankind, doubt lest the liberal geniality of this age be spurious. They are small Pizarros in their way – by the very princeliness of men's geniality stunned into distrust of it.'

'Far be such distrust from you and me, my genial friend,' cried the other fervently; 'fill up, fill up!'

'Well, this all along seems a division of labour,' smiled the cosmopolitan. 'I do about all the drinking, and you do about all – the genial. But yours is a nature competent to do that to a large population. And now, my friend,' with a peculiarly grave air, evidently foreshadowing something not unimportant, and very likely of close personal interest; 'wine, you know, opens the heart, and –'

'Opens it!' with exultation, 'it thaws it right out. Every heart is ice-bound till wine melt it, and reveal the tender grass and sweet herbage budding below, with every dear secret, hidden before like a dropped jewel in a snow-bank, lying there unsuspected through winter till spring.'

'And just in that way, my dear Charlie, is one of my little secrets now to be shown forth.'

'Ah!' eagerly moving round his chair 'what is it?'

'Be not so impetuous, my dear Charlie. Let me explain. You see, naturally, I am a man not over-gifted with assurance; in general, I am, if anything, diffidently reserved; so, if I shall presently seem otherwise, the reason is, that you, by the geniality you have evinced in all your talk, and especially the noble way in which, while affirming your good opinion of men, you intimated that you never could prove false to any man, but most by your indignation at a particularly illiberal passage in Polonius' advice – in short, in short,' with extreme embarrassment, 'how shall I express what I mean, unless I add that by your whole character you impel me to throw myself upon your nobleness; in one word, put confidence in you, a generous confidence?'

'I see, I see,' with heightened interest, 'something of moment you wish to confide. Now, what is it, Frank? Love affair?'

'No, not that.'

'What, then, my *dear* Frank? Speak – depend upon me to the last. Out with it.'

'Out it shall come, then,' said the cosmopolitan, 'I am in want, urgent want, of money.'

A METAMORPHOSIS MORE SURPRISING THAN
ANY IN OVID

———— • ————

'In want of money!' pushing back his chair as from a suddenly-disclosed man-trap or crater.

'Yes,' naïvely assented the cosmopolitan, 'and you are going to loan me fifty dollars. I could almost wish I was in need of more, only for your sake. Yes, my dear Charlie, for your sake; that you might the better prove your noble kindliness, my dear Charlie.'

'None of your dear Charlies,' cried the other, springing to his feet, and buttoning up his coat, as if hastily to depart upon a long journey.

'Why, why, why?' painfully looking up.

'None of your why, why, whys!' tossing out a foot, 'go to the devil, sir! Beggar, impostor! – never so deceived in a man in my life.'

SHOWING THAT THE AGE OF MAGIC AND
MAGICIANS IS NOT YET OVER

While speaking or rather hissing those words, the boon companion underwent much such a change as one reads of in fairy-books. Out of old materials sprang a new creature. Cadmus glided into the snake.

The cosmopolitan rose, the traces of previous feeling vanished; looked steadfastly at his transformed friend a moment, then, taking ten half-eagles from his pocket, stooped down, and laid them, one by one, in a circle round him; and, retiring a pace, waved his long tasselled pipe with the air of a necromancer, an air heightened by his costume, accompanying each wave with a solemn murmur of cabalistical words.

Meantime, he within the magic-ring stood suddenly rapt, exhibiting every symptom of a successful charm – a turned cheek, a fixed attitude, a frozen eye; spell-bound, not more by the waving wand than by the ten invincible talismans on the floor.

'Reappear, reappear, reappear, oh, my former friend! Replace this hideous apparition with thy blest shape, and be the token of thy return the words, "My dear Frank."'

'My dear Frank,' now cried the restored friend, cordially stepping out of the ring, with regained self-possession regaining lost identity, 'My dear Frank, what a funny man you are; full of fun as an egg of meat. How could you tell me that absurd story of your being in need? But I relish a good joke too well to spoil it by letting on. Of course, I humoured the thing; and, on my side, put on all the cruel airs you would have me. Come, this little episode of fictitious estrangement will but enhance the delightful reality. Let us sit down again, and finish our bottle.'

'With all my heart,' said the cosmopolitan, dropping the necromancer with the same facility with which he had assumed it. 'Yes,' he added, soberly picking up the gold pieces, and returning them with a chink to his pocket, 'yes, I am something of a funny man now and then; while for you, Charlie,' eyeing him in tenderness, 'what you say about your humouring the thing is true enough; never did man second a joke better than you did just now. You played your part better than I did mine; you played it, Charlie, to the life.'

'You see, I once belonged to an amateur play company; that accounts for it. But come, fill up, and let's talk of something else.'

'Well,' acquiesced the cosmopolitan, seating himself, and quietly brimming his glass, 'what shall we talk about?'

'Oh, anything you please,' a sort of nervously accommodating.

'Well, suppose we talk about Charlemont?'

'Charlemont? What's Charlemont? Who's Charlemont?'

'You shall hear, my dear Charlie,' answered the cosmopolitan. 'I will tell you the story of Charlemont, the gentleman-madman.'

33

WHICH MAY PASS FOR WHATEVER IT MAY
PROVE TO BE WORTH

But ere be given the rather grave story of Charlemont, a reply must in civility be made to a certain voice which methinks I hear, that in view of past chapters, and more particularly the last, where certain antics appear, exclaims: How unreal all this is! Who did ever dress or act like your cosmopolitan? And who, it might be returned, did ever dress or act like harlequin?

Strange, that in a work of amusement, this severe fidelity to real life should be exacted by any one, who, by taking up such a work, sufficiently shows that he is not unwilling to drop real life, and turn, for a time, to something different. Yes, it is, indeed, strange that any one should clamour for the thing he is weary of; that any one, who, for any cause, finds real life dull, should yet demand of him who is to divert his attention from it, that he should be true to that dullness.

There is another class, and with this class we side, who sit down to a work of amusement tolerably as they sit at a play, and with much the same expectations and feelings. They look that fancy shall evoke scenes different from those of the same old crowd round the custom-house counter, and same old dishes on the boarding-house table, with characters unlike those of the same old acquaintances they meet in the same old way every day in the same old street. And as, in real life, the proprieties will not allow people to act out themselves with that unreserve permitted to the stage; so, in books of fiction, they look not only for more entertainment, but, at bottom, even for more reality, than real life itself can show. Thus, though they want novelty, they want nature, too;

but nature unfettered, exhilarated, in effect transformed. In this way of thinking, the people in a fiction, like the people in a play, must dress as nobody exactly dresses, talk as nobody exactly talks, act as nobody exactly acts. It is with fiction as with religion: it should present another world, and yet one to which we feel the tie.

If, then, something is to be pardoned to well-meant endeavour, surely a little is to be allowed to that writer who, in all his scenes, does but seek to minister to what, as he understands it, is the implied wish of the more indulgent lovers of entertainment, before whom harlequin can never appear in a coat too parti-coloured, or cut capers too fantastic.

One word more. Though every one knows how bootless it is to be in all cases vindicating one's self, never mind how convinced one may be that he is never in the wrong; yet, so precious to man is the approbation of his kind, that to rest, though but under an imaginary censure applied to but a work of imagination, is no easy thing. The mention of this weakness will explain why all such readers as may think they perceive something inharmonious between the boisterous hilarity of the cosmopolitan with the bristling cynic, and his restrained good-nature with the boon-companion, are now referred to that chapter where some similar apparent inconsistency in another character is, on general prin-ciples, modestly endeavoured to be apologized for.

34

IN WHICH THE COSMOPOLITAN TELLS THE
STORY OF THE GENTLEMAN-MADMAN

'Charlemont was a young merchant of French descent, living in St Louis – a man not deficient in mind, and possessed of that sterling and captivating kindliness, seldom in perfection seen but in youthful bachelors, united at times to a remarkable sort of gracefully devil-may-care and witty good-humour. Of course, he was admired by everybody, and loved, as only mankind can love, by not a few. But in his twenty-ninth year a change came over him. Like one whose hair turns gray in a night, so in a day Charlemont turned from affable to morose. His acquaintances were passed without greeting; while, as for his confidential friends, them he pointedly, unscrupulously, and with a kind of fierceness, cut dead.

'One, provoked by such conduct, would fain have resented it with words as disdainful; while another, shocked by the change, and, in concern for a friend, magnanimously overlooking affronts, implored to know what sudden, secret grief had distempered him. But from resentment and from tenderness Charlemont alike turned away.

'Ere long, to the general surprise, the merchant Charlemont was gazetted, and the same day it was reported that he had withdrawn from town, but not before placing his entire property in the hands of responsible assignees for the benefit of creditors.

'Whither he had vanished none could guess. At length, nothing being heard, it was surmised that he must have made away with himself – a surmise, doubtless, originating in the remembrance of the change some months previous to his bankruptcy – a change of a sort only to be ascribed to a mind suddenly thrown from its balance.

'Years passed. It was spring-time, and lo, one bright morning, Charlemont lounged into the St Louis coffee-houses – gay, polite, humane, companionable, and dressed in the height of costly elegance. Not only was he alive, but he was himself again. Upon meeting with old acquaintances, he made the first advances, and in such a manner that it was impossible not to meet him half-way. Upon other old friends, whom he did not chance casually to meet, he either personally called, or left his card and compliments for them; and to several, sent presents of game or hampers of wine.

'They say the world is sometimes harshly unforgiving, but it was not so to Charlemont. The world feels a return of love for one who returns to it as he did. Expressive of its renewed interest was a whisper, an inquiring whisper, how now, exactly, so long after his bankruptcy, it fared with Charlemont's purse. Rumour, seldom at a loss for answers, replied that he had spent nine years in Marseilles in France, and there acquiring a second fortune, had returned with it, a man devoted henceforth to genial friendships.

'Added years went by, and the restored wanderer still the same; or, rather, by his noble qualities, grew up like golden maize in the encouraging sun of good opinions. But still the latent wonder was, what had caused that change in him at a period when, pretty much as now, he was, to all appearance, in the possession of the same fortune, the same friends, the same popularity. But nobody thought it would be the thing to question him here.

'At last, at a dinner at his house, when all the guests but one had successively departed; this remaining guest, an old acquaintance, being just enough under the influence of wine to set aside the fear of touching upon a delicate point, ventured, in a way which perhaps spoke more favourably for his heart than his tact, to beg of his host to explain the one enigma of his life. Deep melancholy overspread the before cheery face of Charlemont; he sat for some moments tremulously silent; then pushing a full decanter towards the guest, in a choked voice, said: "No, no! when by art, and care, and time, flowers are made to bloom over a grave, who would seek to dig all up again only to know the mystery? – The wine." When both glasses were filled, Charlemont took his, and lifting it, added lowly: "If ever, in days to come, you shall see ruin at hand, and, thinking you understand mankind, shall tremble for your friendships, and tremble for your pride; and, partly through love for the one and fear for the other, shall resolve to be beforehand with the world, and save it from a sin by prospectively taking that sin to yourself, then will you do as one I now dream of once did, and like him will you suffer; but how fortunate and how grateful should you be, if like him, after all that had happened, you could be a little happy again."

'When the guest went away, it was with the persuasion, that though outwardly restored in mind as in fortune, yet, some taint of Charlemont's old malady survived, and that it was not well for friends to touch one dangerous string.'

IN WHICH THE COSMOPOLITAN STRIKINGLY
EVINCES THE ARTLESSNESS OF HIS NATURE

—————•◆•—————

'Well, what do you think of the story of Charlemont?' mildly asked he who had told it.

'A very strange one,' answered the auditor, who had been such not with perfect ease, 'but is it true?'

'Of course not; it is a story which I told with the purpose of every story-teller – to amuse. Hence, if it seem strange to you, that strangeness is the romance; it is what contrasts it with real life; it is the invention, in brief, the fiction as opposed to the fact. For do but ask yourself, my dear Charlie,' lovingly leaning over towards him, 'I rest it with your own heart now, whether such a forereaching motive as Charlemont hinted he had acted on in his change – whether such a motive, I say, were a sort of one at all justified by the nature of human society? Would you, for one, turn the cold shoulder to a friend – a convivial one, say, whose pennilessness should be suddenly revealed to you?'

'How can you ask me, my dear Frank? You know I would scorn such meanness.' But rising somewhat disconcerted – 'really, early as it is, I think I must retire; my head,' putting up his hand to it, 'feels unpleasantly; this confounded elixir of logwood, little as I drank of it, has played the deuce with me.'

'Little as you drank of this elixir of logwood? Why, Charlie, you are losing your mind. To talk so of the genuine, mellow old port. Yes, I think that by all means you had better away, and sleep it off. There – don't apologize – don't explain – go, go – I understand you exactly. I will see you to-morrow.'

IN WHICH THE COSMOPOLITAN IS ACCOSTED BY A MYSTIC, WHEREUPON ENSUES PRETTY MUCH SUCH TALK AS MIGHT BE EXPECTED

As, not without some haste, the boon companion withdrew, a stranger advanced, and touching the cosmopolitan, said: 'I think I heard you say you would see that man again. Be warned; don't you do so.'

He turned, surveying the speaker; a blue-eyed man, sandy-haired, and Saxon-looking; perhaps five and forty; tall, and, but for a certain angularity, well made; little touch of the drawing-room about him, but a look of plain propriety of a Puritan sort, with a kind of farmer dignity. His age seemed betokened more by his brow, placidly thoughtful, than by his general aspect, which had that look of youthfulness in maturity, peculiar sometimes to habitual health of body, the original gift of nature, or in part the effect or reward of steady temperance of the passions, kept so, perhaps, by constitution as much as morality. A neat, comely, almost ruddy cheek, coolly fresh, like a red clover-blossom at coolish dawn – the colour of warmth preserved by the virtue of chill. Toning the whole man, was one-knows-not-what of shrewdness and mythiness, strangely jumbled; in that way, he seemed a kind of cross between a Yankee peddler and a Tartar priest, though it seemed as if, at a pinch, the first would not in all probability play second fiddle to the last.

'Sir,' said the cosmopolitan, rising and bowing with slow dignity, 'if I cannot with unmixed satisfaction hail a hint pointed at one who has just been clinking the social glass with me, on the other hand, I am not disposed to underrate the motive which, in the present case, could alone have prompted such an intimation.

My friend, whose seat is still warm, has retired for the night, leaving more or less in his bottle here. Pray, sit down in his seat, and partake with me; and then, if you choose to hint aught further unfavourable to the man, the genial warmth of whose person in part passes into yours, and whose genial hospitality meanders through you – be it so.'

'Quite beautiful conceits,' said the stranger, now scholastically and artistically eyeing the picturesque speaker, as if he were a statue in the Pitti Palace; 'very beautiful,' then with the gravest interest, 'yours, sir, if I mistake not, must be a beautiful soul – one full of all love and truth; for where beauty is, there must those be.'

'A pleasing belief,' rejoined the cosmopolitan, beginning with an even air, 'and to confess, long ago it pleased me. Yes, with you and Schiller, I am pleased to believe that beauty is at bottom incompatible with ill, and therefore am so eccentric as to have confidence in the latent benignity of that beautiful creature, the rattlesnake, whose lithe neck and burnished maze of tawny gold, as he sleekly curls aloft in the sun, who on the prairie can behold without wonder?'

As he breathed these words, he seemed so to enter into their spirit – as some earnest descriptive speakers will – as unconsciously to wreathe his form and side-long crest his head, till he all but seemed the creature described. Meantime, the stranger regarded him with little surprise, apparently, though with much con-templativeness of a mystical sort, and presently said: 'When charmed by the beauty of that viper, did it never occur to you to change personalities with him? to feel what it was to be a snake? to glide unsuspected in grass? to sting, to kill at a touch; your whole beautiful body one iridescent scabbard of death? In short, did the wish never occur to you to feel yourself exempt from knowledge, and conscience, and revel for a while in the care-free, joyous life of a perfectly instinctive, unscrupulous, and ir-responsible creature?'

'Such a wish,' replied the other, not perceptibly disturbed, 'I must confess, never consciously was mine. Such a wish, indeed, could hardly occur to ordinary imaginations, and mine I cannot think much above the average.'

'But now that the idea is suggested,' said the stranger, with infantile intellectuality, 'does it not raise the desire?'

'Hardly. For though I do not think I have any uncharitable prejudice against the rattlesnake, still, I should not like to be one. If I were a rattlesnake now, there would be no such thing as being genial with men – men would be afraid of me, and then I should be a very lonesome and miserable rattlesnake.'

'True, men would be afraid of you. And why? Because of your rattle, your hollow rattle – a sound, as I have been told, like the shaking together of small, dry skulls in a tune of the Waltz of Death. And here we have another beautiful truth. When any creature is by its make inimical to other creatures, nature in effect labels that creature, much as an apothecary does a poison. So that whoever is destroyed by a rattlesnake, or other harmful agent, it is his own fault. He should have respected the label. Hence that significant passage in Scripture, "Who will pity the charmer that is bitten with a serpent?"'

'*I* would pity him,' said the cosmopolitan, a little bluntly, perhaps.

'But don't you think,' rejoined the other, still maintaining his passionless air, 'don't you think, that for a man to pity where nature is pitiless, is a little presuming?'

'Let casuists decide the casuistry, but the compassion the heart decides for itself. But, sir,' deepening in seriousness, 'as I now for the first realize, you but a moment since introduced the word irresponsible in a way I am not used to. Now, sir, though, out of a tolerant spirit, as I hope, I try my best never to be frightened at any speculation, so long as it is pursued in honesty, yet, for once, I must acknowledge that you do really, in the point cited, cause me uneasiness; because a proper view of the universe, that view which is suited to breed a proper confidence, teaches, if I err not, that since all things are justly presided over, not very many living agents but must be some way accountable.'

'Is a rattlesnake accountable?' asked the stranger, with such a preternaturally cold, gemmy glance out of his pellucid blue eye, that he seemed more a metaphysical merman than a feeling man; 'is a rattlesnake accountable?'

'If I will not affirm that it is,' returned the other, with the caution of no inexperienced thinker, 'neither will I deny it. But if we suppose it so, I need not say that such accountability is neither to you, nor me, nor the Court of Common Pleas, but to something superior.'

He was proceeding, when the stranger would have interrupted him; but as reading his argument in his eye, the cosmopolitan, without waiting for it to be put into words, at once spoke to it. 'You object to my supposition, for but such it is, that the rattlesnake's accountability is not by nature manifest; but might not much the same thing be urged against man's? A *reductio ad absurdum*, proving the objection vain. But if now,' he continued, 'you consider what capacity for mischief there is in a rattlesnake (observe, I do not charge it with being mischievous, I but say it has the capacity), could you well avoid admitting that that would be no symmetrical view of the universe which should maintain that, while to man it is forbidden to kill, without judicial cause, his fellow, yet the rattlesnake has an implied permit of unaccountability to murder any creature it takes capricious umbrage at – man included? – But,' with a wearied air, 'this is no genial talk; at least it is not so to me. Zeal at unawares embarked me in it. I regret it. Pray, sit down, and take some of this wine.'

'Your suggestions are new to me,' said the other, with a kind of condescending appreciativeness, as of one who, out of devotion to knowledge, disdains not to appropriate the least crumb of it, even from a pauper's board; 'and, as I am a very Athenian in hailing a new thought, I cannot consent to let it drop so abruptly. Now, the rattlesnake –'

'Nothing more about rattlesnakes, I beseech,' in distress; 'I must positively decline to re-enter upon that subject. Sit down, sir, I beg, and take some of this wine.'

'To invite me to sit down with you is hospitable,' collectedly
acquiescing now in the change of topics; 'and hospitality being
fabled to be of oriental origin, and forming, as it does, the subject
of a pleasing Arabian romance, as well as being a very romantic
thing in itself – hence I always hear the expressions of hospitality
with pleasure. But, as for the wine, my regard for that beverage is
so extreme, and I am so fearful of letting it sate me, that I keep my
love for it in the lasting condition of an untried abstraction.
Briefly, I quaff immense draughts of wine from the page of Hafiz,
but wine from a cup I seldom as much as sip.'

The cosmopolitan turned a mild glance upon the speaker, who,
now occupying the chair opposite him, sat there purely and
coldly radiant as a prism. It seemed as if one could almost hear
him vitreously chime and ring. That moment a waiter passed,
whom, arresting with a sign, the cosmopolitan bid go bring a
goblet of ice-water. 'Ice it well, waiter,' said he; 'and now,'
turning to the stranger, 'will you, if you please, give me your
reason for the warning words you first addressed to me?'

'I hope they were not such warnings as most warnings are,' said
the stranger; 'warnings which do not forewarn, but in mockery
come after the fact. And yet something in you bids me think now,
that whatever latent design your impostor friend might have had
upon you, it as yet remains unaccomplished. You read his label.'

'And what did it say? "This is a genial soul." So you see you
must either give up your doctrine of labels, or else your prejudice
against my friend. But tell me,' with renewed earnestness, 'what
do you take him for? What is he?'

'What are you? What am I? Nobody knows who anybody is.
The data which life furnishes, towards forming a true estimate of
any being, are as insufficient to that end as in geometry one side
given would be to determine the triangle.'

'But is not this doctrine of triangles someway inconsistent with
your doctrine of labels?'

'Yes; but what of that? I seldom care to be consistent. In a
philosophical view, consistency is a certain level at all times,

maintained in all the thoughts of one's mind. But, since nature is nearly all hill and dale, how can one keep naturally advancing in knowledge without submitting to the natural inequalities in the progress? Advance into knowledge is just like advance upon the Grand Erie Canal, where, from the character of the country, change of level is inevitable; you are locked up and locked down with perpetual inconsistencies, and yet all the time you get on; while the dullest part of the whole route is what the boatmen call the "long level" – a consistently flat surface of sixty miles through stagnant swamps.'

'In one particular,' rejoined the cosmopolitan, 'your simile is, perhaps, unfortunate. For, after all these weary lockings-up and lockings-down, upon how much of a higher plain do you finally stand? Enough to make it an object? Having from youth been taught reverence for knowledge, you must pardon me if, on but this one account, I reject your analogy. But really you someway bewitch me with your tempting discourse, so that I keep straying from my point unawares. You tell me you cannot certainly know who or what my friend is; pray, what do you conjecture him to be?'

'I conjecture him to be what, among the ancient Egyptians, was called a –' using some unknown word.

'A –! And what is that?'

'A – is what Proclus, in a little note to his third book on the theology of Plato, defines as – –' coming out with a sentence of Greek.

Holding up his glass, and steadily looking through its transparency, the cosmopolitan rejoined: 'That, in so defining the thing, Proclus set it to modern understandings in the most crystal light it was susceptible of, I will not rashly deny; still, if you could put the definition in words suited to perceptions like mine, I should take it for a favour.'

'A favour!' slightly lifting his cool eyebrows; 'a bridal favour I understand, a knot of white ribbons, a very beautiful type of the purity of true marriage; but of other favours I am yet to learn;

and still, in a vague way, the word, as you employ it, strikes me as unpleasingly significant in general of some poor, unheroic submission to being done good to.'

Here the goblet of iced-water was brought, and, in compliance with a sign from the cosmopolitan, was placed before the stranger, who, not before expressing acknowledgments, took a draught, apparently refreshing – its very coldness, as with some is the case, proving not entirely uncongenial.

At last, setting down the goblet, and gently wiping from his lips the beads of water freshly clinging there as to the valve of a coral-shell upon a reef, he turned upon the cosmopolitan, and, in a manner the most cool, self-possessed, and matter-of-fact possible, said: 'I hold to the metempsychosis; and whoever I may be now, I feel that I was once the stoic Arrian, and have inklings of having been equally puzzled by a word in the current language of that former time, very probably answering to your word *favour*.'

'Would you favour me by explaining?' said the cosmopolitan, blandly.

'Sir,' responded the stranger, with a very slight degree of severity, 'I like lucidity, of all things, and am afraid I shall hardly be able to converse satisfactorily with you, unless you bear it in mind.'

The cosmopolitan ruminatingly eyed him awhile, then said: 'The best way, as I have heard, to get out of a labyrinth, is to retrace one's steps. I will accordingly retrace mine, and beg you will accompany me. In short, once again to return to the point: for what reason did you warn me against my friend?'

'Briefly, then, and clearly, because, as before said, I conjecture him to be what, among the ancient Egyptians –'

'Pray, now,' earnestly deprecated the cosmopolitan, 'pray, now, why disturb the repose of those ancient Egyptians? What to us are their words or their thoughts? Are we pauper Arabs, without a house of our own, that, with the mummies, we must turn squatters among the dust of the Catacombs?'

'Pharaoh's poorest brick-maker lies proudlier in his rags than the Emperor of all the Russias in his hollands,' oracularly said the stranger; 'for death, though in a worm, is majestic; while life, though in a king, is contemptible. So talk not against mummies. It is a part of my mission to teach mankind a due reverence for mummies.'

Fortunately, to arrest these incoherencies, or rather, to vary them, a haggard, inspired-looking man now approached – a crazy beggar, asking alms under the form of peddling a rhapsodical tract, composed by himself, and setting forth his claims to some rhapsodical apostleship. Though ragged and dirty, there was about him no touch of vulgarity; for, by nature, his manner was not unrefined, his frame slender, and appeared the more so from the broad, untanned frontlet of his brow, tangled over with a dishevelled mass of raven curls, throwing a still deeper tinge upon a complexion like that of a shrivelled berry. Nothing could exceed his look of picturesque Italian ruin and dethronement, heightened by what seemed just one glimmering peep of reason, insufficient to do him any lasting good, but enough, perhaps, to suggest a torment of latent doubts at times, whether his addled dream of glory were true.

Accepting the tract offered him, the cosmopolitan glanced over it, and, seeming to see just what it was, closed it, put it in his pocket, eyed the man a moment, then, leaning over and presenting him with a shilling, said to him, in tones kind and considerate: 'I am sorry, my friend, that I happen to be engaged just now; but, having purchased your work, I promise myself much satisfaction in its perusal at my earliest leisure.'

In his tattered, single-breasted frock-coat, buttoned meagerly up to his chin, the shatter-brain made him a bow, which, for courtesy, would not have misbecome a viscount, then turned with silent appeal to the stranger. But the stranger sat more like a cold prism than ever, while an expression of keen Yankee cuteness, now replacing his former mystical one, lent added icicles to his aspect. His whole air said: 'Nothing from me.' The repulsed petitioner threw a look full of resentful pride and cracked disdain upon him, and went his way.

'Come, now,' said the cosmopolitan, a little reproachfully, 'you ought to have sympathized with that man; tell me, did you feel no fellow-feeling? Look at his tract here, quite in the transcendental vein.'

'Excuse me,' said the stranger, declining the tract, 'I never patronize scoundrels.'

'Scoundrels?'

'I detected in him, sir, a damning peep of sense – damning, I say; for sense in a seeming madman is scoundrelism. I take him for a cunning vagabond, who picks up a vagabond living by adroitly playing the madman. Did you not remark how he flinched under my eye?'

'Really,' drawing a long, astonished breath, 'I could hardly have divined in you a temper so subtlely distrustful. Flinched? to be sure he did, poor fellow; you received him with so lame a welcome. As for his adroitly playing the madman, invidious critics might object the same to some one or two strolling magi of these days. But that is a matter I know nothing about. But, once more, and for the last time, to return to the point: why sir, did you warn me against my friend? I shall rejoice, if, as I think it will prove, your want of confidence in my friend rests upon a basis equally slender with your distrust of the lunatic. Come, why did you warn me? Put it, I beseech, in few words, and those English.'

'I warned you against him because he is suspected for what on these boats is known – so they tell me – as a Mississippi operator.'

'An operator, ah? he operates, does he? My friend, then, is something like what the Indians call a Great Medicine, is he? He operates, he purges, he drains off the repletions.'

'I perceive, sir,' said the stranger, constitutionally obtuse to the pleasant drollery, 'that your notion, of what is called a Great Medicine, needs correction. The Great Medicine among the Indians is less a bolus than a man in grave esteem for his politic sagacity.'

'And is not my friend politic? Is not my friend sagacious? By your own definition, is not my friend a Great Medicine?'

'No, he is an operator, a Mississippi operator; an equivocal character. That he is such, I little doubt, having had him pointed out to me as such, by one desirous of initiating me into any little novelty of this western region, where I never before travelled. And, sir, if I am not mistaken, you also are a stranger here (but, indeed, where in this strange universe is not one a stranger?) and that is a reason why I felt moved to warn you against a companion who could not be otherwise than perilous to one of a free and trustful disposition. But I repeat the hope, that, thus far at least, he has not succeeded with you, and trust that, for the future, he will not.'

'Thank you for your concern; but hardly can I equally thank you for so steadily maintaining the hypothesis of my friend's objectionableness. True, I but made his acquaintance for the first to-day, and know little of his antecedents; but that would seem no just reason why a nature like his should not of itself inspire confidence. And since your own knowledge of the gentleman is not, by your account, so exact as it might be, you will pardon me if I decline to welcome any further suggestions unflattering to him. Indeed, sir,' with friendly decision, 'let us change the subject.'

37

THE MYSTICAL MASTER INTRODUCES THE
PRACTICAL DISCIPLE

'Both, the subject, and the interlocutor,' replied the stranger rising, and waiting the return towards him of a promenader, that moment turning at the further end of his walk.

'Egbert!' said he, calling.

Egbert, a well-dressed, commercial-looking gentleman of about thirty, responded in a way strikingly deferential, and in a moment stood near, in the attitude less of an equal companion apparently than a confidential follower.

'This,' said the stranger, taking Egbert by the hand and leading him to the cosmopolitan, 'this is Egbert, a disciple. I wish you to know Egbert. Egbert was the first among mankind to reduce to practice the principles of Mark Winsome – principles previously accounted as less adapted to life than the closet. Egbert,' turning to the disciple, who, with seeming modesty, a little shrank under these compliments, 'Egbert, this,' with a salute towards the cosmopolitan, 'is, like all of us, a stranger. I wish you, Egbert, to know this brother stranger; be communicative with him. Particularly if, by anything hitherto dropped, his curiosity has been roused as to the precise nature of my philosophy, I trust you will not leave such curiosity ungratified. You, Egbert, by simply setting forth your practice, can do more to enlighten one as to my theory, than I myself can by mere speech. Indeed, it is by you that I myself best understand myself. For to every philosophy are certain rear parts, very important parts, and these, like the rear of one's head, are best seen by reflection. Now, as in a glass, you, Egbert, in your life, reflect to me the more important part of my system, he, who approves you, approves the philosophy of Mark Winsome.'

Though portions of this harangue may, perhaps, in the phraseology seem self-complacent, yet no trace of self-complacency was perceptible in the speaker's manner, which throughout was plain, unassuming, dignified, and manly; the teacher and prophet seemed to lurk more in the idea, so to speak, than in the mere bearing of him who was the vehicle of it.

'Sir,' said the cosmopolitan, who seemed not a little interested in this new aspect of matters, 'you speak of a certain philosophy, and a more or less occult one it may be, and hint of its bearing upon practical life; pray, tell me, if the study of this philosophy tends to the same formation of character with the experiences of the world?'

'It does; and that is the test of its truth; for any philosophy that, being in operation contradictory to the ways of the world, tends to produce a character at odds with it, such a philosophy must necessarily be but a cheat and a dream.'

'You a little surprise me,' answered the cosmopolitan; 'for, from an occasional profundity in you, and also from your allusions to a profound work on the theology of Plato, it would seem but natural to surmise that, if you are the originator of any philosophy, it must needs so partake of the abstruse, as to exalt it above the comparatively vile uses of life.'

'No uncommon mistake with regard to me,' rejoined the other. Then meekly standing like a Raphael: 'If still in golden accents old Memnon murmurs his riddle, none the less does the balance-sheet of every man's ledger unriddle the profit or loss of life. Sir,' with calm energy, 'man came into this world, not to sit down and muse, not to befog himself with vain subtleties, but to gird up his loins and to work. Mystery is in the morning, and mystery in the night, and the beauty of mystery is everywhere; but still the plain truth remains, that mouth and purse must be filled. If, hitherto, you have supposed me a visionary, be undeceived. I am no one-ideaed one, either; no more than the seers before me. Was not Seneca a usurer? Bacon a courtier? and Swedenborg, though with one eye on the invisible, did he not keep the other on the main chance? Along with whatever else it may be given me to be, I am a man of serviceable knowledge, and a man of the world. Know me for such. And as for my disciple here,' turning towards him, 'if you look to find any soft Utopian-isms and last year's sunsets in him, I smile to think how he will set you right. The doctrines I have taught him will, I trust, lead him neither to the mad-house nor the poor-house, as so many other doctrines have served credulous sticklers. Furthermore,' glancing upon him paternally, 'Egbert is both my disciple and my poet. For poetry is not a thing of ink and rhyme, but of thought and act, and, in the latter way, is by any one to be found anywhere, when in useful action sought. In a word, my disciple here is a thriving young merchant, a practical poet in the West India trade. There,' presenting Egbert's hand to the cosmopolitan, 'I join you, and leave you.' With which words, and without bowing, the master withdrew.

38

THE DISCIPLE UNBENDS, AND CONSENTS TO
ACT A SOCIAL PART

——◆·◆——

In the master's presence the disciple had stood as one not ignorant of his place; modesty was in his expression, with a sort of reverential depression. But the presence of the superior withdrawn, he seemed lithely to shoot up erect from beneath it, like one of those wire men from a toy snuff-box.

He was, as before said, a young man of about thirty. His countenance of that neuter sort, which, in repose, is neither prepossessing nor disagreeable; so that it seemed quite uncertain how he would turn out. His dress was neat, with just enough of the mode to save it from the reproach of originality; in which general respect, though with a readjustment of details, his costume seemed modelled upon his master's. But, upon the whole, he was, to all appearances, the last person in the world that one would take for the disciple of any transcendental philosophy; though, indeed, something about his sharp nose and shaved chin seemed to hint that if mysticism, as a lesson, ever came in his way, he might, with the characteristic knack of a true New-Englander, turn even so profitless a thing to some profitable account.

'Well,' said he, now familiarly seating himself in the vacated chair, 'what do you think of Mark? Sublime fellow, ain't he?'

'That each member of the human guild is worthy respect, my friend,' rejoined the cosmopolitan, 'is a fact which no admirer of that guild will question; but that, in view of higher natures, the word sublime, so frequently applied to them, can, without confusion, be also applied to man, is a point which man will decide for himself; though, indeed, if he decide it in the affirmative, it is not for me to object. But I am curious to know more of that philosophy of which, at present, I have but inklings. You, its first disciple among men, it seems, are peculiarly qualified to expound it. Have you any objections to begin now?'

'None at all,' squaring himself to the table. 'Where shall I begin? At first principles?'

'You remember that it was in a practical way that you were represented as being fitted for the clear exposition. Now, what you call first principles, I have, in some things, found to be more or less vague. Permit me, then, in a plain way, to suppose some common case in real life, and that done, I would like you to tell me how you, the practical disciple of the philosophy I wish to know about, would, in that case, conduct.'

'A business-like view. Propose the case.'

'Not only the case, but the persons. The case is this: There are two friends, friends from childhood, bosom-friends; one of whom, for the first time, being in need, for the first time seeks a loan from the other, who, so far as fortune goes, is more than competent to grant it. And the persons are to be you and I: you, the friend from whom the loan is sought – I, the friend who seeks it; you, the disciple of the philosophy in question – I, a common man, with no more philosophy than to know that when I am comfortably warm I don't feel cold, and when I have the ague I shake. Mind, now, you must work up your imagination, and, as much as possible, talk and behave just as if the case supposed were a fact. For brevity, you shall call me Frank, and I will call you Charlie. Are you agreed?'

'Perfectly. You begin.'

The cosmopolitan paused a moment, then, assuming a serious and care-worn air, suitable to the part to be enacted, addressed his hypothesized friend.

39

THE HYPOTHETICAL FRIENDS

'Charlie, I am going to put confidence in you.'

'You always have, and with reason. What is it, Frank?'

'Charlie, I am in want – urgent want of money.'

'That's not well.'

'But it *will* be well, Charlie, if you loan me a hundred dollars. I would not ask this of you, only my need is sore, and you and I have so long shared hearts and minds together, however unequally on my side, that nothing remains to prove our friendship but, with the same inequality on my side, to share purses. You will do me the favour, won't you?'

'Favour? What do you mean by asking me to do you a favour?'

'Why, Charlie, you never used to talk so.'

'Because, Frank, you on your side, never used to talk so.'

'But won't you loan me the money?'

'No, Frank.'

'Why?'

'Because my rule forbids. I give away money, but never loan it; and of course the man who calls himself my friend is above receiving alms. The negotiation of a loan is a business transaction. And I will transact no business with a friend. What a friend is, he is socially and intellectually; and I rate social and intellectual friendship too high to degrade it on either side into a pecuniary make-shift. To be sure there are, and I have, what is called business friends; that is, commercial acquaintances, very convenient persons. But I draw a red-ink line between them and my friends in the true sense – my friends social and intellectual. In brief, a true friend has nothing to do with loans; he should have a soul above loans. Loans are such unfriendly accommodations as are to be had from the soulless corporation of a bank, by giving the regular security and paying the regular discount.'

'An *unfriendly* accommodation? Do those words go together handsomely?'

'Like the poor farmer's team, of an old man and a cow – not handsomely, but to the purpose. Look, Frank, a loan of money on interest is a sale of money on credit. To sell a thing on credit may be an accommodation, but where is the friendliness? Few men in their senses, except operators, borrow money on interest, except upon a necessity akin to starvation. Well, now, where is the friendliness of my letting a starving man have, say, the money's worth of a barrel of flour upon the condition that, on a given day, he shall let me have the money's worth of a barrel and a half of flour; especially if I add this further proviso, that if he fail so to do, I shall then, to secure to myself the money's worth of my barrel and his half barrel, put his heart up at public auction, and, as it is cruel to part families, throw in his wife's and children's?'

'I understand,' with a pathetic shudder; 'but even did it come to that, such a step on the creditor's part, let us, for the honour of human nature, hope, were less the intention than the contingency.'

'But, Frank, a contingency not unprovided for in the taking beforehand of due securities.'

'Still, Charlie, was not the loan in the first place a friend's act?'

'And the auction in the last place an enemy's act. Don't you see? The enmity lies couched in the friendship, just as the ruin in the relief.'

'I must be very stupid to-day, Charlie, but really, I can't understand this. Excuse me, my dear friend, but it strikes me that in going into the philosophy of the subject, you go somewhat out of your depth.'

'So said the incautious wader-out to the ocean; but the ocean replied: "It is just the other way, my wet friend," and drowned him.'

'That, Charlie, is a fable about as unjust to the ocean, as some of Aesop's are to the animals. The ocean is a magnanimous element, and would scorn to assassinate a poor fellow, let alone taunting him in the act. But I don't understand what you say about enmity couched in friendship, and ruin in relief.'

'I will illustrate, Frank. The needy man is a train slipped off the rail. He who loans him money on interest is the one who, by way of accommodation, helps get the train back where it belongs; but then, by way of making all square, and a little more, telegraphs to an agent, thirty miles a-head by a precipice, to throw just there, on his account, a beam across the track. Your needy man's principal-and-interest friend is, I say again, a friend with an enmity in reserve. No, no, my dear friend, no interest for me. I scorn interest.'

'Well, Charlie, none need you charge. Loan me without interest.'

'That would be alms again.'

'Alms, if the sum borrowed is returned?'

'Yes; an alms, not of the principal, but the interest.'

'Well, I am in sore need, so I will not decline the alms. Seeing that it is you, Charlie, gratefully will I accept the alms of the interest. No humiliation between friends.'

'Now, how in the refined view of friendship can you suffer yourself to talk so, my dear Frank? It pains me. For though I am not of the sour mind of Solomon, that, in the hour of need, a stranger is better than a brother; yet I entirely agree with my sublime master, who, in his Essay on Friendship, says so nobly, that if he want a terrestrial convenience, not to his friend celestial (or friend social and intellectual) would he go; no: for his terrestrial convenience, to his friend terrestrial (or humbler business friend) he goes. Very lucidly he adds the reason: Because, for the superior nature, which on no account can ever descend to do good, to be annoyed with requests to do it, when the inferior one, which by no instruction can ever rise above that capacity, stands always inclined to it – this is unsuitable.'

'Then I will not consider you as my friend celestial, but as the other.'

'It racks me to come to that; but, to oblige you, I'll do it. We are business friends; business is business. You want to negotiate a loan. Very good. On what paper? Will you pay three per cent a month? Where is your security?'

'Surely you will not exact those formalities from your old schoolmate – him with whom you have so often sauntered down the groves of Academe, discoursing of the beauty of virtue, and the grace that is in kindliness – and all for so paltry a sum. Security? Our being fellow-academics, and friends from child-hood up, is security.'

'Pardon me, my dear Frank, our being fellow-academics is the worst of securities; while, our having been friends from childhood up is just no security at all. You forget we are now business friends.'

'And you, on your side, forget, Charlie, that as your business friend I can give you no security; my need being so sore that I cannot get an indorser.'

'No indorser, then, no business loan.'

'Since then, Charlie, neither as the one nor the other sort of friend you have defined, can I prevail with you; how if, combining the two, I sue as both?'

'Are you a centaur?'

'When all is said then, what good have I of your friendship, regarded in what light you will?'

'The good which is in the philosophy of Mark Winsome, as reduced to practice by a practical disciple.'

'And why don't you add, much good may the philosophy of Mark Winsome do me? Ah,' turning invokingly, 'what is friend-ship, if it be not the helping hand and the feeling heart, the good Samaritan pouring out at need the purse as the vial!'

'Now, my dear Frank, don't be childish. Through tears never did man see his way in the dark. I should hold you unworthy that sincere friendship I bear you, could I think that friendship in the ideal is too lofty for you to conceive. And let me tell you, my dear Frank, that you would seriously shake the foundations of our love, if ever again you should repeat the present scene. The philosophy, which is mine in the strongest way, teaches plain-dealing. Let me, then, now, as at the most suitable time, candidly disclose certain circumstances you seem in ignorance of. Though our friendship began in boyhood, think not that, on my side at least, it began injudiciously. Boys are little men, it is said. You, I juvenilely picked out for my friend, for your favourable points at the time; not the least of which were your good manners, handsome dress, and your parents' rank and repute of wealth. In short, like any grown man, boy though I was, I went into the market and chose me my mutton, not for its leanness, but its fatness. In other words, there seemed in you, the schoolboy who always had silver in his pocket, a reasonable probability that you would never stand in lean need of fat succour; and if my early impression has not been verified by the event, it is only because of the caprice of fortune producing a fallibility of human expectations, however discreet.'

'Oh, that I should listen to this cold-blooded disclosure!'

'A little cold blood in your ardent veins, my dear Frank, wouldn't do you any harm, let me tell you. Cold-blooded? You say that, because my disclosure seems to involve a vile prudence on my side. But not so. My reason for choosing you in part for the points I have mentioned, was solely with a view of preserving inviolate the delicacy of the connection. For – do but think of it – what more distressing to delicate friendship, formed early, than your friend's eventually, in manhood, dropping in of a rainy night for his little loan of five dollars or so? Can delicate friendship stand that? And, on the other side, would delicate friendship, so long as it retained its delicacy, do that? Would you not instinctively say of your dripping friend in the entry, "I have been deceived, fraudulently deceived, in this man; he is no true friend that, in platonic love to demand love-rites?"'

'And rites, doubly rights, they are, cruel Charlie!'

'Take it how you will, heed well how, by too importunately claiming those rights, as you call them, you shake those foundations I hinted of. For though, as it turns out, I, in my early friendship, built me a fair house, on a poor site; yet such pains and cost have I lavished on that house, that, after all, it is dear to me. No, I would not lose the sweet boon of your friendship, Frank. But beware.'

'And of what? Of being in need? Oh, Charlie! you talk not to a god, a being who in himself holds his own estate, but to a man who, being a man, is the sport of fate's wind and wave, and who mounts towards heaven or sinks towards hell, as the billows roll him in trough or on crest.'

'Tut! Frank. Man is no such poor devil as that comes to – no poor drifting sea-weed of the universe. Man has a soul; which, if he will, puts him beyond fortune's finger and the future's spite. Don't whine like fortune's whipped dog, Frank, or by the heart of a true friend, I will cut ye.'

'Cut me you have already, cruel Charlie, and to the quick. Call to mind the days we went nutting, the times we walked in the woods, arms wreathed about each other, showing trunks invined like the trees – oh, Charlie!'

'Pish! we were boys.'

'Then lucky the fate of the first-born of Egypt, cold in the grave ere maturity struck them with a sharper frost. – Charlie?'

'Fie! you're a girl.'

'Help, help, Charlie, I want help!'

'Help? to say nothing of the friend, there is something wrong about the man who wants help. There is somewhere a defect, a want, in brief, a need, a crying need, somewhere about that man.'

'So there is, Charlie. – Help, help!'

'How foolish a cry, when to implore help, is itself the proof of undesert of it.'

'Oh, this, all along, is not you, Charlie, but some ventriloquist who usurps your larynx. It is Mark Winsome that speaks, not Charlie.'

'If so, thank heaven, the voice of Mark Winsome is not alien but congenial to my larynx. If the philosophy of that illustrious teacher find little response among mankind at large, it is less that they do not possess teachable tempers, than because they are so unfortunate as not to have natures predisposed to accord with him.'

'Welcome, that compliment to humanity,' exclaimed Frank with energy, 'the truer because unintended. And long in this respect may humanity remain what you affirm it. And long it will; since humanity, inwardly feeling how subject it is to straits, and hence how precious is help, will, for selfishness' sake, if no other, long postpone ratifying a philosophy that banishes help from the world. But Charlie, Charlie! speak as you used to; tell me you will help me. Were the case reversed, not less freely would I loan you the money than you would ask me to loan it.'

'*I* ask? *I* ask a loan? Frank, by this hand, under no circumstances would I accept a loan, though without asking pressed on me. The experience of China Aster might warn me.'

'And what was that?'

'Not very unlike the experience of the man that built himself a palace of moon-beams, and when the moon set was surprised that his palace vanished with it. I will tell you about China Aster. I wish I could do so in my own words, but unhappily the original story-teller here has so tyrannized over me, that it is quite impossible for me to repeat his incidents without sliding into his style. I forewarn you of this, that you may not think me so maudlin as, in some parts, the story would seem to make its narrator. It is too bad that any intellect, especially in so small a matter, should have such power to impose itself upon another, against its best exerted will, too. However, it is satisfaction to know that the main moral, to which all tends, I fully approve. But, to begin.'

40

IN WHICH THE STORY OF CHINA ASTER IS, AT SECOND-HAND, TOLD BY ONE WHO, WHILE NOT DISAPPROVING THE MORAL, DISCLAIMS THE SPIRIT OF THE STYLE

▬▶▬

'China Aster was a young candle-maker of Marietta, at the mouth of the Muskingum — one whose trade would seem a kind of subordinate branch of that parent craft and mystery of the hosts of heaven, to be the means, effectively or otherwise, of shedding some light through the darkness of a planet benighted. But he made little money by the business. Much ado had poor China Aster and his family to live; he could, if he chose, light up from his stores a whole street, but not so easily could he light up with prosperity the hearts of his household.

'Now, China Aster, it so happened, had a friend, Orchis, a shoemaker; one whose calling it is to defend the understandings of men from naked contact with the substance of things: a very useful vocation, and which, spite of all the wiseacres may prophesy, will hardly go out of fashion so long as rocks are hard and flints will gall. All at once, by a capital prize in a lottery, this useful shoemaker was raised from a bench to a sofa. A small nabob was the shoemaker now, and the understandings of men, let them shift for themselves. Not that Orchis was, by prosperity, elated into heartlessness. Not at all. Because, in his fine apparel, strolling one morning into the candlery, and gaily switching about at the candle-boxes with his gold-headed cane — while poor China Aster, with his greasy paper cap and leather apron, was selling one candle for one penny to a poor orange-woman, who, with the patronizing coolness of a liberal customer, required it to be carefully rolled up and tied in a half sheet of paper — lively Orchis, the woman being gone, discontinued his gay switchings and said: "This is poor business for you, friend China Aster; your capital is too small. You must drop this vile tallow and hold up pure spermaceti to the world. I tell you what it is, you shall have one thousand dollars to extend with. In fact, you must make money, China Aster. I don't like to see your little boy paddling about without shoes, as he does."

'"Heaven bless your goodness, friend Orchis," replied the candle-maker, "but don't take it ill if I call to mind the word of my uncle, the blacksmith, who, when a loan was offered him, declined it, saying: 'To ply my own hammer, light though it be, I think best, rather than piece it out heavier by welding to it a bit of a neighbour's hammer, though that may have some weight to spare; otherwise, were the borrowed bit suddenly wanted again, it might not split off at the welding, but too much to one side or the other.'"

'"Nonsense, friend China Aster, don't be so honest; your boy is barefoot. Besides, a rich man lose by a poor man? Or a friend be the worse by a friend? China Aster, I am afraid that, in leaning over into your vats here, this morning, you have spilled out your wisdom. Hush! I won't hear any more. Where's your desk? Oh, here." With that, Orchis dashed off a check on his bank, and off-handedly presenting it, said: "There, friend China Aster, is your one thousand dollars; when you make it ten thousand, as you soon enough will (for experience, the only true knowledge, teaches me that, for every one, good luck is in store), then, China Aster, why, then you can return me the money or not, just as you please. But, in any event, give yourself no concern, for I shall never demand payment."

'Now, as kind heaven will so have it that to a hungry man bread is a great temptation, and, therefore, he is not too harshly to be blamed, if, when freely offered, he take it, even though it be uncertain whether he shall ever be able to reciprocate; so, to a poor man, proffered money is equally enticing, and the worst that can be said of him, if he accept it, is just what can be said in the other case of the hungry man. In short, the poor candle-maker's scrupulous morality succumbed to his unscrupulous necessity, as is now and then apt to be the case. He took the check, and was about carefully putting it away for the present, when Orchis, switching about again with his gold-headed cane, said: "By-the-way, China Aster, it don't mean anything, but suppose you make a little memorandum of this; won't do any harm, you know." So China Aster gave Orchis his note for one thousand dollars on demand. Orchis took it, and looked at it a moment, "Pooh, I told you, friend China Aster, I wasn't going ever to make any *demand*." Then tearing up the note, and switching away again at the candle-boxes, said, carelessly; "Put it at four years." So China Aster gave Orchis his note for one thousand dollars at four years. "You see I'll never trouble you about this," said Orchis, slipping it in his pocket-book, "give yourself no further thought, friend China Aster, than how best to invest your money. And don't forget my hint about spermaceti. Go into that, and I'll buy all my light of you," with which encouraging words, he, with wonted, rattling kindness, took leave.

'China Aster remained standing just where Orchis had left him; when, suddenly, two elderly friends, having nothing better to do, dropped in for a chat. The chat over, China Aster, in greasy cap and apron, ran after Orchis, and said: "Friend Orchis, heaven will reward you for your good intentions, but here is your check, and now give me my note."

'"Your honesty is a bore, China Aster," said Orchis not without displeasure. "I won't take the check from you."

'"Then you must take it from the pavement, Orchis," said China Aster; and, picking up a stone, he placed the check under it on the walk.

'"China Aster," said Orchis, inquisitively eyeing him, "after my leaving the candlery just now, what asses dropped in there to advise with you, that now you hurry after me, and act so like a fool? Shouldn't wonder if it was those two old asses that the boys nickname Old Plain Talk and Old Prudence."

'"Yes, it was those two, Orchis, but don't call them names."

'"A brace of spavined old croakers. Old Plain Talk had a shrew for a wife, and that's made him shrewish; and Old Prudence, when a boy, broke down in an apple-stall, and that discouraged him for life. No better sport for a knowing spark like me than to hear Old Plain Talk wheeze out his sour old saws, while Old Prudence stands by, leaning on his staff, wagging his frosty old pow, and chiming in at every clause."

'"How can you speak so, friend Orchis, of those who were my father's friends?"

'"Save me from my friends, if those old croakers were Old Honesty's friends. I call your father so, for every one used to. Why did they let him go in his old age on the town? Why, China Aster, I've often heard from my mother, the chronicler, that those two old fellows, with Old Conscience – as the boys called the crabbed old quaker, that's dead now – they three used to go to the poor-house when your father was there, and get round his bed, and talk to him for all the world as Eliphaz, Bildad, and Zophar did to poor old pauper Job. Yes, Job's comforters were Old Plain Talk, and Old Prudence, and Old Conscience, to your poor old father. Friends? I should like to know who you call foes? With their everlasting croaking and reproaching they tormented poor Old Honesty, your father, to death."

'At these words, recalling the sad end of his worthy parent, China Aster could not restrain some tears. Upon which Orchis said: "Why, China Aster, you are the dolefulest creature. Why don't you, China Aster, take a bright view of life? You will never get on in your business or anything else, if you don't take the bright view of life. It's the ruination of a man to take the dismal one." Then, gaily poking at him with his gold-headed cane, "Why don't you, then? Why don't you be bright and hopeful, like me? Why don't you have confidence, China Aster?"

'"I'm sure I don't know, friend Orchis," soberly replied China Aster, "but may be my not having drawn a lottery prize, like you, may make some difference."

'"Nonsense! before I knew anything about the prize I was gay as a lark, just as gay as I am now. In fact, it has always been a principle with me to hold to the bright view."

'Upon this, China Aster looked a little hard at Orchis, because the truth was, that until the lucky prize came to him, Orchis had gone under the nickname of Doleful Dumps, he having been beforetimes of a hypochondriac turn, so much so as to save up and put by a few dollars of his scanty earnings against that rainy day he used to groan so much about.

'"I tell you what it is, now, friend China Aster," said Orchis, pointing down to the check under the stone, and then slapping his pocket, "the check shall lie there if you say so, but your note shan't keep it company. In fact, China Aster, I am too sincerely your friend to take advantage of a passing fit of the blues in you. You *shall* reap the benefit of my friendship." With which, buttoning up his coat in a jiffy, away he ran, leaving the check behind.

'At first, China Aster was going to tear it up, but thinking that this ought not to be done except in the presence of the drawer of the check, he mused a while, and picking it up, trudged back to the candlery, fully resolved to call upon Orchis soon as his day's work was over, and destroy the check before his eyes. But it so happened that when China Aster called, Orchis was out, and, having waited for him a weary time in vain, China Aster went home, still with the check, but still resolved not to keep it another day. Bright and early next morning he would a second time go after Orchis, and would, no doubt, make a sure thing of it, by finding him in his bed; for since the lottery-prize came to him, Orchis, besides becoming more cheery, had also grown a little lazy. But as destiny would have it, that same night China Aster had a dream, in which a being in the guise of a smiling angel, and holding a kind of cornucopia in her hand, hovered over him, pouring down showers of small gold dollars, thick as kernels of corn. "I am Bright Future, friend China Aster," said the angel, "and if you do what friend Orchis would have you do, just see what will come of it." With which Bright Future, with another swing of her cornucopia, poured such another shower of small gold dollars upon him, that it seemed to bank him up all round, and he waded about in it like a maltster in malt.

'Now, dreams are wonderful things, as everybody knows – so wonderful, indeed, that some people stop not short of ascribing them directly to heaven; and China Aster, who was of a proper turn of mind in everything, thought that in consideration of the dream, it would be but well to wait a little, ere seeking Orchis again. During the day, China Aster's mind dwelling continually upon the dream, he was so full of it, that when Old Plain Talk dropped in to see him, just before dinner time, as he often did, out of the interest he took in Old Honesty's son, China Aster told all about his vision, adding that he could not think that so radiant an angel could deceive; and, indeed, talked at such a rate that one would have thought he believed the angel some beautiful human philanthropist. Something in this sort Old Plain Talk understood him, and, accordingly, in his plain way, said: "China Aster, you tell me that an angel appeared to you in a dream. Now what does that amount to but this, that you dreamed an angel appeared to you? Go right away, China Aster, and return the check as I advised you before. If friend Prudence were here, he would say just the same thing." With which words Old Plain Talk went off to find friend Prudence, but not succeeding, was returning to the candlery himself, when, at a distance mistaking him for a dun who had long annoyed him, China Aster in a panic barred all his doors, and ran to the back part of the candlery, where no knock could be heard.

'By this sad mistake, being left with no friend to argue the other side of the question, China Aster was so worked upon at last, by musing over his dream, that nothing would do but he must get the check cashed, and lay out the money the very same day in buying a good lot of spermaceti to make into candles, by which operation he counted upon turning a better penny than he ever had before in his life; in fact, this he believed would prove the foundation of that famous fortune which the angel had promised him.

'Now, in using the money, China Aster was resolved punctually to pay the interest every six months till the principal should be returned, howbeit not a word about such a thing had been breathed by Orchis; though, indeed, according to custom, as well as law, in such matters, interest would legitimately accrue on the loan, nothing to the contrary having been put in the bond. Whether Orchis at the time had this in mind or not, there is no sure telling; but, to all appearance, he never so much as cared to think about the matter, one way or other.

'Though the spermaceti venture rather disappointed China Aster's sanguine expectations, yet he made out to pay the first six months' interest, and though his next venture turned out still less prosperously, yet by pinching his family in the matter of fresh meat, and what pained him still more, his boys' schooling, he contrived to pay the second six months' interest, sincerely grieved that integrity, as well as its opposite, though not in an equal degree, costs something, sometimes.

'Meanwhile, Orchis had gone on a trip to Europe by advice of a physician; it so happening that, since the lottery-prize came to him, it had been discovered to Orchis that his health was not very firm, though he had never complained of anything before but a slight ailing of the spleen, scarce worth talking about at the time. So Orchis, being abroad, could not help China Aster's paying his interest as he did, however much he might have been opposed to it; for China Aster paid it to Orchis's agent, who was of too business-like a turn to decline interest regularly paid in on a loan.

'But overmuch to trouble the agent on that score was not again to be the fate of China Aster; for, not being of that skeptical spirit which refuses to trust customers, his third venture resulted, through bad debts, in almost a total loss — a bad blow for the candle-maker. Neither did Old Plain Talk, and Old Prudence neglect the opportunity to read him an uncheerful enough lesson upon the consequences of his disregarding their advice in the matter of having nothing to do with borrowed money. "It's all just as I predicted," said Old Plain Talk, blowing his old nose with his old bandana. "Yea, indeed is it," chimed in Old Prudence, rapping his staff on the floor, and then leaning upon it, looking with solemn forebodings upon China Aster. Low-spirited enough felt the poor candle-maker; till all at once who should come with a bright face to him but his bright friend, the angel, in another dream. Again the cornucopia poured out its treasure, and promised still more. Revived by the vision, he resolved not to be down-hearted, but up and at it once more – contrary to the advice of Old Plain Talk, backed as usual by his crony, which was to the effect, that, under present circumstances, the best thing China Aster could do, would be to wind up his business, settle, if he could, all his liabilities, and then go to work as a journeyman, by which he could earn good wages, and give up, from that time henceforth, all thoughts of rising above being a paid subordinate to men more able than himself, for China Aster's career thus far plainly proved him the legitimate son of Old Honesty, who, as every one knew, had never shown much business-talent, so little, in fact, that many said of him that he had no business to be in business. And just this plain saying Plain Talk now plainly applied to China Aster, and Old Prudence never disagreed with him. But the angel in the dream did, and, maugre Plain Talk, put quite other notions into the candle-maker.

'He considered what he should do towards re-establishing him-self. Doubtless, had Orchis been in the country, he would have aided him in this strait. As it was, he applied to others; and as in the world, much as some may hint to the contrary, an honest man in misfortune still can find friends to stay by him and help him, even so it proved with China Aster, who at last succeeded in borrowing from a rich old farmer the sum of six hundred dollars, at the usual interest of money-lenders, upon the security of a secret bond signed by China Aster's wife and himself, to the effect that all such right and title to any property that should be left her by a well-to-do-childless uncle, an invalid tanner, such property should, in the event of China Aster's failing to return the borrowed sum on the given day, be the lawful possession of the money-lender. True, it was just as much as China Aster could possibly do to induce his wife, a careful woman, to sign this bond; because she had always regarded her promised share in her uncle's estate as an anchor well to windward of the hard times in which China Aster had always been more or less involved, and from which, in her bosom, she never had seen much chance of his freeing himself. Some notion may be had of China Aster's standing in the heart and head of his wife, by a short sentence commonly used in reply to such persons as happened to sound her on the point. "China Aster," she would say, "is a good husband, but a bad business man!" Indeed, she was a connection on the maternal side of Old Plain Talk's. But had not China Aster taken good care not to let Old Plain Talk and Old Prudence hear of his dealings with the old farmer, ten to one they would, in some way, have interfered with his success in that quarter.

'It has been hinted that the honesty of China Aster was what mainly induced the money-lender to befriend him in his misfortune, and this must be apparent; for, had China Aster been a different man, the money-lender might have dreaded lest, in the event of his failing to meet his note, he might some way prove slippery – more especially as, in the hour of distress, worked upon by remorse for so jeopardizing his wife's money, his heart might prove a traitor to his bond, not to hint that it was more than doubtful how such a secret security and claim, as in the last resort would be the old farmer's, would stand in a court of law. But though one inference from all this may be, that had China Aster been something else than what he was, he would not have been trusted, and, therefore, he would have been effectually shut out from running his own and wife's head into the usurer's noose; yet those who, when everything at last came out, maintained that, in this view and to this extent, the honesty of the candle-maker was no advantage to him, in so saying, such persons said what every good heart must deplore, and no prudent tongue will admit.

'It may be mentioned, that the old farmer made China Aster take part of his loan in three old dried-up cows and one lame

horse, not improved by the glanders. These were thrown in at a
pretty high figure, the old money-lender having a singular prejudice in regard to the high value of any sort of stock raised on his
farm. With a great deal of difficulty, and at more loss, China
Aster disposed of his cattle at public auction, no private purchaser
being found who could be prevailed upon to invest. And now,
raking and scraping in every way, and working early and late,
China Aster at last started afresh, nor without again largely and
confidently extending himself. However, he did not try his hand
at the spermaceti again, but, admonished by experience, returned
to tallow. But, having bought a good lot of it, by the time he got
it into candles, tallow fell so low, and candles with it, that his
candles per pound barely sold for what he had paid for the tallow.
Meantime, a year's unpaid interest had accrued on Orchis' loan,
but China Aster gave himself not so much concern about that as
about the interest now due to the old farmer. But he was glad that
the principal there had yet some time to run. However, the
skinny old fellow gave him some trouble by coming after him
every day or two on a scraggy old white horse, furnished with a
musty old saddle, and goaded into his shambling old paces with a
withered old raw hide. All the neighbours said that surely Death
himself on the pale horse was after poor China Aster now. And
something so it proved; for, ere long, China Aster found himself
involved in troubles mortal enough.

'At this juncture Orchis was heard of. Orchis, it seemed, had
returned from his travels, and clandestinely married, and, in a
kind of queer way, was living in Pennsylvania among his wife's
relations, who, among other things, had induced him to join a
church, or rather semi-religious school, of Come-Outers; and
what was still more, Orchis, without coming to the spot himself,
had sent word to his agent to dispose of some of his property in
Marietta, and remit him the proceeds. Within a year after, China
Aster received a letter from Orchis, commending him for his
punctuality in paying the first year's interest, and regretting the
necessity that he (Orchis) was now under of using all his dividends;

so he relied upon China Aster's paying the next six months' interest, and of course with the back interest. Not more surprised than alarmed, China Aster thought of taking steamboat to go and see Orchis, but he was saved that expense by the unexpected arrival in Marietta of Orchis in person, suddenly called there by that strange kind of capriciousness lately characterizing him. No sooner did China Aster hear of his old friend's arrival than he hurried to call upon him. He found him curiously rusty in dress, sallow in cheek, and decidedly less gay and cordial in manner, which the more suprised China Aster, because, in former days, he had more than once heard Orchis, in his light rattling way, declare that all he (Orchis) wanted to make him a perfectly happy, hilarious, and benignant man, was a voyage to Europe and a wife, with a free development of his inmost nature.

'Upon China Aster's stating his case, his rusted friend was silent for a time; then, in an odd way, said that he would not crowd China Aster, but still his (Orchis') necessities were urgent. Could not China Aster mortgage the candlery? He was honest, and must have moneyed friends; and could he not press his sales of candles? Could not the market be forced a little in that particular? The profits on candles must be very great. Seeing, now, that Orchis had the notion that the candle-making business was a very profitable one, and knowing sorely enough what an error was here, China Aster tried to undeceive him. But he could not drive the truth into Orchis – Orchis being very obtuse here, and, at the same time, strange to say, very melancholy. Finally, Orchis glanced off from so unpleasing a subject into the most unexpected reflections, taken from a religious point of view, upon the unstableness and deceitfulness of the human heart. But having, as he thought, experienced something of that sort of thing, China Aster did not take exception to his friend's observations, but still refrained from so doing, almost as much for the sake of sympathetic sociality as anything else. Presently, Orchis, without much ceremony, rose, and saying he must write a letter to his wife, bade his friend good-bye, but without warmly shaking him by the hand as of old.

'In much concern at the change, China Aster made earnest inquiries in suitable quarters, as to what things, as yet unheard of, had befallen Orchis, to bring about such a revolution; and learned at last that, besides travelling, and getting married, and joining the sect of Come-Outers, Orchis had somehow got a bad dyspepsia, and lost considerable property through a breach of trust on the part of a factor in New York. Telling these things to Old Plain Talk, that man of some knowledge of the world shook his old head, and told China Aster that, though he hoped it might prove otherwise, yet it seemed to him that all he had communicated about Orchis worked together for bad omens as to his future forbearance – especially, he added with a grim sort of smile, in view of his joining the sect of Come-Outers; for, if some men knew what was their inmost natures, instead of coming out with it, they would try their best to keep it in, which, indeed, was the way with the prudent sort. In all which sour notions Old Prudence, as usual, chimed in.

'When interest-day came again, China Aster, by the utmost exertions, could only pay Orchis' agent a small part of what was due, and a part of that was made up by his children's gift money (bright tenpenny pieces and new quarters, kept in their little money-boxes), and pawning his best clothes, with those of his wife and children, so that all were subjected to the hardship of staying away from church. And the old usurer, too, now beginning to be obstreperous, China Aster paid him his interest and some other pressing debts with money got by, at last, mortgaging the candlery.

'When next interest-day came round for Orchis, not a penny could be raised. With much grief of heart, China Aster so informed Orchis' agent. Meantime the note to the old usurer fell due, and nothing from China Aster was ready to meet it; yet, as heaven sends its rain on the just and unjust alike, by a coincidence not unfavourable to the old farmer, the well-to-do uncle, the tanner, having died, the usurer entered upon possession of such part of his property left by will to the wife of China Aster. When still the next interest-day for Orchis came round, it found China Aster worse off than ever; for besides his other troubles, he was now weak with sickness. Feebly dragging himself to Orchis' agent, he met him in the street, told him just how it was; upon which the agent, with a grave enough face, said that he had instructions from his employer not to crowd him about the interest at present, but to say to him that about the time the note would mature, Orchis would have heavy liabilities to meet, and therefore the note must at that time be certainly paid, and, of course, the back interest with it; and not only so, but, as Orchis had had to allow the interest for good part of the time, he hoped that, for the back interest, China Aster would, in reciprocation, have no objections to allowing interest on the interest annually. To be sure, this was not the law; but, between friends who accommodate each other, it was the custom.

'Just then, Old Plain Talk with Old Prudence turned the corner, coming plump upon China Aster as the agent left him; and whether it was a sun-stroke, or whether they accidentally ran against him, or whether it was his being so weak, or whether it was everything together, or how it was exactly, there is no telling, but poor China Aster fell to the earth, and, striking his head sharply, was picked up senseless. It was a day in July; such a light and heat as only the midsummer banks of the inland Ohio know. China Aster was taken home on a door; lingered a few days with a wandering mind, and kept wandering on, till at last, at dead of night, when nobody was aware, his spirit wandered away into the other world.

'Old Plain Talk and Old Prudence, neither of whom ever omitted attending any funeral, which, indeed, was their chief exercise – these two were among the sincerest mourners who followed the remains of the son of their ancient friend to the grave.

'It is needless to tell of the executions that followed; how that the candlery was sold by the mortgagee; how Orchis never got a penny for his loan; and how, in the case of the poor widow, chastisement was tempered with mercy; for though she was left penniless, she was not left childless. Yet, unmindful of the alleviation, a spirit of complaint, at what she impatiently called the bitterness of her lot and the hardness of the world, so preyed upon her, as ere long to hurry her from the obscurity of indigence to the deeper shades of the tomb.

'But though the straits in which China Aster had left his family had, besides apparently dimming the world's regard, likewise seemed to dim its sense of the probity of its deceased head, and though this, as some thought, did not speak well for the world, yet it happened in this case, as in others, that though the world may for a time seem insensible to that merit which lies under a cloud, yet, sooner or later, it always renders honour where honour is due; for, upon the death of the widow, the freemen of Marietta, as a tribute of respect for China Aster, and an expression of their conviction of his high moral worth, passed a resolution, that until they attained maturity, his children should be considered the town's guests. No mere verbal compliment, like those of some public bodies; for on the same day, the orphans were officially installed in that hospitable edifice where their worthy grandfather, the town's guest before them, had breathed his last breath.

'But sometimes honour may be paid to the memory of an honest man, and still his mound remain without a monument. Not so, however, with the candle-maker. At an early day Plain Talk had procured a plain stone, and was digesting in his mind what pithy word or two to place upon it, when there was discovered, in China Aster's otherwise empty wallet, an epitaph, written, probably, in one of those disconsolate hours, attended with more or less mental aberration, perhaps, so frequent with him for some months prior to his end. A memorandum on the back expressed the wish that it might be placed over his grave. Though with the sentiment of the epitaph Plain Talk did not disagree, he himself being at times of a hypochondriac turn – at least, so many said – yet the language struck him as too much drawn out; so after consultation with Old Prudence, he decided

upon making use of the epitaph, yet not without verbal retrench-
ments. And though, when these were made, the thing still
appeared wordy to him, nevertheless, thinking that, since a dead
man was to be spoken about, it was but just to let him speak for
himself, especially when he spoke sincerely, and when, by so
doing, the more salutary lesson would be given, he had the
retrenched inscription chiselled as follows upon the stone:

HERE LIE

THE REMAINS OF

CHINA ASTER THE CANDLE-MAKER,

WHOSE CAREER

WAS AN EXAMPLE OF THE TRUTH OF SCRIPTURE, AS FOUND

IN THE

SOBER PHILOSOPHY

OF

SOLOMON THE WISE;

FOR HE WAS RUINED BY ALLOWING HIMSELF TO BE PERSUADED,

AGAINST HIS BETTER SENSE,

INTO THE FREE INDULGENCE OF CONFIDENCE

AND

AN ARDENTLY BRIGHT VIEW OF LIFE,

TO THE EXCLUSION

OF

THAT COUNSEL WHICH COMES BY HEEDING

THE

OPPOSITE VIEW.

'This inscription raised some talk in the town, and was rather
severely criticized by the capitalist – one of a very cheerful turn –
who had secured his loan to China Aster by the mortgage; and
though it also proved obnoxious to the man who, in town-meet-
ing, had first moved for the compliment to China Aster's memory,
and, indeed, was deemed by him a sort of slur upon the candle-
maker, to that degree that he refused to believe that the candle-
maker himself had composed it, charging Old Plain Talk with the

authorship, alleging that the internal evidence showed that none but that veteran old croaker could have penned such a jeremiade – yet, for all this, the stone stood. In everything, of course, Old Plain Talk was seconded by Old Prudence; who, one day going to the graveyard, in great-coat and over-shoes – for, though it was a sunshiny morning, he thought that, owing to heavy dews, dampness might lurk in the ground – long stood before the stone, sharply leaning over on his staff, spectacles on nose, spelling out the epitaph word by word; and, afterwards meeting Old Plain Talk in the street, gave a great rap with his stick, and said: "Friend Plain Talk, that epitaph will do very well. Nevertheless, one short sentence is wanting." Upon which, Plain Talk said it was too late, the chiselled words being so arranged, after the usual manner of such inscriptions, that nothing could be interlined. "Then," said Old Prudence, "I will put it in the shape of a postscript." Accordingly, with the approbation of Old Plain Talk, he had the following words chiselled at the left-hand corner of the stone, and pretty low down:

The root of all was a friendly loan.'

41

ENDING WITH A RUPTURE OF THE
HYPOTHESIS

——••——

'With what heart,' cried Frank, still in character, 'have you told me this story? A story I can no way approve; for its moral, if accepted, would drain me of all reliance upon my last stay, and, therefore, of my last courage in life. For, what was that bright view of China Aster but a cheerful trust that, if he but kept up a brave heart, worked hard, and ever hoped for the best, all at last would go well? If your purpose, Charlie, in telling me this story, was to pain me, and keenly, you have succeeded; but, if it was to destroy my last confidence, I praise God you have not.'

'Confidence?' cried Charlie, who, on his side, seemed with his whole heart to enter into the spirit of the thing, 'what has confidence to do with the matter? That moral of the story, which I am for commending to you, is this: the folly, on both sides, of a friend's helping a friend. For was not that loan of Orchis to China Aster the first step towards their estrangement? And did it not bring about what in effect was the enmity of Orchis? I tell you, Frank, true friendship, like other precious things, is not rashly to be meddled with. And what more meddlesome between friends than a loan? A regular marplot. For how can you help that the helper must turn out a creditor? And creditor and friend, can they ever be one? no, not in the most lenient case; since, out of lenity to forgo one's claim, is less to be a friendly creditor than to cease to be a creditor at all. But it will not do to rely upon this lenity, no, not in the best man; for the best man, as the worst, is subject to all mortal contingencies. He may travel, he may marry, he may join the

Come-Outers, or some equally untoward school or sect, not to speak of other things that more or less tend to new-cast the character. And were there nothing else, who shall answer for his digestion, upon which so much depends?'

'But Charlie, dear Charlie –'

'Nay, wait. – You have hearkened to my story in vain, if you do not see that, however indulgent and right-minded I may seem to you now, that is no guarantee for the future. And into the power of that uncertain personality which, through the mutability of my humanity, I may hereafter become, should not common sense dissuade you, my dear Frank, from putting yourself? Consider. Would you, in your present need, be willing to accept a loan from a friend, securing him by a mortgage on your homestead, and do so, knowing that you had no reason to feel satisfied that the mortgage might not eventually be transferred into the hands of a foe? Yet the difference between this man and that man is not so great as the difference between what the same man may be to-day and what he may be in days to come. For there is no bent of heart or turn of thought which any man holds by virtue of an unalterable nature or will. Even those feelings and opinions deemed most identical with eternal right and truth, it is not impossible but that, as personal persuasions, they may in reality be but the result of some chance tip of Fate's elbow in throwing her dice. For, not to go into the first seeds of things, and passing by the accident of parentage predisposing to this or that habit of mind, descend below these, and tell me, if you change this man's experiences or that man's books, will wisdom go surety for his unchanged convictions? As particular food begets particular dreams, so particular experiences or books particular feelings or beliefs. I will hear nothing of that fine babble about development and its laws; there is no development in opinion and feeling but the developments of time and tide. You may deem all this talk idle, Frank; but conscience bids me show you how fundamental the reasons for treating you as I do.'

'But Charlie, dear Charlie, what new notions are these? I thought that man was no poor drifting weed of the universe, as you phrased it; that, if so minded, he could have a will, a way, a thought, and a heart of his own? But now you have turned everything upside down again, with an inconsistency that amazes and shocks me.'

'Inconsistency? Bah!'

'There speaks the ventriloquist again,' sighed Frank, in bitterness.

Ill pleased, it may be, by this repetition of an allusion little flattering to his originality, however much so to his docility, the disciple sought to carry it off by exclaiming: 'Yes, I turn over day and night, with indefatigable pains, the sublime pages of my master, and unfortunately for you, my dear friend, I find nothing *there* that leads me to think otherwise than I do. But enough: in this matter the experience of China Aster teaches a moral more to the point than anything Mark Winsome can offer, or I either.'

'I cannot think so, Charlie; for neither am I China Aster, nor do I stand in his position. The loan to China Aster was to extend his business with; the loan I seek is to relieve my necessities.'

'Your dress, my dear Frank, is respectable; your cheek is not gaunt. Why talk of necessities when nakedness and starvation beget the only real necessities?'

'But I need relief, Charlie; and so sorely, that I now conjure you to forget that I was ever your friend, while I apply to you only as a fellow-being, whom, surely, you will not turn away.'

'That I will not. Take off your hat, bow over to the ground, and supplicate an alms of me in the way of London Streets, and you shall not be a sturdy beggar in vain. But no man drops pennies into the hat of a friend, let me tell you. If you turn beggar, then, for the honour of noble friendship, I turn stranger.'

'Enough,' cried the other, rising, and with a toss of his shoulders seeming disdainfully to throw off the character he had assumed. 'Enough. I have had my fill of the philosophy of Mark Winsome as put into action. And moonshiny as it in theory may be, yet a very practical philosophy it turns out in effect, as he himself engaged I should find. But, miserable for my race should I be, if I thought he spoke truth when he claimed, for proof of the soundness of his system, that the study of it tended to much the same formation of character with the experiences of the world. – Apt disciple! Why wrinkle the brow, and waste the oil both of life and the lamp, only to turn out a head kept cool by the under ice of the heart? What your illustrious magian has taught you, any poor, old, broken–down, heart-shrunken dandy might have lisped. Pray, leave me, and with you take the last dregs of your inhuman philosophy. And here, take this shilling, and at the first woodlanding buy yourself a few chips to warm the frozen natures of you and your philosopher by.'

With these words and a grand scorn the cosmopolitan turned on his heel, leaving his companion at a loss to determine where exactly the fictitious character had been dropped, and the real one, if any, resumed. If any, because, with pointed meaning, there occurred to him, as he gazed after the cosmopolitan, these familiar lines:

> All the world's a stage,
> And all the men and women merely players;
> They have their exits and their entrances,
> And one man in his time plays many parts.

42

UPON THE HEEL OF THE LAST SCENE, THE COSMOPOLITAN ENTERS THE BARBER'S SHOP, A BENEDICTION ON HIS LIPS

'Bless you, barber!'

Now, owing to the lateness of the hour, the barber had been all alone until within the ten minutes last passed; when, finding himself rather dullish company to himself, he thought he would have a good time with Souter John and Tam O'Shanter, otherwise called Somnus and Morpheus, two very good fellows, though one was not very bright, and the other an arrant rattle-brain, who, though much listened to by some, no wise man would believe under oath.

In short, with back presented to the glare of his lamps, and so to the door, the honest barber was taking what are called cat-naps, and dreaming in his chair; so that, upon suddenly hearing the benediction above, pronounced in tones not unangelic, starting up, half awake, he stared before him, but saw nothing, for the stranger stood behind. What with cat-naps, dreams, and bewilderments, therefore, the voice seemed a sort of spiritual manifestation to him; so that, for the moment, he stood all agape, eyes fixed, and one arm in the air.

'Why, barber, are you reaching up to catch birds there with salt?'

'Ah!' turning round disenchanted, 'it is only a man, then.'

'*Only* a man? As if to be but man were nothing. But don't be too sure what I am. You call me *man*, just as the townsfolk called the angels who, in man's form, came to Lot's house; just as the Jew rustics called the devils who, in man's form, haunted the tombs. You can conclude nothing absolute from the human form, barber.'

'But I can conclude something from that sort of talk, with that sort of dress,' shrewdly thought the barber, eyeing him with regained self-possession, and not without some latent touch of apprehension at being alone with him. What was passing in his mind seemed divined by the other, who now, more rationally and gravely, and as if he expected it should be attended to, said: 'Whatever else you may conclude upon, it is my desire that you conclude to give me a good shave,' at the same time loosening his neck-cloth. 'Are you competent to a good shave, barber?'

'No broker more so, sir,' answered the barber, whom the business-like proposition instinctively made confine to business-ends his views of the visitor.

'Broker? What has a broker to do with lather? A broker I have always understood to be a worthy dealer in certain papers and metals.'

'He, he!' taking him now for some dry sort of joker, whose jokes, he being a customer, it might be as well to appreciate, 'he, he! You understand well enough, sir. Take this seat, sir,' laying his hand on a great stuffed chair, high-backed and high-armed, crimson-covered, and raised on a sort of dais, and which seemed but to lack a canopy and quarterings, to make it in aspect quite a throne, 'take this seat, sir.'

'Thank you,' sitting down; 'and now, pray, explain that about the broker. But look, look – what's this?' suddenly rising, and pointing, with his long pipe, towards a gilt notification swinging among coloured fly-papers from the ceiling, like a tavern sign, 'No Trust? No trust means distrust; distrust means no confidence. Barber,' turning upon him excitedly, 'what fell suspiciousness prompts this scandalous confession? My life!' stamping his foot, 'if but to tell a dog that you have no confidence in him be matter for affront to the dog, what an insult to take that way the whole haughty race of man by the beard! By my heart, sir! but at least you are valiant; backing the spleen of Thersites with the pluck of Agamemnon.'

'Your sort of talk, sir, is not exactly in my line,' said the barber, rather ruefully, being now again hopeless of his customer, and not without return of uneasiness; 'not in my line, sir,' he emphatically repeated.

'But the taking of mankind by the nose is; a habit, barber, which I sadly fear has insensibly bred in you a disrespect for man. For how, indeed, may respectful conceptions of him coexist with the perpetual habit of taking him by the nose? But, tell me, though I, too, clearly see the import of your notification, I do not, as yet, perceive the object. What is it?'

'Now you speak a little in my line, sir,' said the barber, not unrelieved at this return to plain talk; 'that notification I find very useful, sparing me much work which would not pay. Yes, I lost a good deal, off and on, before putting that up,' gratefully glancing towards it.

'But what is its object? Surely, you don't mean to say, in so many words, that you have no confidence? For instance, now,' flinging aside his neckcloth, throwing back his blouse, and reseating himself on the tonsorial throne, at sight of which proceeding the barber mechanically filled a cup with hot water from a copper vessel over a spirit-lamp, 'for instance, now, suppose I say to you, "Barber, my dear barber, unhappily I have no small change by me to-night, but shave me, and depend upon your money to-morrow" – suppose I should say that now, you would put trust in me, wouldn't you? You would have confidence?'

'Seeing that it is you, sir,' with complaisance replied the barber, now mixing the lather, 'seeing that it is *you*, sir, I won't answer that question. No need to.'

'Of course, of course – in that view. But, as a supposition – you would have confidence in me, wouldn't you?'

'Why – yes, yes.'

'Then why that sign?'

'Ah, sir, all people ain't like you,' was the smooth reply, at the same time, as if smoothly to close the debate, beginning smoothly to apply the lather, which operation, however, was, by a motion, protested against by the subject, but only out of a desire to rejoin, which was done in these words:

'All people ain't like me. Then I must be either better or worse
than most people. Worse, you could not mean; no, barber, you
could not mean that; hardly that. It remains, then, that you think
me better than most people. But that I ain't vain enough to
believe; though, from vanity, I confess, I could never yet, by my
best wrestlings, entirely free myself; nor, indeed, to be frank, am I
at bottom over anxious to – this same vanity, barber, being so
harmless, so useful, so comfortable, so pleasingly preposterous a
passion.'

'Very true, sir; and upon my honour, sir, you talk very well.
But the lather is getting a little cold, sir.'

'Better cold lather, barber, than a cold heart. Why that cold
sign? Ah, I don't wonder you try to shirk the confession. You feel
in your soul how ungenerous a hint is there. And yet, barber, now
that I look into your eyes – which somehow speak to me of the
mother that must have so often looked into them before me – I
dare say, though you may not think it, that the spirit of that
notification is not one with your nature. For look now, setting
business views aside, regarding the thing in an abstract light; in
short, supposing a case, barber; supposing, I say, you see a stranger,
his face accidentally averted, but his visible part very respectable-
looking; what now, barber – I put it to your conscience, to your
charity – what would be your impression of that man, in a moral
point of view? Being in a signal sense a stranger, would you, for
that, signally set him down for a knave?'

'Certainly not, sir; by no means,' cried the barber, humanely resentful.

'You would upon the face of him –'

'Hold, sir,' said the barber, 'nothing about the face; you remember, sir, that is out of sight.'

'I forgot that. Well then, you would, upon the *back* of him,
conclude him to be, not improbably, some worthy sort of person;
in short, an honest man; wouldn't you?'

'Not unlikely I should, sir.'

'Well now – don't be so impatient with your brush, barber –

suppose that honest man meet you by night in some dark corner of the boat where his face would still remain unseen, asking you to trust him for a shave – how then?'

'Wouldn't trust him, sir.'

'But is not an honest man to be trusted?'

'Why – why – yes, sir.'

'There! don't you see, now?'

'See what?' asked the disconcerted barber, rather vexedly.

'Why, you stand self-contradicted, barber; don't you?'

'No,' doggedly.

'Barber,' gravely, and after a pause of concern, 'the enemies of our race have a saying that insincerity is the most universal and inveterate vice of man – the lasting bar to real amelioration, whether of individuals or of the world. Don't you now, barber, by your stubbornness on this occasion, give colour to such a calumny?'

'Hity-tity!' cried the barber, losing patience, and with it respect; 'stubbornness?' Then clattering round the brush in the cup, 'Will you be shaved, or won't you?'

'Barber, I will be shaved, and with pleasure; but, pray, don't raise your voice that way. Why, now, if you go through life gritting your teeth in that fashion, what a comfortless time you will have.'

'I take as much comfort in this world as you or any other man,' cried the barber, whom the other's sweetness of temper seemed rather to exasperate than soothe.

'To resent the imputation of anything like unhappiness I have often observed to be peculiar to certain orders of men,' said the other pensively, and half to himself, 'just as to be indifferent to that imputation, from holding happiness but for a secondary good and inferior grace, I have observed to be equally peculiar to other kinds of men. Pray, barber,' innocently looking up, 'which think you is the superior creature?'

'All this sort of talk,' cried the barber, still unmollified, 'is, as I told you once before, not in my line. In a few minutes I shall shut up this shop. Will you be shaved?'

'Shave away, barber. What hinders?' turning up his face like a flower.

The shaving began, and proceeded in silence, till at length it became necessary to prepare to relather a little – affording an opportunity for resuming the subject, which, on one side, was not let slip.

'Barber,' with a kind of cautious kindliness, feeling his way, 'barber, now have a little patience with me; do; trust me, I wish not to offend. I have been thinking over that supposed case of the man with the averted face, and I cannot rid my mind of the impression that, by your opposite replies to my question at the time, you showed yourself much of a piece with a good many other men – that is, you have confidence, and then again, you have none. Now, what I would ask is, do you think it sensible standing for a sensible man, one foot on confidence and the other on suspicion? Don't you think, barber, that you ought to elect? Don't you think consistency requires that you should either say "I have confidence in all men," and take down your notification; or else say "I suspect all men," and keep it up?'

This dispassionate, if not deferential, way of putting the case, did not fail to impress the barber, and proportionately conciliate him. Likewise, from its pointedness, it served to make him thoughtful; for, instead of going to the copper vessel for more water, as he had purposed, he halted half-way towards it, and, after a pause, cup in hand, said: 'Sir, I hope you would not do me injustice. I don't say, and can't say, and wouldn't say, that I suspect all men; but I *do* say that strangers are not to be trusted, and so,' pointing up to the sign, 'no trust.'

'But look, now, I beg, barber,' rejoined the other deprecatingly, not presuming too much upon the barber's changed temper; 'look, now; to say that strangers are not to be trusted, does not that imply something like saying that mankind is not to be trusted; for the mass of mankind, are they not necessarily strangers to each individual man? Come, come, my friend,' winningly, 'you are no Timon to hold the mass of mankind untrustworthy.

Take down your notification; it is misanthropical; much the same sign that Timon traced with charcoal on the forehead of a skull stuck over his cave. Take it down, barber; take it down to-night. Trust men. Just try the experiment of trusting men for this one little trip. Come now, I'm a philanthropist, and will insure you against losing a cent.'

The barber shook his head dryly, and answered, 'Sir, you must excuse me. I have a family.'

'So you are a philanthropist, sir,' added the barber with an illuminated look; 'that accounts, then, for all. Very odd sort of man the philanthropist. You are the second one, sir, I have seen. Very odd sort of man, indeed, the philanthropist. Ah, sir,' again meditatively stirring in the shaving-cup, 'I sadly fear, lest you philanthropists know better what goodness is, than what men are.' Then, eyeing him as if he were some strange creature behind cage-bars, 'So you are a philanthropist, sir.'

'I am Philanthropos, and love mankind. And, what is more than you do, barber, I trust them.'

Here the barber, casually recalled to his business, would have replenished his shaving-cup, but finding now that on his last visit to the water-vessel he had not replaced it over the lamp, he did so now; and, while waiting for it to heat again, became almost as sociable as if the heating water were meant for whisky-punch; and almost as pleasantly garrulous as the pleasant barbers in romances.

'Sir,' said he, taking a throne beside his customer (for in a row there were three thrones on the dais, as for the three kings of Cologne, those patron saints of the barber), 'sir, you say you trust men. Well, I suppose I might share some of your trust, were it not for this trade, that I follow, too much letting me in behind the scenes.'

'I think I understand,' with a saddened look; 'and much the same thing I have heard from persons in pursuits different from yours – from the lawyer, from the congressman, from the editor, not to mention others, each, with a strange kind of melancholy vanity, claiming for his vocation the distinction of affording the surest inlets to the conviction that man is no better than he should be. All of which testimony, if reliable, would, by mutual corroboration, justify some disturbance in a good man's mind. But no, no; it is a mistake – all a mistake.'

'True, sir, very true,' assented the barber.

'Glad to hear that,' brightening up.

'Not so fast, sir,' said the barber; 'I agree with you in thinking that the lawyer, and the congressman, and the editor, are in error, but only in so far as each claims peculiar facilities for the sort of knowledge in question; because, you see, sir, the truth is, that every trade or pursuit which brings one into contact with the facts, sir, such trade or pursuit is equally an avenue to those facts.'

'*How* exactly is that?'

'Why, sir, in my opinion – and for the last twenty years I have, at odd times, turned the matter over some in my mind – he who comes to know man, will not remain in ignorance of man. I think I am not rash in saying that; am I, sir?'

'Barber, you talk like an oracle – obscurely, barber, obscurely.'

'Well, sir,' with some self-complacency, 'the barber has always been held an oracle, but as for the obscurity, that I don't admit.'

'But pray, now, by your account, what precisely may be this mysterious knowledge gained in your trade? I grant you, indeed, as before hinted, that your trade, imposing on you the necessity of functionally tweaking the noses of mankind, is, in that respect, unfortunate, very much so; nevertheless, a well-regulated imagination should be proof even to such a provocation to improper conceits. But what I want to learn from you, barber, is, how does the mere handling of the outside of men's heads lead you to distrust the inside of their hearts?'

'What, sir, to say nothing more, can one be for ever dealing in macassar oil, hair dyes, cosmetics, false moustaches, wigs, and toupees, and still believe that men are wholly what they look to be? What think you, sir, are a thoughtful barber's reflections, when, behind a careful curtain, he shaves the thin, dead stubble off a head, and then dismisses it to the world, radiant in curling auburn? To contrast the shamefaced air behind the curtain, the fearful looking forward to being possibly discovered there by a prying acquaintance, with the cheerful assurance and challenging pride with which the same man steps forth again, a gay deception, into the street, while some honest, shock-headed fellow humbly gives him the wall. Ah, sir, they may talk of the courage of truth, but my trade teaches me that truth sometimes is sheepish. Lies, lies, sir, brave lies are the lions!'

'You twist the moral, barber; you sadly twist it. Look, now; take it this way: A modest man thrust out naked into the street, would he not be abashed? Take him in and clothe him; would not his confidence be restored? And in either case, is any reproach involved? Now, what is true of the whole, holds proportionably true of the part. The bald head is a nakedness which the wig is a coat to. To feel uneasy at the possibility of the exposure of one's nakedness at top, and to feel comforted by the consciousness of having it clothed – these feelings, instead of being dishonourable to a bald man, do, in fact, but attest a proper respect for himself and his fellows. And as for the deception, you may as well call the fine roof of a fine chateau a deception, since, like a fine wig, it also is an artificial cover to the head, and equally, in the common eye, decorates the wearer. – I have confuted you, my dear barber; I have confounded you.'

'Pardon,' said the barber, 'but I do not see that you have. His coat and his roof no man pretends to palm off as a part of himself, but the bald man palms off hair, not his, for his own.'

'Not *his*, barber? If he have fairly purchased his hair, the law will protect him in its ownership, even against the claims of the head on which it grew. But it cannot be that you believe what you say, barber; you talk merely for the humour. I could not think so of you as to suppose that you would contentedly deal in the impostures you condemn.'

'Ah, sir, I must live.'

'And can't you do that without sinning against your conscience, as you believe? Take up some other calling.'

'Wouldn't mend the matter much, sir.'

'Do you think, then, barber, that, in a certain point, all the trades and callings of men are much on a par? Fatal, indeed,' raising his hand, 'inexpressibly dreadful, the trade of the barber, if to such conclusions it necessarily leads. Barber,' eyeing him not without emotion, 'you appear to me not so much a misbeliever, as a man misled. Now, let me set you on the right track; let me restore you to trust in human nature, and by no other means than the very trade that has brought you to suspect it.'

'You mean, sir, you would have me try the experiment of taking down that notification,' again pointing to it with his brush; 'but, dear me, while I sit chatting here, the water boils over.'

With which words, and such a well-pleased, sly, snug, expression, as they say some men have when they think their little stratagem has succeeded, he hurried to the copper vessel, and soon had his cup foaming up with white bubbles, as if it were a mug of new ale.

Meantime, the other would have fain gone on with the discourse; but the cunning barber lathered him with so generous a brush, so piled up the foam on him, that his face looked like the yeasty crest of a billow, and vain to think of talking under it, as for a drowning priest in the sea to exhort his fellow-sinners on a raft. Nothing would do, but he must keep his mouth shut. Doubtless, the interval was not, in a meditative way, unimproved; for, upon the traces of the operation being at last removed, the cosmopolitan rose, and, for added refreshment, washed his face and hands; and having generally readjusted himself, began, at last, addressing the barber in a manner different, singularly so, from his previous one. Hard to say exactly what the manner was, any more than to hint it was a sort of magical; in a benign way, not wholly unlike the manner, fabled or otherwise, of certain creatures in nature, which have the power of persuasive fascination – the power of holding another creature by the button of the eye, as it

were, despite the serious disinclination, and, indeed, earnest protest, of the victim. With this manner the conclusion of the matter
was not out of keeping; for, in the end, all argument and expostu-
lation proved vain, the barber being irresistibly persuaded to agree
to try, for the remainder of the present trip, the experiment of
trusting men, as both phrased it. True, to save his credit as a free
agent, he was loud in averring that it was only for the novelty of
the thing that he so agreed, and he required the other, as before
volunteered, to go security to him against any loss that might
ensue; but still the fact remained, that he engaged to trust men, a
thing he had before said he would not do, at least not unreservedly.
Still the more to save his credit, he now insisted upon it, as a last
point, that the agreement should be put in black and white,
especially the security part. The other made no demur; pen, ink,
and paper were provided, and grave as any notary the cosmopolitan sat down, but, ere taking the pen, glanced up at the
notification, and said: 'First down with that sign, barber – Timon's
sign, there; down with it.'

This, being in the agreement, was done – though a little
reluctantly – with an eye to the future, the sign being carefully
put away in a drawer.

'Now, then, for the writing,' said the cosmopolitan, squaring
himself. 'Ah,' with a sigh, 'I shall make a poor lawyer, I fear.
Ain't used, you see, barber, to a business which, ignoring the
principle of honour, holds no nail fast till clinched. Strange,
barber,' taking up the blank paper, 'that such flimsy stuff as this
should make such strong hawsers; vile hawsers, too. Barber,'
starting up, 'I won't put it in black and white. It were a reflection
upon our joint honour. I will take your word, and you shall take
mine.'

'But your memory may be none of the best, sir. Well for you,
on your side, to have it in black and white, just for a memorandum
like, you know.'

'That, indeed! Yes, and it would help *your* memory, too,
wouldn't it, barber? Yours, on your side, being a little weak, too,

I dare say. Ah, barber! how ingenious we human beings are; and how kindly we reciprocate each other's little delicacies, don't we? What better proof, now, that we are kind, considerate fellows, with responsive fellow-feelings – eh, barber? But to business. Let me see. What's your name, barber?'

'William Cream, sir.'

Pondering a moment, he began to write; and, after some corrections, leaned back, and read aloud the following:

AGREEMENT
Between
FRANK GOODMAN, Philanthropist, and Citizen of the World,
and
WILLIAM CREAM, Barber of the Mississippi steamer, Fidèle.

The first hereby agrees to make good to the last any loss that may come from his trusting mankind, in the way of his vocation, for the residue of the present trip; PROVIDED that William Cream keep out of sight for the given term, his notification of 'NO TRUST', and by no other mode convey any, the least hint or intimation, tending to discourage men from soliciting trust from him, in the way of his vocation, for the time above specified; but, on the contrary, he do, by all proper and reasonable words, gestures, manners, and looks, evince a perfect confidence in all men, especially strangers; otherwise, this agreement to be void.

Done, in good faith, this 1st day of April, 18—, at a quarter to twelve o'clock, P.M., in the shop of said William Cream, on board the said boat, Fidèle.

'There, barber; will that do?'

'That will do,' said the barber, 'only now put down your name.'

Both signatures being affixed, the question was started by the barber, who should have custody of the instrument; which point, however, he settled for himself, by proposing that both should go together to the captain, and give the document into his hands – the barber hinting that this would be a safe proceeding, because the captain was necessarily a party disinterested, and, what was more, could not, from the nature of the present case, make anything by a breach of trust. All of which was listened to with some surprise and concern.

'Why, barber,' said the cosmopolitan, 'this don't show the right spirit; for me, I have confidence in the captain purely because he is a man; but he shall have nothing to do with our affair; for if you have no confidence in me, barber, I have in you. There, keep the paper yourself,' handing it magnanimously.

'Very good,' said the barber, 'and now nothing remains but for me to receive the cash.'

Though the mention of that word, or any of its singularly numerous equivalents, in serious neighbourhood to a requisition upon one's purse, is attended with a more or less noteworthy effect upon the human countenance, producing in many an abrupt fall of it – in others, a writhing and screwing up of the features to a point not undistressing to behold, in some, attended with a blank pallor and fatal consternation – yet no trace of any of these symptoms was visible upon the countenance of the cosmopolitan, notwithstanding nothing could be more sudden and unexpected than the barber's demand.

'You speak of cash, barber; pray in what connection?'

'In a nearer one, sir,' answered the barber, less blandly, 'than I thought the man with the sweet voice stood, who wanted me to trust him once for a shave, on the score of being a sort of thirteenth cousin.'

'Indeed, and what did you say to him?'

'I said, "Thank you, sir, but I don't see the connection."'

'How could you so unsweetly answer one with a sweet voice?'

'Because, I recalled what the son of Sirach says in the True Book: "An enemy speaketh sweetly with his lips"; and so I did what the son of Sirach advises in such cases: "I believed not his many words."'

'What, barber, do you say that such cynical sort of things are in the True Book, by which, of course, you mean the Bible?'

'Yes, and plenty more to the same effect. Read the Book of Proverbs.'

'That's strange, now, barber; for I never happen to have met with those passages you cite. Before I go to bed this night, I'll inspect the Bible I saw on the cabin-table, to-day. But mind, you mustn't quote the True Book that way to people coming in here; it would be impliedly a violation of the contract. But you don't know how glad I feel that you have for one while signed off all that sort of thing.'

'No, sir; not unless you down with the cash.'

'Cash again! What do you mean?'

'Why, in this paper here, you engage, sir, to insure me against a certain loss, and –'

'Certain? Is it so *certain* you are going to lose?'

'Why, that way of taking the word may not be amiss, but I didn't mean it so. I meant a *certain* loss; you understand, a CERTAIN loss; that is to say, a certain loss. Now then, sir, what use your mere writing and saying you will insure me, unless beforehand you place in my hands a money-pledge, sufficient to that end?'

'I see; the material pledge.'

'Yes, and I will put it low; say fifty dollars.'

'Now what sort of a beginning is this? You, barber, for a given time engage to trust man, to put confidence in men, and, for your first step, make a demand implying no confidence in the very man you engage with. But fifty dollars is nothing, and I would let you have it cheerfully, only I unfortunately happen to have but little change with me just now.'

'But you have money in your trunk, though?'

'To be sure. But you see – in fact, barber, you must be consistent. No, I won't let you have the money now; I won't let you violate the inmost spirit of our contract, that way. So good-night, and I will see you again.'

'Stay, sir' – humming and hawing – 'you have forgotten something.'

'Handkerchief? – gloves? No, forgotten nothing. Good-night.'

'Stay, sir – the – the shaving.'

'Ah, I *did* forget that. But now that it strikes me, I shan't pay you at present. Look at your agreement; you must trust. Tut! against loss you hold the guarantee. Good-night, my dear barber.'

With which words he sauntered off, leaving the barber in a maze, staring after.

But it holding true in fascination as in natural philosophy, that nothing can act where it is not, so the barber was not long now in being restored to his self-possession and senses; the first evidence of which perhaps was, that, drawing forth his notification from the drawer, he put it back where it belonged; while, as for the agreement, that he tore up; which he felt the more free to do from the impression that in all human probability he would never again see the person who had drawn it. Whether that impression proved well-founded or not, does not appear. But in after days, telling the night's adventure to his friends, the worthy barber always spoke of his queer customer as the man-charmer – as certain East Indians are called snake-charmers – and all his friends united in thinking him QUITE AN ORIGINAL.

44

IN WHICH THE LAST THREE WORDS OF THE LAST CHAPTER ARE MADE THE TEXT OF DISCOURSE, WHICH WILL BE SURE OF RECEIVING MORE OR LESS ATTENTION FROM THOSE READERS WHO DO NOT SKIP IT

QUITE AN ORIGINAL. A phrase, we fancy, rather oftener used by the young, or the unlearned, or the untravelled, than by the old, or the well-read, or the man who has made the grand tour. Certainly, the sense of originality exists at its highest in an infant, and probably at its lowest in him who has completed the circle of the sciences.

As for original characters in fiction, a grateful reader will, on meeting with one, keep the anniversary of that day. True, we sometimes hear of an author who, at one creation, produces some two or three score such characters; it may be possible. But they can hardly be original in the sense that Hamlet is, or Don Quixote, or Milton's Satan. That is to say, they are not, in a thorough sense, original at all. They are novel, or singular, or striking, or captivating, or all four at once.

More likely, they are what are called odd characters; but for that, are no more original, than what is called an odd genius, in his way, is. But, if original, whence came they? Or where did the novelist pick them up?

Where does any novelist pick up any character? For the most part, in town, to be sure. Every great town is a kind of man-show, where the novelist goes for his stock, just as the agriculturist goes to the cattle-show for his. But in the one fair, new species of quadrupeds are hardly more rare, than in the other are new species of characters — that is, original ones. Their rarity may still the more appear from this, that, while characters, merely singular, imply but singular forms, so to speak, original ones, truly so, imply original instincts.

In short, a due conception of what is to be held for this sort of personage in fiction would make him almost as much of a prodigy there, as in real history is a new law-giver, a revolutionizing philosopher, or the founder of a new religion.

In nearly all the original characters, loosely accounted such in works of invention, there is discernible something prevailingly local, or of the age; which circumstance, of itself, would seem to invalidate the claim, judged by the principles here suggested.

Furthermore, if we consider, what is popularly held to entitle characters in fiction to being deemed original, is but something personal – confined to itself. The character sheds not its characteristic on its surroundings, whereas, the original character, essentially such, is like a revolving Drummond light, raying away from itself all round it – everything is lit by it, everything starts up to it (mark how it is with Hamlet), so that, in certain minds, there follows upon the adequate conception of such a character, an effect, in its way, akin to that which in Genesis attends upon the beginning of things.

For much the same reason that there is but one planet to one orbit, so can there be but one such original character to one work of invention. Two would conflict to chaos. In this view, to say that there are more than one to a book, is good presumption there is none at all. But for new, singular, striking, odd, eccentric, and all sorts of entertaining and instructive characters, a good fiction may be full of them. To produce such characters, an author, beside other things, must have seen much, and seen through much: to produce but one original character, he must have had much luck.

There would seem but one point in common between this sort of phenomenon in fiction and all other sorts; it cannot be born in the author's imagination – it being as true in literature as in zoology, that all life is from the egg.

In the endeavour to show, if possible, the impropriety of the phrase, *Quite an Original*, as applied by the barber's friends, we have, unawares, been led into a dissertation bordering upon the prosy, perhaps upon the smoky. If so, the best use the smoke can be turned to, will be, by retiring under cover of it, in good trim as may be, to the story.

THE COSMOPOLITAN INCREASES IN
SERIOUSNESS

In the middle of the gentlemen's cabin burned a solar lamp, swung from the ceiling, and whose shade of ground glass was all round fancifully variegated, in transparency, with the image of a horned altar, from which flames rose, alternate with the figure of a robed man, his head encircled by a halo. The light of this lamp, after dazzlingly striking on marble, snow-white and round – the slab of a centre-table beneath – on all sides went rippling off with ever-diminishing distinctness, till, like circles from a stone dropped in water, the rays died dimly away in the furthest nook of the place.

Here and there, true to their place, but not to their function, swung other lamps, barren planets, which had either gone out from exhaustion, or been extinguished by such occupants of berths as the light annoyed, or who wanted to sleep, not see.

By a perverse man, in a berth not remote, the remaining lamp would have been extinguished as well, had not a steward forbade, saying that the commands of the captain required it to be kept burning till the natural light of day should come to relieve it. This steward, who, like many in his vocation, was apt to be a little free-spoken at times, had been provoked by the man's pertinacity to remind him, not only of the sad consequences which might, upon occasion, ensue from the cabin being left in darkness, but, also of the circumstance that, in a place full of strangers, to show one's self anxious to produce darkness there, such an anxiety was, to say the least, not becoming. So the lamp – last survivor of many – burned on, inwardly blessed by those in some berths, and inwardly execrated by those in others.

Keeping his lone vigils beneath his lone lamp, which lighted his book on the table, sat a clean, comely, old man, his head snowy as the marble, and a countenance like that which imagination ascribes to good Simeon, when, having at last beheld the Master of Faith, he blessed him and departed in peace. From his hale look of greenness in winter, and his hands ingrained with the tan, less, apparently, of the present summer, than of accumulated ones past, the old man seemed a well-to-do farmer, happily dismissed, after a thrifty life of activity, from the fields to the fireside – one of those who, at three-score-and-ten, are fresh-hearted as at fifteen; to whom seclusion gives a boon more blessed than knowledge, and at last sends them to heaven untainted by the world, because ignorant of it; just as a countryman putting up at a London inn, and never stirring out of it as a sight-seer, will leave London at last without once being lost in its fog, or soiled by its mud.

Redolent from the barber's shop, as any bridegroom tripping to the bridal chamber might come, and by his look of cheeriness seeming to dispense a sort of morning through the night, in came the cosmopolitan; but marking the old man, and how he was occupied, he toned himself down, and trod softly, and took a seat on the other side of the table, and said nothing. Still there was a kind of waiting expression about him.

'Sir,' said the old man, after looking up puzzled at him a moment, 'sir,' said he, 'one would think this was a coffee-house, and it was war-time, and I had a newspaper here with great news, and the only copy to be had, you sit there looking at me so eager.'

'And so you *have* good news there, sir – the very best of good news.'

'Too good to be true,' here came from one of the curtained berths.

'Hark!' said the cosmopolitan. 'Some one talks in his sleep.'

'Yes,' said the old man, 'and you – *you* seem to be talking in a dream. Why speak you, sir, of news, and all that, when you must see this is a book I have here – the Bible, not a newspaper?'

'I know that; and when you are through with it – but not a moment sooner – I will thank you for it. It belongs to the boat, I believe – a present from a society.'

'Oh, take it, take it!'

'Nay, sir, I did not mean to touch you at all. I simply stated the fact in explanation of my waiting here – nothing more. Read on, sir, or you will distress me.'

This courtesy was not without effect. Removing his spectacles, and saying he had about finished his chapter, the old man kindly presented the volume, which was received with thanks equally kind. After reading for some minutes, until his expression merged from attentiveness into seriousness, and from that into a kind of pain, the cosmopolitan slowly laid down the book, and turning to the old man, who thus far had been watching him with benign curiosity, said: 'Can you, my aged friend, resolve me a doubt – a disturbing doubt?'

'There are doubts, sir,' replied the old man, with a changed countenance, 'there are doubts, sir, which, if man have them, it is not man that can solve them.'

'True; but look, now, what my doubt is. I am one who thinks well of man. I love man. I have confidence in man. But what was told me not a half-hour since? I was told that I would find it written – "Believe not his many words – an enemy speaketh sweetly with his lips" – and also I was told that I would find a good deal more to the same effect, and all in this book. I could not think it; and, coming here to look for myself, what do I read? Not only just what was quoted, but also, as was engaged, more to the same purpose, such as this: "With much communication he will tempt thee; he will smile upon thee, and speak thee fair, and say What wantest thou? If thou be for his profit he will use thee; he will make thee bare, and will not be sorry for it. Observe and take good heed. When thou hearest these things, awake in thy sleep."'

'Who's that describing the confidence-man?' here came from the berth again.

'Awake in his sleep, sure enough, ain't he?' said the cosmopolitan, again looking off in surprise. 'Same voice as before, ain't it? Strange sort of dreamy man, that. Which is his berth, pray?'

'Never mind *him*, sir,' said the old man anxiously, 'but tell me, truly, did you, indeed, read from the book just now?'

'I did,' with changed air, 'and gall and wormwood it is to me, a truster in man; to me a philanthropist.'

'Why,' moved, 'you don't mean to say, that what you repeated is really down there? Man and boy, I have read the good book this seventy years, and don't remember seeing anything like that. Let me see it,' rising earnestly, and going round to him.

'There it is; and there – and there' – turning over the leaves, and pointing to the sentences one by one; 'there – all down in the "Wisdom of Jesus, the Son of Sirach."'

'Ah!' cried the old man, brightening up, 'now I know. Look,' turning the leaves forward and back, till all the Old Testament lay flat on one side, and all the New Testament flat on the other, while in his fingers he supported vertically the portion between, 'look, sir, all this to the right is certain truth, and all this to the left is certain truth, but all I hold in my hand here is apocrypha.'

'Apocrypha?'

'Yes; and there's the word in black and white,' pointing to it. 'And what says the word? It says as much as "not warranted"; for what do college men say of anything of that sort? They say it is apocryphal. The word itself, I have heard from the pulpit, implies something of uncertain credit. So if your disturbance be raised from aught in this apocrypha,' again taking up the pages, 'in that case think no more of it, for it's apocrypha.'

'What's that about the Apocalypse?' here a third time came from the berth.

'He's seeing visions now, ain't he?' said the cosmopolitan, once more looking in the direction of the interruption. 'But, sir,' resuming, 'I cannot tell you how thankful I am for your reminding me about the apocrypha here. For the moment its being such escaped me. Fact is, when all is bound up together, it's sometimes confusing. The uncanonical part should be bound distinct. And, now that I think of it, how well did those learned doctors who rejected for us this whole book of Sirach. I never read anything so calculated to destroy man's confidence in man. This son of Sirach even says – I saw it but just now: "Take heed of thy friends"; not, observe, thy seeming friends, thy hypocritical friends, thy false friends, but thy *friends*, thy real friends – that is to say, not the truest friend in the world is to be implicitly trusted. Can Roche-foucault equal that? I should not wonder if his view of human nature, like Machiavelli's, was taken from this Son of Sirach. And to call it wisdom – the Wisdom of the Son of Sirach! Wisdom, indeed? What an ugly thing wisdom must be! Give me the folly that dimples the cheek, say I, rather than the wisdom that curdles the blood. But no, no; it ain't wisdom; it's apocrypha, as you say, sir. For how can that be trustworthy that teaches distrust?'

'I tell you what it is,' here cried the same voice as before, only more in less of mockery, 'if you two don't know enough to sleep, don't be keeping wiser men awake. And if you want to know what wisdom is, go find it under your blankets.'

'Wisdom?' cried another voice with a brogue; 'arrah, and is't wisdom the two geese are gabbling about all this while? To bed with ye, ye divils, and don't be after burning your fingers with the likes of wisdom.'

'We must talk lower,' said the old man; 'I fear we have annoyed these good people.'

'I should be sorry if wisdom annoyed any one, said the other; 'but we will lower our voices, as you say. To resume: taking the thing as I did, can you be surprised at my uneasiness in reading passages so charged with the spirit of distrust?'

'No, sir, I am not surprised,' said the old man; then added: 'from what you say, I see you are something of my way of thinking – you think that to distrust the creature, is a kind of distrusting of the Creator. Well, my young friend, what is it? This is rather late for you to be about. What do you want of me?'

These questions were put to a boy in the fragment of an old

linen coat, bedraggled and yellow, who, coming in from the deck
barefooted on the soft carpet, had been unheard. All pointed and
fluttering, the rags of the little fellow's red-flannel shirt, mixed
with those of his yellow coat, flamed about him like the painted
flames in the robes of a victim in *auto-da-fé*. His face, too, wore
such a polish of seasoned grime, that his sloe-eyes sparkled from
out it like lustrous sparks in fresh coal. He was a juvenile peddler,
or *marchand*, as the polite French might have called him, of
traveller's conveniences; and, having no allotted sleeping-place,
had, in his wanderings about the boat, spied, through glass doors,
the two in the cabin; and, late though it was, thought it might
never be too much so for turning a penny.

Among other things, he carried a curious affair – a miniature
mahogany door, hinged to its frame, and suitably furnished in all
respects but one, which will shortly appear. This little door he
now meaningly held before the old man, who, after staring at it a
while, said: 'Go thy ways with thy toys, child.'

'Now, may I never get so old and wise as that comes to,'
laughed the boy through his grime; and, by so doing, disclosing
leopard-like teeth, like those of Murillo's wild beggar-boy's.

'The divils are laughing now, are they?' here came the brogue
from the berth. 'What do the divils find to laugh about in
wisdom, begorrah? To bed with ye, ye divils, and no more of ye.'

'You see, child, you have disturbed that person,' said the old
man; 'you mustn't laugh any more.'

'Ah, now,' said the cosmopolitan, 'don't, pray, say that; don't
let him think that poor Laughter is persecuted for a fool in this
world.'

'Well,' said the old man to the boy, 'you must, at any rate,
speak very low.'

'Yes, that wouldn't be amiss, perhaps,' said the cosmopolitan;
'but, my fine fellow, you were about saying something to my
aged friend here; what was it?'

'Oh,' with a lowered voice, coolly opening and shutting his
little door, 'only this: when I kept a toy-stand at the fair in

Cincinnati last month, I sold more than one old man a child's rattle.'

'No doubt of it,' said the old man. 'I myself often buy such things for my little grandchildren.'

'But these old men I talk of were old bachelors.'

The old man stared at him a moment; then, whispering to the cosmopolitan: 'Strange boy, this; sort of simple, ain't he? Don't know much, hey?'

'Not much,' said the boy, 'or I wouldn't be so ragged.'

'Why, child, what sharp ears you have!' exclaimed the old man.

'If they were duller, I would hear less ill of myself,' said the boy.

'You seem pretty wise, my lad,' said the cosmopolitan; 'why don't you sell your wisdom, and buy a coat?'

'Faith,' said the boy, 'that's what I did to-day, and this is the coat that the price of my wisdom bought. But won't you trade? See, now, it is not the door I want to sell; I only carry the door round for a specimen, like. Look now, sir,' standing the thing up on the table, 'supposing this little door is your state-room door; well,' opening it, 'you go in for the night; you close your door behind you – thus. Now, is all safe?'

'I suppose so, child,' said the old man.

'Of course it is, my fine fellow,' said the cosmopolitan.

'All safe. Well. Now, about two o'clock in the morning, say, a soft-handed gentleman comes softly and tries the knob here – thus; in creeps my soft-handed gentleman; and hey, presto! how comes on the soft cash?'

'I see, I see, child,' said the old man; 'your fine gentleman is a fine thief, and there's no lock to your little door to keep him out'; with which words he peered at it more closely than before.

'Well, now,' again showing his white teeth, 'well, now, some of you old folks are knowing 'uns, sure enough; but now comes the great invention,' producing a small steel contrivance, very simple but ingenious, and which, being clapped on the inside of the little door, secured it as with a bolt. 'There now,' admiringly holding it off at arm's length, 'there now, let that soft-handed gentleman come now a' softly trying this little knob here, and let him keep a' trying till he finds his head as soft as his hand. Buy the traveller's patent lock, sir, only twenty-five cents.'

'Dear me,' cried the old man, 'this beats printing. Yes, child, I will have one, and use it this very night.'

With the phlegm of an old banker pouching the change, the boy now turned to the other: 'Sell you one, sir?'

'Excuse me, my fine fellow, but I never use such blacksmiths' things.'

'Those who give the blacksmith most work seldom do,' said the boy, tipping him a wink expressive of a degree of indefinite knowingness, not uninteresting to consider in one of his years. But the wink was not marked by the old man, nor, to all appearances, by him for whom it was intended.

'Now then,' said the boy, again addressing the old man. 'With your traveller's lock on your door tonight, you will think yourself all safe, won't you?'

'I think I will, child.'

'But how about the window?'

'Dear me, the window, child. I never thought of that. I must see to that.'

'Never you mind about the window,' said the boy, 'nor, to be honour bright, about the traveller's lock either (though I ain't sorry for selling one), do you just buy one of these little jokers,' producing a number of suspender-like objects, which he dangled before the old man; 'money-belts, sir; only fifty cents.'

'Money-belt? never heard of such a thing.'

'A sort of pocket-book,' said the boy, 'only a safer sort. Very good for travellers.'

'Oh, a pocket-book. Queer looking pocket-books though, seems to me. Ain't they rather long and narrow for pocket-books?'

'They go round the waist, sir, inside,' said the boy. 'Door open or locked, wide awake on your feet or fast asleep in your chair, impossible to be robbed with a money-belt.'

'I see, I see. It *would* be hard to rob one's money-belt. And I was told to-day the Mississippi is a bad river for pick-pockets. How much are they?'

'Only fifty cents, sir.'

'I'll take one. There!'

'Thank-ee. And now there's a present for ye,' with which, drawing from his breast a batch of little papers, he threw one before the old man, who, looking at it, read *Counterfeit Detector*.

'Very good thing,' said the boy, 'I give it to all my customers who trade seventy-five cents' worth; best present can be made them. Sell you a money-belt, sir?' turning to the cosmopolitan.

'Excuse me, my fine fellow, but I never use that sort of thing; my money I carry loose.'

'Loose bait ain't bad,' said the boy, 'look a lie and find the truth; don't care about a Counterfeit Detector, do ye? or is the wind East, d'ye think?'

'Child,' said the old man in some concern, 'you mustn't sit up any longer, it affects your mind; there, go away, go to bed.'

'If I had some people's brains to lie on, I would,' said the boy, 'but planks is hard, you know.'

'Go, child – go, go!'

'Yes, child – yes, yes,' said the boy, with which roguish parody, by way of congé, he scraped back his hard foot on the woven flowers of the carpet, much as a mischievous steer in May scrapes back his horny hoof in the pasture; and then with a flourish of his hat – which, like the rest of his tatters, was, thanks to hard times, a belonging beyond his years, though not beyond his experience, being a grown man's cast-off beaver – turned, and with the air of a young Caffre, quitted the place.

'That's a strange boy,' said the old man, looking after him. 'I wonder who's his mother; and whether she knows what late hours he keeps?'

'The probability is,' observed the other, 'that his mother does not know. But if you remember, sir, you were saying something, when the boy interrupted you with his door.'

'So I was. – Let me see,' unmindful of his purchases for the moment, 'what, now, was it? What was that I was saying? Do *you* remember?'

'Not perfectly, sir; but, if I am not mistaken, it was something like this: you hoped you did not distrust the creature; for that would imply distrust of the Creator.'

'Yes, that was something like it,' mechanically and unintelligently letting his eye fall now on his purchases.

'Pray, will you put your money in your belt to-night?'

'It's best, ain't it?' with a slight start. 'Never too late to be cautious. "Beware of pick-pockets" is all over the boat.'

'Yes, and it must have been the Son of Sirach, or some other morbid cynic, who put them there. But that's not to the purpose. Since you are minded to it, pray, sir, let me help you about the belt. I think that, between us, we can make a secure thing of it.'

'Oh no, no, no!' said the old man, not unperturbed, 'no, no, I wouldn't trouble you for the world,' then, nervously folding up the belt, 'and I won't be so impolite as to do it for myself, before you, either. But, now that I think of it,' after a pause, carefully taking a little wad from a remote corner of his vest pocket, 'here are two bills they gave me at St Louis, yesterday. No doubt they are all right; but just to pass time, I'll compare them with the Detector here. Blessed boy to make me such a present. Public benefactor, that little boy!'

Laying the Detector square before him on the table, he then, with something of the air of an officer bringing by the collar a brace of culprits to the bar, placed the two bills opposite the Detector, upon which, the examination began, lasting some time, prosecuted with no small research and vigilance, the forefinger of the right hand proving of lawyer-like efficacy in tracing out and pointing the evidence, whichever way it might go.

After watching him a while, the cosmopolitan said in a formal voice, 'Well, what say you, Mr Foreman; guilty, or not guilty? – Not guilty, ain't it?'

'I don't know, I don't know,' returned the old man, perplexed, 'there's so many marks of all sorts to go by, it makes it a kind of uncertain. Here, now, is this bill,' touching one, 'it looks to be a three dollar bill on the Vicksburgh Trust and Insurance Banking Company. Well, the Detector says –'

'But why, in this case, care what it says? Trust and Insurance! What more would you have?'

'No; but the Detector says, among fifty other things, that, if a good bill, it must have, thickened here and there into the substance of the paper, little wavy spots of red; and it says that they must have a kind of silky feel, being made by the lint of a red silk handkerchief stirred up in the paper-maker's vat – the paper being made to order for the company.'

'Well, and is –'

'Stay. But then it adds, that sign is not always to be relied on; for some good bills get so worn, the red marks get rubbed out. And that's the case with my bill here – see how old it is – or else it's a counterfeit, or else – I don't see right – or else – dear, dear me – I don't know what else to think.'

'What a peck of trouble that Detector makes for you now; believe me, the bill is good; don't be so distrustful. Proves what I've always thought, that much of the want of confidence, in these days, is owing to these Counterfeit Detectors you see on every desk and counter. Puts people up to suspecting good bills. Throw it away, I beg, if only because of the trouble it breeds you.'

'No: it's troublesome, but I think I'll keep it. – Stay, now, here's another sign. It says that, if the bill is good, it must have in one corner, mixed in with the vignette, the figure of a goose, very small, indeed, all but microscopic; and, for added precaution, like the figure of Napoleon outlined by the tree, not observable, even if magnified, unless the attention is directed to it. Now, pore over it as I will, I can't see this goose'

'Can't see the goose? why, I can; and a famous goose it is. There' (reaching over and pointing to a spot in the vignette).

'I don't see it – dear me – I don't see the goose. Is it a real goose?'

'A perfect goose; beautiful goose.'

'Dear, dear, I don't see it.'

'Then throw that Detector away, I say again; it only makes you purblind; don't you see what a wild-goose-chase it has led you? The bill is good. Throw the Detector away.'

'No; it ain't so satisfactory as I thought for, but I must examine this other bill.'

'As you please, but I can't in conscience assist you any more; pray, then, excuse me.'

So, while the old man with much painstakings resumed his work, the cosmopolitan, to allow him every facility, resumed his reading. At length, seeing that he had given up his undertaking as hopeless, and was at leisure again, the cosmopolitan addressed some gravely interesting remarks to him about the book before him, and, presently, becoming more and more grave, said, as he turned the large volume slowly over on the table, and with much difficulty traced the faded remains of the gilt inscription giving the name of the society who had presented it to the boat, 'Ah, sir, though every one must be pleased at the thought of the presence in public places of such a book, yet there is something that abates the satisfaction. Look at this volume; on the outside, battered as any old valise in the baggage-room; and inside, white and virgin as the hearts of lilies in bud.'

'So it is, so it is,' said the old man sadly, his attention for the first directed to the circumstance.

'Nor is this the only time,' continued the other, 'that I have observed these public Bibles in boats and hotels. All much like this – old without, and new within. True, this aptly typifies that internal freshness, the best mark of truth, however ancient; but then, it speaks not so well as could be wished for the good book's esteem in the minds of the travelling public. I may err, but it seems to me that if more confidence was put in it by the travelling public, it would hardly be so.'

With an expression very unlike that with which he had bent over the Detector, the old man sat meditating upon his companion's remarks awhile; and, at last, with a rapt look, said: 'And yet, of all people, the travelling public most need to put trust in that guardianship which is made known in this book.'

'True, true,' thoughtfully assented the other.

'And one would think they would want to, and be glad to,' continued the old man kindling; 'for, in all our wanderings through this vale, how pleasant, not less than obligatory, to feel that we need start at no wild alarms, provide for no wild perils; trusting in that Power which is alike able and willing to protect us when we cannot ourselves.'

His manner produced something answering to it in the cosmopolitan, who, leaning over towards him, said sadly: 'Though this is a theme on which travellers seldom talk to each other, yet, to you, sir, I will say, that I share something of your sense of security. I have much moved about the world, and still keep at it; nevertheless, though in this land, and especially in these parts of it, some stories are told about steamboats and railroads fitted to make one a little apprehensive, yet, I may say that, neither by land nor by water, am I ever seriously disquieted, however, at times, transiently uneasy; since, with you, sir, I believe in a Committee of Safety, holding silent sessions over all, in an invisible patrol, most alert when we soundest sleep, and whose beat lies as much through forests as towns, along rivers as streets. In short, I never forget that passage of Scripture which says, "Jehovah shall be thy confidence." The traveller who has not this trust, what miserable misgiving must be his; or, what vain, short-sighted care must he take of himself.'

'Even so,' said the old man, lowly.

'There is a chapter,' continued the other, again taking the book, 'which, as not amiss, I must read you. But this lamp, solar-lamp as it is, begins to burn dimly.'

'So it does, so it does,' said the old man with changed air, 'dear me, it must be very late. I must to bed, to bed! Let me see,' rising and looking wistfully all round, first on the stools and settees, and then on the carpet, 'let me see, let me see; – is there anything I have forgot, – forgot? Something I a sort of dimly remember. Something, my son – careful man – told me at starting this morning, this very morning. Something about seeing to – something before I got into my berth. What could it be? Something for safety. Oh, my poor old memory?'

'Let me give a little guess, sir. Life-preserver?'

'So it was. He told me not to omit seeing I had a life-preserver in my state-room; said the boat supplied them, too. But where are they? I don't see any. What are they like?'

'They are something like this, sir, I believe,' lifting a brown stool with a curved tin compartment underneath; 'yes, this, I think, is a life-preserver, sir; and a very good one, I should say, though I don't pretend to know much about such things, never using them myself.'

'Why, indeed, now! Who would have thought it? *that* a life-preserver? That's the very stool I was sitting on, ain't it?'

'It is. And that shows that one's life is looked out for, when he ain't looking out for it himself. In fact, any of these stools here will float you, sir, should the boat hit a snag, and go down in the dark. But, since you want one in your room, pray take this one,' handing it to him. 'I think I can recommend this one; the tin part,' rapping it with his knuckles, 'seems so perfect – sounds so very hollow.'

'Sure it's *quite* perfect, though?' Then, anxiously putting on his spectacles, he scrutinized it pretty closely – 'well soldered? quite tight?'

'I should say so, sir; though, indeed, as I said, I never use this sort of thing myself. Still, I think that in case of a wreck, barring sharp-pointed timbers, you could have confidence in that stool for a special providence.'

'Then, good-night, good-night; and Providence have both of us in its good keeping.'

'Be sure it will,' eyeing the old man with sympathy, as for the moment he stood, money-belt in hand, and life-preserver under arm, 'be sure it will, sir, since in Providence, as in man, you and I equally put trust. But, bless me, we are being left in the dark here. Pah! what a smell, too.'

'Ah, my way now,' cried the old man, peering before him, 'where lies my way to my state-room?'

'I have indifferent eyes, and will show you; but, first, for the good of all lungs, let me extinguish this lamp.'

The next moment, the waning light expired, and with it the waning flames of the horned altar, and the waning halo round the robed man's brow; while in the darkness which ensued, the cosmopolitan kindly led the old man away. Something further may follow of this Masquerade.

NOTES

The numerals introducing each note refer to page numbers only. Full details of works referred to here only by author or title and author can be found in the Bibliography on pp. xxxix–xliv.

CONTENTS

4. *the age of magic and magicians* [title of ch. 32]. The first editions read 'music and magicians'; the error is here corrected.

I

7. *Manco Capac* Spanish spelling of Manqo Qhapaq, founder of the Incan dynasty in the thirteenth century, and a mythical figure to later people of the Andes. He is reputed to have emerged from the earth.

7. *extremest sense . . . stranger* This man, the deaf mute, is possibly the first manifestation of the Confidence Man. Helen Trimpi argues in her book that he represents Benjamin Lundy (1789–1839), a Quaker strongly opposed to slavery.

7. *Fidèle* Although on one level it is straightforwardly ironic, Melville's use of the name, meaning 'Faithful', also refers to the appearance-and-reality motif. In Shakespeare's *Cymbeline*, Imogen takes the name of Fidèle, and in Wycherley's *The Plain Dealer* (1677), Fidelia is a disguised woman. In Beethoven's 1805 opera *Fidelio*, Leonora takes that name in disguise. Also, Melville knew of the ambiguous name 'Faith' in Hawthorne's 'Young Goodman Brown' (the Confidence Man appears later as Frank Goodman). Edwin Fussell notes that there was a boat called *Fidelity*, listed as destroyed (*Frontier*, p. 307n.).

7. *chevaliers* Cf. 'chevalier d'industrie', term for a common swindler or adventurer.

8. *Meason . . . Murrel . . . brothers Harpe* Outlaws. The most notorious

was Murrell, also spelt Murrel or Murel (*fl.* 1804–44), who led a gang of around a thousand members in the Southwest. The gang carried out various acts of outlawry, including Negro-stealing. The first editions had the name 'Measan', here corrected.

8. *Charity thinketh no evil* Along with the other mottoes on the slate, from 1 Corinthians 1:13.

9. *Shield-like bearing his slate before him* Ephesians 6:14: 'Stand therefore, having your loins girt about with truth, and having on the breastplate of righteousness.'

2

12. *Casper Hauser* Celebrated figure (1812–33) of mysterious origins, brought before the Nuremberg authorities in 1828. Cf. the later references to Peter the Wild Boy and Hairy Orson (see pp. 130 and 174 and notes).

12. *Spirit-rapper* A term of contempt in Melville's work; see the sketch 'The Apple-Tree Table'. In 'I and My Chimney' the narrator's wife is characterized partly by her willingness to believe in the 'Spirit Rapping philosophy', the vogue of which, as is indicated in 'The Apple-Tree Table', was started by the Fox sisters. Leah and Margaret Fox started to develop spirit-rapping in 1848, and during the 1850s the sisters were celebrated public performers, along with their younger sister, Kate. The extraordinary popularity of the activity is reflected in the publication of *The Spirit-Rapper* (1854) by Orestes Brownson, which, Edwin Fussell suggests, influenced *The Confidence-Man* (*Frontier*, p. 308n.).

12. *daylight Endymion* Endymion was bewitched by Selene (Diana) and made to sleep for ever.

12. *Jacob dreaming at Luz* Jacob dreamt of a ladder connecting heaven and earth, and commemorated the dream with a stone. See Genesis 28:11–15.

13. *Ving-King-Ching, in the Flowery Kingdom* Although 'the Flowery Kingdom' is a well-known epithet for China (a literal translation of the Chinese Hwa-Kwo), 'Ving-King-Ching' is Melville's own term for the Grand Imperial Canal.

13. *coiner* Counterfeiter.

13. *Corcovado* The first editions read 'Cocovarde'.

14. *Chaucer's Canterbury pilgrims* Who also set forth in April.

14. *Dives and Lazarus* The story of the rich man and Lazarus the poor man

with sores is given in Luke 16:19–31. Lazarus recurs in the novel (see pp. 60 and 113) and Dives is mentioned once more (p. 89).

14. *blacklegs* Swindlers. The modern usage of those working while others strike did not appear until later in the nineteenth century.

14. *clay-eaters* A derogatory term for poor Southerners, with whom the practice of clay-eating was especially associated.

14. *Anacharsis Cloots congress* Jean-Baptiste du Val-de-Grâce, Baron de Cloots (1755–94), who adopted the pseudonym 'Anacharsis', was a Prussian who took part in the French Revolution and led a delegation of foreigners (termed by him the 'embassy of the human race') to the French National Assembly. He is mentioned in Carlyle's *French Revolution* (1837), and his name appears in both *Moby-Dick* and *Billy Budd* as a kind of Melville shorthand for the ship as microcosm.

3

15. *Newfoundland dog* Melville himself owned one, and the association between the Black and the dog appears also in *Mardi* (ch. 30), and in 'Benito Cereno'.

15. *Black Guinea* H. Bruce Franklin suggests in his edition that the name indicates a counterfeit. This is supposition, though 'guinea dropper' was a term for a sharper, and the word 'black', in 'blacklegs', has already been associated with deception (p. 14). Blacks were often nicknamed 'Guinea' on account of their supposed origin; see *White-Jacket* (ch. 90), where the purser's slave is automatically termed thus.

16. *baker's oven* Perhaps a joking reference to the diabolic nature of Black Guinea; there was a rock formation called Devil's Oven beneath St Louis. (See J. W. Nichol, 'Melville and the Midwest'.)

17. *some discharged custom house officer ... suspecting everything and everybody* Perhaps a wry reference to Nathaniel Hawthorne. He had been discharged from his post as Surveyor in the Salem Custom House in 1849 (he used his experience of the position in his introduction to *The Scarlet Letter*), and was left in serious financial straits. In 'Hawthorne and His Mosses' (1850) Melville noted Hawthorne's 'great power of blackness', his concentration on the dark side of human nature.

17. *The will of man is by his reason swayed A Midsummer Night's Dream*, II, ii, 115. The context renders the statement ironic, in that the

speaker, Lysander, is under the influence of Puck's juice. On the *Fidèle*, nothing is quite what it seems.

19. *dar is aboard here . . . as is a sodjer* Guinea's list seems to introduce the other identities the Confidence Man will adopt, but he lists more identities than there are manifestations.

19. *ge'mman wid a weed* The English first edition had an explanatory footnote ('Crape on his hat'), which has here been excluded.

19. *Episcopal clergyman . . . Methodist minister* H. Bruce Franklin notes in his edition that both here are true to their churches; the Episcopalian appeals to higher authority, while the Methodist tries to settle the matter personally. Murrel (also a Tennessean) and Harpe often took the disguise of ministers.

20. *Canada thistle* The *Cirsium arvense*; literally, 'cursed thistle', introduced to the US from France via Canada. It is legally considered a 'noxious weed'. True to Guinea's words, a 'ge'mman wid a weed' soon appears.

20. *betrays a fool with a kiss* An oblique reference to Judas' betrayal of Christ, with Melville suggesting the association between April Fool's Day and the Passion. See Mark 14:44–6.

20. *the old Adam* Original sin, inherent in us because of Adam; cf. *Henry V*, I, i, 50: 'Consideration, like an angel, came / And whipped the offending Adam out of him.' The phrase 'the old Adam of resentment' is used in 'Bartleby'.

21. *this ship of fools* A significant phrase possibly indicating the satirical literary tradition to which *The Confidence-Man* belongs. The tradition originated with Sebastian Brandt's *Narrenshiff* in 1494.

22. *Timon* Melville's interest in the Athenian misanthrope was strong, and derived from Shakespeare's play (1607). Reviews of *The Confidence-Man* labelled it 'Timonist'.

22. *Jeremy Diddler* The chief character in *Raising the Wind* (1803), a farce by James Kenney. Probably the origin of the term 'to diddle'; Poe assumes as much in 'Diddling Considered as One of the Exact Sciences' (1843).

4

25. *Don't you know me?* Michael S. Reynolds points out that the routine of pretended prior acquaintance was a common strategy of the confidence man whose activities were reported by the New York

Herald. (See the Introduction to the present edition, p. xv, and Reynolds, 'The Prototype for Melville's Confidence Man'.)

25. *a long weed on his hat* To show that he is in mourning. William M. Ramsey suggests that Melville is referring to one of Barnum's hoaxes. In 1850 Barnum exhibited a black who claimed to have found a weed which would gradually turn blacks white. While the man did change colour daily, the hoax was that the man was a white who had been painted black. If we are to assume that the 'man with the weed' is also Black Guinea, then he also has changed colour. (See Ramsey, 'Melville's and Barnum's Man with a Weed'.) In her book Helen Trimpi has identified the man with the weed, John Ringman, as William Cullen Bryant (1794–1878), a distinguished poet and one of the founders of the Republican Party.

26. *Virginia* Although the first editions read 'Pennsylvania', Wheeling (now in West Virginia) was then in Virginia. In his 1970 Ph.D. dissertation, Watson G. Branch suggested that the mistake arose from a confusion of abbreviations, 'Pa' and 'Va'.

26. *Werther's Charlotte* A reference to *The Sorrows of Young Werther* (1774, rev. 1787) by Goethe. Melville almost certainly knew of Thackeray's parody of Werther's first view of Charlotte, since it appeared in the same issue of *Putnam's Monthly* as an episode of 'Benito Cereno'. The parody begins:

> Werther had a love for Charlotte
> Such as words could never utter;
> Would you know how he first met her?
> She was cutting bread and butter.

27. *erased from the tablet* See Melville's story 'The Paradise of Bachelors and the Tartarus of Maids' (1855), where the idea of the *tabula rasa* is examined further.

27. *potter's clay* Isaiah 64:8.

28. *you are a mason* One of the strategies actually used by the original confidence man. (See note to p. 25: *Don't you know me?*)

29. *Black Rapids Coal Company* A possible reference to Hell.

30. *from the stock's descent . . . no second fate* An echo of Milton, *Paradise Lost*, II, 14–17:

> . . . From this descent
> Celestial vertues rising, will appear
> More glorious and more dread then from no fall,
> And trust themselves to fear no second fate

Thus Satan exhorts the fallen angels. (See Henry F. Pommer, *Milton and Melville*, p. 31.)

5

33. *almost transformed into another being* Signalling the changing character and identity of the Confidence Man, who is indeed a 'transfer-agent'.

33. *Greek characters* Denoting his membership of a student fraternity.

33. *a sophomore* The English first edition had an explanatory footnote ('A student in his second year') which has here been excluded.

34. *a black and shameful period lies before me* There is no exact corresponding passage in Tacitus, though several are similar. Elizabeth Foster quotes from *Histories*, i, 2: 'I enter upon a time rich in catastrophes, full of fierce battles and civic strife . . .' (translated by George Gilbert Ramsay).

34. *there is a subtle man . . . deceived* Melville's quotation is an amalgam of Ecclesiasticus 19:20, 23, 25 and 26. The same apocryphal book appears in ch. 45.

35. *this book . . . drown it for you* Cf. *The Tempest*, V, i, 56–7, where Prospero resolves to drown his book, abjuring his 'rough magic'.

35. *Auburn and Greenwood* Auburn is in Cambridge, Massachusetts, Greenwood in Brooklyn, New York. Elizabeth Foster suggests that Melville is referring to the 'graveyard' school of poets, which included Robert Blair, Edward Young and others.

35. *Akenside* Mark Akenside, *The Pleasures of Imagination* (1744), revised as *The Pleasures of the Imagination* (1757), a blank verse poem extolling the benevolence of the universe and the status quo.

35. *fraternal* Although the first editions read 'paternal', the Northwestern-Newberry editors proposed 'fraternal' as more relevant to the context.

36. *Astrea* Daughter of Zeus and Themis. She lived on earth until, horrified at human impiety, she left for the skies, where she became the constellation Virgo.

6

37. *man in a gray coat* The next manifestation of the Confidence Man. In her book Helen Trimpi has associated the man in gray with Theodore Parker (1810–60). Parker was a religious leader,

abolitionist and social reformer, with a special interest in the reform
of prisons and education.

37. *Seminoles* The widows and orphans resulted from the Seminole
Wars of 1816–18 and 1835–42. (The war is also mentioned in
White-Jacket, ch. 15.) Hershel Parker points out in his edition that
Melville is referring back to Cotton Mather's equation of the
Indians with devils.

37. *Look, you . . . look, you* H. Bruce Franklin suggests in his edition
that since the man with the wooden leg used almost this exact
construction in ch. 3, the Confidence Man's opponents may also be
players in the masquerade.

38. *I myself . . . ashore* One of the hints of the protean identity of the
Confidence Man.

40. *Benedicts* Married men, especially those recently married.

40. *with . . . satisfaction hobbled away* Cf. the description of Appolyon in
Hawthorne's 'The Celestial Railroad' (1846), one of the likely
sources for *The Confidence-Man*.

42. *cried the one-legged man* The first editions read 'one-eyed', here
corrected. However, if one accepts Helen Trimpi's identification of
the wooden-legged man with the newspaper editor William Gordon
Bennett, 'one-eyed' may not be a mistake, since Bennett was
caricatured with one eye turned in. (See Trimpi, *Melville's
Confidence Men*, p. 59.)

42. *Caffre* Or Kafir; infidel. William M. Ramsey notes that in 1846
Barnum had exhibited 'twin Caffres' – in fact, two dressed-up
albino blacks – and that there are 'twin Caffres' in Melville's novel:
both Black Guinea and the boy peddler (p. 292) are likened to
Caffres. (See Ramsey, 'Melville's and Barnum's Man with a Weed'.)

7

45. *A GENTLEMAN WITH GOLD SLEEVE-BUTTONS* Elizabeth
Foster argues that this man is the 'only one in the novel . . . neither
dupe . . . knave, cynic or hard-hearted egoist. He is the ideal, the
all-good . . .' In Poe's 'Diddling Considered as one of the Exact
Sciences' a similarly well-dressed figure appears; he is a confidence
man. William Norris suggested that he was a portrait of the
millionaire manufacturer and politician Abbott Lawrence. (See
Norris, 'Abbott Lawrence in *The Confidence-Man*: American Success
or American Failure'.)

46. *for that, probably . . . him* The first editions excluded 'him'. The passage seems corrupt and I have followed the Northwestern-Newberry editors' suggestion as the most obvious way of restoring sense to it.

46. *hands nature had dyed black* Unlike those of Black Guinea? The English first edition has the obviously corrupt 'died', here emended to correspond to the American first edition.

46. *like the Hebrew governor* Pontius Pilate; see Matthew 27:24, where Pilate, like the gentleman, keeps his hands clean. The reference contradicts Elizabeth Foster's benign view of the character. (See note to chapter heading on p. 305.)

46. *Wilberforce* William Wilberforce (1759–1833), who led agitation against the slave-trade. But, with his attendant black servant, the man with the gold sleeve-buttons appears as an ironic 'kind of Wilberforce'.

47. *scarcely for a righteous man . . . dare to die* Romans 5:7: 'For scarcely for a righteous man will one die: yet peradventure for a good man some would even dare to die.'

48. *confederation . . . that of the states* Deeply ironic in the 1850s, considering the division between the states that was to lead to civil war.

48. *Socrates . . . soul is a harmony* The idea recurs in his teachings; see Plato's *Republic*, *Phaedo* and *Protagoras*. Socrates also believed that men were wicked not from will but from innate evil.

49. *World's Fair in London* Actually the Great Exhibition, held in London's Crystal Palace in 1851. Barnum's 1851 April Fool's trick involved sending people telegrams that dispatched them on fools' errands. One victim was invited to the World's Fair in London. (See P. T. Barnum, *Life of P. T. Barnum Written by Himself* [London: Sampson Low, 1855], pp. 308–9.)

49. *charity is not like a pin* Melville refers to an example used by Adam Smith to illustrate the advantages of the division of Labour (see *The Wealth of Nations*, ed. R. H. Campbell and A. S. Skinner. [Oxford, 1976], vol. 1, pp. 14–15). In *Redburn* (ch. 18), Wellingborough Redburn falls asleep while trying to read the book.

49. *my Protean easy-chair* Suitable for a protean Confidence Man? Elizabeth Foster notes that at the 1851 Great Exhibition in London several types of such reclining chairs were exhibited.

49. *glass house* The Crystal Palace.

50. *Fourier* French utopian (1772–1837). His ideas influenced the Brook Farm project, a cooperative community near Boston (1841–7).

Hawthorne was involved in the project and wrote of it in his novel *The Blithedale Romance* (1852).

53. *Sarah . . . Abraham* On being told that Sarah would bear a child, Abraham laughed at God (Genesis 17:16–17).

53. *confidence to remove . . . mountains* 1 Corinthians 13:2: '. . . and though I have all faith, so that I could remove mountains, and have not charity, I am nothing.'

53. *millennial promise* After God's victory, Satan will be unable to deceive the nations for a thousand years (Revelation 20:1–3); an ironic reference to the World's Charity scheme.

53. *gestures that were a Pentecost* Referring to the gift of tongues given to the Apostles by the Holy Ghost (Acts 2:1–11).

8

57. *as the apostle . . . things* St Paul, in 2 Corinthians 7:16: 'I rejoice therefore that I have confidence in you in all things.'

9

58. *ruddy-cheeked man* John Truman, here introduced, has been identified by Helen Trimpi in her book as Thurlow Weed (1797–1882). Weed was a newspaper editor and co-founder of the Republican Party.

60. *spurious Jeremiahs* Cf. ch. 24, 'I have heard of Jeremy the prophet.'

60. *Heraclituses . . . Lazaruses* Believing that all things are in a state of flux, Heraclitus was known as the 'weeping philosopher'. The Lazarus referred to here is the beggar in Luke 16:19–31. (See also note to p. 14.)

61. *Good-Enough-Morgan* In 1826 William Morgan of Batavia, New York, disappeared, having threatened to publish the secrets of the Freemasons. Murder by the Freemasons was strongly suspected but never proved. When a drowned corpse was found and believed to be that of Morgan, the supposed identification was used in an election campaign in order to impugn the masonic candidate. It was said that the corpse was a 'good enough Morgan' for the purpose of election publicity. The phrase came to mean an adequate substitute. In this novel of mysterious appearances and disappearances, the case of the disappearing Morgan forms an interesting contrast to the appearances of Casper

Hauser and Peter and the Wild Boy (see pp. 12 and 130 and notes).

61. *I fancy these gloomy souls . . . bore!* Not only has the Collegian picked up the anti-gloomy sentiments of the 'man with the weed' but, with his cigar, he becomes a pictorial pun on a man with a weed.

61. *a musty old Seneca* Lucius Annaeus Seneca (c. 4 BC–AD 65): bloody tragedian, tutor to Nero and Stoic philosopher. He is mentioned in ch. 37 as a notorious usurer.

62. *the maxim of Lord Bacon* In the Dedication to the 1625 edition of *Essays, Counsels, Civil and Moral*, Bacon wrote 'My essays . . . come home, to men's business, and bosoms.' He was not a lord, though the mistake was common (in 'Ligeia' Poe refers similarly to 'Lord Bacon').

62. *The New Jerusalem* A common swindle. In Dickens's widely read *Martin Chuzzlewit* (1844), Martin and Mark Tapley set off for Eden, which turns out to be a fever-ridden swamp. (See also the reference to 'Eden' on p. 156 and note.) In 1839 the Mormons had founded the city of Nauvoo, by the Mississippi river in Illinois. By 1845 it was the largest city in Illinois, but its prosperity was only apparent and, after local antagonism, the Mormons left the city by December 1846. The New Jerusalem itself is described in Revelation 21–2.

63. *read my title clear* From a hymn by Isaac Watts:

> When I can read my title clear
> To mansions in the skies,
> I'll bid farewell to every fear,
> And wipe my weeping eyes.

63. *two fugitives, who had swum over naked* In Part I of Bunyan's *The Pilgrim's Progress* (1678), Christian and Hopeful swim over to the Celestial City.

63. *Arimanius* In Zoroastrianism, Arimanius, also known as Ahriman, represented the evil principle, as opposed to the good represented by Ormazd. The English first edition read 'Ariamus', while the American had 'Ariamius'; both are here corrected.

10

64. *ODE ON THE INTIMATIONS OF DISTRUST* Playing on the title of Wordsworth's 'Ode: Intimations of Immortality' (1807).

Wordsworth's optimism and his belief in a benign nature were
repugnant to Melville, as evident from the story 'Cock-A-Doodle-
Doo!'; a pointed satire on Wordsworth's 'Resolution and
Independence' (1807).

66. *drawn up against the side* The English first edition read 'against his
side', here corrected to correspond with the American edition.

68. *Don't know him* A curious denial of Ringman.

11

70. *true friendliness ... independent of works* Melville refers to the
religious controversy that had raged since the Reformation over
whether salvation could come through good works or by faith
alone. In the character of Falsgrave from *Pierre* Melville satirized
those who had faith without performing good works.

71. *Nature ... had meal and bran Cymbeline*, IV, ii, 26–7: 'Nature hath
meal and bran, contempt and grace.'

71. *Zimmermann or Torquemada* Johann Georg, Ritter von Zimmerman
(1728–95), a Swiss philosophical writer who wrote in praise of
solitude. He is mentioned again (ch. 23). Torquemada (1420–98),
the Spanish Inquisitor General, had figured also in *White-Jacket*
(ch. 70).

12

73. *Thrasea* Thrasea Peatus, Publius Clodius. Roman senator (d.
AD 66) who opposed Nero because of disgust at his vices and was
consequently forced to commit suicide. H. Bruce Franklin notes in
his edition that Thrasea's saying is recorded in Pliny, Bk VIII,
Epistle 22.

73. *Goneril* Egbert S. Oliver put forward the idea that Goneril is based
on the actress Fanny Kemble Butler, Melville's Pittsfield neighbour
between 1849 and 1851. In her 1954 edition of *The Confidence-Man*
Elizabeth Foster dismissed the proposal as 'untenable' (p. 311). (See
Oliver, 'Melville's Goneril and Fanny Kemble'.) The name, taken
from *King Lear*, highlights certain aspects of the story – for example,
the father–daughter relation and the theme of unfounded jealousy.

74. *dried sticks of blue clay* 'Clay-eaters' are included in the list of
passengers (p. 14).

74. *She was taciturn* H. Bruce Franklin notes in his edition the association between Goneril's taciturnity and the man with the weed's aversion to Tacitus.

74. *she had a strange way of touching* On the significance of touching in the novel, see William M. Ramsey, 'Touching Scenes in *The Confidence-Man*'.

13

78. *THE MAN WITH THE TRAVELLING-CAP ... OPTIMISTS* In his manifestation as the man with the weed, the Confidence Man has told the story of Goneril to the merchant. The merchant has retold it to another of the Confidence Man's avatars, the man with the book, who now proceeds to doubt its veracity.

78. *a grave American savan* Elizabeth Foster suggests this is John Quincy Adams, who related a similar incident. (See *Memoirs of J. Q. Adams, 1795–1848* [12 vols., Philadelphia, 1874–6], vol. III, p. 217.) Humphry Davy is mentioned in *Mardi* (ch. 19). Again, the anecdote reflects the distinction between appearance and reality.

80. *Still, he was far from ... not permissible* In an attempt to make sense of this tortuous sentence, the Northwestern-Newberry editors dropped 'not'. However, the emendation is at least debatable and the passage is here left intact.

81. *the secure Malakoff of confidence* The fortress of Malakhov at Sevastopol was considered impregnable, but was captured by the French during the Crimean War (September 1855). Elizabeth Foster argues that the reference to 'secure' Malakoff is evidence that the novel was written before the fort's fall. However, there could be an ironic allusion to the destruction of apparent security.

83. *black, brightening. Seriously, I* The first editions read 'black, brightening seriously, I', which is here emended.

14

84. *run and read* Habbakuk 2:2: 'Write the vision, and make it plain upon tables, that he may run that readeth it.'

85. *caterpillar ... butterfly* Mistakenly reversed in the first editions and here emended.

85. *of life. As elsewhere, experience* The first editions read 'life as elsewhere.

Experience', but since some emendation here is needed, I have followed the suggestion of the Northwestern-Newberry editors.

85. *experience is the only guide* For the sophomore, experience 'is the only teacher' (p. 62).

85. *as no one man's experience can be* The first editions read 'as no one man can be'; since that makes no sense, emendation is required.

85. *the duck-billed beaver of Australia* The platypus. For some time after its discovery in 1797, it was considered to be a hoax. Barnum exhibited one in 1842.

86. *fearfully and wonderfully made* Psalms 139:14: 'I will praise thee; for I am fearfully and wonderfully made.'

15

88. *pine barrens* Tracts of semi-desert wooded with pine trees.

88. *the associate penguin and pelican.* In the Third Sketch of *The Encantadas*, Melville commented on these as freaks of nature. The penguin is the 'most ambiguous and least lovely creature yet discovered by man'. The pelican is called a 'penitential bird'.

88. *Philadelphian regularity* The streets of Philadelphia were noted for their right-angled meetings. They here contrast with the aforementioned crooked streets of Boston (p. 86).

89. *Procrustean beds* In Greek legend the robber Procrustes placed his victims on an iron bed. They were then either stretched or mutilated to fit it. H. Bruce Franklin notes in his edition that there is a direct contrast with the Protean easy chair, and that the barber was described as 'crusty', being 'newly out of bed' (p. 9).

89. *Orpheus* In Greek mythology his singing opened hell so that he could be reunited with his wife Eurydice.

89. *Dives* In torment, after death, the rich man known as Dives begged that Lazarus give him water (Luke 16:19–31). The list of the *Fidèle's* passengers included Dives and Lazarus (see p. 14 and note).

90. *Cant, gammon . . . devils!* The miser is speaking in rogue's cant, in which 'gammon' is both nonsense and a thief's accomplice, to 'bubble' is to cheat, to 'fetch' is to steal, and to 'gouge' is to swindle. In *Pierre* (Book XVI, iii) cant is described as 'the foulest of all human lingoes, that dialect of sin and death'.

91. *I wish, my friend, the herb-doctor* The Northwestern-Newberry editors revise this to read 'I wish my friend the herb-doctor' on the grounds that the Confidence Man would not address the miser as

'friend' and that the irony of the Confidence Man referring to his later manifestation is otherwise lost. However, the copy-text punctuation is here maintained, since Truman does elsewhere address the miser in a friendly way, and the irony of the Confidence Man's reference to a later appearance is already there in the very mention of the herb-doctor.

91.   *He's aboard somewhere* The English first edition reads 'abroad', which is here corrected to correspond with the American edition.

91.   *confidence in me . . . great gain* 1 Timothy 6:6: '. . . godliness with contentment is great gain.'

92.   *I confide . . . my distrust* In Mark 9:24, Christ exorcizes a boy and illustrates the power of belief. The boy's father cries out, 'Lord I believe; help thou my unbelief.'

92.   *ten hoarded eagles* An eagle was a ten-dollar gold coin minted between 1795 and 1933, so called because the reverse depicted an eagle.

93.   *My gold, my gold* Cf. *The Merchant of Venice*, II, viii, 15ff., where Shylock's reaction to the loss of Jessica is reported. Melville's miser bears a general resemblance to Shylock, and the themes of deception, trust, appearance and money are prominent in *The Confidence-Man*, as in Shakespeare's play. See, for example, Bassanio's speech beginning 'So may the outward shows be least themselves' (III, ii, 73ff.).

16

94.   *a seventy-four* A 74-gun warship.

94.   *the daedal boat* Skilfully made; the adjective derives from the name of Daedalus the artificer, again suggesting the theme of appearance and reality.

94.   *surtout* Overcoat. The herb-doctor, who here enters the story, has been identified by Helen Trimpi in her book as Charles Sumner. Sumner (1811–74) was an ardent abolitionist and worked for many causes such as prison reform and world peace.

94.   *good Samaritans erring* The parable of the good Samaritan is told in Luke 10:30–37 and referred to in ch. 39.

95.   *I am mute* While reflecting the 'dumb show' of the patient, the phrase also lends support to the argument that the deaf mute of ch. 1 is the first appearance of the Confidence Man.

95.   *Calvin Edson* A 'living skeleton' displayed by Barnum. He is mentioned again on p. 156.

96. *Pharaoh's vain sorcerers* Exodus 7:11; the sorcerers are powerless to prevent the plagues called down on Egypt.

96. *Solomon the Wise . . . hyssop on the wall* See 1 Kings 4:33: 'And he spake of trees, from the cedar tree that is in Lebanon even unto the hyssop that springeth out of the wall.'

97. *'Medea gathered . . . Aeson' The Merchant of Venice*, V, i, 12–14. Aeson, the elderly father of Jason, was rejuvenated by Medea's use of a herbal potion.

97. *Priessnitz* Vincent Priessnitz (1799–1851), Silesian author of a book on hydrotherapy; Franklin notes that he died while undertaking his own water-cure.

97. *get strength by confidence* Isaiah 30:15: '. . . in quietness and in confidence shall be your strength.'

99. *a book entitled 'Nature in Disease'* The title of a collection of essays by Jacob Bigelow, MD (1854). Among other achievements, Bigelow (1787–1879) founded Auburn cemetery, mentioned in ch. 5.

101. *truth will out* Cf. *Merchant of Venice*, II, ii, 73.

102. *Prove all the vials . . . true* 1 Thessalonians 5:21: 'Prove all things; hold fast to that which is good.'

102. *Iapis in Virgil* The first English edition reads 'Iapus', here corrected.

102. *This is no mortal work . . . power divine* A slightly altered version of Dryden's translation of the *Aeneid*, XII, 632–3; Dryden has 'hands divine'.

17

104. *haunted Cock Lane in London* In 1762 unexplained noises heard at 33 Cock Lane, Smithfield, were popularly believed to have been made by a ghost. Melville knew of the story from Boswell's *Life of Johnson*, where it appears in the entry for 25 June 1763. Johnson was a member of a group that had investigated and exposed the haunting as a hoax, though Johnson himself was represented at the time as a believer in the ghost. Melville visited Cock Lane in November 1849, and referred several times to the ghost of Cock Lane and Johnson's supposed credulity: see *Moby-Dick*, ch. 69; 'The Apple-Tree Table'; and *Journal up the Straits*, p. 54 (3 January 1857). (See also the reference to Dr Johnson on p. 188 and note.)

104. *invalid Titan* In Greek mythology the Titans were a family of giants.

105. *with bead tassel-work* The first editions read 'lead tassel-work', which is almost certainly a mistake. The Northwestern-Newberry editors proposed 'bead' rather than 'lead'.

105. *a little Cassandra* The daughter of Priam. She was blessed with the gift of prophecy, but cursed always to be disbelieved.

105. *Hey diddle, diddle* An appropriate song for a 'Jeremy Diddler' (p. 22). Poe also uses the rhyme in 'Diddling Considered as one of the Exact Sciences' (1843).

106. *the Mexican war* Fought between 1846 and 1848, it was caused mainly by the US annexation of Texas as part of an aggressive expansionist policy. The military victory resulted in the gain of a vast area in what is now the US Southwest and West. In 1847 Melville had satirized General Zachary Taylor in a series of sketches using the style and character of Barnum.

106. *Adam to the thunder* God's voice is often associated with thunder; see Genesis 1:9, 3:8–10

106. *the scales of indifference . . . eyes* The curing of St Paul's blindness is recorded in Acts 9:18; 'And immediately there fell from his eyes as it had been scales.'

18

109. *Asmodeus* In the apocryphal Book of Tobit, Asmodeus represents a demon and is especially associated with marital discord. (See *Paradise Lost*, IV, 167–71.) Asmodeus is also a demon in Le Sage's novel *Le Diable Boiteux* (1707), adaptations of which played in New York in the mid-nineteenth century. In the novel, Asmodeus opens up the roofs of the city houses to reveal the private lives of the inhabitants.

109. *as Hamlet says . . . curiously* That is, Horatio, in *Hamlet*, V, i, 200: 'T'were to consider too curiously, to consider so.'

112. *knave, fool, and genius all together* An emendation of the first editions, which read 'altogether'.

112. *Jesuit emissaries* The Jesuits were reputed to travel in disguise and disseminate Papism, and this supposed intrigue caused a series of panics. (See Ernest Tuveson 'The Creed of the Confidence Man'.) Tuveson cites a passage on Jesuit disguises from *The Jesuits* by R. Fülop-Miller (New York: Capricorn Books, 1963), and in their respective editions Hershel Parker and H. Bruce Franklin cite useful sources for the issue.

113. *Molino del Rey? Resaca de la Palma?* Battles in the Mexican War,
      fought respectively on 8 September 1847 and 9 May 1846.

113. *Tombs!* The Hall of Justice in New York City, used as a prison.
      Melville's Bartleby dies there, and the climax of his novel *Pierre* is
      also set in 'the city prison'.

113. *you are Lazarus . . . the other Lazarus* Lazarus of Bethany was raised
      from the dead (John 11–12), while Lazarus the poor man with
      sores (Luke 16:19–31) has already been mentioned (see p. 14 and
      note). In *Mardi* (ch. 78), Babbalanja considers it odd that 'in
      Mohi's chronicles' the man raised from the dead made no revelation
      concerning the experience of death.

114. *the noble cripple, Epictetus* Stoic philosopher (55–135). He was born
      a slave, was lame from youth and suffered ill health his entire life.
      He can be compared to Black Guinea in these respects.

114. *The Happy Man* Melville had already written ironically of 'The
      Happy Failure' (1854).

115. *still correspond . . . Mrs Fry* Even though she had been dead at least
      ten years as Melville was writing. Elizabeth Fry (1780–1845) was
      an English Quaker minister and philanthropist concerned with
      prison reform and the condition of vagrants.

115. *New York . . . cooper* H. Bruce Franklin suggests in his edition
      that there is a reference to the writer James Fenimore Cooper,
      from Cooperstown, New York. Several commentators have
      suggested that the character of Pitch, soon to appear, is a sketch
      of Cooper.

115. *a political meeting in the Park* Probably City Hall Park, where
      Melville's brother Gansevoort had made political speeches.

115. *pavior* A street-paver.

118. *Buena Vista . . . General Scott . . . Contreras* Further battles of the
      Mexican War, respectively dated 22–23 February and 19–20 August
      1847. General Winfield Scott (1788–1866) took over the direction
      of the war from Zachary Taylor and led the US troops into
      Mexico City.

118. *Charity never faileth* One of the deaf mute's mottoes from
      I Corinthians 1:13.

120. *apparent calamities* In 'Compensation' (1841) Emerson argues that
      incidents and misfortunes that seem overwhelming may later
      assume the aspect of a 'guide or genius'. The series of privations

experienced by Thomas Fry seem designed specifically to ridicule
Emerson's optimistic confidence.

120.   *those who are loved are chastened* Hebrews 12:6: 'For whom the Lord
       loveth he chasteneth.' See also Proverbs 13:24, Revelation, 3:19.

20

126.   *you'll hear from him, all right* An emendation of the pointless
       reading in the first editions, 'you'll hear from him. All right.'

126.   *Mammoth Cave* A renowned cave in Kentucky. A group of
       consumptives had occupied the cave in 1843 in the vain hope that
       it would help cure them. In *Moby-Dick*, the whale's stomach is
       compared to the same cave (ch. 74).

127.   *four boxes for nothing* In fact, it is getting two boxes for nothing.
       Melville may simply be confused here; he described himself as 'a
       sorry arithmetician' (Jay Leyda, *The Melville Log*, p. 610). In ch. 99
       of *Moby-Dick*, Flask's arithmetic also goes sadly awry as he
       calculates the number of cigars that may be bought for $16.

128.   *not quarters ... sweated* Pistareens were Spanish coins in
       US circulation, worth about 17 cents rather than the 25 cents in
       the US quarter. Coins would be clipped or sweated to remove
       some of the silver. In effect the miser ends up paying less than
       $1.36 for the $2 box.

21

129.   *file* Slang for a pickpocket, but here probably with only the
       meaning of 'wretch'.

129.   *Yarbs and natur ... you think?* The first editions omit the question
       mark here added.

129.   *a shaggy spencer ... bear's-skin* That is, a short double-breasted
       jacket made of coarse, shaggy wool. Pitch, who appears here, has
       been variously identified; several critics suggested that he represents
       the writer James Fenimore Cooper, while in her book Helen
       Trimpi has identified him with Thomas Hart Benton (1782–1858).
       Benton was an enthusiast of westward expansion and a democrat
       who, although opposing slavery, refused to join the Republican
       party after its formation in 1854.

129.   *a double-barrelled gun in hand* Wellingborough Redburn similarly

travels armed on a river boat; like Pitch, he 'clicks the lock' (*Redburn*, ch. 2).

129.   *Hoosier* An awkward or ungainly rustic.

130.   *poets . . . to green pastures* An echo of Milton's 'Lycidas', at the end of which the poet looks forward to 'fresh Woods and Pastures new'.

130.   *Peter the Wild Boy* (?1712–85). The boy was discovered near Hamelin in 1724, unable to talk and apparently wild. He was brought to England by George I in an attempt to test the theory of innate ideas. The case is similar to that of Casper Hauser (see p. 12 and note).

130.   *come to us and the mercury* The Missourian is referring to the often bitter nineteenth-century dispute between those who extolled the curative properties of minerals and those who favoured the use of herbs.

130.   *Confession of Faith* Christopher S. Durer suggests that this phrase was possibly taken from Rousseau's *Emile*, Book IV: 'The Profession of Faith of a Savoyard Vicar'. (See Durer, 'Melville's *The Confidence-Man*, and Jean-Jacques Rousseau.)

131.   *broad off upon the waters . . . back after many days* Cf. Ecclesiastes 11:1: 'Cast thy bread upon the waters: for thou shalt find it after many days.'

131.   *the Siamese twins* The originals were Chang and Eng, born in Siam in 1811 and displayed by Barnum. Melville's use of the phrase 'less strong' suggests asymmetrical Siamese twins, with one dependent on the other.

132.   *Is it not to nature* The English first edition's 'It is not to nature' is here corrected to correspond with the American first edition.

133.   *Lint her out* That is, stuff lint into chinks and cracks.

134.   *the dungeoned Italian we read of* Elizabeth Foster suggests a reference to the Abbé Faria in *The Count of Monte Cristo*. Dumas's novel had been translated into English in 1846.

136.   *the freer of the two* H. Bruce Franklin notes in his edition that the Missourian's statement has been used as evidence for the identification with James Fenimore Cooper, who, while professing his detestation of slavery, argued that the slave in America was better off than the European peasantry, as far as animal needs were concerned.

136.   *then am I what you say* Melville's opposition to slavery was consistent and is expressed powerfully in chs. 157–62 of *Mardi*. In ch. 157 the travellers arrive at Vivenza (the United States) and read

the monument to liberty and equality. However, a hieroglyphic below the main inscription makes an exception; all are born free and equal 'Except-the-tribe-of-Hamo'. As Media points out, 'That nullifies the other.' They proceed to visit the 'South of Vivenza', where Melville satirizes some of the apologists for slavery.

136. *the moderate man ... useless for right* An echo of Revelation 3:16: '... because thou art ... neither cold nor hot, I will spue thee out of my mouth.'

137. *Who is your master, pray?* Cf. Pope's epigram, 'I am his Highness's dog at Kew; / pray tell me Sir, whose dog are you?' In the next chapter, the Philosophical Intelligence representative appears 'with a sort of canine deprecation' and a brass plate around his neck.

137. *Cape Girardeau* In Missouri, about 140 miles down river from St Louis. The first editions read 'Giradeau', here and subsequently corrected.

22

138. *IN THE POLITE SPIRIT ... DISPUTATIONS* Cicero's *Tusculan Disputations* (45 BC) are indeed polite; not so the following 'disputations'.

138. *Philosophical Intelligence Office* An 'intelligence office' was a current term for a domestic employment agency. In 'Hawthorne and His Mosses' Melville had praised Hawthorne's short story 'The Intelligence Office'. Helen Trimpi argues in her book that the Philosophical Intelligence Officer, the next appearance of the Confidence Man, represents Horace Greeley (1811–72), a newspaper editor who supported the Republican Party.

138. *baker-kneed man* Knock-kneed, a condition supposedly typical of bakers. The term also has connotations of effeminacy.

139. *Alton* In Illinois, about 30 miles north of St Louis. At this time, Illinois was a 'free' state, where slavery was not permitted.

139. *I'm a Mede and Persian* Daniel 6:8: '... the law of the Medes and Persians, which altereth not.'

140. *Accommodate?* In 2 *Henry IV*, III, ii, 66–79, Bardolph and Shallow repeat this word in a similar way.

140. *cousin-german* A first or full cousin.

140. *patient continuance in well-doing* Romans 2:7: 'To them who by patient continuance in well doing seek for glory and honour and immortality, eternal life.'

140. *Praise-God-Barebones* Praisegod Barbon, Barebone or Barebones

(1596?–1679). An English Anabaptist and a member of Cromwell's parliament. After the Restoration he was confined for a time in the Tower.

141. *Horace ... servants* Horace (65–8 BC) refers often to the untrustworthiness of slaves.

142. *a perfect Chesterfield* The boy's politeness here masks his dishonesty. Philip Dormer Stanhope (1694–1773) wrote a series of letters (published in 1774) to his natural son, advocating manners and politeness. (In his celebrated dismissal, Dr Johnson said that 'they teach the morals of a whore, and the manners of a dancing master'. See Boswell's *Life*, 1754.)

144. *the child is father of the man* From Wordsworth's 'My Heart Leaps Up'. The short poem is also used as the epigraph to the 'Ode: Intimations of Immortality', with which Melville plays in ch. 10. The phrase here glances back at Chesterfield's letters to his (publicly unacknowledged) son.

145. *A wet sheet and a flowing sea!* From a poem with that title by Alan Cunningham (1784–1842).

148. *dropped overnight in Eden* Even this is not straightforward, considering the Eden of *Martin Chuzzlewit*, into which Martin and Mark are 'dropped'. (See the references to 'The New Jerusalem' and 'Cairo' on pp. 62 and 156 respectively, and notes.)

150. *visit upon the butterfly ... caterpillar* But cf. Exodus 20:5: '... visiting the inquity of the fathers upon the children unto the third and fourth generation.'

151. *founder of La Trappe ... Loyola* Abbot de Rancé (1626–1700) founded the reformed Cistercians, known as the Trappists, making it the order of austerity. St Ignatius Loyola (1491–1556) founded the Jesuits. Both men underwent conversion from worldliness at around the age of thirty, as did St Augustine (354–430), soon to be mentioned. In *White-Jacket* Loyola is associated with Torquemada (ch. 70).

151. *What's wisdom itself ... the form of table-talk?* A reference to the Last Supper; see John 13–17, Matthew 26:20–29, Mark, 14:17–25, Luke 22:14–38.

152. *St Augustine on Original Sin* Augustine revised the church's teaching on Original Sin by emphasizing that total depravity resulted from Adam's fall. Thus, the human will to do good is limited. Augustine's development of the doctrine resulted logically in the concept of predestination and directly influenced Calvin.

152. *this mild summer's eve* Although it is an April day?

153. *your marines ... say anything* Used to indicate a tall tale. The
saying probably dates back to Pepys, but was variously used in the
early nineteenth century. (See Byron, *The Island* [1823], Canto II,
xxi; Scott, *Redgauntlet* [1824]: 'Tell that to the marines – the sailors
won't believe it.') In *White-Jacket* Melville wrote of the 'mutual
contempt, and even hatred' necessarily existing between the
Marines and the sailors (ch. 89).

153. *reformado boys* Boys out of reform school.

155. *Devil's Joke* John W. Nichol, in 'Melville and the Midwest',
points out that in this area there were rock formations known as
'Devil's Oven' and 'Devil's Tea Table'.

23

156. *Cairo* Dickens's Eden in *Martin Chuzzlewit* was based on the area
around Cairo, infamous for its unhealthy environment. Reaching
Cairo is a significant point of transition in *The Confidence-Man*,
signalling the novel's division into two parts. (See also references
to 'The New Jerusalem' and 'Eden' on pp. 62 and 148 respectively,
and notes.)

156. *Yellow Jack* Yellow fever.

156. *hand ... not lost its cunning* Psalms 137:5: 'If I forget thee, O
Jerusalem, let my right hand forget her cunning.'

156. *audibly mumbles* The English first edition had dropped the
American edition's 'audibly', here restored.

156. *Apemantus' dog* In Shakespeare's *Timon of Athens*, Apemantus is a
cynical philosopher, friend of Timon. He actually has no dog (see
IV, iii, 199); the narrator is punning on 'cynic' and 'dog'.
Apemantus' dog would be doubly cynical.

156. *Crossbones* An emblem of death.

157. *Suspicion, the warder* In *Milton and Melville*, Henry F. Pommer
suggests the reference to *Paradise Lost*, III, 686–9:

> And oft, though wisdom wake, suspicion sleeps
> At wisdom's gate, and to simplicitie
> Resigns her charge, while goodness thinks no ill
> Where no ill seems.

Satan has disguised himself and learnt how to reach Eden. (See
Pommer, *Milton and Melville*, p. 64.)

157. *Talleyrand ... Machiavelli ... Rosicrucian* References indicating

the cunning and secrecy of the Intelligence Office man: Charles-Maurice de Talleyrand-Périgord (1754–1838), the renowned diplomat; Niccolò Machiavelli (1469–1527), the deceptive opportunist. The Rosicrucians are a worldwide secret society claiming to possess esoteric knowledge; they were probably founded during the Renaissance.

157.   *beast that windeth . . . belly* After the temptation of Adam and Eve, the serpent was condemned to go thus. See Genesis 3:14.

24

158.   *our Fair* A reference to the Vanity Fair of *Pilgrim's Progress* and also to Hawthorne's 'The Celestial Railroad'. (See John W. Shroeder, 'Sources and Symbols for Melville's *Confidence Man*.')

158.   *a liberalist, in dress* Nathalia Wright argued that the Confidence Man resembles Steadfast Dodge, a character in James Fenimore Cooper's novel *Homeward Bound* (1838). (See 'The Confidence Men of Melville and Cooper: An American Indictment'.) The Cosmopolitan's international dress recalls the 'Anacharsis Cloots congress' of ch. 1.

159.   *in blast* alight and smoking.

159.   *Signor Marzetti* During the 1840s Joseph Marzetti played the role of an ape in several New York pantomimes.

159.   *fortiter in re . . . sauviter in modo* Strongly in deed, gently in manner, The phrase occurs in Chesterfield's *Letters*, cxciv.

160.   *A cosmopolitan . . . No man is a stranger* John Bryant usefully outlines the issues suggested by this phrase. (See '"Nowhere a Stranger": Melville and Cosmopolitanism'.) In her book Helen Trimpi associates him with Henry Ward Beecher (1813–87), the abolitionist who was at the time the most popular preacher in the United States. He was noted for his unorthodox dress and manners.

160.   *the Lunar Mountains* In East Africa. During the nineteenth century they were considered legendary.

160.   *Ladrone* A highway robber.

160.   *that good dish, man* According to John W. Shroeder, the Devil was reputed to eat the human soul (see Shroeder, 'Sources and Symbols for Melville's *The Confidence-Man*').

160.   *London-Dock-Vault connoisseur* The London dock vaults housed wines from all over the world. In *White-Jacket* the men find some barrels of 'London Dock' (port) floating in the sea (ch. 37).

161. *hide his light under the bushel* A reference to part of the Sermon on the Mount (Matthew 5:14–15).

161. *Life is a pic-nic en costume* While recovering from exhaustion and illness Melville attended such a picnic in September 1855. It has been suggested that the event helped give Melville the idea for *The Confidence-Man*. (See Leon Howard, *Herman Melville: A Biography*, p. 226.) Like the hypothetical man here, Melville was 'in plain clothes' (Jay Leyda, *The Melville Log*, p. 507).

161. *the worthy old woman of Goshen* Goshen, which gave its name to several US towns, was the area of Egypt untouched by the plagues (Exodus 7–9). H. Bruce Franklin notes in his edition that 'a number of limericks used the name as the key riming word, and there may well be one about an old woman of Goshen'.

161. *shoats* Young pigs, less than one year old.

161. *a green Christmas, inauspicious to the old* Part of an old proverb, 'a green Yule makes a fat churchyard' – that is, a mild winter is often followed by a severe spring.

162. *a jug of Santa Cruz* Rum, from Santa Cruz in the West Indies.

163. *Mr Megrims* That is, Zimmerman as Mr Migraine, a megrim being a kind of neuralgia. (See also note to p. 71: *Zimmermann* . . .)

163. *Hume's on Suicide . . . Bacon's on Knowledge* Hume's posthumously published *Essay on Suicide* (1783) presents arguments for the justification of suicide. In *Redburn* (ch. 58) Hume's calm acceptance of death is praised. No specific work by Bacon seems intended.

163. *Rabelais's pro-wine Koran* A reference to *Gargantua and Pantagruel* (1532–52) by Rabelais (?1494–1553). Gargantua himself is born at the end of a drinking scene, and the characters go on a quest for the 'oracle of the Holy Bottle'. The oracle's advice is, 'Drink.' The influence of Rabelais on Melville has often been noted, and *The Confidence-Man* itself was considered 'Rabelaisian'. In the Islamic Koran intoxicating drinks and prohibited.

163. *Jeremy Taylor* Theologian (1613–67) and Bishop of Down and Connor.

165. *Now be frank* The Cosmopolitan later assumes the name Frank.

166. *my friends nigh Primrose Hill* Associated with duels and with the 1678 murder of Sir Edmund Berry Godfrey. Melville visited Primrose Hill during his 1849 trip to London.

166. *Diogenes . . . flower-market . . . Timon* The Cosmopolitan is contrasting Diogenes the cynic (*c.* 412–323 BC), who lived in a jar in the market place, with Timon, who chose a cave in the woods.

166. *Diogenes . . . a cosmopolitan* However, Diogenes did say, 'I am a
      citizen of the world,' and is reputed to have originated the term
      'cosmopolitan'.

166. *an Ishmael* Ishmael was cast out by his father Abraham; see Genesis
      16–17; 21:6–21; 25:8–18. The wandering Ishmael figure recurs
      frequently in the works of Melville, most notably in *Moby-Dick*.

25

168. *abord* Manner of approach.

168. *Colonel John Moredock* The Indian-hater who will be described in
      the subsequent chapters.

168. *the beauty . . . less in the fit than the cut* That is, the man's ill-fitting
      clothes are stolen.

169. *eye like Lochiel's* Sir Ewen or Evan Cameron of Lochiel (1629–
      1719), Scottish hunter and warrior. He is said to have killed the last
      wolf in Britain. Perhaps indeed, 'where the wolves are killed off,
      the foxes increase' (p. 8).

169. *hated Indians like snakes* Indian-hating was a well-established fact of
      frontier life. (See Appendix B, and Edwin Fussell, *Frontier*.) In his
      1849 review of Parkman's *California and Oregon Trail* Melville
      wrote, 'It is too often the case, that civilized beings sojourning
      among savages soon come to regard them with disdain and
      contempt. But though in many cases this feeling is almost natural,
      it is not defensible; and it is wholly wrong.'

170. *I admire Indians* Ambiguous confirmation of the Cosmopolitan's
      identity as the Devil, since the earliest Americans considered the
      Indians devils.

170. *Pocahontas . . . Auraucanians* The Cosmopolitan's list of Indians is a
      mixture of those friendly and those hostile to the whites.
      Pocahontas rescued John Smith, was kidnapped by the English and
      married to John Rolfe. She died during a visit to England in 1617
      (and is buried in Kent). Massasoit (d. 1661) was a chief of the
      Wampanoag. The tribe lived peacefully after a 1621 treaty with
      the Plymouth settlers. Massasoit's son Philip (d. 1676) was a later
      leader of the Wampanoag who fought the English in 'King Philip's
      War' (1675–6), in which he was killed and his tribe virtually
      destroyed. Tecumseh (1768–1813) was a Shawnee chief who
      attempted to unite all the Indian tribes, but they were defeated by
      the United States forces, led by Harrison, at the Battle of

Tippecanoe in 1811. He sided with the British in the war of 1812, during which he was killed. Red-Jacket (*c.* 1756–1830) was one of the leaders of the Seneca tribe. He was largely friendly towards whites, receiving his name from the British army jacket that he wore. James Logan (1725–80), who had a white father and a native mother, lived in peace with the whites until the massacre of his family in 1774. He subsequently waged war on the whites, and he fought on the side of the British in the Revolutionary War. The Five Nations were a confederacy of the Iroquois tribes who fought with the English against the French and the Revolutionaries. The Araucanians, a tribe from central Chile, fought against the Incas in the fifteenth century and later against the Spanish. During the 1850s they were defending their independence from Chile.

170.   *a white stone* Used to mark a memorable day or event. See Genesis 28:11–15; Revelation 2:17.

171.   *James Hall, the judge* A circuit judge in Illinois (1793–1868) who wrote fiction and essays on the West. For the chapters on Indian-hating, Melville drew heavily upon ch. 6 of the second volume of Hall's *Sketches of History, Life and Manners in the West* (Philadelphia, 1835). See Appendix B.

171.   *press . . . impressive . . . impressible* H. Bruce Franklin notes in his edition that the play on words here foreshadows the elaborate puns on 'press' in chs. 29–30.

26

173.   *ROUSSEAU* Jean-Jacques Rousseau (1712–78), philosopher who supported the idea of the Noble Savage.

174.   *Hairy Orson* In the fifteenth-century French Romance, Orson, the twin brother of Valentine, is carried off by a bear. He is raised as a wild man, while Valentine is raised at court. Orson belongs to the same myth of the 'wild boy' as Casper Hauser and Peter (see pp. 12 and 130 and notes).

174.   *the Emperor Julian in Gaul* Roman Emperor (361–3). Before becoming Emperor he had been in charge of Gaul and Britain. He shared the hardships of his troops and was fatally wounded in battle.

175.   *the theory of the Peace Congress* A variety of international gatherings in the nineteenth century were devoted to the attainment of world peace. The movements developed into organizations such as the

American Peace Society (1828), and the League of Universal Brotherhood (1846). 'Universal Peace Congresses' were held between 1848 and 1853 in Britain and Europe.

175.   *the Newgate Calendar or the Annals of Europe* The Newgate Calendar, or *The Malefactor's Bloody Register* chronicled lurid crimes. It was first published about 1744. *The Annals of Europe*, published annually between 1739 and 1744, detailed the events of each year.

175.   *As the twig is bent the tree's inclined* From Pope's *Moral Essays* (1732), Epistle I, 149–50: "'Tis education forms the common mind, / Just as the twig is bent, the tree's inclined.'

176.   *Moyamensing* The Philadelphia County Prison.

176.   *a treaty-breaker like an Austrian* During the revolutionary year 1848 the Austrian government made a series of concessions to the people; these were later revoked.

176.   *now a Palmer* William Palmer (1824–56), known as the 'Rugeley poisoner' and responsible for the deaths, among others, of his wife, his brother and a friend. His trial received wide publicity and he was hanged in June 1856. Melville's reference indicates the date that this part of the novel was written. Poisoners recur in this part of the novel. (See Barry C. Chabot, 'Melville's *The Confidence-Man*: A "Poisonous" Reading'.)

176.   *Jeffries ... bloody death* Judge George Jeffreys (1648–89), the notoriously severe and unjust judge. Among other atrocities he was responsible for sentencing to death over three hundred men at the 'Bloody Assizes' following Monmouth's rebellion in 1685, and for the transportation, torture and imprisonment of many more.

176.   *Manitou* There were two Manitous recognized by certain Indian tribes, one being the spirit of evil, the other a spiritual force for good.

177.   *the Bloody Ground, Kentucky* Kentucky was the first state west of the Alleghenies to be settled by pioneers, and in *Sketches of History, Life and Manners in the West* Hall had claimed that the Indian name applied to the territory meant 'dark and bloody ground' (Vol. I, p. 234). The name Kentucky is usually considered to derive from the Iroquois *kentake*, 'meadowland'.

177.   *Mocmohoc* There was no known native American of that name, which can be taken to mean 'mock Mohawk'. With regard to Melville's use of contemporary Indian burlesques, see William M. Ramsey, 'The Moot Points of Melville's Indian-Hating'.

177.   *Caesar Borgia* Cesare Borgia (1475–1507), the Duke of Valentinois and Romagna, son of Pope Alexander VI. He was notorious for

his treachery, and is praised on account of it by Machiavelli in *The Prince*.

178. *Daniel Boone* The almost mythical frontiersman (1734–1820) and legendary discoverer of Kentucky. He claimed that his two sons and his brother had been killed by Indians. Melville referred to his solitariness and his longevity in *Moby-Dick* (ch. 88).

180. *An intenser Hannibal* Hannibal (247–183 BC) swore at the age of nine always to be an enemy of Rome.

180. *a Spaniard turned monk* In 'Benito Cereno' Don Benito is a Spaniard who turns monk.

180. *Leather-stocking* Like 'Pathfinder' (p. 174), one of the names of Natty Bumppo, hero of James Fenimore Cooper's 'Leather-stocking' novels (1823–41). This character was based in part on the figure of Daniel Boone. Melville warmly admired Cooper's work.

180. *gone to his long home* Ecclesiastes 12:5: '. . . man goeth to his long home, and the mourners go about the streets.'

180. *ascetic* The English first edition read 'asthetic', here amended in accordance with the American first edition.

181. *Senegal* In 'Benito Cereno' Senegal symbolized primitive evil.

181. *calenture* A kind of delirium known to affect sailors. It often results in drowning, because of the delusion that the sea is a field.

181. *calumet* The ornamental pipe used in Indian rituals.

27

182. *ENGLISH MORALIST . . . GOOD HATER* Dr Johnson, on Bathurst: 'Dear Bathurst (said he to me one day) was a man to my very heart's content: he hated a fool, and he hated a rogue, and he hated a *whig*; he was a very good *hater*' (Hesther Lynch Piozzi, *Anecdotes of the Late Samuel Johnson* [London: T. Cadell, 1786], p. 83). The phrase recurs in *Mardi* (ch. 13).

182. *a new Arcadia* Arcadia, a region of Greece, was idealized as a place of pastoral contentment.

183. *the rock of the Grand Tower* A 75-feet-high rock standing out into the river from the Missouri shore, between the mouth of the Ohio River and St Louis.

184. *the voice calling through the garden* Genesis 3:8; Adam and Eve hear God after they have eaten the apple.

184. *a number* The first editions read ' murder', which is clearly wrong.

The emendation to 'a number' was first suggested by Hershel
Parker in 1963 (see 'The Metaphysics of Indian-hating').

185.   *Hull's dubious surrender at Detroit* General William Hull (1753–
       1825) surrendered Detroit to the British in August 1812 without
       attempting resistance. At a court martial he was acquitted of
       treason but found guilty of cowardice and un-officer-like conduct.
       Although sentenced to death, he was pardoned by President
       Madison.

28

188.   *Dr Johnson ... don't believe it* Dr Johnson said that he did not
       believe in the Lisbon earthquake 'for six months' (Hesther Lynch
       Piozzi, *Anecdotes of the Late Samuel Johnson* [London: T. Cadell,
       1786], p. 141). The earthquake occurred on All Saints' Day, 1
       November 1755; the churches were crowded and an estimated
       30,000 people were killed, with some 9,000 buildings destroyed.
       The event was a setback to those adhering to optimistic and
       benign views of God and nature; hence Dr Johnson's wilful
       incredulity is akin to the Cosmopolitan's disbelief in Indian-hating.
       Some optimists found cause for celebration in the event, as
       signifying God's overall design, a view satirized by Voltaire in
       both his *Poem on the Lisbon Disaster* (1756) and in *Candide* (1759).
       The earthquake itself is experienced by Candide and Pangloss;
       they survive, though Pangloss is hanged in an *auto-da-fé* when the
       townspeople are angered by his optimism. *Candide* and *The
       Confidence-Man* are comparable, at least as satires on optimism. (See
       also the note to p. 104: *haunted Cock Lane in London*.)

189.   *Can a misanthrope ... cigar* In *White-Jacket* Melville wrote that 'a
       bunch of cigars' is a 'symbol of brotherly love' (ch. 91).

189.   *Cold regards ... word for it* Hershel Parker suggests in his edition
       that Melville 'may be wryly altering' a passage from Amaso
       Delano's *Voyages* (Boston: 1817), p. 328. Delano's book had been
       used extensively by Melville in 'Benito Cereno'.

190.   *Let us drink ... Sansovine* From 'Bacchus in Tuscany' by Leigh
       Hunt (1825). Melville slightly misquotes ll. 246–7, which read:
       'And drink of the wine of the vine benign / That sparkles warm in
       Sansovine.' The first editions read 'Zansovine', here corrected.

190.   *When mermaid songs ... resolute* In *Mardi* (ch. 122) Melville
       ridiculed Barnum's mermaid exhibits.

29

191. *Charles Arnold Noble* On board ship, a 'Charley Noble' was the galley funnel, thus named after a Commodore Noble who insisted that the funnel be kept clean and bright. H. Bruce Franklin notes in his edition that a common trick played on landsmen was to send them off to find 'Charley Noble'. He also says that John Seelye has brought to his attention that in Poe's story 'Thou Art the Man' a mysterious stranger appears called Charley Goodfellow. This name is combined in those of Charles Noble and Frank Goodman.

192. *Brinvillierses* A reference to the Marquise de Brinvilliers (1630–76), a Frenchwoman who poisoned her father, sister and two brothers. One of the allegations against her was that she tested the poison on patients in the hospitals she charitably visited. She was subsequently executed. Melville wrote a poem entitled 'The Marchioness of Brinvilliers' emphasizing the conflict between appearance and reality.

192. *Hebe's cheek* Hebe was the Greek Goddess of youth and spring, as well as being the cup-bearer to the Gods. She contrasts ironically with the Marquise de Brinvilliers.

194. *the Rochefoucaultites* Those endorsing the maxims of François, Duc de La Rochefoucauld (1613–80).

194. *but nine good jokes . . . Sodom* Abraham bargained until God promised not to destroy Sodom if ten righteous men could be found there. See Genesis 18:23–32. H. Bruce Franklin suggests in his edition that the 'nine good jokes' could refer to the number of avatars of the Confidence Man. *The Confidence-Man* was Melville's ninth novel.

195. *a man may smile, and smile . . . villain* Hamlet, I, v, 107–8: 'Meet it is I set it down / That one may smile, and smile, and be a villain.' Cf. *Pierre*, Book IV, v: '. . . a smile is the chosen vehicle of all ambiguities.'

195. *the voice of the people is the voice of truth* The Latin proverb 'Vox populi, vox Dei' is attributed to Alcuin (c. 735–804), *Works*, Epistle 127.

195. *Aristotle . . . Phalaris!* Melville here makes his own hoax and links it to a celebrated seventeenth-century controversy. Both Elizabeth Foster and H. Bruce Franklin report that the remark attributed to Aristotle does not appear in his works. In the sixth century BC Phalaris was a tyrant of Acragas in Sicily. While notorious for his

cruelty, there is no evidence of the story Melville relates. In the seventeenth century Phalaris became the subject of controversy after Charles Boyle had edited what were supposedly Phalaris' letters (they were forgeries). The dispute, involving Boyle, Wotton, Temple and Bentley, was used by Swift in *The Battle of the Books* (1704).

197. *a kind of poetry . . . chant* Possibly a reference to the free verse of Whitman's *Leaves of Grass* (1855, 1856).

197. *Jack Cade* The rebel leader (d. 1450) who appears in Shakespeare's *2 Henry VI*.

197. *Kossuth and Mazzini* Lajos Kossuth (1802–94) led the Hungarian revolution against Austria in 1848, but failed when Austria received the support of Russia. He visited the USA in 1851–2 while attempting to raise support for the revolutionary cause and received warm ovations. (He is referred to also in 'I and My Chimney'.) Guiseppi Mazzini (1805–72) fought for the liberation of Italy and was involved in the Roman revolution of 1848. The series of European revolutions is outlined in *Mardi* (ch. 153).

198. *Paul* St Paul, the recurring figure whose letter to the Corinthians was the source of the deaf mute's text in ch. 1.

198. *force and light* Perhaps a reference to 'sweetness and light' from Swift's *The Battle of the Books* (1704).

198. *parhelion* A 'mock sun' caused when ice crystals in the atmosphere refract sunlight.

198. *sovereign of England . . . Defender of the Faith* Defensor Fidei was the title given to Henry VIII by Pope Leo X in 1521. It became ironic after Henry's break with the Roman Church.

30

199. *Praise be unto the press* In *Melville's Use of the Bible* Nathalia Wright demonstrates how this first paragraph imitates Biblical language and formulas. For example, see Proverbs 23:29–30.

199. *not Faust's, but Noah's* Johann Faust or Fust (*c.* 1400–1467), was a German printer and partner of Gutenberg. After their partnership ended in 1455 he continued to use Gutenberg's press. Noah's press was the wine press; see Genesis 9:20–27.

199. *Madeira or Mitylene* Both used here for their association with wine. Madeira is in the North Atlantic, Mitylene, or Mytilene, is the capital of the Greek island of Lesbos. In *White-Jacket* (ch. 37) the *Neversink* visited the island of Madeira so that wines could be taken aboard.

200. *a Catawba vine* Catawba is a white wine made mainly in Ohio and New York State. Longfellow's poem 'Catawba Wine' celebrates the drink.

200. *in guise of an apple . . . ashes* Melville here refers to the legendary 'Apple of Sodom', or Dead Sea Fruit, which resembled the apple but had an interior of ashes. He uses the image several times for desolation; see the first sketch of 'The Encantadas' and *Clarel*, II, canto xxviii.

202. *the advice of Polonius to Laertes Hamlet*, I, iii, 59–80. The Polonius figure representing worldly wisdom was a frequent target of Melville's, characterized also by Chesterfield and (in *Israel Potter*, chs. 7–8) Benjamin Franklin. The type was fictionalized in *Pierre* as Plinlimmon and Falsgrave. The idea that Christian actions are impossible in a worldly context recurs in Melville; see Plinlimmon's pamphlet in *Pierre* (Book XIV, iii).

202. *Malvolios* The Puritan type satirized by Shakespeare in *Twelfth Night*. Other examples of Shakespeare's scorn of the Puritans are in *All's Well That Ends Well* (I, iii, 88), and *The Winter's Tale* (IV, ii, 45–6).

203. *'The friends thou hast . . . steel' Hamlet* I, iii, 62–3, in Pope's edition, which amends the generally accepted 'hoops' to 'hooks'.

203. *sell all thou hast . . . poor* Matthew 19:21.

204. *This Shakespeare . . . reliable* In 'Hawthorne and His Mosses' Melville wrote: 'Through the mouths of the dark characters of Hamlet, Timon, Lear, and Iago, he craftily says, or sometimes insinuates the things, which we feel to be so terrifically true, that it were all but madness for any good man, in his own proper character, to utter, or even hint of them.'

205. *Shakespeare has got to be a kind of deity* Cf. 'Hawthorne and His Mosses': 'this absolute and unconditional adoration of Shakespeare has grown to be a part of our Anglo-Saxon superstitions . . . You must believe in Shakespeare's unapproachability, or quit the country.'

205. *Autolycus* The rogue from *The Winter's Tale*.

205. *what a fool is Honesty . . . gentlemen The Winter's Tale*, IV, iv, 586–7. Autolycus is an appropriate figure to be quoted by a confidence man; but see also the debate between Pollixenes and Perdita concerning the natural and the artificial (IV, iv, 70–97), a debate reflecting that between Pitch and the herb-doctor.

206. *punk* Decayed wood.

206. *To humâne minds* The first editions read 'human minds', the

emendation made by the Northwestern-Newberry editors is followed here.

207. *Madness, to be mad with anything* Cf. *Moby-Dick* (ch. 136): 'Madness! To be enraged with a dumb thing, Captain Ahab, seems blasphemous.'

207. *loan losing both itself and friend Hamlet* I, iii, 75–6: 'Neither a borrower, nor a lender be; / For loan oft loses both itself and friend.'

208. *Why, bless you, Charlie* The first editions read 'Frank'; Leon Howard first noticed the error (see *Herman Melville: A Biography* p. 232).

208. *freely drink it, it has* The English first edition read 'freely drink, it has', which corrected the American 'freely drink, it it has' but lost the intended sense of the original edition.

209. *he who loves not wine* Cf. Falstaff's speech in praise of wine (*2 Henry IV*, IV, iii 84–124).

209. *free-and-easies* Saloons, or the gatherings in them.

209. *Pizarro* Francisco Pizarro (*c.* 1471–1541), the Spanish conquistador who plundered the Incas from 1532 onwards, securing an immense amount of gold. He murdered the Inca king Atahualpa.

210. *Jack Ketch* The barbarous executioner (d.1686) whose name has become synonymous with that of hangman; cf. the name of the character in Punch and Judy.

211. *throwing stones at people ... Timon* In *Timon of Athens* Timon throws a stone at Apemantus (IV, iii, 372) before giving gold to the bandits.

211. *fiddle in hand ... a'dancing* Cf. the happy fiddler Hautboy in 'The Fiddler' (1854), who has renounced the responsibilities of serious art.

31

214. *A METAMORPHOSIS ... OVID* A general reference to Ovid's *Metamorphoses*. There is possibly also a reference to Joseph G. Baldwin's fictional character Ovid Bolus, who is a skilled liar and an early confidence man. See Baldwin, *The Flush Times of Alabama and Mississippi* (New York: 1853), and Susan Kuhlmann, *Knave, Fool, and Genius* (pp. 30–31).

32

215. *Cadmus glided into the snake* Cadmus killed a dragon sacred to Mars

and sowed its teeth, from which sprang a harvest of hostile soldiers. In old age he and his wife Harmonia were turned into serpents. Hawthorne had told the story of Cadmus and the dragon's teeth in *Tanglewood Tales* (1853); this is indeed a metamorphosis that 'one reads of in fairy-books'.

215.   *ten half-eagles* A half-eagle was a five-dollar gold piece issued between 1795 and 1916.

215.   *full of fun as an egg of meat* Cf. *Romeo and Juliet*, III i, 24: 'The head is as full of quarrels as an egg is full of meat.'

216.   *Charlemont, the gentleman-madman* The story of Charlemont's disappearance and reappearance has affinities with Melville's story 'Jimmy Rose' (1855), and with Hawthorne's 'Wakefield' (1835) and *The Blithedale Romance* (1852).

33

218.   *Though everyone knows . . . no easy thing* Hershel Parker suggests in his edition that this is an oblique reference to the reception of Melville's earlier works, including *Pierre*.

34

219.   *Charlemont was gazetted* Was officially declared a bankrupt.

35

222.   *elixir of logwood* That is, dyed water.

36

223.   *IN WHICH THE COSMOPOLITAN . . . EXPECTED* Elizabeth Foster, noting that Melville originally entitled this chapter 'The Practical Mystic', surmises that he intended to keep Winsome and Egbert as one person. Egbert S. Oliver's identification of Winsome and Egbert as Emerson and Thoreau is now generally accepted (see 'Melville's Picture of Emerson and Thoreau in *The Confidence-Man*').

224.   *a statue in the Pitti Palace* In Florence; it is famed for its statuary.

Melville later visited it; see *Journal Up the Straits*, pp. 145–6 (24 March 1857).

224. *you and Schiller* The writer, dramatist and poet Johann Cristoph Friedrich von Schiller (1759–1805). Schiller proposed a relation between beauty and goodness. Carlyle wrote a biography of him, published in 1825.

224. *all but seemed the creature described* Elizabeth Foster noted the relation between this passage and that describing the serpent tempting Eve in *Paradise Lost*, IX, 499–525.

225. *Who will pity . . . serpent* Ecclesiasticus 12:13.

225. *the compassion the heart decides* The English first edition reads 'the compassion of the heart decides', which lost the sense of the American edition reading, here restored.

227. *the page of Hafiz* Shams ud-din Mohammed Hafiz, Persian poet and philosopher of the fourteenth century. Emerson translated some of Hafiz's poems from German and wrote an essay on Persian poetry.

227. *I seldom care to be consistent* In 'Self-Reliance' (1841) Emerson wrote: 'A foolish consistency is the hobgoblin of little minds, adored by little statesmen and philosophers and divines. With consistency a great soul simply has nothing to do.'

228. *using some unknown word* Ridiculing the supposed Transcendentalist habit of using unintelligible words.

228. *Proclus* A Greek neo-Platonic philosopher (410–485) who influenced Emerson. Melville made fun of him in *Mardi*; see Merton M. Sealts, Jr., 'Melville's Neoplatonical Originals', *Modern Language Notes*, LXVII (1952), 80–86.

229. *the stoic Arrian* Flavius Arrianus (95–175), Greek historian who wrote two books on Epictetus.

230. *talk not against mummies* The reference to mummies immediately precedes the possible appearance of Poe, who wrote variously of them; see 'Some Words with a Mummy' (1845).

230. *a haggard, inspired-looking man* Probably a reference to Poe, with his pamphlet 'Eureka'. (See Harrison Hayford, 'Poe in *The Confidence-Man*'.)

231. *strolling magi of these days* Hershel Parker suggests in his edition a possible reference to Emerson's success on the lecture circuit.

37

234. *meekly standing like a Raphael* Henry F. Pommer pointed out the

use of *Paradise Lost*, VII, 217: 'To whom thus *Raphael* answer'd heav'nly meek' (*Milton and Melville*, p. 72).

234. *in golden accents old Memnon murmurs* Memnon, son of Aurora and Tithonus, was killed by Achilles in the Trojan war. A statue near Thebes was named Memnon by the Greeks; at dawn it would make a musical sound, considered to be Memnon's greeting to his mother. Melville tells the story in *Pierre*, Book VII, vi.

235. *Seneca a usurer* Lucius Annaeus Seneca (*c.* 3 BC–AD 65). He was notorious as a usurer, made possible partly through the favour of Nero, to whom he was a tutor.

235. *Bacon a courtier* Having been knighted in 1603, Bacon was successively Solicitor-General (1607), Attorney-General (1613), Privy Councillor (1616), Keeper of the Seal (1617) and Lord Chancellor (1618). He declared himself guilty of corrupt practices such as accepting bribes.

235. *Swedenborg* Emanuel Swedenborg (1688–1772), Swedish philosopher and mystic. Prior to his visions from God in 1743 he was, as Winsome indicates, a practical man, being an engineer and mining inspector. Emerson included him in *Representative Men* (1850). In 'I and My Chimney' Melville links Swedenborgianism to the 'Spirit Rapping Philosophy'.

235. *West India trade* Strictly, sugar, rum or slavery; possibly, a play with the initials: wit.

38

237. *when I am comfortably warm . . . shake* H. Bruce Franklin notes in his edition that in the first chapter of *Walden* Thoreau reduces human needs to 'Food Shelter Clothing and Fuel'.

237. *you shall call me Frank* Mirroring the previous 'Charlie', who was asked for 50 dollars. Melville is suggesting that there is little difference between the Transcendentalists and Charlie Noble the Mississippi operator.

39

238. *my rule forbids* The conversation here satirizes the sentiments of Thoreau's *Week on the Concord and Merrimack Rivers* ('Wednesday'), *Walden* ('Visitors') and Emerson's 'Essay on Friendship'.

240. *the sour mind of Solomon* Proverbs 18:24, 27:10. Melville regarded Solomon as the author of Proverbs, Ecclesiastes, and the Song of Songs, and Ishmael praises him highly in ch. 96 of *Moby-Dick*. Melville referred to Proverbs 18:24 when he inscribed a copy of *The Whale* for his brother-in-law in 1854. (See Jay Leyda, *The Melville Log*, p. 483.)

240. *sublime master ... Essay on Friendship* In this essay Emerson distinguished, as outlined here, between different levels of friendship.

241. *good Samaritan* See Luke 10:30–37. As well as assisting the unfortunate traveller, the Samaritan left money for him.

243. *the first-born of Egypt* Exodus 12:29.

244. *China Aster* The name suggests the common flower, as opposed to the rarer 'Orchis'. The name 'aster' also suggests 'star', ironically for the failing candle-maker. There was a children's magazine called *The China Aster*. The story of China Aster has provoked a variety of interpretations. See works by Foster, Fussell, Rogin, Chase, Hoffman, Sattelmeyer and Barbour cited in the Bibliography.

40

245. *Marietta ... Muskingum* Marietta, in Ohio, is situated at the junction of the Muskingum and Ohio rivers; it is named after Marie Antoinette. H. Bruce Franklin points out in his edition that Melville is punning on the derivation of 'musk' from the Sanskrit word for 'testicle', complementing 'orchis' as the Greek word for testicle.

245. *light up from his stores a whole street* In the autobiographical strain of China Aster's story, this is a possible reference to the 1853 fire at Harper's, which destroyed unsold copies of Melville's works. The reference is also to the failure of Melville to provide adequately for his family.

248. *Eliphaz, Bildad, and Zophar* Job's 'comforters'; see Job 2:11–32. The Quaker Captain Bildad is one of the part-owners of the *Pequod*.

254. *Death himself on the pale horse* Revelation 6:8: 'And I looked, and behold a pale horse, and his name that sat upon him was Death.'

254. *a church ... of Come-Outers* The sect, which flourished in New England around 1840, comprised a group of religious enthusiasts

who had separated from the established churches. They included abolitionists who advocated 'coming out' of the church and the state over the issue of slavery.

41

263. *Inconsistency? Bah!* Egbert reveals himself as a true disciple of Winsome; cf. the latter's statement (p. 227). The Emersonian attitude to contradiction expressed in 'Self-Reliance' was also echoed in Whitman's 1855 'Song of Myself': 'Do I contradict myself?/Very well then . . . I contradict myself;/I am large . . . I contain multitudes' (ll. 1314–16). In *Mardi* (ch. 143), Babbalanja says 'the sum of my inconsistencies makes up my consistency. And to be consistent to oneself is often to be inconsistent to Mardi. Common consistency implies unchangeableness, but much of the wisdom here below lives in a state of transition.'

264. *All the world's a stage As You Like It*, II, vii, 139–42. The American first edition printed 'Who' for 'They' in line 141, which was corrected in the English edition.

42

265. *Souter John and Tam O'Shanter . . . Somnus and Morpheus* In Robert Burns's poem 'Tam O'Shanter' Tam and his friend Souter Johnny get drunk and Tam sees the devil. Somnus and his son Morpheus are the Roman gods of sleep and dreams.

265. *catch birds there with salt* A possible warning to the reader. Melville refers to the teasing advice given to children, to catch a bird by putting salt on its tail. In ch. 7 of *Tale of a Tub* (1704) Swift wrote, '. . . men catch knowledge, by throwing their wiч at the posteriors of a book, as boys do sparrows with flinging salt on their tails.' Swift's title for this section, 'A Digression in Praise of Digressions', has already been echoed in Melville's playful titles for chs. 11, 14, 33, 43 and 44. Melville may also be implicitly comparing the transfixed barber with Lot's wife, who was turned into a pillar of salt.

265. *the townsfolk called the angels* The angels who went into Lot's house in Sodom were attacked by a lustful mob; see Genesis 19:1–11.

265. *the devils who . . . haunted the tombs* See Matthew 8:28–34 and Mark 5:2–20. The men were possessed by the devils; Christ exorcizes the spirits and places them in a herd of swine.

266. *the spleen of Thersites ... pluck of Agamemnon* Although both appear in the *Iliad*, Melville is more likely referring to their appearance in Shakespeare's *Troilus and Cressida*. Thersites is the bitter cynic who undermines the courage and heroism of Achilles.

271. *Timon traced with charcoal ... cave* A reference to *Timon of Athens*, V, iv, 69–73. Although Shakespeare makes no reference to an inscribed skull, a soldier brings an impression of the misanthropical inscription from Timon's gravestone.

271. *I have a family* Parker points out that the barber neatly reverses Christ's exhortation to followers to desert family and wealth. See Matthew 19:29 and Mark 10:29–30.

43

272. *I am Philanthropos, and love mankind* A contrast with Timon in *Timon of Athens*, IV, iii, 51: 'I am Misanthropos and hate mankind.'

272. *the pleasant barbers in romances* H. Bruce Franklin notes in his edition that this chapter plays on many supposed characteristics of barbers, such as their loquaciousness, and that Figaro is the most famous barber in romance. Man-of-war barbers are described in *White-Jacket* (ch. 84).

272. *the three Kings of Cologne ... barber* The supposed relics of the three magi who brought gifts to the infant Jesus are held at Cologne. The Northwestern-Newberry editors change 'barber' to 'traveler' since the Kings were patrons of travellers, and Melville's handwriting may have been misread. However, 'barber' is here retained, since Melville could easily be punning on the barber's use of cologne. Melville had visited Cologne Cathedral in 1849. See Jay Leyda, *The Melville Log*, pp. 344–5, and Herman Melville, *Journal of a Visit to London etc.*, pp. 61–2.

274. *dishonourable to a bald man* The original editions read 'bold' but the context requires 'bald'.

278. *An enemy speaketh sweetly ... believed not his many words* Ecclesiasticus 12:16, 13:11.

279. *fifty dollars ... little change with me* However, he has already shown his 'ten half-eagles' to Charlie Noble (p. 215).

280. *man-charmer ... snake-charmers* An earlier draft of this chapter's title was 'In which the Cosmopolitan ... earns the title of the man-charmer ... in the same sense that certain East Indians are called

snake-charmers . . .' See Elizabeth Foster's edition, p. 384, and the Northwestern-Newberry edition, p. 489.

44

281.   *QUITE AN ORIGINAL* The phrase was applied to the 'mysterious impostor' on the first page.

281.   *original characters in fiction* Cf. *Pierre*, Book XVIII, i: 'The world is forever babbling of originality; but there never yet was an original man, in the sense intended by the world; the first man himself . . . not being an original; the only original author being God.'

282.   *the founder of a new religion* H. Bruce Franklin notes in his edition that Manco Capac, mentioned on the first page, was such a one.

282.   *a revolving Drummond light* The British engineer Captain Thomas Drummond (1797–1840) invented the lime-light that was used in lighthouses from 1825. P. T. Barnum brought the first Drummond lights to New York in order to advertise his American Museum.

282.   *which in Genesis attends upon the beginning of things* A reference to God's utterance, 'Let there be light', at the creation of the universe (Genesis 1:2–5). From now to the end of the novel, Melville uses references to lights and lamps, from the powerful Drummond light to the weakening solar lamp, ending with the extinguishing of the lamp.

282.   *but one such original character . . . invention* A hint to the reader that the various Confidence Man figures are all one.

45

284.   *a solar lamp* A lamp with a tubular wick, allowing air both inside and outside the flame. Also called an Argand lamp.

284.   *a horned altar . . . encircled by a halo* Elizabeth Foster notes that Melville is referring to the light of the Old and the New Testaments, evident in the symbol of the horned altar and the old man with the halo. The four-horned altar was made for worship and sacrifice, and God's instructions for it are precise (Exodus 27:1–2). References to the horned altar recur in the Bible: for instance, Leviticus 4:17–18, 8:15, 9:9, 16:18; I Kings 1:50–51, 2:28; Psalms 118:27; Revelation 9:13.

285.   *good Simeon . . . departed in peace* Luke 2:25–35.

285. *as any bridegroom tripping to the bridal chamber* The bridegroom is a common designation of Christ, and is further relevant here because of the parable of the virgins; see Matthew 9:15, 25:1–13.

285. *the Bible, not a newspaper* To support the view that the old man is being led away to death, Robert Paul Lamb cites Jewish folklore, according to which the Angel of Death cannot take a man's life if he is reading the Bible. (See Lamb, 'The Place of *The Confidence-Man* in Melville's Career'.)

286. *what was told me not a half-hour since* On p. 277 the agreement between the Cosmopolitan and the barber was timed at 11.45 p.m. Since it was the barber who used the quotation from Ecclesiasticus, the possible implication is that All Fools' Day is over.

286. *more to the same purpose* The scriptural selections derive from Ecclesiasticus 13:4–13. The warnings from this book directly contrast with the exhortations from 1 Corinthians used in ch. 1.

286. *he will make thee bare* The original editions read 'bear'; Elizabeth S. Foster noted the error.

287. *Wisdom of Jesus, the Son of Sirach* The Book of Ecclesiasticus.

287. *apocrypha . . . Apocalypse* Apocrypha means 'hidden', apocalypse, 'revealed'.

288. *Take heed of thy friends* Ecclesiasticus 6:13.

288. *only more in less of mockery* The Northwestern-Newberry edition substitutes 'now' for 'more' to help clarify the sense.

289. *painted flames . . . in auto-da-fé* During the Spanish Inquisition, victims of *autos-da-fé* ('acts of faith') were dressed in clothes depicting the torment of hell. The last Mexican *auto-da-fé* had taken place only recently, in 1850, and fear of the Inquisition and the *auto-da-fé* is evident in the Lima setting for ch. 54 of *Moby-Dick*. Melville appears to have considered dedicating *The Confidence-Man* to 'victims of Auto da Fé, judging by a note he made on his working list of chapter titles.

289. *a miniature mahogany door* H. Bruce Franklin suggests in his edition the relevance of Revelation 3:8: 'I have set before thee an open door, and no man can shut it.'

289. *Murillo's wild beggar-boy's* The Spanish religious painter Bartolomé Esteban Murillo (1617–82), who often used peasants as subjects. Melville refers to him similarly in *Redburn* (ch. 29).

291. *Money-belt? never heard of such a thing* The money-belt was quite a recent innovation; the term's first recorded use is in 1846. In ch. 1 the chevalier was 'ex-officio a peddler of money-belts'.

292. *Counterfeit Detector* A publication that described worthless and

counterfeit currency in order to assist in its detection. Since banks were unregulated, they could, like the 'Vicksburgh Trust and Insurance Banking Company', issue their own paper money. However, sometimes the counterfeit detectors were themselves untrustworthy. See Ted N. Weissbuch, 'A Note on the Confidence Man's Counterfeit Detector', *ESQ*, 19 (1960), 16–18. The existence of the Detectors reflected a growing concern at the amount and variety of paper money being circulated in the 1850s.

292. *look a lie and find the truth* Originally a Spanish proverb, '*Di mentira y sacarás verdad*'; used by Francis Bacon in *Promos*, no. 610 (*c.* 1594) as 'Tell a lie to know a truth.'

296. *a Committee of Safety* While this phrase refers primarily to God and the angels, there is also an allusion to the three separate Committees of Public Safety that functioned after the French Revolution. A Committee of Safety was also established for a short time in Vienna in 1848.

296. *Jehovah shall be thy confidence* Proverbs 3:26.

297. *a brown stool* A kind of chamber pot supplied for the use of passengers; the scatological allusion is obvious. In *Gulliver* (3, vi) Swift writes, 'Men are never so serious, thoughtful or intent as when they are at stool.'

298. *Something further . . . Masquerade* The concluding line of the novel has often been taken to suggest that Melville intended a sequel.

APPENDIX A

'THE RIVER'

In all there are 26 MS fragments relating to *The Confidence-Man*. Of these, two pages comprise a descriptive passage not included in the published text. It seems to be a kind of prologue to *The Confidence-Man*, though written in an expansive style differing from the novel's restrained tone; perhaps Melville felt that its vein was inappropriate to the novel's dark themes.

The manuscript is also interesting because it raises the possibility that one of Melville's sources for some passages in *The Confidence-Man* was Timothy Flint's *A Condensed Geography and History of the Western States; or, The Mississippi Valley* (Cincinnati, 1828). Melville may have been indebted to Volume I of this work for descriptions of the West and the Mississippi. The proposal of Flint's work as a source, however, is complicated by several factors. Melville does not take particular words and phrases from Flint, as he did from the work of Hall (see Appendix B). Further, Flint's work appeared in different editions with various titles, and a selection from Flint had appeared in an anonymous pamphlet, *Description of Banvard's Panorama of the Mississippi River* (1847). For further information, see John D. Seelye, 'Timothy Flint's "Wicked River" and *The Confidence-Man*', *PMLA*, LXXVIII (1963), 75–9, and the Northwestern–Newberry edition of *The Confidence-Man*, pp. 401–11, 490–99 and 511–18.

Since Melville's handwriting is notoriously difficult to decipher, in transcribing 'The River' I am very much indebted to its previous editors, and especially to the suggested readings made by the editors of the Northwestern–Newberry edition. I am also happy to thank the Houghton Library, University of Harvard, for providing me with a photograph copy of the manuscript, and for permission to use it here. Since Melville's manuscript is a rough draft, not a fair copy, I have taken the liberty of regularizing his spelling and punctuation where necessary.

THE RIVER

As the word Abraham means the father of a great multitude of men, so the word Mississippi means the father of a great multitude of waters. His tribes stream in from east and west, exceeding fruitful the lands they enrich. In this granary of a continent, this basin of the Mississippi, must not the nations be greatly multiplied and blest?

Above the Falls of St Anthony, for the most part he winds evenly on between banks of flags or through tracts of pine over marble sands in waters so clear that the deepest fish have the visible flight of the bird. Undisturbed as the lowly life in its bosom feeds the lordly life on its shores, the coroneted elk and the deer, while in the walrus form of some couched rock in the channel, furred over with moss, the furred bear on the marge seems to eye his amphibious brother. Wood and wave wed, man is remote. The unsung time, the Golden Age of the billow.

By his Fall, though he rise not again, the unhumbled river ennobles himself, now deepens, now proudly expands, now first forms his character and begins that career whose majestic amenity, if not overborne by fierce onsets of torrents, shall end only with ocean.

Like a larger Susquehannah, like a long-drawn bison herd, he browses on through the prairie, here and there expanding into archipelagoes cycladean in beauty, while, fissured and verdant, a long China Wall, the bluffs sweep bluely away. Glad and content, the sacred river glides on.

But at St Louis the course of this dream is run. Down on it like a Pawnee from ambush foams the yellow-painted Missouri. The calmness is gone, the grouped isles disappear, the shores are jagged and rent, the hue of the water is clayed, the before moderate current is rapid and vexed. The peace of the Upper River seems broken in the Lower, nor is it ever renewed.

The Missouri would seem rather an hostile element than a filial flood. Larger, stronger than the father of waters, like Jupiter he dethrones his sire and reigns in his stead. Under the benign name Mississippi it is in truth the Missouri that now rolls to the Gulf, the Missouri that with the Timon snows from his solitudes freezes the warmth of the genial zones, the Missouri that by open assault or artful sap sweeps away forest and field, grave-yard and town, the Missouri that not a tributary but an invader enters the sea, long disdaining to yield his white wave to the blue.

APPENDIX B
JAMES HALL'S *SKETCHES*

———•··•———

It was Elizabeth S. Foster who first noted Melville's use of James Hall's *Sketches of History, Life, and Manners, in the West* (Philadelphia: 1835). Melville took Chapter 6 of Volume II as a source for the story of Moredock the Indian-hater (see *The Confidence-Man*, Chapters 26 and 27). The recognition of source material is important since, unusually for Melville, very little seems to have been used in the making of *The Confidence-Man*. Indeed, the Hall chapter is the single unequivocal source that has been identified. Other parts of Hall's work may have been used, though not so closely. For instance, in Volume II, Chapter 7, directly after the Indian-hating chapter, Hall discusses the Harpe brothers and Meason, referred to also by Melville. In Volume I, pp. 233–45, Hall wrote about Daniel Boone and Kentucky, defending Boone from charges of misanthropy in a way similar to the Cosmopolitan's defence of Pitch: 'He was not a misanthrope, who retired to the woods because he was disgusted with the world, but a man of social and benevolent feelings, of mild and unassuming manners, and of strict integrity.'

The extract printed here, pp. 74–82 of the first edition, is significant for any attempt to throw light on Melville's inclusion of the Indian-hater in the novel. For the debate on this issue, see the book by Fussell and the articles by Bellis, Parker, Pearce, Ramsey, Shroeder and Sussman cited in the Bibliography.

CHAPTER 6

Indian hating – Some of the sources of this animosity – Brief account of Col. Moredock

The violent animosity which exists between the people of our frontier and the Indians, has long been a subject of remark. In the early periods of the history of our country, it was easily accounted for, on the ground of mutual aggression. The whites were continually encroaching upon the aborigines, and the latter avenging their wrongs by violent and sudden hostilities. The philanthropist is surprised, however, that such feelings should prevail now, when these atrocious wars have ceased, and when no immediate cause of enmity remains; at least upon our side. Yet the fact is, that the dweller upon the frontier continues to regard the Indian with a degree of terror and hatred, similar to that which he feels towards the rattlesnake or panther, and which can neither be removed by argument, nor appeased by any thing but the destruction of its object.

In order to understand the cause and the operation of these feelings, it is necessary to recollect that the backwoodsmen are a peculiar race. We allude to the pioneers, who, keeping continually in the advance of civilization, precede the denser population of our country in its progress westward, and live always upon the frontier. They are the descendants of a people whose habits were identically the same as their own. Their fathers were pioneers. A passion for hunting, and a love for sylvan sports, have induced them to recede continually before the tide of emigration, and have kept them a separate people, whose habits, prejudices, and modes of life have been transmitted from father to son with but little change. From generation to generation they have lived in contact with the Indians. The ancestor met the red men in battle upon the shores of the Atlantic, and his descendants have pursued the footsteps of the retreating tribes, from year to year, throughout a whole century, and from the eastern limits of our great continent to the wide prairies of the west.

America was settled in an age when certain rights, called those of *discovery* and *conquest*, were universally acknowledged; and when the possession of a country was readily conceded to the strongest. When more accurate notions of moral right began, with the spread of knowledge, and the dissemination of religious truth, to prevail in public opinion, and regulate the public acts of our government, the pioneers were but slightly affected by the wholesome contagion of such opinions. Novel precepts in morals were not apt to reach men who mingled so little with society in its more refined state, and who shunned the restraints, while they despised the luxuries of social life.

The pioneers, who thus dwelt ever upon the borders of the Indian hunting grounds, forming a barrier between savage and civilized men, have received but few accessions to their numbers by emigration. The great tide of emigration, as it rolls forward, beats upon them and rolls them onward, without either swallowing them up in its mass, or mingling its elements with theirs. They accumulate by natural increase; a few of them return occasionally to the bosom of society, but the great mass moves on.

It is not from a desire of conquest, or thirst of blood, or with any premeditated hostility against the savage, that the pioneer continues to follow him from forest to forest, ever disputing with him the right to the soil, and the privilege of hunting game. It is simply because he shuns a crowded population, delights to rove uncontrolled in the woods, and does not believe that an Indian, or any other man has a right to monopolize the hunting grounds, which he considers free to all. When the Indian disputes the propriety of this invasion upon his ancient heritage, the white man feels himself injured, and stands, as the southern folks say, upon his reserved rights.

The history of the borders of England and Scotland, and of all dwellers upon frontiers, who come often into hostile collision, shows, that between such parties an intense hatred is created. It is national antipathy, with the addition of private feud and personal injury. The warfare is carried on by a few individuals, who become known to each other, and a few prominent actors on each side soon become distinguished for their prowess or ferocity. When a state of public war ostensibly ceases, acts of violence continue to be perpetrated from motives of mere mischief, or for pillage or revenge.

Our pioneers have, as we have said, been born and reared on the frontier, and have, from generation to generation, by successive removals, remained in the same relative situation in respect to the Indians and to our own government. Every child thus reared, learns to hate an Indian, because he always hears him spoken of as an enemy. From the cradle, he listens continually to horrid tales of savage violence, and becomes familiar with narratives of aboriginal cunning and ferocity. Every family can number some of its members or relatives among the victims of a midnight massacre, or can tell of some acquaintance who has suffered a dreadful death at the stake. Traditions of horses stolen, and cattle driven off, and cabins burned, are numberless; are told with great minuteness, and listened to with intense interest. With persons thus reared, hatred towards an Indian becomes a part of their nature, and revenge an instinctive principle. Nor does the evil end here. Although the backwoodsmen, properly so called, retire before that tide of emigration which forms the more stationary population, and eventually fills the country with inhabitants, they usually remain for a time in contact with the first of those who, eventually, succeed them, and impress their own sentiments upon the latter. In the formation of each of the western territories and states, the backwoodsmen have, for a while, formed the majority of the population, and given the tone to public opinion.

If we attempt to reason on this subject, we must reason with a due regard to facts, and to the known principles of human nature. Is it to be wondered at, that a man should fear and detest an Indian, who has been always accustomed to hear him described only as a midnight prowler, watching to murder the mother as she bends over her helpless children, and tearing, with hellish malignity, the babe from the maternal breast? Is it strange, that he whose mother has fallen under the savage tomahawk, or whose father has died a lingering death at the stake, surrounded by yelling fiends in human shape, should indulge the passion of revenge towards the perpetrators of such atrocities? They know the story only as it was told to them. They have only heard one side, and that with all the exaggerations of fear, sorrow, indignation and resentment. They have heard it from the tongue of a father, or from the lips of a mother, or a sister, accompanied with all the particularity which the tale could receive from the vivid impressions of an eye-witness, and with all the eloquence of deeply awakened feeling. They have heard it perhaps at a time when the war-whoop still sounded in the distance, when the rifle still was kept in preparation, and the cabin door was carefully secured with each returning night.

Such are some of the feelings, and of the facts, which operate upon the inhabitants of our frontiers. The impressions which we have described are handed down from generation to generation, and remain in full force long after all danger from the savages has ceased, and all intercourse with them been discontinued.

Besides that general antipathy which pervades the whole community under such circumstances, there have been many instances of individuals who, in consequence of some personal wrong, have vowed eternal hatred to the whole Indian race, and have devoted nearly all of their lives to the fulfilment of a vast scheme of vengeance. A familiar instance is before us in the life of a gentleman, who was known to the writer of this article, and whose history we have often heard repeated by those who were intimately conversant with all the events. We allude to the late Colonel John Moredock, who was a member of the territorial legislature of Illinois, a distinguished militia officer, and a man universally known and respected by the early settlers of that region. We are surprised that the writer of a sketch of the early history of Illinois, which we published some months ago, should have omitted the name of this gentleman, and some others, who were famed for deeds of hardihood, while he has dwelt upon the actions of persons who were comparatively insignificant.

John Moredock was the son of a woman who was married several times, and was as often widowed by the tomahawk of the savage. Her husbands had been pioneers, and with them she had wandered from one territory to another, living always on the frontier. She was at last left a widow, at Vincennes, with a large family of children, and was induced to join a party about to remove to Illinois, to which region a few American families had then recently removed. On the eastern side of Illinois there were no settlements of whites; on the shore of the Mississippi a few spots were occupied by the French; and it was now that our own backwoodsmen began to turn their eyes to this delightful country, and determined to settle in the vicinity of the French villages. Mrs Moredock and her friends embarked at Vincennes in boats, with the intention of descending the Wabash and Ohio rivers, and ascending the Mississippi. They proceeded in safety until they reached the Grand Tower on the Mississippi, where, owing to the difficulty of the navigation for ascending boats, it became necessary for the boatmen to land, and drag their vessels round a rocky point, which was swept by a violent current. Here a party of Indians, lying in wait, rushed upon them, and murdered the whole party. Mrs Moredock was among the victims, and *all* her children, except John, who was proceeding with another party.

John Moredock was just entering upon the years of manhood, when he was thus left in a strange land, the sole survivor of his race. He resolved upon executing vengeance, and immediately took measures to discover the actual perpetrators of the massacre. It was ascertained that the outrage was committed by a party of twenty or thirty Indians, belonging to different tribes, who had formed themselves into a lawless predatory band. Moredock watched the motions of this band for more than a year, before an opportunity suitable for his purpose occurred. At length he learned, that they were hunting on the Missouri side of the river, nearly opposite to the recent settlements of the Americans. He raised a party of young men and pursued them; but that time they escaped. Shortly after, he sought them at the head of another party, and had the good fortune to discover them one evening, on an island, whither they had retired to encamp the more securely for the night. Moredock and his friends, about equal in numbers to the Indians, waited until the dead of night, and then landed upon the island, turning adrift their own canoes and those of the enemy, and determined to sacrifice their own lives, or to extermi-nate the savage band. They were completely successful. Three only of the Indians escaped, by throwing themselves into the river; the rest were slain, while the whites lost not a man.

But Moredock was not satisfied while one of the murderers of his mother remained. He had learned to recognize the names and persons of the three that had escaped, and these he pursued with secret, but untiring diligence, until they all fell by his own hand. Nor was he yet satisfied. He had now become a hunter and a warrior. He was a square-built, muscular man, of remarkable strength and activity. In athletic sports he had few equals; few men would willingly have encountered him in single combat. He was a man of determined courage, and great coolness and steadi-ness of purpose. He was expert in the use of the rifle and other weapons; and was complete master of those wonderful and num-berless expedients by which the woodsman subsists in the forest, pursues the footsteps of an enemy with unerring sagacity, or conceals himself and his design from the discovery of a watchful foe. He had resolved never to spare an Indian, and though he made no boast of this determination, and seldom avowed it, it became the ruling passion of his life. He thought it praiseworthy to kill an Indian; and would roam through the forest silently and alone, for days and weeks, with this single purpose. A solitary red man, who was so unfortunate as to meet him in the woods, was sure to become his victim; if he encountered a party of the enemy, he would either secretly pursue their footsteps until an opportunity for striking a blow occurred, or, if discovered, would elude them by his superior skill. He died about four years ago, an old man, and it is supposed never in his life failed to embrace an opportunity to kill a savage.

The reader must not infer, from this description, that Colonel Moredock was unsocial, ferocious, or by nature cruel. On the contrary, he was a man of warm feelings, and excellent disposition. At home he was like other men, conducting a large farm with industry and success, and gaining the good will of all his neighbours by his popular manners and benevolent deportment. He was cheerful, convivial, and hospitable; and no man in the territory was more generally known, or more universally respected. He was an officer in the ranging service during the war of 1813–14, and acquitted himself with credit; and was afterwards elected to the command of the militia of his county, at a time when such an office was honourable, because it imposed responsibility, and required the exertion of military skill. Colonel Moredock was a member of the legislative council of the territory of Illinois, and at the formation of the state government, was spoken of as a candidate for the office of governor, but refused to permit his name to be used.

There are many cases to be found on the frontier, parallel to that just stated, in which individuals have persevered through life, in the indulgence of a resentment founded either on a personal wrong suffered by the party, or a hatred inherited through successive generations, and perhaps more frequently on a combination of these causes. In a fiction, written by the author, and founded on some of these facts, he has endeavoured to develop and illustrate this feeling through its various details.

READ MORE IN PENGUIN

In every corner of the world, on every subject under the sun, Penguin represents quality and variety – the very best in publishing today.

For complete information about books available from Penguin – including Puffins, Penguin Classics and Arkana – and how to order them, write to us at the appropriate address below. Please note that for copyright reasons the selection of books varies from country to country.

In the United Kingdom: Please write to *Dept. EP, Penguin Books Ltd, Bath Road, Harmondsworth, West Drayton, Middlesex UB7 0DA*

In the United States: Please write to *Consumer Sales, Penguin Putnam Inc., P.O. Box 12289 Dept. B, Newark, New Jersey 07101-5289*. VISA and MasterCard holders call 1-800-788-6262 to order Penguin titles

In Canada: Please write to *Penguin Books Canada Ltd, 10 Alcorn Avenue, Suite 300, Toronto, Ontario M4V 3B2*

In Australia: Please write to *Penguin Books Australia Ltd, P.O. Box 257, Ringwood, Victoria 3134*

In New Zealand: Please write to *Penguin Books (NZ) Ltd, Private Bag 102902, North Shore Mail Centre, Auckland 10*

In India: Please write to *Penguin Books India Pvt Ltd, 11 Community Centre, Panchsheel Park, New Delhi 110017*

In the Netherlands: Please write to *Penguin Books Netherlands bv, Postbus 3507, NL-1001 AH Amsterdam*

In Germany: Please write to *Penguin Books Deutschland GmbH, Metzlerstrasse 26, 60594 Frankfurt am Main*

In Spain: Please write to *Penguin Books S. A., Bravo Murillo 19, 1° B, 28015 Madrid*

In Italy: Please write to *Penguin Italia s.r.l., Via Benedetto Croce 2, 20094 Corsico, Milano*

In France: Please write to *Penguin France, Le Carré Wilson, 62 rue Benjamin Baillaud, 31500 Toulouse*

In Japan: Please write to *Penguin Books Japan Ltd, Kaneko Building, 2-3-25 Koraku, Bunkyo-Ku, Tokyo 112*

In South Africa: Please write to *Penguin Books South Africa (Pty) Ltd, Private Bag X14, Parkview, 2122 Johannesburg*

READ MORE IN PENGUIN

A CHOICE OF CLASSICS

READ MORE IN PENGUIN

A CHOICE OF CLASSICS

READ MORE IN PENGUIN

A CHOICE OF CLASSICS

Thomas Wentworth Higginson	**Army Life in a Black Regiment**
William Dean Howells	**The Rise of Silas Lapham**
Gilbert Imlay	**The Emigrants**
Sarah Orne Jewett	**The Country of the Pointed Firs**
Herman Melville	**Billy Budd, Sailor and Other Stories**
	The Confidence-Man
	Moby-Dick
	Pierre
	Redburn
	Typee
Thomas Paine	**Common Sense**
	The Rights of Man
	The Thomas Paine Reader
Edgar Allan Poe	**Comedies and Satires**
	The Fall of the House of Usher
	The Narrative of Arthur Gordon Pym **of Nantucket**
	The Science Fiction of Edgar Allan Poe
Jacob A. Riis	**How the Other Half Lives**
Elizabeth Stoddard	**The Morgesons**
Harriet Beecher Stowe	**Uncle Tom's Cabin**
Henry David Thoreau	**Walden/Civil Disobedience**
	Week on the Concord and Merrimack
Mark Twain	**The Adventures of Huckleberry Finn**
	The Adventures of Tom Sawyer
	A Connecticut Yankee at King Arthur's **Court**
	Life on the Mississippi
	The Prince and the Pauper
	Pudd'nhead Wilson
	Roughing It
	Short Stories
	A Tramp Abroad
	Tales, Speeches, Essays and Sketches
Walt Whitman	**The Complete Poems**
	Leaves of Grass